*What fires the blood, twists the mind, and
drives a person to kill?*

FURY

"THE RAYMOND CHANDLER OF SEATTLE."
San Antonio Express-News

"FORD HAS COME UP WITH
ANOTHER WINNER . . .
Suspenseful, realistic, and fast-moving, the first
Frank Corso novel is certain not to be the last."
Dallas Morning News

"CORSO IS DEFINITELY FORD'S HOTTEST
CHARACTER TO DATE . . .
[*FURY*] reminds me, pleasantly, of the early Michael
Connolly novels, and that's rare praise . . . This
story has a lot of good twists in a terrific plot
with great characters."
Toronto Globe —

"G.M. FO—
UNT—
And he continu—
colorful major an—   mystery
fiction. Filled w—   and black humor,
FURY is a very entertaining read."
Milwaukee Journal Sentinel

"A BREAKNECK-PACED, SMOOTHLY WRITTEN,
AND DISTINCTLY UNCOMIC THRILLER."
Seattle Times

"*FURY* IS A WINNER—
great ticking-bomb suspense, a wonderful sense of
place, fine writing, and flesh-and-bones characters,
especially Ford's new kick-ass hero, Frank Corso.
G.M. Ford is must reading."
Harlan Coben

"SHARP AND TOUGH . . .
Frank Corso makes a winning debut . . . There's
a love story here, too, tender and solid, that
sneaks up on the reader and on the couple in
question. Only a master could serve up such a
fine story and then some . . . This one could push
Ford onto mystery bestseller charts."
Publishers Weekly (*Starred Review*)

"FRANK CORSO IS IRRESISTIBLE.
Part Sam Spade, part Hunter S. Thompson . . .
Ingeniously written, *FURY* holds up a funhouse
mirror on our criminal justice system and the reflected
image is as scary as it is hilarious. When you get this
much substance, depth, and rollicking entertainment
between the cover of one book, you know you're in
the hands of a superior storyteller."
Martha C. Lawrence

"FORD WRITES WITH A TOUGHNESS LEAVENED
BY GRACE AND WIT."
Margaret Maron

Also by G. M. Ford

FURY
BLACK RIVER
A BLIND EYE

The Leo Waterman Series

WHO IN HELL IS WANDA FUCA?
CAST IN STONE
THE BUM'S RUSH
SLOW BURN
LAST DITCH
THE DEADER THE BETTER

G. M. FORD

AVON BOOKS
An Imprint of HarperCollinsPublishers

This is a work of fiction. Names, characters, places, and incidents are products of the author's imagination or are used fictitiously and are not to be construed as real. Any resemblance to actual events, locales, organizations, or persons, living or dead, is entirely coincidental.

AVON BOOKS
An Imprint of HarperCollins*Publishers*
10 East 53rd Street
New York, New York 10022-5299

Copyright © 2001 by G. M. Ford
Excerpt from *Black River* copyright © 2002 by G. M. Ford
ISBN: 0-380-80421-2
www.avonbooks.com

First Avon Books paperback printing: June 2002
First William Morrow hardcover printing: May 2001

Avon Trademark Reg. U.S. Pat. Off. and in Other Countries, Marca Registrada, Hecho en U.S.A.
HarperCollins ® is a registered trademark of HarperCollins Publishers Inc.

Printed in the U.S.A.

10 9 8 7 6 5 4 3

In this dreary and comfortless region, it was no inconsiderable piece of good fortune to find a little cove in which we could take shelter, and a small spot of level ground on which we could erect our tent. . . .

—From the journals of Captain George Vancouver

FURY

A Pound of Flesh

God only knows where he found an orange-plaid suit.
Probably some retro consignment joint up on Broadway. Jacket two sizes too small, with the shoulders
sticking up like epaulets. Trousers six inches too short,
like he was expecting a flood or something. Big
cuffs . . . brogans . . . no socks.

His lawyer, Myron Mendenhal, on the other hand,
was the very soul of sartorial elegance. Natty in a
charcoal-gray three-piece. Pinky ring, with a diamond
as big as the Ritz. A habitual cuff shooter who kept the
Rolex double diamond tastefully in view at all times.
After all, when one tilled the personal injury end of the
legal field, it was merely good business to look as pros-
perous as possible.

Mendenhal had already stated his case. Two or three
times, in fact. On behalf of his client, he was filing a
lawsuit against both the city of Seattle and the state of
Washington. Wrongful and malicious prosecution.
Three million in compensatory damages. Ten million
in punitive damages. Each. Individual civil actions to
follow.

Only reason he was still talking was so his client
wouldn't. Last time Bozo'd opened his trap, all hell

had broken loose. A guy in the front row had lost his composure and tried to crawl over the table at them. He'd clawed halfway through the forest of microphones before the female cop grabbed him by the belt and jerked him to the floor. Took four officers to get him out of the room and ten minutes to get the electronics back in order. The echo of the man's anguished cries still ruffled the drapes, and a scent of spent hormones hovered in the air like gunsmoke. No doubt about it; Myron Mendenhal was prepared to run his mouth for as long as it took.

"How do you compensate a man for three years of his life?" he asked. "Is there some dollar figure that can repair the heart of a man who has lived for years under the specter of his own imminent death? Who has lain upon the table of death? I think not. Can we—"

The client leaned toward the mikes. "If it ain't me or him, just gonna be somebody else, you know."

"Excuse me?" one of the reporters lining the wall said.

Mendenhal covered the nearest mikes with his arm and whispered something to his client. First, imploring. Then, insisting. The audience caught its collective breath when the client reached over and clamped his big hand over Mendenhal's nose and mouth. With the bug-eyed lawyer still squirming behind his half-acre palm, the client curled his rubbery lips and scooted his chair closer to the alphabet-soup collection of microphones.

"Said there's always gonna be somebody out there killin' bitches. Bitches and mo' bitches is gonna be dyin' all over the damn place, till you-all up to your damn ass in dead bitches."

Seven separate cameras recorded the onset of what happened next. The man sitting front-row center slowly got to his feet. He ran both hands over his face, like he was wiping away spiderwebs. He turned his back on Mendenhal and his client. Leaned over and appeared to whisper in the ear of the woman seated in the chair beside him. By then, the half dozen rent-a-cops stationed around the hotel ballroom were all moving his way, but it was too late.

When the man straightened up, he was holding a WWII-vintage Colt forty-five automatic in both hands. With tears in his eyes, he looked out over the crowded ballroom and uttered a single syllable. And then he turned toward the front of the room, raised the gun, and began pulling the trigger.

Run the NBC tape and you can see the client take four direct hits in the chest. Each time the force rocks his chair up onto two legs, only to have his weight slam it back to earth. Slow it down and you can see the impact of the bullets as they tear through the garish fabric of his suit. Watch the second slug go high left, taking off part of the shoulder, painting the side of Myron Mendenhal's face with a high-pressure spray of blood and bone. Stop it right after the third impact dents the suit; run a couple more frames. Then, right before your eyes, seems like all at once, the plaid fades to red and the client falls slowly from his chair with that odd, enigmatic smile still frozen on his lips.

By that time, the ballroom is in complete panic. When the man with the gun turns back toward the crowd, only the brass-balls NBC cameraman keeps it rolling. Everybody else hits the deck. The rest of the network footage looks like *The Blair Witch Project*.

People who were there—and God knows half the city claims to have been present at the time—say the air was instantly sucked from the room, leaving the lungs scratched and dry, in that awful silent moment when the guy put the gun in his mouth and pulled the trigger.

Chapter 1

In the year when summer never came, the spring rains lasted through July and then into August and September, until finally, with the leaves still green on the trees, people bowed to the inevitable and abandoned their memories of the sun.

More out of habit than duty, Bill Post flicked his eyes toward the street. Just in time to see her dismount the number 30 bus and step awkwardly out into a gray, driving rain. He watched as she pulled the hood low on her head and sloshed her big brown shoes across the sidewalk toward the front doors. Once inside, she removed her green raincoat and shook it out over the black rubber runner. He couldn't remember ever seeing anyone go to that much trouble to keep water off the floor. Like somebody was going to make her clean it up or something.

In other years, he might have mentioned the rain, and they would have nurtured the bond that forms among those who suffer together. Not this year, though. This year, spring and summer had come and gone like wishes, washing any expectation of relief so far downstream that the state of the weather was no longer considered polite conversation.

From behind the security desk he asked, "Something I can help you with?"

She seemed startled by the sound of his voice. "I hope so," she said. "I need to see a Mr. Frank Corso. He's a writer . . . a reporter here." She draped the dripping coat over her arm and approached the desk.

"Is Mr. Corso in?"

"Not that I ever seen," the guard said with a chuckle. "The guy I replaced said he used to see him once in a while, but I been here just under two years and he ain't never been in during my shift. Night crew says he comes in sometimes to see Mrs. Van Der Hoven, but I personally ain't never seen him myself." He leaned back in his chair.

When he tilted his head forward and looked at her through the upper half of his bifocals, he instantly realized he was supposed to know who she was. He sat up straight. Closed the travel brochures he'd been reading and stuffed them in the top drawer. Tried to let it come to him, but wasn't surprised when he couldn't put a name to the face. In recent months, he seldom could. Hell, if he didn't hang his car keys on the same hook in the kitchen every night, he couldn't find the damn things in the morning.

"Maybe somebody else could help you, Miss . . . ?" He left it a question.

She looked like she was going to cry. "Mr. Corso *has* to see me." She said it like daytime TV. "You tell him Leanne Samples is downstairs and needs to talk with him on a matter of life and death."

The name did it. It was her all right. The girl from the TV. He kicked himself for not recognizing her right away and wondered again if he shouldn't discuss his failing memory with his doctor. He picked up the phone. Who? Mr. Hawes? He was the honcho. The managing editor and all that jazz. Yeah. Last button on the right.

Natalie Van Der Hoven pulled her head back and looked down her nose at Bennett Hawes, her managing editor. She was in her mid-sixties, with a face from an ancient coin. Pointed and haughty like a hawk, with a "fear of God" gaze to match. Wrought-iron hair and shoulders wider than most men's. Machete murderers jumped to their feet and doffed their caps when she entered a room. She had that kind of style.

"You can't be serious," she said.

"That's all she'll say. She lied at the trial. That and how she won't cooperate with us unless Corso writes the story."

Always impeccable, in a Nordstrom three-piece suit, Hawes claimed to be five-nine, but in reality stood about five foot seven. He wore what remained of his sandy hair combed completely across his scalp and sprayed in place. Worked out five days a week at the gym up the street. Everything he did, he did quickly.

She raised an eyebrow. "Surely she can be persuaded."

He scratched the back of his neck. "I don't think so," he said.

"You explained that Mr. Corso no longer works directly for the paper?"

"The distinction between direct and indirect employees seems to be lost on Miss Samples. As far as she's concerned, she reads his column in the paper twice a month, so he works here."

"Did you explain Mr. Corso's aversion to the lime-light? That he hasn't been seen in public since he hit the bestseller list?"

Hawes nodded disgustedly. "She doesn't care. We either produce Corso today or she takes her story up the road." He turned his palms toward the ceiling. "Why she wants Corso is beyond me."

"Did you ask?"

Hawes made a sour face. "She said it was because he was"— he used his fingers to make quotation marks in the air—"*nice* to her back then." Jamming his hands in his pockets, he paced across the room.

"Do we have a number for Mr. Corso?"

"I was hoping you had one," he said.

She shook her head. "When Mr. Corso wants to chat, he calls me."

"What about his agent?"

"Some woman in New York named Vance."

"She'll have a number."

"Not that she'll share with us," Mrs. V. said. "I've tried before."

"I went down to accounting. We send his checks to a P.O. box in the U District." Hawes's normal pacing suddenly took on the air of a strut. She searched him with her eyes. "You think you know something, don't you?" she said.

He kept his face as bland as a cabbage. "I might," he admitted.

"Come on now, Bennett," she prompted. "Out with it."

A smile escaped his thin lips. "While I was down in

accounting, I went through his expense file. Gave me an idea how we might be able to find him quickly," he said.

"Oh?" she said. "At one time, people made careers of trying to find our Mr. Corso. What makes you think you can run him to ground?"

"They never had to pay his expenses."

"Such as?"

"Such as Corso hired a local private eye a couple of times. I know because we paid the guy's bill. I think the guy probably knows where to find Corso."

"Who would that be?"

"Guy named Leo Waterman."

"Bill Waterman's boy?"

"Yeah."

She managed a small smile. "I haven't seen Leo since he was in short pants," she said. "As you know, his father and my late husband, Edmund, were quite close. What makes you think Leo could find Mr. Corso?"

"I saw the two of them having a beer together one time, when I stopped for cigarettes. Over on Eastlake, a neighborhood dive called the Zoo."

"That's all?"

"You know how Corso is. He hates everybody. For him, having a beer with somebody is like a long-term relationship."

"He's not *that* bad, Bennett," she scoffed. "That's just his act."

Hawes made a noise with his lips. "If that arrogance of his is an act, he ought to get an Academy Award."

"It's just his way of protecting himself."

Hawes snorted. "By this time, if anybody out there still wanted him dead, he'd be dead."

"Not *physically*. Emotionally."

Hawes scowled. "Christ, I feel like I'm on *Oprah*." He crossed the room. "So, what do you want to do?"

"I don't see how we have a choice here," she said after a moment. "The Himes execution is six days off. Not only do we have a moral obligation to the public, but I don't have to tell you what a story such as this could mean to the paper."

No . . . she didn't. An exclusive like this could go a long way toward rescuing the *Sun*. If not financially, then at least in terms of restoring some measure of credibility.

"Problem is, even if we do find him, he won't do it," Hawes said. "Why should he?" He kept pacing the room, slowly shaking his head. "Last time I looked, that new book of his was number seven on the *New York Times* bestseller list. He doesn't do interviews of any kind. He doesn't sign books. He sure as hell doesn't need the money anymore. Why in God's name would he open himself up to all that abuse? Quite frankly, I'm amazed he still sends in his columns."

Mrs. V. smiled. "Mr. Corso and I have an agreement," she said. "And Mr. Corso is an unusually honorable man."

"Lotta people don't think so."

"Lots of people like professional wrestling," she said.

Hawes snorted and shook his head. "He'd have to be crazy to get involved in something like this. The whole *New York Times* libel thing is going to end up right back on the front page. No way he's going to let that happen."

"Ironic, isn't it?" Mrs. V. said.

"What's that?"

"That the same mighty newspaper that so publicly fired Mr. Corso for fabricating a story now gives him free publicity for his fictionalized reporting efforts."

Bennett Hawes was beyond wistful irony. He paced the room at breakneck speed. "Even if I do find him, he's just going to tell me to kiss his ass," he blurted out. "Excuse my French, but you know he and I aren't exactly . . . ," he said.

Bennett Hawes had been managing editor for twenty-one years prior to Corso's arrival. He'd lobbied long and hard for Corso not to be hired. First time they met, he'd asked Corso for an explanation of New York. Corso told him he didn't have one. "Then I'll never be sure I can trust you," Hawes had said. Corso said he didn't blame him. Said he wouldn't hire himself either. Fortunately or unfortunately, depending on your outlook, Mrs. V. had insisted.

"I know," Mrs. V. said.

She opened the top drawer of her desk, pulled out a piece of pale blue notepaper and a matching envelope. He couldn't see what she wrote, but whatever it was fit on a single line. She then reached down into her bottom drawer and fingered her way to what she was looking for. Found it. A scrap of white paper folded in thirds. She signed her name to the note, folded the page in half, slipped the white scrap inside, and sealed the envelope. "If he can find him, have Leo give this to Mr. Corso."

Chapter 2

The hunted develop an eye for detail. An inner lens for imprinting the lay of familiar land or the fall of shadows at a certain time of day. He spotted the silhouette as soon as he turned the corner. A guy waiting by the women's showers. He stopped the car. Shifted into reverse and then backed to the far end of the lot.

As he got out and walked to the back of the car, he flicked his eyes in the guy's direction. Big son of a bitch . . . whoever he was. He opened the hatchback and bent down as if to remove something from the car. Then quickly duck-walked between parked cars until he reached the opposite side of the shower building.

He slipped off his boat shoes and pulled a steel ballpoint pen from the pocket of his raincoat. With his shoes stuffed into his coat pockets, he peeked around the short side of the building. Empty. He covered the distance and then peeked again. The guy still stood in the eaves, peering out at the Datsun through the beaded curtain of rain that ran headlong from the gutterless roof.

He took two silent steps forward, grabbed the guy by the back of his hair, and jammed the point of the pen into the hollow behind the big guy's ear. The guy made a surprisingly fast move to duck and turn, but Corso moved with him, increasing the pressure on the pen until it threatened to burst his eardrum, lifting him up onto his tiptoes, as if he were climbing a ladder.

"Easy now . . . easy now," the big guy chanted in a strained tenor.

Corso recognized the voice. Pulled the pen back and spun the guy around. The guy rubbed behind his ear. Scowled. "What the hell's with the Apache routine, Frank?" he asked. "You could seriously piss a guy off with that kind of shit."

"Apache, my ass. I should be asking you what's with the lurking routine?"

The big guy patted the hair at the back of his head. His face was red. "I'm a professional lurker, Frank. Remember? I'm a detective. Lurkers Are Us."

Corso slipped his shoes onto his feet, shouldered his way past the guy, and headed back to the car. The guy followed Corso into the rain.

"You don't generate much paperwork, Frank," he said to Corso's back. "You don't exactly leave a guy a lot of choices when it comes to finding you."

"Might lead some guys to figure I don't want to be found," Corso said. He stuck his head inside the car.

"Took me damn near two hours yammering on the phone," the guy complained as he ambled through the downpour.

"Come over here and make your big ass useful," Corso said.

The big man crossed the parking lot to Corso's side.

Both men stood six-four, but that was where the similarities ended. Corso had a loose-jointed, raw-boned quality about him. Leo Waterman was big all over. Fingers twice the size of Corso's. One of those guys you could hit with a shovel, only to have him rise from the ground, smiling at you, with blood on his teeth. That was Leo's edge, what made him a good private investigator. By the time you figured out he was about three times as smart as you'd imagined, it was too late. You were screwed. Worse yet, if you had a problem with it, Leo doubled as his own complaint department.

Corso straightened up. Heaved a sigh. Looked the big man in the eye.

"How you been, Leo?" Corso asked.

"Hangin' in there, Frank."

Corso clapped him on the shoulder. "Good to see you again. How's Rebecca?"

"Dating a gynecologist."

"Sorry to hear that, Leo. You guys were together a long time."

Leo looked off into the distance. "Yeah," he said. "Almost twenty years. She says I'm not 'emotionally available.' "

"What's that mean?"

"Damned if I know," Leo said. "I've been trying to work up a picture of it for the past four months so's I could fake it."

"Sorry to hear it," Corso said again.

Leo made a face. "Not only am I back to eating my own cooking, but I'm so horny the crack of dawn better be careful around me," he said.

"A gynecologist, huh?"

"He's thirty," Leo said. "Named Brendan."

"I remember when thirty sounded so old," Corso mused.

"Yeah, me too," Leo said miserably.

They stood for a moment, sharing a silent grimace with the rain.

"Grab ahold here," Corso said.

Leo stepped around the corner of the car. A Rolls marine battery. Two hundred or so pounds of lead and acid with a plastic handle at each end.

Together the two men carried the battery down the ramp to the dock. Set it down while Corso unlocked the chain-link gate to C dock and then lugged it all the way out to the end. By the time they set the load down, Corso was heeled so far over on one side his knuckles threatened to drag on the dock and his hand felt as if it was being cut in two. Leo didn't seem to notice either Corso's discomfort or the weight of the load. Corso reckoned how if he were Brendan the gynecologist, he'd make it a point to stay a long way from Leo.

Leo looked the boat over. Whistled. "Yours, huh?" he asked.

Corso allowed how it surely was.

"This true-crime writing shit must really pay," Leo said. "Maybe I oughta pen my memoirs." He walked along the slip, taking the boat in. "How big?"

"Fifty-one feet," Corso said. "A Monk design."

"A beauty."

"Think of it as my house and it won't seem so extravagant," Corso said. "I live aboard." Corso stepped up onto his combination dock box and boarding stairs. "Come on," he said, stepping over the rail onto the deck.

Leo reached down, grabbed both of the handles, and, without so much as a grunt, set the battery on the rail. Corso thought he might have detected the hint of a smile forming on Leo's lips. Corso spread his feet wide, grabbed the handles, and pulled upward. Nothing. Corso looked down at Leo, who was openly grinning now.

"Awkward angle," Corso said.

Leo just kept smiling. Annoyed now, Corso yanked the battery for all he was worth, getting just enough clearance to allow the load to bang down onto the deck between his feet. The big boat rocked from the impact, but he still had his toes. Thank God for inch-and-a-half-thick teak decks.

Corso slid the door open and stepped into the boat. Leo climbed aboard. Still smiling. "Ya didn't hurt yourself, did ya, Frank?"

"Stop grinning at me, goddamn it," Corso snapped.

Leo used a massive hand to wipe the smile from his face, then nodded at the battery. "Where's this baby go?" he asked.

Corso pointed to the floor beneath his feet. "Down in the engine room," he said.

"Why don't we put it down there? Wouldn't want you to sink the damn boat. It's way too pretty for that."

Corso had spent just enough time around Leo to know this was the only chance he was going to get. With Leo, it wasn't a good idea to go all demure at a time like this. You made any noise about how you could handle it on your own and Leo was just the guy to give you a wink and allow how he knew all along you could.

Corso grabbed a D-ring in the teak-planked floor and pulled up a four-by-four-foot section of floor. Before he could set the hatch aside and lend a hand, Leo swung the battery over to the edge of the opening. He dropped to his knees, then down onto his belly, grabbed the handles, and managed to set the battery down gently in the engine compartment. As he worked the hatch back into place, Corso thought, once again, that if he were Dr. Stirrups he'd make it a point to give Leo a wide berth.

"So," Leo said. "You want to know who's looking for you?"

"Nope," Corso said. "Couldn't give less of a shit. As soon as I get that battery installed, I'm firing up and heading to the islands for a couple of weeks. A little cruising. A little fishing. Maybe some writing."

"Not even curious?"

"Just tell 'em that you told me whatever you were supposed to tell me."

"Actually, I wasn't supposed to tell you anything."

Leo reached into the pocket of his coat and produced a pale blue envelope. "I was just asked to give you this. You don't want to read it, don't."

Corso knew the stationery right away. "Shit," he said and snatched the envelope.

"Mind if I look around?" Leo asked.

Distracted, Corso told him to go for it. He held the envelope but didn't open it.

He vividly recalled the day her first note had arrived in the mail. He'd been sitting on a trunk in the East Village apartment, eating cornflakes out of an empty margarine tub. Waiting for the lease to expire at the end of the month and wondering what in hell he was going to do with the rest of his life. It was two weeks after the front-page saga of his disgrace and firing, and about ten days after Cynthia had packed in their lives and fled, leaving only the trunk, a brass end table, and a pile of partially addressed wedding invitations adrift on the mantel.

Bent in half and stuffed into the top of his mailbox. A plain manila envelope with a baby blue note that read:

Dear Mr. Corso,

If you would be interested in discussing a position with the Seattle Sun, *please use the attached ticket to fly to Seattle on July 9, 1998. A room has been booked for you at the Sorrento Hotel. Confirmation #032011134. I look forward to seeing you at 9 A.M. on July 10, 1998, at the Seattle Sun Building, 2376 Western Avenue, Seattle, WA.*

Natalie Van Der Hoven
Owner-Publisher
Seattle Sun

A bit odd, to be sure, but . . . I mean, why not? Wasn't like he'd had other offers. The way Corso saw it, for the next thirty years or so, he'd be lucky to land a job writing copy for a union newsletter. Why not, indeed?

She never asked him for an explanation of the New York fiasco. Just said she was a longtime fan. She also had a rather audacious plan. The kind of leap of faith only attempted by the desperate. She was willing to bet that Corso's syndication readers would follow him, regardless of what had happened in the past. She offered to give him back his press credentials. Said she'd make him the *Seattle Sun*'s roving reporter. He could call his own shots. Thousand bucks a column. Expenses agreed upon in advance. No bennies.

What she wanted in return was all of his syndication revenues. After New York? Hell, it was a no-brainer. Like that old Billy Preston song: "Nothin' from nothin' leaves nothin'." So Corso had agreed. The deal had worked out for both of them. Over the past three years, she'd built Corso's syndication numbers nearly back to where they had been before his firing. The extra revenue was a major factor in keeping the *Seattle Sun* afloat. As for Corso, he'd rebuilt some measure of confidence in his own sanity and had finally finished the book he'd started ten years earlier. When *Those Who Favor Fire* had gone to the top of the bestseller lists last year, they'd negotiated the weekly column back to twice a month. Two grand a pop.

He used his thumb to rip open the flap of the envelope. Written in her crisp schoolteacher hand it read: *Same story. This time the marker is mine.* Signed *Natalie Van Der Hoven.* A scrap of white paper waffled to the floor. Corso heaved a heavy sigh and dropped the note on the chart table. Left the paper on the floor. He knew what it said. Read the note again. Same story? Walter Leroy Himes?

Leo was out on the stern checking out the view of Lake Union and foggy Queen Anne Hill beyond. A floatplane roared north, bouncing across the choppy green water until it lurched into the sky and disappeared over Gasworks Park.

"Hey," Corso yelled. Leo stepped over and poked his head into the cabin.

"Himes is scheduled for execution on Saturday, right?" Corso asked.

Leo made a move like he was giving himself an injection. "Yeah," he said. "Midnight. Walter Leroy boots up the cosmic Kool-Aid over in Walla Walla."

For over eleven weeks in 1998, a serial killer had shaken Seattle like a maraca. Eight bodies in eighty days. Eight girls strangled, raped, and thrown into Dumpsters like urban litter. Taken from crowded places, where the volume of traffic alone should have made abductions impossible. As the weeks passed and the bodies became more frequent, the killer began to take on almost mythic properties. The media started calling him the Trashman. By the end, the streets were deserted after dark, and the pressure on the Seattle Police Department to find the killer was unrelenting.

SPD had now called in the county, the state, and the FBI. They hunted and harangued and profiled and pontificated, until, like clockwork, the sixth girl was found dead in an alley below the Pike Street Market. And then the seventh girl turned up. Hysteria reigned. A chorus called for the ouster of the chief of police. Others wanted the National Guard to safeguard the streets. Then, just when they feared another body was due to be found, they finally got lucky.

Two uniformed officers in a patrol car came upon an eighteen-year-old girl, Leanne Samples, staggering down a snow-covered service road in Volunteer Park, her panties missing in action, her face scratched and bleeding, her blouse torn to shreds and hanging at her wrists. When finally calm enough to talk, she told the officers that she'd been dragged into the bushes and had been in the process of being raped when the sound

of the squad car caused her attacker to flee. The officers called for an aide car and all the backup in the
world.

About the time Leanne Samples arrived at Harborview Medical Center, nearly a hundred cops and
FBI agents swept through the park like fire ants. They
found her white cotton panties beneath a dormant
azalea; they also found the owner of a local auto-body
shop getting a blow job from a fifteen-year-old runaway boy from Saginaw, Michigan. Most significant,
however, they found a homeless transient by the name
of Walter Leroy Himes playing with himself in the
men's room behind the bandshell.

By the time detectives arrived at Harborview Medical Center, Leanne's parents, who were members of a
Christian fundamentalist congregation, had put a stop
to her medical treatment. Seems they and their
brethren didn't hold with any of that scientific hocus-
pocus. No fluid workups, no DNA testing. No nothing.
The Devil's handiwork and all that, you know.

Faced with the total loss of forensic evidence, the
desperate detectives showed Leanne a five-year-old
mug shot of Walter Leroy Himes. After some prod-
ding, she said yes, that was the man who'd tried to rape
her. Two days later, Leanne picked Walter Leroy
Himes out of a six-man lineup. The rest, as they say,
was history. Hell, Himes made it easy for them.

Walter Leroy Himes was, after all, everything a
murdering scumbag was supposed to be. For starters,
he was every bit as ugly as he was big. A mouth-
breather with big red lips and truly lamentable personal hygiene. Not only was he uneducated, but he was
stupid besides. Refusing a lawyer until the last mo-

ment, when Judge Spearbeck stuck him with a wet-behind-the-ears public defender who had no idea how to deal with a client who wouldn't shut up in court, who wound up duct-taped to his chair, wearing a bright orange ball gag the judge ordered from the sex shop up the street from the courthouse. The capper was that Himes turned out to have an extensive record of sex offenses. Three county convictions for public nudity back in his native North Carolina. Seems he liked to wave his winkie at schoolkids. Worse yet, he'd recently done nineteen months at the Twin Rivers Correctional Facility for fondling an eleven-year-old girl in a downtown mini-mart. He had been released from prison a scant three weeks before the killings began. If ever a man was a natural to catch a rap, it was Walter Leroy Himes. And catch it he did. Big time. Eight counts of aggravated murder. Eight death sentences.

Leo stepped into the salon, sliding the teak door closed behind him. "What do you think?" he asked. "Now that Judgment Day is close at hand, you figure old Walter Leroy wishes he hadn't kept referring to the governor as 'the chink'?"

Corso thought it over. "If Himes was wired for regret, he wouldn't be on death row at all," he said finally. Leo nodded in silent agreement.

The state of Washington has never been particularly anxious to enforce its death penalty. Had Himes had sense enough to keep his mouth shut, they would have locked him up and let him appeal until he rotted. Not Himes though. No . . . Himes immediately tried to waive his right to appeal and demanded his death sentence be carried out posthaste. Claimed his maker knew he hadn't killed those girls. Figured when he got to wherever he was going, first thing he'd do was he'd rape those eight, what he called "stuck-up bitches," good and proper. Give 'em an eternity of what he figured they'd been asking for anyway. Way Himes saw it, since he was an innocent man, they owed it to him. Needless to say, such pronouncements did little to enhance Walter Leroy's popularity.

Such quantum stupidity quite naturally attracted the attention of the ACLU, which then had spent the last three years and the better part of four million dollars exhausting every legal avenue in an ill-fated effort to save Walter Leroy Himes from both the state of Washington and himself.

Leo ambled back through the boat to Corso's side. "Just for my peace of mind, Frank, who owns the Datsun?"

"Why?"

"'Cause you don't. You don't even have a Washington driver's license. If you owned a car or had a license, I'd have been here two hours ago."

"It's a dock car. Parking got to be so damn bad a bunch of us chipped in and bought it. You just sign up to use it whenever you need it. I need a car for anything serious, I rent one."

"No phone number, listed or not. No utility bills under your own name. No library card. No traffic tickets. No tax bills. You don't take any of the papers. No magazine subscriptions. No cable TV. You're not on-line with any of the local Internet providers. You're a regular Ted Kaczynski, you know that, Corso?"

Corso grinned. "So . . . just for *my* peace of mind, how *did* you find me?"

"Pizza," Leo said. "Pagliacci's has everybody in

town who's ever ordered a pizza in their database." He
eyed Corso. "Anchovy . . . Jesus, man."

Corso washed his hands in the sink and then dried
them with a paper towel.

"Since you just fucked up my fishing plans and quite
possibly my life, how about you giving me a ride down
to the *Sun*? Somebody else is signed up for the car this
afternoon." His tone had a resigned quality Leo had
never heard before.

Leo held up a moderating hand. "I don't know what
this is about, Frank, and quite honestly, I don't give a
shit, but whatever it is—if you don't want to do it, then
don't."

"Easier said than done."

"I gave up guilt for Lent," Leo said. "Maybe you
ought to do the same."

"What if you're actually guilty?" Corso asked.

"There's always denial."

"Let's go," Corso said.

They were halfway back to the gate when Leo said,
"Whaddya think, Frank? You figure gynecologists—
you know—know stuff that the rest of us don't?"

Corso pulled open the gate. "What kind of stuff?"

Leo waved a big hand. "You know . . .
techniques . . ." He shot Corso a quick glance. "You
know . . . like in bed."

"How long did you say it took you to find me?"

"Couple hours. Why?"

"How long do you think it would have taken Brendan the gynecologist?"

Leo gave the question serious consideration.

"Sorry I asked," the big guy said.

Chapter 3

Monday, September 17
2:58 P.M.   Day 1 of 6

Looked kinda like an older version of that karate movie guy. Steven Somethingorother. The guy with the long black ponytail. Bill Post tried to recall the actor's name. Yeah . . . Steven Something. The guy pulled the door open and strode into the lobby. Without so much as a by-your-leave, he took a hard left and headed for the elevator. What the hell . . .

Post scrambled out from behind the desk. "Hey . . . hey . . . there," he said. "This is a full security area, you can't just . . ." Bill Post reached out and grabbed the guy by the shoulder. Next thing he knew, ponytail had ahold of his hand. With his thumb, the guy found some pressure point in the soft meat between Post's thumb and forefinger, sending an electric shock up the length of the old man's arm. The arm dropped uselessly to Post's side. "Damn." Post flapped his wing like an injured bird.

"Now there's no cause to be . . . ," the old man sputtered. Rubbing his hand and trying to shake some feeling back into his palsied arm. "I can get the cops down here, if you want. You think you're Mr.—"

Ponytail pulled something out of the pocket of his black overcoat with one hand and pushed the elevator button with the other. A press credential. With his working arm, Post reached for the laminated card but the guy pulled it back, out of reach. A muted ding announced the elevator's arrival. He tilted his head back, squinted at the card: THE *SEATTLE SUN*. Frank Corso. The picture had short hair, but it was him all right.

Post began to stammer. "Oh . . . well, then . . . yes . . . sorry, Mr. Corso."

Corso stepped into the elevator.

"I'm supposed to send you to the second-floor lunchroom," Post said.

The door slid shut.

Post turned and headed back to his desk. The elevator bell sounded again.

"Hey," a voice called.

Post turned back. Corso again.

"Sorry about the hand," he said. "You okay?"

Post stopped trying to shake the feeling back into his arm.

"It's nothin'," he said. "I'll be fine."

"I'm a little jumpy sometimes," Corso explained. "I think maybe I spend a little too much time alone."

Post said he understood. Watched as Corso got back in the elevator and the steel door again slid closed. Post went back to massaging his arm as he stood and stared at the door for a moment. "Seagal. That's it, damnit. He looks like Steven Seagal."

He smiled as he started back toward his desk.

"Nothin' wrong with my memory. No, sir. Nothin' at all."

The minute he pulled open the door, Corso knew what was going on. Six days before Walter Leroy Himes's scheduled execution and she'd changed her tune. What he couldn't fathom, however, was what it had to do with him. Sure, he'd covered the trial for the *Sun*. His first big story in Seattle and damn near his last. He'd spoken to Leanne a couple of times. Interviewed her once. So what?

Fresh from the debacle in New York, Corso had found himself the only person in the Pacific Northwest who thought Himes had gotten the shaft and had insisted on writing a dissent. It started: "If Walter Leroy Himes hadn't existed, local law enforcement surely would have invented him." Hawes, on the other hand, quite rightly saw any dissent whatsoever as a public relations nightmare and had refused the piece. Corso went upstairs. Reminded Mrs. V. of their agreement. Mrs. V. said, "Run it," and the most unpopular piece of journalism in the city's history had appeared on page one the next morning.

Public furor had been costly. From Corso's end, the piece had motivated a couple of outraged rednecks from Kent to damn near beat him to death with tire irons. As for the paper, the *Seattle Sun* lost four thousand subscribers, 8 percent of its advertising revenue, and thus was forced to abandon its century-old broadsheet format. If Hawes had had his way, it would have cost Corso his job. Maybe his life. Corso was amazed when Mrs. V. chalked it off to experience. He'd gone to her office and handed her his handwritten IOU. "I owe you another one," he'd said. She'd agreed and tucked the slip of paper away for a rainy day. Like today.

Hawes read the girl's startled expression. Looked back over his shoulder and then got to his feet. He said something to Leanne. She nodded. Hawes crossed the room to Corso's side. He gestured with his head and then led Corso over to an uninhabited corner of the room.

"She says she lied at the Himes trial."

"So what?"

"That's all she'll say. She insists on talking to you."

"Why me?"

Hawes sneered at him. "Funny, but I've been asking myself that very question."

"I don't need this shit," Corso said.

Hawes had his jaw clamped so hard he looked like a largemouth bass.

Corso removed his coat and folded it over his left arm. "Tell Mrs. V. I'll be up when I get through chatting with Leanne." Hawes nodded. Corso excused himself and walked across the room. Leanne squirmed in her seat. From six feet away, Corso could see that the rim of the paper Pepsi cup in front of her had been picked to shreds. Two other similarly shredded cups leaned against the wall. Bits of waxed paper littered the table.

Instead of taking Hawes's seat across the table from Leanne, Corso slid onto the bench next to her. Eyes wide, she scooted over by the wall. "Long time no see, Miss Samples," he said. She nodded. "It is still *Miss* Samples, isn't it?"

Leanne managed an uncertain smile and said why of course it was still Miss.

"I thought maybe some young man might have spirited you away by now," he said. "Off to the Casbah or something."

The young woman reddened and hid her face with her hands.

"Stop it," she said with a giggle.

She hadn't changed a great deal. Same wide-open face and deep-set eyes. Her brown hair was, if anything, thicker, and she might have lost a little weight. She was, what? Twenty-one or so now. She'd been something like eighteen at the time. Probably not the PC nomenclature anymore, but, back then, Corso had decided that "slow" was the proper term for Leanne Samples. Eventually, Leanne got to the right answer. It just took her a bit longer than it did most folks.

"Leanne . . . ," Corso began. "I hope you won't mind if we get right down to business here." She nodded. "Did you tell Mr. Hawes that Mr. Himes did not attempt to rape you? Is that what you told him?" Before she could answer, Corso waved a finger in her face. "Because . . . if you are . . . I mean, girl, I've got to tell you right up front what a serious matter you're getting yourself into here."

She was chewing her thumb. Moving her head up and down.

"I did," she said softly.

The bench squeaked as Corso leaned back against the wall. His scalp tingled.

"Now why would a nice girl like you want to do a thing like that, Leanne? Why would you want to go and tell a lie about something so important?"

She thought it over. "I was scared," she said finally.

"Scared of what?"

"Of my parents."

"Why would you be afraid of your parents?"

"I thought I was pregnant."

"Pregnant by whom?"

She shrugged. "Some boy from school." She pulled her hand from her mouth and waved it as if she were shooing a fly. "You remember my parents . . ." She looked pleadingly at Corso. He nodded. "They'd go crazy," she said. "They'd . . ."

"So you . . ."

"So I went to the park. I tore up my clothes . . . scratched myself . . ." Unconsciously, she brought her fingertips to her cheek. "You know, to make it look like I was attacked. So . . . you know . . . in case I turned out to be pregnant . . . I could say I'd been . . ."

"What did you think the cops would do?" he pressed.

"There weren't supposed to be any police," she blurted out.

The lunchroom fell silent around them. She looked around. She started her thumb to her mouth, caught herself, jammed it back in her lap.

"I was just going to go home and tell my parents. That was all," she whispered. "They'd keep the shame in the family. It's their way." She waved her hand again. "The policemen just drove up. I didn't—"

"You identified a picture of Mr. Himes."

"They kept asking me to look again and look again and look again. I didn't know what else to do," she whined.

"You picked him out of a lineup."

"He was the man in the picture," she said. "I thought—"

"You testified in court," Corso interrupted.

She began to cry. "They're going to kill him. I never thought . . . I thought—"

"You thought what?" Corso pushed.

Her shoulders shook as she began to sob. "I thought he was a bad man and that they would put him away where he could get better and not hurt anybody."

Over the top of her head, he could see that the room had nearly stopped again as people realized who they were. The air was still and electrically charged, like in the seconds before a cloudburst.

"Have you been to the authorities?"

Her eyes again filled with tears. When she nodded, droplets rolled down her cheeks. "They didn't believe me. They said I'd have to go to jail."

Corso wasn't surprised. Recanting testimony was nearly impossible. Careers were at stake even in low-profile cases. In a case as emotionally charged as Walter Leroy Himes's, God only knew how far they'd go to cover their collective asses.

"Who did you talk to?" he asked.

She picked her purse up from the floor. Her hand came out with a business card. County seal. Assistant District Attorney. Timothy Beal.

"And then they brought some other men in. They said I was a liar."

She began to cry in earnest now. Corso waited as she found a twisted Kleenex in her coat pocket and applied it to her dripping nose. With the other hand, she fumbled in her purse and produced a yellowed and much-fingered piece of newsprint. "I showed them your article about how Mr. Himes was innocent. And you know what?" She didn't wait for an answer. "They said you were a liar too. That you got fired for printing lies.

And that was why you were working here instead of wherever you used to work."

Corso kept his mouth shut.

"Did you?" she insisted.

"Did I what? Get fired for fabricating a story? Yes, I did."

"Not that," she whined. "Did you lie?"

"Not on purpose," he said.

"You made a mistake?"

He grudgingly nodded. "In some way I still don't understand, I must have gotten sloppy. Overconfident, maybe . . . something like that."

Corso recalled Cynthia's face, watching it melt like a cake in the rain as he told her the real story of what he thought had happened. And then the silence and the look of pity as she asked, "You don't really think anyone is going to believe that, do you?" After that she began to rave about how if he'd just admit to making a mistake, maybe he could salvage what was left of his career. About how telling the story he'd just told her would accomplish nothing except to get him branded as not only a liar but as a paranoid schizophrenic as well. Corso had never told the story again. Not to Ben Gardner, his editor at the *New York Times* who fired him, and not to Mrs. V. here at the *Seattle Sun* when she hired him. So why, he wondered, did he feel compelled to tell Leanne Samples?

"Leanne," he said, "what happened to me back in New York is a very complicated story." He looked into her eyes. They were nearly black. "I say that not because I think you'll have any trouble understanding it. I say it because I don't understand the details of it myself. All I know for sure is that it happened."

She sat up straight, as if she were at school. Said she understood.

"I was writing a series about a very rich and powerful man." Corso paused. Took a deep breath. "He invited me to his office one day. Real polite and everything. Had a catered lunch there for us." Corso gathered himself. "After lunch—over coffee—he told me to stop. No more writing about him, he said." Corso snapped his fingers. "Just like that. 'Stop,' he told me. He said he'd squash me like a bug if I didn't." Corso ground his thumb on the table for emphasis.

Leanne cringed. "But you didn't stop, did you?" she said hopefully.

"No," Corso said. "I didn't. I kept picking at it."

She looked at her own thumb. "And he—"

"Like a bug." Corso sighed. "People got fired," he said. "Some of them held me responsible for ruining their lives."

"How?" she asked.

Yeah . . . that was the double jeopardy question, wasn't it? How could such a thing have happened? To a raw rookie, maybe. But to a seasoned investigative reporter? He wakes up one day and a whole raft of otherwise respectable people are suddenly conspiring against him. Spare us. We wanna hear that crap, we'll watch *The X-Files*.

"Money and pride," Corso said after a moment. "He had enough money to be truly dangerous, and I had enough pride to be truly stupid."

"Mama says money won't buy happiness," Leanne said.

"What's your mama have to say about pride?" he asked.

"Mama always says that 'pride goeth before a fall.'"

"I'm living proof your mama is right," Corso said.

"I knew you wouldn't lie on purpose."

"Thanks," Corso said with a chuckle. "You're now executive vice president of the Frank Corso Fan Club."

"Do you really have a fan club?" He'd forgotten how earnest she could be. Made a mental note to be careful about joking with her.

"Here we are," Corso said. "All of us."

She laughed again and used the Kleenex to dab at her eyes.

"If you don't mind me asking, Leanne, why me?"

She shrugged but didn't answer. She had an odd way of stepping back inside herself. Almost like she had a closet back there somewhere where she could go to hide.

"Well, then, I'll have to assume it's my boyish charm and rugged good looks," Corso said. "You probably didn't know this, Leanne, but women regularly swoon at the very sight of me. As a matter of fact, it's pretty amazing that you're still conscious."

Leanne laughed behind her hand. Told him again to stop it. Then suddenly got serious. "You always treated me nice like this. Like I mattered. Always listened to me like I was somebody important. Not like I was a spaz, like the others do. So . . . will you, please?" she pleaded.

"Will I what?"

"Will you make them listen to me?"

Corso thought about it. With the exception of Himes's ACLU lawyer, nobody but nobody was going to want any part of this story. In six days, dozens of heartbroken souls were finally scheduled to be granted some small measure of relief. A flawed but final resolution to a three-year-old nightmare and . . . what? Somebody was going to come along and say, Oops . . . waitaminute . . . there's been a minor glitch here. Back to square one. Feel free to return to your grieving.

Corso's insides suddenly had that sheet-metal feel. The feeling he'd first experienced in New York and had carried with him, on and off, ever since. A cold, dull ache in the pit of his stomach, as if he'd swallowed ball bearings. A pain that only subsided when he was floating alone on deep, green water.

He got to his feet and looked to the windows on the far side of the room. Outside, the steel-wool sky engulfed Queen Anne Hill. A steady rain coated the streets, leaving the cars to hiss along inside silver canopies of mist.

"Come on," he said.

Halfway down the hall to the elevator, Blaine Newton came across the red-tile floor toward Corso and Leanne, holding his oversize lunch bag by his side. Newton was about thirty and already lapping over his belt. Blaine Newton had been, for the past few years, Hawes's pet-reporter project. Another fancy dresser from the University of Washington journalism department, where Hawes moonlighted as an assistant professor. He was a better writer than a reporter. Next in line for the metro-crime beat, whenever Nathan Hopkins could be persuaded to retire. Corso disliked him on principle. When he recognized Corso, his big pink cheeks very nearly squeezed his eyes shut.

"Finally find yourself a date, Corso?"

"I'm saving it for Judith. She's all I can handle."

"Har-har," Newton barked. "Very funny."

"Give us a chorus of '*Danke Schoen,*'" Corso said as they passed.

Newton stopped in his tracks. "What the hell is that supposed to mean? You always say that like it's supposed to be a big joke or something."

Corso kept walking. "Ask Judith," he said.

"You're so funny," Newton said to his back.

Leanne leaned in and whispered, "Who's Judith?"

"His wife," Corso said in a loud voice. "She's very demanding."

Leanne giggled and squeezed his arm. When the elevator opened, Corso stepped aside and allowed her to enter first.

Chapter 4

The pictures on her desk made the facts of her life clear. Sons in college? Two. Husbands in residence? None. Violet Rogers was a sturdily built, no-nonsense woman of forty-five. Motherly, she wore her long hair braided and wound around her head like shiny black ropes.

The sound of the elevator pulled her eyes from the computer screen to the sliding door. "Why, Mr. Corso," she said with a smile. "It's been far too long."

She removed an earpiece from the side of her head and got to her feet. They shook hands. "Violet," Corso said, "this is Leanne Samples."

"I know . . . I know. It's not often we have such a celebrity up here."

Leanne blushed and began to stammer, "Oh . . . I'm not a celebrity . . . no, please . . ."

Corso inclined his head toward Mrs. V.'s office and raised his eyebrow. Violet instantly picked up on his drift. She took Leanne by the hand.

"What can I get you, honey?" she asked. "Coffee? Tea?"

Leanne swiveled her head around the room. "Is there a . . . a facilities on this floor?"

Violet emitted a deep, booming laugh. "Honey, this is the executive floor. We've got a facilities you won't believe. You just come along with me."

Corso watched the women wade through the ankle-deep carpet and disappear around the corner. Without knocking, he pulled open the door and stepped into Natalie Van Der Hoven's office. Bennett Hawes was pacing the center of the room with his hands jammed in his pants. Mrs. V. was seated behind her ornate ma-hogany desk opening mail with a silver letter opener.

"Thank you for coming, Mr. Corso," she said.

Corso crossed the room and shook the woman's hand. "Nice to see you again, Mrs. V.," he said. "You're the only thing about this business I miss."

"You flatter me, Mr. Corso."

"It's true," Corso insisted.

"I'm enchanted that you think so."

"You wanna tell us what she said, or what?" Hawes huffed.

Corso gave them the short version of what Leanne had told him. As always, Hawes refused to tilt his head back far enough to maintain eye contact with Corso and listened while staring at Corso's shirtfront.

From a newspaperman's point of view, one question now begged an answer. Mrs. V. was all over it. "Who else has she told?"

Corso handed her the ADA's business card.

"And how was her information received?" she asked.

"Just as you'd imagine. They threatened her and threw her out."

"You think they'll go public?" Hawes asked.

"No way. They'll stonewall for as long as they can."

"And she told nobody else?" Hawes pressed.

"She says the Beal guy called in a couple of suits. I'm guessing cops."

"So we print what? 'Himes Innocent'?" Hawes asked sarcastically.

"We print 'State's Witness Says She Lied' " Mrs. V. said.

Before Hawes could open his mouth, Corso said, "She's all the case they had."

Natalie Van Der Hoven sighed and rocked back in her chair. She knew where this was going. May as well let them work it out of their systems, she thought.

"He confessed," Hawes insisted.

According to the arresting officer, as he and Himes stood together in the corridor outside central booking, Himes had admitted to killing the girls.

"Himes always claimed the cop was lying."

"The killings stopped, goddamn it," Hawes spat out. "Let's not waste our time arguing about all this crap again. From the day they picked that slimeball up, there's never been another Trashman killing, period." He dotted the air with his index finger.

"No period," Corso said. "As I recall, they found the eighth victim several days after Himes was arrested."

"She was killed beforehand," Hawes said. "Took that long to find her."

"That's not how I remember it," Corso said quickly. "I seem to recall there was some reason or other why the time of death couldn't be established for the last girl."

"They had other forensic material," Hawes insisted.

"If they had a match, they'd have used it."

The official word on the forensics had been that although they had collected a great deal of forensic material, the fact that the victims had been found in Dumpsters raised the unfortunate specter of outside contamination to such a level that any competent defense attorney could easily get the forensics excluded. As far as Corso was concerned, in the end, Leanne Samples was the state's case.

"They had Himes dead to rights," Hawes persisted.

"The FBI sure as hell didn't think so," Corso countered.

Hawes made a disgusted face. "Oh, don't start that crap again."

"I'll tell you again—same thing I told you back then—the Bureau doesn't miss photo opportunities. I've worked around them a lot."

Hawes got theatrical now. Parading around with his hands on his hips. "Back before you were a famous true-crime writer. Back when you were the golden boy of the *New Yaaaawk Times*," he mocked. "Haaaaaavard scholar. Nieeeeeeman Fellow."

Corso swallowed his anger, took a deep breath. "Yeah, Bennett, way back then . . . And you know as well as I do, that's why local law enforcement hates working with them. No matter who breaks the case, they take the credit. Hell, it was a couple of Oklahoma troopers who pulled Timothy McVeigh over and made the collar. You remember seeing those good old boys up at the podium when they announced the arrest?" Before the older man could open his mouth, Corso said, "Yeah . . . me neither."

Bennett Hawes sighed and turned his back to Corso. He walked to the right side of the desk and sat heavily in the matching red leather chair. His face was sour. "And that tells you Himes was innocent?"

"No," Corso said. "What it tells me is that the FBI wanted nothing to do with the case against Walter Leroy Himes. That they wanted to distance themselves from the whole thing. I'm telling you, if Miss Samples out there keeps telling her present tale, we're about to see the biggest public ass covering since Pontius Pilate."

Mrs. V. slapped a palm on her desktop. The resounding silenced the men. "Enough," she said. "I've heard it all before. Ad nauseam," she added.

"And you remember what happened," Hawes snapped. "We're less than a week from a final resolution and I'm telling you"—he waved his arm at the skyline of the city—"these people want their pound of flesh. If they don't get Himes, they're gonna settle for whoever brings them the bad news."

No doubt about it. The execution frenzy was building to a peak. Just inside the prison gates, a herd of mobile television units aimed their concave eyes at the sky. Outside the gates of the prison, a tent city was growing. UPI estimated that by the time Himes was administered the lethal injection, three to four thousand souls would be gathered outside the gates to speed him on his way to eternity.

Corso knew the execution crowds. The foam baseball caps and the battered motor homes. He'd rubbed elbows with the soapbox preachers and the legions of lonely women. He'd personally witnessed two electrocutions and a hanging. All part of being in a business

where a phone call could drag you from the sanctity of
your bed and send you kicking amid the rubble of a
bombed-out building, watching your tasseled feet
slide amid the blood and the baby shoes and the broken bricks of other people's lives. The way Corso saw
it, if you had the nerve to insert yourself into such mo-
ments of personal tragedy, the least you could do was
not watch from the bleachers. You had to get down on
the field and play. You owed it to both the living and
the dead.

"Where is Miss Samples?" Mrs. V. demanded.

"Outside with Violet," Corso said.

She pushed a button on her phone. "Violet, would
you please send in Miss Samples?" Violet said it
would be her pleasure. A few seconds later, the door
eased open.

Leanne Samples stopped in the doorway, one hand
gripping each side of the opening, like Samson about
to pull down the temple. Her eyes darted around the
room, taking in the gallery of mutton-chopped fore-
bears whose portraits lined the walls. Her gaze finally
came to rest on the portrait of Natalie Van Der Hoven
that hung behind her desk. Mrs. V. got to her feet.
"Please come in," Mrs. V. prompted. Leanne stayed
put, staring at the portraits. "The paper has been in my
family for over a hundred years," Mrs. V. tried.

Leanne let go of the doorway and took several tentative steps into the room. Hawes slipped behind her,
closed the door, gently placed a hand on her shoulder,
and began to aim her to one of the chairs to the right of
Mrs. V.'s desk. Leanne, however, was having none of
it. She shook off his hand and made a beeline for

Corso, who, in the manner of a matador, eased the young woman past the edge of the desk and into the guest chair. She sat, halfway into the seat, leaning forward, her hands clasped in her lap.

"Can I get you something?" Mrs. V. inquired. "Coffee? A soft drink? A bottled water?" Leanne shook her head.

"A hundred years is a long time," she said after a moment.

"And quite a responsibility," Mrs. V. added. "The portraits make me feel as if they're all watching over me. Making sure I do the right thing."

"That's why I came here today," Leanne said.

Mrs. V. settled back into her seat. "To do the right thing?"

Leanne nodded. "I had to. I couldn't let somebody—Mr. Himes—be dead on account of me."

"I owe it to all of my readers to make sure that what I print in this paper is accurate." Mrs. V. locked Leanne with her gaze. The young woman seemed to steel herself, sitting up straight. Stilling her hands.

"What I told Mr. Corso is true." She looked back over her shoulder at Corso. He gave her a nod. "I lied about Mr. Himes, and now I have to fix it."

"That won't be easy," Mrs. V. said.

"I know," Leanne said softly.

"This is a very serious matter," Hawes added.

"I know," she said again, softer this time.

"Then I'm certain you will want to—" Mrs. V. began.

Leanne exploded like a cherry bomb. "No," she shouted. "Don't you dare start telling me what I want. I *know* what I want." She looked over at Hawes. "My whole life people have been telling me what I really want or what I really mean—like I'm such a retard I don't even know what's going on inside of me."

She turned finally to Corso. "Mr. Corso . . . he just listens to me like he listens to everybody else."

Natalie Van Der Hoven looked to Corso for an explanation.

"She means I treat everybody like they're retarded," he said.

Leanne covered her mouth and laughed. Mrs. V. returned to her seat behind the desk, leaned forward, pushed the red button on her phone. "Violet, could you come in here, please?"

"Yes, Mrs. Van Der Hoven," crackled the voice.

Mrs. V. looked over at Leanne. "Do you still live with your parents?"

Leanne shook her head. Said she was living in a group home on Harvard Avenue. Transitioning into the workplace, as it were. Place was called Pathways.

The office door opened. Violet stepped in. "Are either of the boys home from college, Violet?" Mrs. V. asked.

"No, Mrs. Van Der Hoven. Not for a couple more weeks."

"How would you feel about spending the next few days in a fancy hotel ordering room service?"

Her face lit up. "I don't believe I understand—" she began.

"Miss Samples is going to be a guest of the paper for a few days. I was wondering if it would be too much of an imposition to ask you to act as her chaperone."

It took a bit of talking, but they worked it out. Leanne suddenly found herself beyond where she'd thought things through and took a little convincing. Violet wouldn't hear of Mrs. V. fielding her own calls and insisted on arranging a suitable temp for herself. They settled on the Carlisle Hotel where the *Sun* had an account they used for out-of-town visitors. They were to get a couple of rooms. Not use their own names. Violet was going to stop at home and gather whatever personal things she might need for an overnight stay. Anything Leanne needed would come out of petty cash. Mrs. V. gave Violet her personal cell phone number and told her to call Pathways as soon as they were settled. Wouldn't want them sending out a search party. Violet was explaining the concept of room service to Leanne as they walked out the door. "Honey, you can order anything!" she said. "You ever had a surf and turf?"

Leanne kept her eyes locked on Corso. He waved. She mustered a tight smile she didn't mean and backed out the door.

Mrs. V. turned to Hawes. "Call Mr. Robbins at the plant. Have him up tonight's street run by fifty percent."

Hawes sighed. "He's gonna say it can't be done."

"He always says it can't be done. Just tell him I said to do it. And tell him I want the first papers in the machines by four-thirty."

They watched as Bennett Hawes hurried out the door.

Chapter 5

Corso sat in the red leather chair and watched the rain close over Elliott Bay like a steel curtain. In the distance, the outline of the westbound Bainbridge Island ferry was little more than a half-erased pencil drawing.

"I don't need this right now," Corso said.

"I know."

"My fifteen minutes of fame are over. I'm no longer the Typhoid Mary of the newspaper business. I can walk up the street for a latte without anybody pointing a camera at me. Hell, I can't even remember the last time anybody threatened to kill me. I like things the way they are. If I've got something that pisses me off, I write a column about it. If it really pisses me off, I write a book. For this, people throw money at me. How bad can things be?"

When she didn't reply, he got to his feet and walked over to the window. Six stories below, in Myrtle Edwards Park, skeletal trees shivered in the wind. Rain skittered across the black asphalt walkways in sweeping silver lines. Beyond the park, Puget Sound hurled itself upon the black boulders of shore, sending plumes of spray high into the dark sky. Corso tried to remember who it was who said that living in Seattle was like being married to a beautiful woman who was sick all the time. Leo, maybe.

"You're going to make me be the one to say it out loud, aren't you?" he asked after a moment. "Not even going to cut me the slack of saying it first."

Natalie Van Der Hoven used class the way Leo used big. As a shield. Corso knew better than to underestimate her. She was a shrewd executive and a practiced negotiator. If you weren't careful, you found yourself nodding at everything she said, not because you agreed but because any sort of disagreement seemed positively rude.

She brought a hand to her throat and did her best Scarlett O'Hara. "Whatever do you mean?"

"That I owe you. That you gave me a job when I was a national leper. After my last employer lost a ten-million-dollar libel judgment on my account. And you take me in and give me a job and what do I do? I screw up again. You damn near lose a newspaper that's been in your family for a hundred years and guess what? You don't fire me, you let me keep my job."

"I'd like to think our relationship has grown beyond a simple case of mutual obligation," she said.

"Don't start with me," Corso scoffed. "You know damn well we're friends, and you know damn well that's not the point."

Corso leaned his forehead against the cool glass. Overhead, a clap of thunder rolled like cannon fire. The tick of rain on the windows rose to a sustained hiss, and then, just as suddenly, abated. Mrs. V. broke the spell.

"I don't suppose I have to tell you what a precarious position the *Sun* finds itself in," she began. "We've reached that unfortunate position on the newspaper food chain where our finances force us to consider our editorial policy." She took a deep breath. "And allowing finances to dictate news is, as we all know, the first step in a slide toward journalistic hell." She looked out, over Corso's head. "A journey, which I say, quite frankly, I have no intention of making. I'll close the doors first."

Something in Corso's reflected face betrayed him. Mrs. V. seemed to read his thoughts. "You're thinking that I already made that mistake, aren't you? You're thinking the Himes case was the first time." Before Corso could lie, she continued, "I quashed the follow-up to your Himes story, quite simply because I thought you were wrong. The public hysteria had nothing to do with my decision. You were new to us. I thought you were overreacting to what had happened to you in New York. It seemed plain to me that you were merely trying a bit too hard to make a new name for yourself." She shrugged. "Human nature, I supposed."

"The screwup was mine," Corso said. "The piece was self-indulgent. Part of the job is knowing which way the wind blows and then tailoring your approach to the weather. I didn't do my job."

"You're too hard on yourself, Mr. Corso," she said.

Down in the park, an elderly Asian woman walked a little brown-and-white dog whose swinging belly nearly dragged on the pavement. With one hand she jerked the leash, as if teaching the dog to heel; with the other she fought to keep her red umbrella from turning inside out in the gale.

"I'm pained to have been forced to prevail upon you in this manner, Mr. Corso. I know what you've been through."

"Pained enough to tell me to forget about it and go fishing?"

"No."

A sudden swirling gust tore the red umbrella from the old woman's hand. She lunged for it, missed, slipped on the wet grass, and went down heavily on her side, dropping the leash as she fell. The dog took off, running after the tumbling umbrella on four-inch legs. The woman struggled to her feet and started after the dog in an arthritic, splay-footed shuffle, waving an arm, shouting.

"I don't want any part of this," Corso said.

"I don't blame you."

The umbrella lodged halfway up the fence on the east side of the park. The little dog hopped on its hind legs in a single-minded frenzy to pull it back to earth. By the time the old woman arrived, her hair was plastered to her head and the umbrella was history. The wind had torn the red fabric free, dropping the metal frame at the base of the fence. She grabbed the leash and nearly fell again as she dragged the dog back onto the pavement. In the deepening gloom, the red nylon waved like a signal flag.

Corso folded his arms across his chest and turned back toward the room. His face was grim and the look in his eyes suggested he might be capable of casual cruelty.

"If I do this . . . this will clear our slate," he said. "Once and for all."

She tapped her manicured fingertips together. "The column too?" she asked.

He thought it over. "Way I see it, the column works out for both of us. The syndication keeps you afloat and the press credentials get me into places I couldn't otherwise get into. I can't see any reason to change that. Unless you want to quit."

"Of course not."

"Well?"

"I suppose I deserve this," she said.

"You suppose correctly."

She fixed him with a steely gaze as she thought over his proposition. "All you have to say is no," she said.

"But we both know I won't, don't we?"

Annoyed now, she arched an eyebrow. "What we both know, Mr. Corso, is that above and beyond either our friendship or our mutual indebtedness"—she waggled a finger at him—"you harbor a certain quixotic spark. . . ."

Corso opened his mouth to protest, but she waved him off. "You say what you want," she said quickly. "It comes out in your columns, in your books. There's a messianic tendency at the very center of you, Mr. Corso. You know it and I know it. You write as if there's a single path to the truth, and you're the only one with a map." She shrugged. "Trust me. It doesn't go unnoticed. I read your hate mail."

"I've always inspired damn little ambivalence," Corso said.

"No doubt."

Corso smiled. "My mama used to say I had enough moral indignation for half a dozen preachers."

Beneath the words, she thought she heard the lazy trace of a drawl. She'd noticed it before. Sometimes when they talked late at night. When he was tired and his guard was down, you could almost hear another voice.

"Your mama had a point," she said.

She watched as his eyes turned inward. "I remember the first time anybody ever told me life wasn't fair," Corso said. "I was three or four . . . something like that. I was pissing and moaning about something not being fair and my aunt Jean leaned over the dinner table and told me how I might as well shut up and get used to the idea."

"And?"

He made eye contact. "I didn't believe it then and I don't believe it now," he said. "If I thought for a minute the world was that arbitrary. I'd go down to my boat and blow my brains out."

A sudden gust of wind rattled the windows. Corso heaved a sigh, cursing silently.

"And you want me to do what?" he asked.

She held up two fingers. "Two things. If Walter Himes didn't kill those young women, then I want to know who did."

"Good thing you don't want much."

"Second, while you're looking into this, I want you to write the stories."

"Hawes is right, you know. Getting between the people and their pound of flesh is going to generate a lot of heat, and having my name on the byline is gonna be like throwing gasoline on the fire."

"I'm aware of that," she said. "The situation, however, is desperate. We've reached the point where we at the *Sun* can no longer concern ourselves with what people may be saying about us as long as they're saying something."

"It's going to get ugly."

"I can handle the heat. Can you?"

"We're gonna find out, aren't we?"

She pulled a small leather-bound pad toward her.

"How much space are you going to need?"

"For the 'Leanne Samples Changes Her Story' story?"

"Yes."

"With a recap . . . probably sixteen hundred words."

"If we're upping the street run, I'm going to need it by nine."

"I'll have it ready," Corso assured her.

"Anything else?"

"Have somebody call Himes's attorney of record and ask if Himes will agree to see me. Tomorrow. As soon as possible."

"He hasn't spoken to the press in nearly two years. What makes you think he'll talk to you?"

"Have whoever calls tell the attorney about the story we're running tomorrow morning. Tell him who wrote it. Remind him of the 'rush to judgment' piece. Run my famous-author status by him. See if maybe that doesn't loosen things up."

"Excellent idea," Mrs. V. said. "As I recall, he wanted to see you rather badly way back when . . ." She let it hang.

"Ask if we can bring a photographer. Somebody other than Harry Dent," he said, naming the *Sun*'s ancient photo editor whose outdated noir style of photography regularly made baby showers look lurid.

"Mr. Dent is the only photographer we have left on staff," she said. She read Corso's pained expression. "He had seniority."

"Who took the shots of the bus accident on Aurora a couple of weeks ago?"

"A freelancer," Mrs. V. said. "A woman named Dougherty, I believe."

Corso recalled the battered metro bus lying on its side. The anguished looks on the faces of the citizens who risked their lives to rescue passengers from the smoldering ruins. Pictures that seemed to jump off the page at the reader.

"Can you get her?"

"Miss Dougherty is . . . as I understand it . . . how shall I put this? I've been led to believe she's somewhat exotic and perhaps a bit . . . forward." She seemed pleased by her choice of words.

Corso chuckled. "We ought to make an interesting pair," he said.

"I'll see what I can do. Anything else?"

Corso gave it some thought. "That's it for right now," he said.

"And you?" Mrs. V. asked of Corso.

"I guess I'm headed downtown. See if I can't scratch up a denial." She looked at him as if he'd broken wind.

"At the *Sun*, we don't generally preview stories," she intoned.

"Neither do I," said Corso, "but, as much as I hate to agree with Hawes twice in the same day, I want to make sure our asses are covered on this one."

She thought it over. "As much as the precedent pains me, you're no doubt right. After all, exclusives like this don't drop on one's doorstep every day."

"Nice touch, by the way, the room at the Carlisle. The watchdog and all," Corso offered with a grin.

She looked offended. "It was my Christian duty.

Could we, after all, have the young woman's group home inundated with the press?"

"As long as we have her to ourselves, we have the story to ourselves."

She gave Corso a wicked smile. "At best, we'll get a day out of the Carlisle," she said. "By this time tomorrow, the hounds will have found her."

"There's lots of hotels."

"My thinking exactly."

She got to her feet, stretched, and then checked her watch.

"You haven't done anything like this in a while."

"I remember how."

"Are you sure you have the stomach for it? It's going to be New York all over again. Whatever personal space you've cut out for yourself in the past couple of years is going to be gone."

"Did I miss the part where you left me a choice?"

She raised an eyebrow. "As you just so poignantly pointed out to me, Mr. Corso, choices come in all sizes and shapes."

"Yeah, but some of them are easier to live with than others."

She smiled that wicked smile again.

"Every form of refuge has its price, Mr. Corso."

Chapter 6

Corner of Fifth and James. The Public Safety Building is notched hard into the side of the hill, sentencing an entire city block to perpetual shade. Connected by a seventh-floor covered walkway to the King County jail, the complex is a remnant of an age when signs on the freeway implored the last person leaving town to please turn out the lights. A pair of ten-story poured-concrete monuments to fiscal restraint, they looked remarkably like waffles standing on end and were quite easily the ugliest buildings in the city's gleaming downtown core.

Two officers at the front desk. Blue shirts, sitting way up high in the power position. Typical city cops. If your aorta wasn't severed, they were going to finish what they were doing before they bothered with you. Corso reached up and dropped a business card faceup in front of the older of the two. When neither of them so much as glanced at the card, Corso asked, "Either of you remember the officers of record in the Trashman killings?"

Without looking up, the young cop said, "Dens-more's the three. I don't—" He suddenly frowned and looked desperately toward his lap, as if the older cop had grabbed him by the balls. The older cop locked his eyes on Corso and said, "You mean back in ninety-eight?" Corso couldn't be sure, but he thought he saw some color drain from the younger man's face. "Yeah," said Corso.

"Chucky Donald was one of them. He's a lieutenant in the East Precinct. Him and whoever was his partner at the time. I think the guy pulled the pin a couple years back." Corso thanked him and wrote Donald's name in his notebook.

"Help you with something?" the older one asked. He now held Corso's card with his fingertips, as if it were radioactive.

"I need to see whoever's in charge of public affairs."

"Dorothy Sheridan," the older cop said. "She's in a meeting."

"Does she have an assistant?"

"Bunches," he said with a sneer. "They're all in the meeting."

Corso searched the cop's face for some indication as to whether the guy was busting his balls for fun. Officer John McCarty, according to the name tag, wasn't, however, offering any hints. When in doubt, keep talking, asking questions—anything to keep a dialogue going. "Do you have a direct number where I could reach Lieutenant Donald at the East Precinct?"

The cop shifted to his left and touched the keyboard. His pockmarked face was bathed in blue light. He pushed a couple of more buttons. "Three, two, nine, three, nine, four, five, extension eleven twenty-nine." The screen went black. For the first time, the younger officer was looking at Corso, who thought he detected a hint of amusement in the guy's eyes. "Was it something I said, fellas?" Corso asked. He pulled open his coat and sniffed at his right armpit. "Deodorant failure?"

Officer McCarty looked only slightly amused when he said, "Happens Lieutenant Donald's in the same meeting."

Corso smiled. He now knew the meeting must be here in the Public Safety Building, otherwise a couple of desk cops wouldn't be privy to it. He took a chance. "Wouldn't be that an ADA name of Timothy Beal is in there with them, would it?" He hunched his shoulders, spread his hands. "Just a guess."

The younger cop checked the screen in front of his face, tapped the keyboard twice, and then looked to McCarty, who leaned over in front of the younger man's video display.

"You read palms on the side?" the older cop asked.

"The bumps on your head," Corso said. "Phrenology."

The cop looked like he was considering adding a few bumps to Corso's head.

"I think you better let me see this Ms. Sheridan."

McCarty weighed his options. "I drag her out of a meeting and this turns out to be crap, there's going to be a problem."

"I understand."

McCarty finally read his way through Corso's card. "Hopkins covers crime for the *Sun*. Says here you write features."

"That's right."

"How long you been with the paper?"

"Three years or so."

"So how come I've never seen you before?"

"Just lucky, I guess," Corso joked. McCarty was not amused.

"Hopkins under the weather?" he asked.

"Not that I know of," Corso said.

McCarty waited for an explanation.

"I need to run a story by someone in authority. To give 'em a chance to confirm or deny." The cop wasn't impressed. "I'm guessing it's the same story they're sitting in there talking about," Corso added.

McCarty got to his feet. Took Corso in from head to toe. Pointed across the room to the built-in bench running along the north wall. "Take a seat over there."

McCarty disappeared through a door behind the desk. Corso planted himself on the blue Naugahyde. The sticky plastic groaned as he slid back. No magazines. No cigarette butts. Just an overgrown jade plant, its thick leaves covered with dust, meandering its way around the dirty window. Corso took his notebook from his coat pocket and had begun to leaf through it when the front doors were pulled open wide.

Deep voices filled the room. SWAT. The storm troopers of the status quo. A full tactical unit, fresh from an operation. Still coming down from the adrenaline rush. Eight jackbooted, armored urban warriors. All in black. Darth Vader helmets. Huge men. Three white, four black, one other. Olympic weight lifters with twenty-inch biceps carrying bulging equipment bags full of body armor. A four-foot steel battering ram swung from the arm of an immense black man who carried what appeared to be an M16 in his other hand. The noise of their walking toward the elevator drowned the rush of the wind and the wet hissing of tires. When the elevator came, only four could fit in the car. Four went. Four waited.

McCarty came out from behind the desk. Clipped a visitor's badge on Corso's collar. "Follow me," he said. Together they crossed to the elevator. The door slid open.

"Hold it, fellas," McCarty said. "Got a priority here."

The SWAT team stopped talking. Didn't move an inch. Made McCarty and Corso squeeze around them and into the elevator. They reminded Corso of those space droids you see on TV. The ones with the tubes coming out of the sides of their heads. Steroid suicide squads, protecting truth, justice, and the American way. Mercifully, the door slid shut. McCarty pushed the button for the eighth floor. "I don't know how the criminals feel about guys like that," Corso said, "but they scare the hell out of me."

"They're supposed to," McCarty said.

She was waiting just outside the elevator. She was pushing forty. Still winning the battle of the bulge. Short blond hair and a bad color sense. She wore a yellow-and-green-plaid sweater and a bright yellow skirt. The yellows didn't quite match and the gold glow lent her complexion a sallow, almost jaundiced tinge.

McCarty held the door open with his arm, handed her Corso's business card.

"And this is about what?" she asked.

"Leanne Samples," Corso said.

She raked her free hand through her hair, thought about running a "Leanne who?" number on Corso and then decided against it. She gestured with her fingers

for Corso to get off the elevator. Corso stepped off. The
door slid shut.

Corso held out his hand. "Frank Corso."

She made no move to shake. "So it says."

Corso put on a smile. "And your name is?"

Her facial expression said "worst-case scenario."
She sighed.

"Dorothy Sheridan. What is it you need, Mr.
Corso?"

He pulled out his notepad. "We're running a story in
tomorrow morning's edition to the effect that Leanne
Samples, who, if you'll recall, was the state's star witness in the Walter Leroy Himes case, that Miss Samples has told both the DA and the SPD that she lied
three years ago when she testified that Mr. Himes had
sexually assaulted her."

"And?"

"And we wanted to give the department the opportunity to comment on the story beforehand. Just as a professional courtesy."

"Anything that may or may not have been said between Miss Samples and any member of the law-
enforcement community would certainly be—"

"I've got her on tape," Corso said, "I've also got a
deadline, so I don't have time to dance, Ms. Sheridan.
Lead, follow, or get out of the way. Confirm, deny, or
tell me 'no comment.'"

Her cheeks reddened. "Are you threatening me?"

"No, ma'am," Corso assured her. "If I were threatening you, my position would be that you either talk to
me or I'll go to print. That would be unethical. This
isn't like that. We're going to print with the story.
That's a given. I'm merely providing the subjects of

the story with an opportunity to comment prior to publication. In the interest of both accuracy and balanced reporting."

She folded her arms so tightly across her chest that her sweater rode up over the waistband of her skirt, revealing a patch of stark-white skin. "Weeeell . . . aren't you just Mr. Smooth. How is it that we haven't crossed swords before?"

"I'm a little out of my beat."

"Which is?"

"Features."

And then she got it. She looked down at the card in her hand and then back at Corso. Inhaled the smile. She knew who he was.

"Stay here," she said. "I'll be right back."

When she looked over her shoulder, Corso was leaning back against the wall. She turned to the right and started down the short hall, turned left at the end.

Corso listened to the clicking of her sensible heels until he thought he detected a change in the sound, then hustled over and peeked around the corner just in time to see the woman disappear down a hall to the left. He tiptoed up to the next corner. Peeked around. Watched as she walked to the center of the corridor, grabbed a door handle on the right side of the hall. The lettering on the door read CONFERENCE ROOM A. She disappeared inside.

Corso checked his watch. Waited a full minute. Started down the hall.

On the left, two rooms. Corso could hear voices. Speaking Spanish. He straightened his jacket and put on his best confident stride. First room held three copy machines. The second, vending machines. Two jani-

tors, both Hispanic. One male, one female; according
to the patches on their blue uniform shirts, Luis and
Carlotta. Corso nodded as he walked past. They nodded back.

He stopped at the door to Conference Room A. The
voices were muffled, the words unintelligible. Corso
checked the hall in both directions. To the left, two
more small rooms and then a dead end. To the right, he
could hear Luis and Carlotta laughing.

Corso leaned his ear against the glass. A familiar
voice said, "I don't give a rat's ass about Walter Leroy
Himes. What I care about is that nothing we do com-
promises the ongoing investigation of these . . ."

Corso didn't catch the rest of it. Two uniformed cops
turned the corner in front of him. The one on the right
pointed at Corso and hollered, "Hey . . . you . . ."

Corso smiled at the cop, waved, and then grabbed
the handle and stepped into Conference Room A.

Chapter 7

Monday, September 17
5:19 P.M.   Day 1 of 6

The mayor stopped in mid-sentence when Dorothy
Sheridan reentered the room. She looked around the
table and sighed. A tough crowd. One of those crowds
you didn't want to be telling anything they didn't want
to hear, which was, of course, precisely what she did
for a living. She told eager reporters that the SPD
wouldn't be releasing information anytime soon. She
told shocked survivors that the remains of their loved
ones couldn't be released until the lab guys were finished. She peered straight-faced into banks of cameras
and claimed the department was developing leads
when she knew damn well they weren't. Still, this was
a rough crowd. Messenger murderers all. Another sigh.
"I've got a live one out there, folks. Guy named Corso
from the *Sun*."

"Where's Hopkins?" Chief of Police Ben Kesey demanded. Kesey was fifty-three, with a great shock of
white hair combed straight back. A master politician,
given to wearing his dress blues as a way of maintaining contact with his officers in the streets, who whis-

pered that he looked like a rear admiral and were so moved by his humility they'd given him a vote of no confidence at the last two union meetings.

"Looks to me like they've sent in the first team," Sheridan said. "This guy Corso is that famous reporter Natalie Van Der Hoven hired after he got canned from the *New York Times* for fabricating a story. He writes books these days."

"A reporter who writes fiction," the mayor mused. "How redundant."

Mayor Stanley Seifort had a scholarly look. Wide, expansive face and enough bare forehead to post bills on. Like his most recent predecessors in the mayor's office, Seifort was, other than possessing a zealous desire to make Seattle into Perfect City, USA, totally devoid of politics.

Sheridan continued to stand behind her chair. "With all due respect, Your Honor, please take my word for it, fact or fiction, credibility or no credibility, this guy is going to be a pain in the butt."

"Why's that?" Seifort asked.

"Because he's not housebroken. We could have asked Nathan Hopkins to hold off on the story and he would have kept it to himself for a day or two. Not this Corso character. He's the type who's never going to be paper-trained. I can tell."

"Why do we have to tell him anything?" Chief Kesey asked. "Tell him to get the hell out of the building."

Dorothy Sheridan worked to keep the impatience out of her voice. Although she was a civilian employee of the SPD, technically Kesey was still her boss. She pictured her daughter Brandy in her new braces. She'd had a migraine for a day and a half after finding out that eighty percent of the braces was going to come out of her own pocket. Had to lie on her bed with a cold rag pressed to her forehead, thinking positive thoughts, picturing her retirement, chanting "twelve down . . . eight to go." She chose her words carefully. "Because the *Sun* is going to press in the morning with Leanne Samples's new story. We have to tell him something. Either that or he prints that we had no comment."

"So . . . tell him no goddamn comment," the chief snapped.

"I'm not sure we want to do that," Dorothy said.

"Why in hell not?" the chief demanded. "Has it gotten to the point where we can't even issue a simple 'No comment'?"

Dorothy was still trying to compose a sentence that did not contain the words "Walter Leroy Himes" when the cute little ADA started waving his arm. Thank God.

Sitting at the center of the long table, Timothy Beal raised his hand like he was in grammar school. "May I say something?" he asked.

Sheridan thought, Go for it, mullet head.

When nobody objected, Beal spoke. "We've been talking about this for an hour and I haven't heard so much as a whisper of the name Walter Leroy Himes. The guy who's scheduled to die by lethal injection less than a week from now. Why is that?"

Sheridan watched as Chucky Donald, who sat directly across from the ADA, winced, as if to say, "Wrong question, dweebus. Bite your tongue." Donald was Kesey's boy. Said to be in line to make captain. Maybe the youngest in history.

Thirty-eight hundred bucks for braces. She'd called her rotten ex. Asked him to pony up some of the cash, reminded him that Brandy was, after all, his kid too. . . . But, you know, the demands of a new family, two kids under three . . . besides which, his paying for braces wasn't in the divorce contract—you're the one who wanted sole custody—he'd have to discuss it with Sheila and you know how Sheila feels about . . . what was a guy gonna do? You understand.

The chief leaned forward, looked down the table at the young ADA. "Listen, Mr. Beal, I don't give a rat's ass about Walter Leroy Himes. What I care about is maintaining the credibility of my department and making damn sure that a highly sensitive, ongoing investigation is not going to be compromised by—"

A shout from the hall broke his train of thought. The conference room door opened. A tall man with a black ponytail stepped into the room, closing the door before turning to the assembled multitude. He showed his perfect teeth and spoke. "Oh, excuse me. I was looking for the men's room," he said.

Bennett Hawes had his notepad out. "Gimme those names again."

Corso counted off on his fingers. "Hizhonor the mayor. Chief Kesey. Dorothy Sheridan and a couple of her assistants in public affairs. I don't know their names. ADA Beal, who's the one Leanne originally told her story to. A nasty cop named Densmore. Another cop named Donald. Charles Donald. A lieutenant from the East Precinct who just happens to be not only one of the arresting officers in the Himes case, but is also the officer to whom Himes supposedly confessed."

"Spelled like the duck?" Hawes asked.

"Yeah."

"Who else?"

"That bald guy who's always standing behind the mayor in photographs."

"Marvin Hale. He's the district attorney," Mrs. V. said.

"That it?" Hawes asked.

"That's all of them," Corso said.

"And you're sure that Miss Samples was the subject of the conversation?"

"Positive."

Hawes looked to Mrs. V. "We'll run the meeting and the refusal to comment as a sidebar to the Samples story."

"I like it," she said.

Hawes snapped his notebook shut. He almost smiled. "So what happened after you claimed you were looking for the john?"

Dorothy Sheridan gestured toward Corso. "The afore-mentioned Mr. Corso," she said. "Making the afore-mentioned pain in the butt of himself."

The mayor rubbed his chin and whispered over his shoulder to the district attorney. A skinny guy in a blue suit jumped to his feet, sending his chair sliding back into the wall. He glared at Dorothy Sheridan. "What the hell is he doing here?"

She stammered. "He . . . I told him to wait . . ."

"It's not her fault," Corso said quickly. "She told me to wait by the elevators. I have a very limited attention span."

Blue Suit blustered his way around the table until he was nose to nose with Corso. His skin was oily. His mean little eyes crawled over Corso like ants. "Turn around," he bellowed. Corso stood still. "You're under arrest for criminal trespass," he said. "Now turn around, you son of a bitch."

"Andy," Kesey said. "Lighten up."

"It's not trespass," Corso said. "I checked in downstairs." He flicked the plastic badge clipped on his collar. "See—I've got a handy-dandy badge."

The guy swung his hand, knocking the badge to the floor. Then poked Corso hard in the chest with his finger. "Didn't I tell you to turn around?" He poked Corso again. Harder. "Densmore," the chief said.

Corso kept his smile locked in place. "You poke me again, Andy, and you're gonna need to wipe your ass with your other hand," he said evenly.

Sharp intake of collective breath. Dead silence. Blue Suit fixed Corso with what he imagined to be his most baleful stare. Bobbed his narrow head up and down. Agreeing with himself. "I'll remember you—you son of a bitch. Don't you think I won't."

"It's always nice to be remembered," Corso said, still smiling.

Densmore balled one hand and used the other to grab Corso by the shirtfront.

"Andy," cautioned the district attorney.

Reluctantly, he let go of Corso's shirt and pointed to the guy in the gray suit. "Donald," he growled, "get him out of here. I swear to God . . . Get him out of here before I . . ." He started back around the table, toward his chair.

Gray Suit got to his feet. Corso pulled out his notebook. "Should I take this to be a no comment, Chief?" he asked. Densmore turned on his heel and started back for Corso.

"Andy," the district attorney said again. Louder this

time. Dorothy Sheridan stepped between the cop and Corso. Her face was white. "Sergeant Densmore, please," she said. He stopped one pace short of Sheridan. Stood there rocking on the balls of his feet. Donald grabbed Corso by the arm.

"Get him the hell out of here," the chief shouted.

Corso let Donald steer him back out into the hall. "Come on," he said. "Let's go." He had a deep, resonant voice reminiscent of a TV anchorman's, and a first-class tan. Couldn't have been much more than thirty. Young for a lieutenant, with one of those youthful faces that linger well past middle age. Thick, Hugh Grant hair. Very trendy. Hawes would have killed for the suit. Italian. Silk. At least a grand and a half, maybe two. Corso checked his feet. Three hundred bucks' worth of Bally loafers. "Andy's a bit testy today," Corso commented.

"Lotta pressure," the cop said. "Move. Let's go."

"You were the arresting officer on the Himes bust," Corso tried.

"Come on," Donald said, herding Corso down the hall and back toward the elevator. Luis and Carlotta were still yukking it up by the Coke machine.

"It's a matter of public record," Corso said. "What's the big deal?"

Donald pushed the elevator button. "The big deal, Mr. Corso, is that you're messing with something you don't understand here."

"What's not to understand? The prime—the only—witness in the case against Walter Leroy Himes now says she lied. The guy's six days from execution. All I want to know is what you guys are going to do about it."

"She wasn't the only witness," Donald said a bit too

quickly. Pushed the button again. Twice. Adjusted his tie. Pushed the button again.

"It was you, wasn't it?" Corso said. "You're the one who supposedly heard Himes confess." Donald didn't answer. Just stood and watched the lighted indicator work its way up to eight. The door slid open. Corso stepped in first. Donald followed. Pushed one. "All you people care about is selling newspapers," he said as the door closed. "You never think about the effects of what you print," he said as the door closed. "You never think about the effects of what you print, as long as you sell papers." Corso kept his mouth shut. He'd heard it a million times before. The truth was that as long as they got a check once a month, most reporters couldn't care less about circulation. Reporters don't write stories to sell papers, they write stories to get their name above the fold on the front page. If the paper has a fold, that is.

"What exactly did Himes say that day?" Corso asked. Donald snorted and shook his head. The elevator door opened. Donald walked him toward the front door. Over his shoulder, Corso caught a glimpse of the two desk cops. McCarty was beet red, whispering some very unsweet nothings in the younger man's ear. Banging his knuckles on the desk to emphasize his point. The young guy was ashen-faced and looked frozen in place. Corso tried to slow down, but it was too late, Donald pushed him out the door into the cold, slanting rain. Corso pulled his collar around his ears and looked back through the glass door. McCarty was still red and still talking, except now he was pointing at Corso.

*　*　*

"What about Himes? Will he see me?"

Bennett Hawes looked like he was passing a kidney stone. "Day after tomorrow. Wednesday. One o'clock," he said.

"A nice call, Mr. Corso," said Mrs. V. "I understand he's turned down everyone else in town."

"Can we bring a photographer?"

"Yeah," Hawes said. "I've got the freelancer you wanted." He crossed the room, punched a button on Mrs. V.'s phone. "Send Miss Dougherty upstairs." He turned back to Corso. "Her name is Meg Dougherty." He said it like he was expecting Corso to recognize the name. "The tattoo girl," he growled. "You remember—couple years back—girl wakes up and finds herself tattooed from head to foot."

Corso remembered the story well. She'd been a successful young photo artist. Already had had a couple of very hot local shows and was beginning to attract national attention. Dating a trendy Seattle tattoo artist. Guy who kinda looked like Billy Idol. You'd see them all the time in the alternative press. Unfortunately, while she's developing photos, he's developing a cocaine habit. She tells him she wants to break it off. He seems to take it well. They agree to have a farewell dinner together. She drinks half a glass of wine and—bam—the lights go out. She wakes up thirty-six hours later in Providence Hospital. In shock. Nearly without vital signs. Tattooed from head to toe with what was rumored to be some pretty weird stuff. A Maori swirl design on her face. The boyfriend nowhere to be found. "They ever find the asshole who did it?" Corso asked.

"Not that I heard," Hawes said.

They stood silently for a moment, as if mourning something lost. Mrs. V. broke the spell. "You'll need to start early, Mr. Corso," she said. "The budget won't manage airplanes for something like this."

"How far is it?" Corso asked.

"Two hundred forty miles," Hawes said.

Mrs. V. said, "I've reserved you a company car."

All heads turned toward the knock at the office door. Hawes started across the office. Didn't get halfway there before she pulled open the door and stepped inside. Twenty-five or so. Six feet with an inch to spare. Pure Seattle Gothic. Black everything. Spider-lady dress down to her ankles and wrists. Doc Martens with soles as thick as bricks. Hair, eyebrows, lipstick. Everything black. She was heavy but nicely shaped. Rubenesque. Full-figured. Whatever you wanted to call it. The facial tattoos Corso remembered from the news photos were either gone or covered up.

Mrs. V. wandered out from behind her desk. Hawes introduced the women to each other first, then turned to Corso. "Frank, this is Meg Dougherty."

She crossed to him. "You write great stuff," she said. "Should be fun working with you."

Up close, the skin on her face had a plastic quality. Shiny and brittle, looking like it had recently been sanded. What Corso had taken to be jewelry was, instead, tattoos. A black barbed-wire bracelet on one wrist and a gold-link bracelet tattooed on the other.

"We're going to drive," Corso said. "So we'll need to leave around seven. It's probably four hours or so each way. That work for you?"

She said it did. "What kinds of shots are we looking at?" she asked.

"A little of everything," Corso said.

"Interiors?"

"Lots of dull metal and dirty linoleum. Overhead fluorescent lights. You'll probably be shooting Himes through two inches of wire-mesh Plexiglas, so you'll want to bring whatever you've got to reduce the glare." She nodded. Corso went on. "Remember that whatever equipment you bring is probably going to get taken apart. Maybe more than once. Maybe even X-rayed. The people I've worked with before don't load the cameras until they're past security."

"Thanks for the tip," she said, "I'd have shown up loaded for bear and wasted forty bucks' worth of film."

"Seven on Wednesday, then," Corso said.

She offered thanks and good-byes all around and was nearly back to the door when Hawes said, "Blaine Newton will be going with you guys."

Unsure whether the remark had been directed at her, Meg Dougherty stopped and turned around. "Excuse me?"

Corso cursed himself. He should have seen it coming. Hawes had his Leanne Samples exclusive. He was willing to take his chances on the rest of it. Clever little bastard knew exactly what Corso would say to the idea of working with Newton. Not only that, but he gets two for the price of one. Gets Corso to renege on his promise to Mrs. V. and then gets to spoon-feed a national story to his personal-reporter project.

"I'm not working with Newton," Corso said.

"You're working with whoever I say you're working with," Hawes said.

"There's a great deal of background work to be done here, Mr. Corso," Mrs. Van Der Hoven said. "Not to mention the day-to-day follow-up. If you're going to be lead man on the story, you're certainly going to require some help."

"No question about it," Corso said. "I'm definitely gonna need some help. But not Blaine Newton. Anybody but Newton."

Hawes's scalp was beginning to glow. "Hey . . . ," he said. "You're not making personnel decisions around here, Corso, I am. You don't like my decisions, feel free to take it up the road. But don't stand here and tell me how to do my job."

Mrs. V. jumped in. "Mr. Hawes believes that Mr. Newton will profit from the experience. That he can learn the rudiments of investigation at your knee . . . so to speak."

Corso kept his gaze on Hawes. Wishing like hell he hadn't let himself get backed into a corner like this but too pissed to keep his mouth shut.

"I'm not working with Newton," Corso said again.

The red glow had worked its way down Hawes's ears. He was smiling like a piranha. Before Corso could open his mouth, another, calmer voice said, "I could do it." Meg Dougherty from the doorway.

"What?" Hawes growled.

"I said, I could help out with the background and follow-up. Right after I got out of college, I did that kind of thing for Barton and Browne," she said, naming the city's largest law firm.

Dead silence.

"Works for me," Corso said in a hurry.

"That's not the goddamn point," Hawes snapped. "We're not talking about what works for you, Corso; we're talking about who and what works for me."

Hawes stood glaring at Corso. Weighing the value of a personal victory versus the magnitude of the story. Tough call. Super Bowls, both.

"What'll it be, Mr. Hawes?" Mrs. V. asked. She checked her watch. "As I see it, we have very little moral or ethical latitude here. We've got something like a hundred hours to do everything we can to see to it that a miscarriage of justice does not take place under our very noses." She folded her arms across her chest. "The decision is yours, Mr. Hawes. But I think you would have to agree that if indeed Mr. Corso has been correct all along and something is rotten here, our chances of getting to the bottom of the matter in the meager time left to us are considerably better with Mr. Corso's help than without."

She was slick. Made it easy for him. He made a re-signed face and forced a strangled "Okay" from between his lips.

Chapter 8

Monday, September 17
7:40 P.M.   Day 1 of 6

"No eat?" the waitress asked.

"Just coffee," Corso said. He wrinkled an eyebrow at Meg Dougherty.

"Two," she added.

The waitress scowled at the pair, stuffed the order pad into her apron, and walked away muttering beneath her breath.

The dim overhead light cast a feeble yellow circle over the center of the table, leaving the rest of the booth bathed in shadows. She thought Corso might have smiled.

"Thanks for bailing me out upstairs," he said.

She waved the notion away. "Just saving my own gig, Corso. I don't do lifeguard work. Believe me, I need the money."

The fall of his hair was silhouetted by the windows. Of his face, only the thick black eyebrows were visible in the gloom.

"You were going to push it, weren't you?" she asked.

"I've got a bad temper," he said. "Gets me in trouble sometimes."

"He was going to fire your ass."

"No," Corso said. "He can't fire me. He wanted me to quit."

"What's the difference?"

"It's a long story."

"I've got time."

"Hawes and I have quite a history," Corso explained. "You walked in on the culmination of something that's been going on for years. It all just sort of came to a head today."

Outside, daylight was losing ground to the elements. Cars on Elliott Avenue had their headlights on at three-fifteen in the afternoon. A ground fog, brown with exhaust fumes, stretched upward, reaching to join the thick gray clouds hovering above.

"You asked for me by name?"

"What makes you say that?"

"Mr. Hawes wouldn't have called me if you hadn't."

"I saw those shots of the bus accident," Corso said. "Good stuff." The waitress reappeared. Slid two steaming white mugs across the table.

"You sure? No eat?"

Corso said they were sure, sending her muttering back into the kitchen, where she began practicing for the national pot-banging finals.

"What do you do other than string for the *Sun*?"

"Anything I can," she answered. "Do quite a bit of work for the *Post Intelligencer* and the *Times*. The alternative rags, when they've got money to spend. I'm working on a photo essay of the club scene for the local PBS affiliate. In my spare time, I'm trying to get somebody interested in helping me put together a new show."

"You said you worked for Barton and Browne?"

"I started out taking accident pictures. Cracks in sidewalks. Faulty steps. That kind of thing. After a while, they started letting me do witness interviews and victim depositions. Right before I left, I was doing background checks on prospective clients."

He had an interesting way of mirroring her actions. Every time she leaned forward into the light, he receded farther into the shadows. If she sat back, he moved forward, as if, for some reason, he needed to maintain a specific distance between them.

"What about you?"

"What about me?" he asked.

"What's all this big mystery thing surrounding you?"

"There's no mystery thing," he said.

"Come on," she countered. "I asked around the newsroom. You're some kind of famous true-crime writer these days. They say you just about killed a reporter who snuck up on you one time. Put him in the hospital for months."

"He was stealing from me," Corso said.

"Stealing what?"

"My privacy."

She searched his eyes for irony. Didn't find it. "They say you haven't been in the building for years. Nobody knows anything about you." She hesitated for a moment. Corso read her mind.

"Except for the libel suit," he said with a sneer.

"That just makes it all the more mysterious," she said. She held a finger to her dark lips. "Famous disgraced reporter turned writer. Syndicated in a couple of hundred papers but works for the lowly *Seattle Sun*. Not part of the regular staff. You're supposed to be like this real dangerous dude who works directly for the owner."

"See . . . people know things about me."

"Phooey," she said. "They say that even back before the books you worked all by yourself. Nobody knew what you were working on. All really hush-hush like."

"I'm very shy."

She laughed out loud at him and, for the first time, felt him tighten up.

"You're not going to be like this all the time, are you?" he asked.

"Like what?"

"Like"—he searched for a neutral word—"inquisitive," he said finally.

"And pushy," she added.

"You said that, I didn't," Corso protested.

"It's what you meant, though, wasn't it?"

"I'm renowned for being able to say exactly what I mean," Corso said.

She cast an annoyed gaze his way, and quickly changed the subject.

"I cried when I read that piece of yours on the housing-project shootings."

She could still see the room, as Corso had described it. The rotting plaster and the peeling paint and the young mother, blank behind her eyes, telling him the story of how her little girl had been killed one morning by a stray bullet as she left for school. Of the surprised look on the little girl's face at the moment of impact and of how her red plastic pencil box had fallen to pieces on the cement steps. And the bumps and the shrill cries of the other children as they ran madly through the apartment, because she no longer allowed them to play outside in the battle zone her project courtyard had become.

Instead of responding, Corso leaned back into the deep shadows and closed his eyes.

"You remember Leanne Samples?" he asked after a moment.

"From the TV this week?"

He told her the story of his day.

"No shit," she said when he finished.

"No shit."

"What do you need me to do?"

"I take it you probably know your way around the courthouse."

"It's been a while, but I remember how."

"Okay then, spend tomorrow down there. I want to take a fresh look at everybody involved with Himes's trial. The judge, the prosecutor, the defense. All of it."

She extricated a spiral-bound notebook from her bag. She wiggled a green golf pencil out from among the coils of wire.

"The judge was a guy named Sheldon Spearbeck." Corso spelled it. "He's still around. I see him on the tube once in a while."

"What do you want to know?" she asked.

"First off," Corso said, "find out about his work habits. Some judges come early and stay late. Others waltz in at noon and are on the golf course every day by two. I want to know where this guy falls on the continuum. I want to know what his caseload was like at the time of the trial."

"I'll look up the dates of the trial and then check

the docket. Then see what kind of case backlog he's got now."

"I want to know how often his decisions are overturned by appellate courts and what the normal rate of overturn is."

"I'll look him up in *Legal Times*," she said.

She wrote for a while and then looked up.

"I want to know how many contempt citations he issues against lawyers and how that number compares with other judges' citations." More hurried scribbling.

"I want to know about his financial status."

"I'll call the election commission," she said without looking up, "have them fax me a copy of his financial statement; then I'll call the Washington State Bar Association and see if any complaints have been filed against him. If so, I'll get copies."

Finally, she looked up. He'd make a lousy poker player, she thought. Wore everything right there on his face. Like right now. He was impressed with what she knew about legal research but just couldn't bring himself to say so.

"What else?" she asked in her best bored voice.

"New page," Corso said. "The prosecutor. I don't remember his name."

"Shouldn't be hard to find," she said.

"I want to know where he ranked in his law school class. I want to know about whatever lawyer jobs he may have had prior to public service. Check his caseload at the time of the trial. Check his caseload now. Find out how many of his cases go to trial and how many are plea-bargained and how those figures square with the norm."

"I'll look at the recent docket. See which defense attorneys have jousted with him lately. Maybe call a few. See what they have to say about him."

"Good idea," Corso said.

She crossed her legs, rested the pad on her knee. She had a cramp in her writing hand but wasn't about to shake it out in front of Corso.

"What about the defense attorney?" she asked.

"Where is he now? How much trial experience did he have at the time? How many capital cases? What was his won-loss record at the time? What was his caseload? We're looking to see if he had the time to be thorough." Corso thought for a second. "And get a copy of his bill to the county. Let's see what that looks like."

She leafed back a couple of pages and read the list back to Corso.

"That it?"

"If you have time, see what you can find out about a police lieutenant named Charles Donald. East Precinct. He was one of Himes's arresting officers and the guy Himes supposedly confessed to. Find out who his partner was at the time of the arrest and where he is now."

"What do you want on Donald?"

Corso thought it over. "When I saw Lieutenant Donald earlier today, he was wearing a couple of thousand dollars' worth of duds, which says to me that either he spends his entire salary on his wardrobe and sleeps in the trunk of his car, or that he has some outside source of income."

"Anything else?" she asked.

"Not that I can think of," Corso said.

She leafed back through her notes. "This is going to take more than one day."

"Take your time. I'll do what I can to see to it you get paid a living wage."

She got to her feet. Something about Corso's manner gave her the urge to make damn sure he wasn't sitting around on his ass while she was out working.

"What are you going to be doing while I'm tearing the courthouse down?"

"I've got to have the Leanne Samples story ready by nine. And then first thing tomorrow morning, I've got an idea about how I might be able to dig us up a story for Wednesday. Which I'm then gonna have to write."

"If I need help or have questions?"

He wrote a telephone number on the back of a business card. Gave it to her.

"I could get a pretty penny for this from one of the tabloids," she joked.

"We are one of the tabloids," he said.

Chapter 9

Tuesday, September 18
10:25 A.M. Day 2 of 6

Special Agent Edward Lewis pushed the earlybird edition of the *Seattle Sun* across the scarred face of the
table. The headline screamed "I LIED." Leanne Samples's story covered pages one through three and then
jumped to page thirteen for the finish and the sidebar.
The street edition had completely sold out by 9:30 A.M.

"Is this your work?" Lewis asked. He had a way of
looking at you over his glasses that seemed to ask you
to consider your answers carefully.

They sat together in an interrogation room on the
eleventh floor of the Henry M. Jackson Federal Building. The room was a low-ceilinged, lime-green rectan-
gle that smelled of piss and desperation. The table was
bolted to the floor. Behind Agent Lewis, the obligatory
mirrored wall loomed like a tunnel. They'd been trading snappy repartee for twenty minutes.

"Sure is," Corso said.

"You must be feeling pretty good about yourself."

Corso shook his head. "Way I see it, there's no 'feel

good' in this one. Just a lot of prolonged pain for a lot
of innocent people."

"That's what you journalists do, isn't it?" Lewis said.

"What's that?"

"Muck around in other people's tragedies."

Corso ignored the barb. "I had a professor once who
said that journalists are charged with writing the first
draft of history. After that, he claimed, the job fell to
editors and historians."

Lewis shrugged. "So then I'm sure you'll understand why the Bureau is going to maintain its distance
here."

"Why's that?"

"We'd prefer to wait for the final edition."

"Walter Leroy Himes doesn't have that option."

"You'll excuse me if I seem callous, Mr. Corso, but I
just can't work up a great deal of remorse over the idea
that Mr. Walter Leroy Himes will soon no longer be
among the living."

"Who can?" Corso said quickly. "Walter Himes is a
big, fat, ugly, child-molesting chunk of dog meat
who's probably committed a barrelful of unchronicled
crimes, and who's spent the past three years belittling
the victims and taunting the survivors." Corso hesitated, held up a hand. "None of which, however, makes
him a mass murderer or a candidate for a lethal injection," he finished.

Lewis curled his lips slightly. "Your capacity for
compassion is noteworthy, Mr. Corso. You sound a bit
like a man of the cloth. Have you ever thought that perhaps you missed your calling?"

"What I think, Agent Lewis, is that tomorrow morning I'm going to print with a story that says that back in ninety-eight the FBI developed a profile of the Trashman murderer and that Walter Leroy Himes wasn't anywhere near a match."

Lewis took a sip of his coffee, then picked up his spoon and began to stir the mixture. He smiled. "You know, Mr. Corso, with your unfortunate past history, I'd be extra careful about what I put into print." Lewis began to read: "January ninety-eight, fired by the *New York Times* for fabricating an investigative story. Subject of the article sues the paper for ten mil . . . eventually settles for three and change. A month later you end up at the *Seattle Sun*. In April of that same year, you're attacked outside your Capital Hill apartment. Coupla guys who took issue with your sympathy for Walter Himes. Left you with a skull fracture, a broken nose, fractured collarbone, five broken fingers, and a severe concussion." Lewis looked up, as if expecting rebuttal from Corso. Corso checked his cuticles.

"Then July ninety-eight." Lewis flipped a page. "You're no longer in the direct employ of the *Sun*. Indicted for first-degree assault."

"Acquitted."

"August . . . same summer. Charged with destruction of property—a fifty-six-hundred-dollar camera and simple assault on the cameraman."

"Acquitted again."

"June ninety-nine—assault with a dangerous weapon. Namely, a boat."

"Some folks think boats have brakes."

"Judge thought you didn't make much of an effort to avoid. He fined you thirty-five hundred dollars and put you on three years' probation."

Lewis removed his glasses, set them on the papers, and massaged the bridge of his nose. "If you'll permit me a professional courtesy, Mr. Corso. If I were you, I think I'd maintain a considerably lower profile. Seems to me that with your recent past and known associates, you're about fresh out of judicial understanding."

"Which known associates would those be?"

Lewis retrieved his glasses. Turned a page. "You're denying your association with Anitole Kashlikov?"

"I know Mr. Kashlikov."

"In what capacity?"

"I hired Mr. Kashlikov as a security consultant."

"To protect you?"

"To teach me how to protect myself."

Lewis fanned the pages.

"Seems he did his job rather well."

"He came highly recommended."

"Perhaps it would surprise you to know that Mr. Kashlikov is a former KGB operative."

"So he said."

"Did he also say that he was personally responsible for what some members of our intelligence community believe to be nearly a hundred killings?"

"He must have skipped that part."

Before the agent could continue, Corso said, "Agent Lewis, much as I appreciate the little rap-sheet retrospective, as *my* professional courtesy, I'm offering you and the Bureau this opportunity to comment on the story before it appears. If you'd prefer not to . . ." Corso spread his hands.

Lewis pointed the spoon at him. "As much as I'm touched by your consideration, Mr. Corso, I'm afraid I must admit to a bit of personal annoyance."

Corso tried to look surprised. "Oh?"

"I mean, it's not every day that a felon comes waltzing into my office and starts throwing around veiled
threats."

Corso pulled his notepad from his back pocket.
"Can I quote you on that?" he asked. "We do like to
provide balanced coverage."

The two men maintained eye contact for a long moment. Lewis blinked first.

"The Bureau was involved in the Himes case in a
purely consultational and tangential manner." He said
it like that was supposed to be the end of it.

"You had two Quantico profilers in town for a
month," Corso said. "They must have been doing
something other than sampling the salmon."

"Profiling is still a new science," Lewis said. "At
best, we can help to narrow down a list of suspects. All
we are able to do is to describe the general type of individual we believe most likely to have committed the
crime, based on the information we've been given by
local law-enforcement authorities." He waved the
spoon. "Sometimes the magic works; sometimes it
doesn't."

Corso got to his feet. Played his hole card. Hoping
like hell that old habits did indeed die hard. "Thanks
for your time, Agent Lewis. I appreciate your seeing
me on such short notice. I thought maybe you'd prefer
being part of the story rather than being forced to recite
the company line every day until it becomes unten-
able." He slapped the side of his head with his palm.
"Can't imagine what I was thinking." He started for the
door. Got all the way across the room, grabbed the
handle.

"You're one arrogant prick, you know that, Corso?"
Lewis said.

It took all of Corso's resolve not to grin. As much as
the Federal Bureau of Investigation loved to hog the
limelight, they hated any hint of blame even more. La-
tent J. Edgar Hooverism: Rule one: *When you secretly
wear a tutu, there's no such thing as paranoia.*

Corso threw his final card. "'Cause you know,
Agent Lewis, when the Bureau has to come back later
on and admit their earlier denials were a crock of shit,
it'll be your ass up there in front of the microphones
explaining away the fertilizer."

Lewis started to speak. Corso raised his voice. ". . .
and then it's gonna be your ass transferred to some
godforsaken outpost where you won't be holding any
further press conferences. That's how they work. You
know the drill better than I do."

Lewis's jaw was set. Corso forced himself to stand
still and shut up.

"I'll have to make some calls," Lewis said finally.

"I'm not waiting in here," Corso said.

The agent's lips curled in a thin smile. "You don't
like the decor?"

"The boogers on the walls are a nice touch," Corso
said.

"We strive for authenticity."

"No attribution. *An unnamed source . . .* That's all."

"Agreed."

"For the time being, the Bureau is neither going to
confirm nor deny."

"Understood."

"And"—he waved two fingers at Corso—"should

we deem it necessary, you will publicly acknowledge that the Bureau has cooperated from the very outset of your investigation."

"Done."

Lewis opened a red spiral-bound case file. "What do you know about profiling?"

"I covered the Wayne Williams trial in Atlanta," Corso said. 1981. His first big story for the *Atlanta Constitution*. The FBI's first big profiling victory. Conventional wisdom insisted the murder of so many black children surely must be a crime with overt racial overtones, perhaps even intended as the prelude to a race war. Despite heavy criticism, the Bureau's newly appointed behavioral specialists steadfastly insisted the perp would turn out to be a soft-spoken black man, who, in all likelihood, lived at home with his parents and who would at some point in the investigation likely offer his services to the investigating officers. About the time Wayne Williams walked up and offered to act as a crime-scene photographer, profiling took a major leap forward. Corso could still see the soft mama's boy with the "I wouldn't hurt a fly" face. And still smell the brown, roiling waters of the Chattahoochee River where Williams threw nearly thirty children after he'd finished mutilating and sexually abusing them.

"Then you know the basics. What we're talking about here is educated guesswork and extensive crime-scene analysis." Lewis leafed to the back of the document. "We postulated a white male between twenty-five and thirty-five." Lewis looked up. So far so good: Himes had been thirty-four at the time of his arrest.

"Employed in some menial capacity," Lewis continued.

"Why employed?" Corso asked. Himes had been long-term homeless, with virtually no work history at all.

Lewis flattened the report with his palm and turned the page toward Corso. A greater Seattle map with bright green dots marking the crime scenes.

"The distance between the crime scenes. Seven miles, north to south. Too far to walk. Had to have a car. A van, we figured."

"Why a van?"

Lewis took off his glasses and massaged the bridge of his nose. "Because of the way he took his time with the victims. He had to have someplace secure where he could have his way with them at his leisure."

"Leisure?"

"That was one of the holdbacks," Lewis said. Holdbacks are significant pieces of signature evidence that investigators "hold back" from the media. Sometimes as a means of weeding out copycat killers and false confessors. Sometimes merely to spare the survivors particularly gruesome details. Lewis went on. "The killer took his time with them. Strangled them some, then sexually assaulted them, then strangled them some more. Then another assault. Got longer and longer as the spree went on. There's evidence to suggest he kept the last three alive overnight." Lewis read Corso's mind. "Ligature shows up as hemorrhages on the victims' eyeballs. The more hemorrhages, the more repetitions of ligature."

Corso felt his breakfast shift. "So he had a car, probably a van. Which means he probably had a driver's license and on some level was getting by in society."

"Most likely," Lewis agreed.

Didn't sound a bit like Walter Leroy. "Why a menial job?" Corso asked.

"Experience suggests that most often this kind of suspect lacks normal interpersonal skills. Probably has a spotty employment history. Has trouble getting along with other people. Has problems with authority. He's usually the guy who eats lunch by himself because he'd rather be alone."

"What else?"

"Probably lives in a dependent relationship with someone from whom he derives monetary support. Most likely a woman. A sister . . . a mother. Probably not a wife. A conflict with the female is most likely what triggered the first murder." Lewis looked up at Corso. "Which, unfortunately, we were not onboard for. They didn't call us in until the third girl was found. That made things a lot harder."

"Why's that?"

"Because abducting women from public places is so high-risk, we would assume that the perp knew the early crime scenes well. Violent offenders usually start off in places where they feel most comfortable and at home. That's why the first crime in a series is so important. Back in eighty-nine, the Quantico boys turned a guy in Alabama who'd killed four women. Found a couple of neighborhood hookers who told them about a customer who couldn't get his rocks off unless they played dead. Bingo."

"Remind me—where was the first body found?"

Lewis rifled through the report. "Susanne Tovar. Twenty-two. Found in a Dumpster behind Julia's Bakery on Eastlake Avenue. January seventh, nineteen ninety-eight." He turned back to the first page. "We didn't come onboard until the twenty-ninth of the month."

"So they missed their best chance."

"Don't get me wrong, we worked the area like a big dog. It stood to reason that he might have been a neighborhood problem for years. Burglaries . . . assaults . . . maybe fires. Killers don't go from shoplifting to serial murders. They generally work their way up to it with a series of increasingly violent crimes, until some stressor in their lives finally pushes them over the top. After that, they're like junkies. It takes more and more to get them off."

"So you would expect the suspect to have a record that reflected a history of escalating violence? Not a kiddie pervert like Himes."

"Exactly," Lewis said. "Crimes against kids exhibit a completely different psychology than crimes against adults."

Walter Leroy Himes had neither a history of violence nor of sex crimes involving other adults. "So," Corso began, "what we would expect to see is a single white man between the ages of twenty-five and thirty-five. A loner, working at some menial job. Nominally, at least, getting along in society. Capable of getting from point A to point B on his own. Probably drives a van of some sort. Most likely lives with his mother or sister. History of increasingly violent acts against adults. Did I leave anything out?"

"A possible religious element."

"Oh?"

"The team felt that the Dumpster angle might have had symbolic overtones. The perp went to a lot of trouble in the way the girls were arranged. In several cases, he rearranged the contents of the Dumpsters so he could lay the girls out the way he wanted. As if he were trying to say something. They had the feeling that the ceremonial nature of the arrangement was his way of justifying his actions. Almost as if by placing his victims just so, the perp was saying that he had a right to do what he was doing."

"That's pretty goddamn crazy," Corso said.

"A lot crazier than Himes has ever been."

"And you shared all this with the Seattle Police Department?"

Lewis leafed back to the front of the report. "SPD received the report on April fifth, nineteen ninety-eight. Three weeks after the arrest. Two months before trial."

Corso flipped through his notes. "A while back you said that the way the Trashman dallied with his victims was 'one of the holdbacks.' Were there others?"

Lewis nodded but didn't speak. "The tags," he said after a moment. Corso waited. "Ovine ear tags," Lewis said. "In the left ear of each victim."

"Ovine?"

"Sheep," Lewis said. "Postmortem, he punched a hole in the earlobe and tagged each of them like livestock. Drew a heart on the tag with Magic Marker." Lewis slid over a glossy photograph from the report. Mercifully, it was an extreme close-up. Dark hair obscuring the eye. The nape of a thin neck dotted by bits of eggshell. A white plastic band, doubled and connected to the left ear by a rivet.

Crooked little heart drawn on the white plastic.

Corso raised his eyes to meet Lewis's. The agent

shrugged. Retrieved the photo. Closed the report. Got to his feet. He started for the door.

"Off the record," Corso said to his back.

Lewis stopped and turned. "Yes?"

"Just between you and me and the wall. You think SPD got the right guy? You think Himes is the Trashman?"

"No way," Lewis said. "I didn't think so then, and I don't think so now."

"The killings stopped."

"Most likely he's in jail for something else. Maybe he moved. Maybe he died." His lips formed a crooked smile. "Look on the bright side, Corso. You've got a whole four days to figure it out."

Chapter 10

"Robert." That voice from downstairs. Sounded like a machine needed oil. He was glad for the sound of the damn radio. Even some lame-ass Doobie Brothers shit about Jesus bein' all right was better than the voice.

"Robert" again. He rolled over and faced the wall. And what the hell was with the Robert shit anyway? How many times he have to tell her? Nobody but her call him Robert. Name be Fury. You ask anybody. They'll tell you that man Fury is a taggin' fool. Look around, man. Fury's name is everywhere.

"Robert." Oh crap, she was coming up the stairs. Maybe she'd forget about the missing tread. Serve her right to bust her ass. He heard her grunt as she stepped over the hole. Shit! He rolled over, swung his legs upward, and put his feet on the floor. Rubbed his eyes with his knuckles. Eyeballs felt like they were full of sand. He cracked his eyes open, glanced at the digital clock on his nightstand: 11:25. On her way to work. Get through the next five minutes and her sorry ass be gone till late.

The door banged open. Bustin' a bigger hole in his beloved Tony Hawk poster.

"Let's go," she said.

"Hey . . . hey," he managed to croak. "What's happening?" She stood there, hands on hips, making that pissy face of hers. "I doan know, Robert. I'm working too damn hard to keep track of what's happening anymore." Oh, man . . . not this shit again. He bent his head and began picking the lint from between his toes. "I'll tell you one thing, though, whatever is happening, happened about three hours ago. Ain't nothing much going to happen, you doan get yourself out of bed in the morning, boy." He tried not to groan. Jesus, ain't got no respect for me at all.

"So where you lookin' for a job today?"

He checked the window. More rain. Can't look for work in the rain.

"Doan gimme that look!" she hollered.

"I din' say nothin'."

"What kind of look is that? Getting a job is what folks do when they ain't going to school no more. No cause to be lookin' at me like that. I'm not the one got myself expelled from Garfield High School. So now you get your butt out there and find yourself a job. You think I'm spending the rest of my life supportin' yourself, you gotta nother think comin'. You hear me, young man? Anotha think comin'."

"I been lookin'," he protested.

"Maybe do something profitable wid your time, insteada hangin' out wid losers like that Tommy Hutton and that other one wid the thing in his tongue, wid them damn spray cans of you-alls, vandalizin' other people's walls and everything."

"I'm lookin', Mom," he said. He unwound himself from the covers and got to his feet, stretched his arms over his head hoping his morning hard-on would drive her out of the room.

"Gonna be late tonight. You be here when I get home. You hear me?"

He wanted to tell her to page him. Call whenever she got through screwin' that fat Korean grocer she work for. Instead, said, "Yeah . . . sure."

She gave him another long dose of the pissy look and said, "This here is serious shit. Robert. Ain't about no job pushin' burgers . . . the question is about what in hell you gonna do wid the rest of your life. And believe me, baby, you listen to your momma here—the rest of your life is a hell of a long time."

No, Robert thought, the question is . . . where in hell am I gonna get eighteen bucks for paint? This kinda shitty weather, nothin' but the best will stick. Cheap shit just roll down, make a puddle on the ground.

She turned and left the room. Left the damn door open. No respect at all.

Chapter 11

She brought the morning paper. Dropped it on the seat between them. "FBI—No Way!" A cup of Starbucks coffee steamed softly between her hands.

"Morning," she said. Her eyes were puffy around the edges, and a faint pillow mark dented her right cheek. "You want to hear what I got yesterday?"

"Too early," Corso growled. "You'd just have to tell me again."

"Good," she said, sipping the coffee, rolling the cup in her hands. She snuggled the cup against her chest, pointed at the paper. "Quarter to seven in the morning and that was the last paper left in the machine," she said.

"Hawes said the plant's got orders to keep printing today's street edition until somebody tells them to stop," Corso said. "CNN was quoting us this morning."

She leaned her head against the window and closed her eyes.

"You want to drive?" he asked, hoping like hell she didn't.

"No" was the last word she said until Corso stopped

for gas on the outskirts of Yakima, two hours later. He was pumping gas when she buzzed the window down and poured out the leftover coffee. "Where are we?" She yawned. Corso told her.

"Halfway?" she growled as she stretched in the seat.

"More or less."

She headed for the ladies' room while Corso pumped gas. She was standing by the passenger door when Corso emerged from the station. Her breath rose in front of her face.

"Cold over here."

"At least it's not raining."

Overhead, a mouse-gray sky moved at warp speed. Sliding east as a single sheet of slate, rolling toward the horizon and the upper Midwest beyond.

"Really different from Seattle."

Two totally different ecosystems. West of the Cascades, along the I-5 corridor, was what most people thought of as the Pacific Northwest. The evergreen rain belt running the length of Oregon, Washington, and British Columbia. Puget Sound, Vancouver Island, rain forests, rocky coasts, software geeks, and the omnipresent latte stands. East of the Cascades was another world. High desert. Scrub pine and manzanita. Creosote bushes and delicate wildflowers. Hot as hell in the summer, cold as hell in the winter. Grapes, fruit trees, pickers, and cowboys.

"You ever been this side of the mountains before?"

"First time," she said.

She watched with amusement as Corso closed his eyes and stretched his back one last time. Held his arms out horizontally and did some twists, then got back in the car. She followed suit. Buckled up. Looked over at Corso. Shook her head. "You're a weird dude, you know that, Corso?"

He started the car. Sort of smiled, but didn't answer, so she dropped her voice an octave and did a bad Corso impression. " 'Why do you say that?' "

"It's the way you never seem to pick up your end of the conversation." She saw his eyebrow move and figured he must be listening. "I tell you I was moved to tears by a piece of your work and your response is to go into a coma and then ask me if I remember Leanne Samples, which—if you don't mind me saying, Corso—wasn't exactly the response I was looking for."

He pushed the accelerator several times, racing the engine in neutral. "If there's a script, maybe you oughta give me a copy," Corso said with a grin.

"Of course there's a script. It's how people get to know one another."

She reached over and turned up the heat. "Today— you know—two minutes ago when I just told you this was the first time I've been over here."

"Yeah? What about it?" he asked.

He pulled the shift lever down into drive and checked back over his shoulder. A tandem livestock carrier roared by, leaving the air full of straw. And then another screaming along in the blurred air of the wake.

"Ninety-nine guys out of a hundred would have taken that as an opportunity to ask me how long I've lived in Washington. Where I came from . . . yadda yadda. Most guys would give me some sort of little geography lesson to show me how much they know. How smart they are. You know, like showing off. That sort of stuff is just what comes next in the conversation."

"I'm not good at small talk," Corso said.

"Of course you are!" She slapped the paper on the seat. "Anybody who can beat an exclusive story like this out of the FBI is the Picasso of small talk."

Corso grunted.

"Hell, you haven't even asked about the goddamn tattoos. I know damn well you must know the story. Everybody knows the goddamn story. All the weird shit I'm supposed to have all over me. By now most guys are tripping all over themselves wondering if all the shit they heard is true."

"Well, is it?"

"What?"

"True that you have some pretty weird shit on you."

"Wouldn't you like to know."

"I'm not saying it never crossed my mind," Corso admitted.

"So why haven't you asked?"

"I didn't want to pry."

"You pry for a living."

"The cops ever find—"

"Brian," she said, shaking her head in the darkness. "Brian Bohannon. They think maybe he's in southern France somewhere. His parents are very wealthy. I'm sure they're supporting him. They see the whole thing as some sort of boyish prank. Can't understand what all the fuss is about. They offered me money not to press charges against him."

"How'd they get them off your face?"

"Lasers," she said. "Dermabrasion."

"What's that?"

"That's where they freeze a section of your face and then sand it."

"Sounds like fun."

"And of course the always exciting chemical peel."

"What's that do?"

"That makes the rest of your face look like a burn victim's, so you can't see where the designs were."

In the darkness, Corso winced. "Hurt?"

She shrugged. "The pain I can handle. It's the money that's killing me," she said. "I've had over twenty treatments so far for my face." She brought her fingertips to her cheek. "They say, in another year or so, I'll just look like I had bad skin as a teenager."

She laughed bitterly.

"Of course, my HMO says the removal procedures are elective and won't pay for it."

"No parents or anybody to help you out?"

He couldn't be sure, but he thought perhaps she laughed. "My parents had other plans for me. They're from a little town in Iowa. Robbinsville, Iowa. Two *b*'s. They didn't approve of my moving to Seattle. They didn't approve of photography as a career for me. They didn't approve of my lifestyle, and they particularly didn't approve of Brian. The way they see it, what happened to me was some kind of divine retribution."

They rode in silence for a moment.

"What the hell was this guy thinking?" Corso asked.

"He was thinking that if he couldn't have me, he was going to make damn sure nobody else was going to have me either. 'Nobody leaves Brian.' That's what he said just as I was passing out. 'Nobody leaves Brian.' Like he was in the third person or something. He left a note in his shop. Said I would remain for all eternity . . . his palette, his personal work of art."

She pulled her jacket over her chest and settled back against the door with her eyes closed. He mashed the accelerator and sent the white Chevy Citation lumbering out onto I-85, rolling south toward the tri-cities and the Columbia River. The eastern Cascades were capped in snow. The low hills were swathed in orchards. Rows of gray, skeletal trees filled the valleys and wound like a bezel around the cut, brown contours of the hills. Apple and pear and peach and cherry. Amputated for winter and huddled together for warmth. The kind of dead, lifeless country that comes alive and green only around the rivers and creeks, and even then after lifetimes of toil. The kind of artificial Eden that, for reasons too many to enumerate, would forever elude the likes of Walter Leroy Himes and his kin.

No . . . Walter Leroy and his ilk were remnants of those folks whose sole contribution to modern society has been an uncanny ability to make sagging front porches look comfortable. Walter was a direct descendant of those untimely souls who, by indolence or ignorance or both, always managed to arrive places a day late and a dollar short, always to find the rich bottomland already under the plow, and themselves relegated to the hardpan at the edge of town, to the steep, deep "gullies and hollers" between hills or to these "touch and go" arid, barren acres where the irrigated prairie suddenly becomes desert and blows away.

His parents came from North Carolina for the trial. From a little hamlet in the extreme northwestern part of the state. Damn near in Virginia, folks said. An "end-of-the-road" town called Husk, North Carolina. Neither had been outside Ashe County before. Christ the Redeemer Reformed Baptist Church held a bake sale and a raffle to raise the money for their pilgrimage. Flew out of Charlotte on a great silver bird.

They sat side by side in the front row. LO-retta-accent-on-the-first-syllable Himes was an immense woman with dyed, cat-black hair and a penchant for wildly flowered tops. No more than a couple of biscuits and a piece of rhubarb pie from four hundred pounds, she sat there every day, frowning and fanning herself with a white plastic fan that had "Jesus Is Coming" stenciled on the back.

Walter Leroy inherited his height from his father, Delroy. Stoop straightened and ironed out, Delroy Himes would have measured at least six-eight. Maybe more. All sinew and bone, loose inside a clean pair of coveralls. Missing a finger from each hand. Everything knotted and twisted and worn out by a lifetime of struggle, he never said a single word. Let his wife do the talking for both of them. As Delroy was undoubtedly aware, LO-retta was more than up to the task.

Every day after the proceedings, she held forth on the courthouse steps. Rain or shine. Talked about how her boy was "tetched" and shouldn't rightly be on trial at all; cried and told about how Walter Lee, as she called him, "dinna have a violet bone in his body." How he "neva shoulda got so far from them thet loved and unnerstood him." 'Bout how Jesus, whose name she miraculously transformed into a three-syllable word, loved her boy and was "just awaitin' to take him on home."

Another two hours and the Chevy crossed the Columbia River just north of Richland. Running fast and smooth and brown . . . navigable all the way up into Idaho.

They crossed the Snake River at Pasco, then turned onto 12 East. Sign said WALLA WALLA 45. Corso reached over and jostled Meg Dougherty awake.

* * *

To the west, a broad butte ran the length of the valley. Rock, milk-chocolate brown, rising as a gentle mound near the bottom, then suddenly straightening to cliffs for the upper hundred feet. Four antennas were spaced along the flat top, their intermittent red lights blinking against the dense gray clouds. The dark sky silhouetted a pair of red-tailed hawks, who rode the cold currents in lazy circles, heads down, feathered fingers making minute adjustments to the ever-changing wind eddies.

To the east, the Walla Walla River running straight as an arrow and the Blue Mountains barely visible through the haze. Corso checked his watch—12:15. Forty-five minutes before they were scheduled to see Walter Leroy Himes.

They were parked forty yards from the front gate of the Washington State Penitentiary. The walls were thirty feet high, concrete with the original river rock peeping through in places. Topped with a maze of coiled razor wire that somehow gleamed without the aid of sunlight. The enclosure must have been half a mile to a side. At each corner a red octagonal guard tower rose above the battlements.

A steady breeze carried mist from the river and the smells of onions and steel. Bright yellow sawhorses divided the parking lot in two, creating a gauntlet through which arriving cars must pass. Half a dozen helmeted county cops manned each side of the division. On one side, the anti–capital punishment crowd milled about, sipping lattes and waving handmade signs, demanding an end to the killing. All Volvos and fancy outdoor gear, they looked out of place on this side of the mountains.

On the other side milled the "eye-for-an-eye" crowd. Wads of chew. Beaten pickup trucks and motor homes. The damaged and the lonely and the lost. The tattered, gone-broke farmers and the slit-eyed fraternity boys who'd finally found a venue worthy of that red anger they carried inside. No surprise. The murder mavens outnumbered the forgiveness folks at least ten to one.

Dougherty and Corso both rolled down their windows. The civilized crowd was chanting something, but Corso couldn't quite make out the words. On Dougherty's side, Lynyrd Skynyrd blared from a scratchy speaker. "*Sweet Home Alabama . . .*"

The nearest cop detached himself from the lines and made his way over to the driver's window. All boots and black leather, behind a gigantic pair of aviator shades. Lose the white helmet, he could take Dougherty to the prom.

"No visitors today," he said. "They're on lockdown."

"We've got an appointment," Corso said. "Corso and Dougherty from the *Seattle Sun*. We're here to see Walter Leroy Himes."

The cop stepped back a pace, turned his head, and spoke into the microphone on his shoulder. After a moment, he leaned down into the window. Put his black-gloved hands on the window frame. "Lemme see some ID," he said. Corso and Dougherty fished around. Found it. Corso handed it over.

Satisfied, the cop handed the ID back to Corso. "Drive down to the gate," he said. "And take it easy. I don't want you to hit one of my officers." He looked down the tube of milling humanity between the car and the front gate. "I'd put the windows up if I were you. The crowd's a little restless today. Couple hours ago, we had a pair of good old boys sneak over into the peaceful section and kick some ass. Now even the loveniks are spoiling for a fight."

The cop backed up, motioned with his arm. Corso eased the car forward. The minute the Chevy began to move, the crowds on both sides of the aisle began to surge toward the barricades. The cops stepped up, waving batons. On the right, one of the barriers tipped, driven onto two legs by the surge of the crowd. Corso felt his throat tighten. A pair of cops wrestled the barrier back in place. Corso pulled his eyes back to the road just in time to see a full can of Bud Lite land on the hood of the Chevy, stopping their breaths. The spewing can bounced high into the air and disappeared. A half dozen similarly slung weapons arched across the gap in front of the car. Aimed, not at the car, this time, but at the protesters on the other side.

On Corso's side the protesters leaned out to wave their signs in his face. Someone poked at the window with a cross-country ski pole. Corso fed the Chevy more gas. Someone screamed the word "murderer." He made out a sign. It said "SHAME."

Twenty yards from the gate, a beer can burst against the passenger window, which cracked but did not break, pulling a gasp from Dougherty and constricting Corso's throat even further.

Then, suddenly, they rolled past the outermost fence and the crowd was gone. Corso's hands shook as he braked the car at the guard gate. He swallowed twice and looked over at Dougherty. She was pale and breathing raggedly. The windshield on her side was

completely covered with something pink. She looked
to Corso, as if for an explanation.

"Strawberry, I think," Corso said.

Death row. Building H of the Washington State Penitentiary at Walla Walla, Washington. All the way at the
back of the enclosure. Newest building in a hundred-
year-old complex about the size of a small New Eng-
land town. A three-story brick building. Gleaming gray
linoleum floors, burnt-orange concrete walls. None of
the   multiple-radio-station,   hip-hop,   honky-tonk
screaming heebie-jeebie chaos of a regular cell block.
Dead-ass silence and lifeless air so thick you felt as if
you needed to swim with your arms as you walked
along the concrete canyons.

The bullet-headed sergeant who'd met them in reception hadn't bothered with introductions. Just said
Himes was a "dead man," so he couldn't leave the row.
Said they had a room on the row where the condemned
met with their lawyers. If they wanted to see him, it
would have to be there. Since then, Corso and
Dougherty had been issued badges, passed through
three checkpoints, three increasingly intimate frisk-
ings, two metal detectors, and were now without shoes,
belts, jewelry, wallets, cell phones, and all the other
identity accoutrements of modern society. Reduced to
visitors eighty-eight and eighty-nine for the day.
Names not even optional.

They'd already been through the camera equipment
twice, but Bullethead still checked the inspection tags
at a small green table outside the entrance to death row,
then handed the camera bag back to Dougherty. He

punched the intercom button to the left of the orange
steel door. "Clear," he said. The door rolled open.

Bullethead walked without swinging his arms. Like
he was on parade or something. He led them through the
door to the first room on the right, selected a key from a
ring attached to his belt, stretched the cable out, and
snapped the lock. He pulled the door open and stood
aside. "I'll be right outside the door," he announced in a
flat, emotionless tone that made it impossible to tell
whether he meant it as admonition or reassurance.

The room was about the size of the bathroom in an
average city apartment and smelled about the same.
Maybe six by eight. That noxious green the government paints everything. A narrow counter ran across
the long wall opposite the door. Two ancient oak chairs
waited, the varnish on their seats worn away by a hundred years of squirming asses. The air had an acrid
quality, as if it were tinctured with adrenaline.

Meg Dougherty's eyes moved toward the door when
it snapped shut. Her face looked shiny and stretched in
the bright fluorescent light. "You okay?" Corso asked.

She took a deep breath. "You should have told me to
wear a suit of armor," she said. "This is . . ." She rolled
her eyes. "I had no idea," she said.

"Prisons are the opposite of everything else in the
world," Corso said.

Meg slung the camera bag up onto the counter just
as the light in the next room burst on. She jumped.
Looked to see if Corso noticed. If he had, he wasn't
letting on. He was focused on the room next door and
fumbling for his notebook.

A mirror image of the room they were in. In between, three inches of wire-reinforced Plexiglas, with

a stainless-steel hole in the center, like a movie theater box office, allowing attorney and client to converse with only a fine screen separating them.

Walter Leroy came into the room at a trot. Just because he was wearing ankle irons didn't mean the guards were going to wait for his big sorry ass. In the old days, when prisoners wore chains twenty-four hours a day, men who'd been free for twenty years carried that distinctive shambling trot to their graves.

Himes stood motionless just inside the doorway while a guard checked the room. Satisfied, the guard leaned over the counter and spoke to Corso. "He looks funny to you it's on account of how he shaves everything off," the guy said. "Wouldn't want you thinking we did that to him."

He was right. Not only was Himes's shaved head gleaming, but his eyebrows were missing also. Corso checked the V of the orange coveralls. Hairless. With his bald head, Himes looked like Crusher, the guy Bugs Bunny always wrestled in the cartoons.

"Every Tuesday and Friday. Shaves every hair offa his body." The guard grinned. "Least all the hairs he can reach," he added with a lewd wink. "You ought to see the position he gets in when he shaves his butt crack. You'd never believe old Walter here was that limber. Would ya, Walter?"

"No, suh," Himes said.

The guard used both hands to plop Walter Lee down into the only chair, then turned again to Corso. His lips twisted into a crooked grin. "I was you, mister, I'd keep well back from the window. Old Walter here don't even own a toothbrush." He scowled down at Himes. "Do ya, Walter?" he asked. Himes kept his gaze on the tabletop.

"No, suh," he said.

"Tell 'em why, Walter."

"Suh?"

"Tell 'em why you ain't brushed your teeth in three years."

"Ain't no point." Himes said it like it had been rehearsed.

"Tell 'em why, Walter."

"Ain't no point 'cause you doan need no teeth in heaven. Onliest things to eat are milk and honey. Nothin' but milk and honey for the righteous."

The guard smiled like a wolf, flicked an amused glance at Corso, and left the room.

Walter Leroy Himes looked up. Smiled. One of his front teeth was completely black. The other, missing entirely. Others had partially rotted away and stood now like rancid pilings. He fixed his eyes on Corso. Blinked a couple of times like a mole.

"You the one, huh?" he said.

"I'm the one," Corso confirmed. "My name is Frank Corso."

In the window's glare, Corso could see Meg Dougherty moving on his left, loading a big square camera. The movement caught Himes's eye. He sat back in the chair. Pulled his head back like somebody was waving a weasel in his face.

"What she doin' here?"

"She's a photographer. Her name's—"

"Doan say," Himes said quickly. "Doan wanna hear no name a hers." He pointed with his manacled hands. "Get her outta here."

"Don't you want your picture in the paper?"

"Get her outta here," he repeated. "Doan like 'em like her."

"How do you like them?" Corso asked.

"Not like her."

"What's wrong with her?"

"Got big milkers," Himes said with no hesitation.

Dougherty stopped twisting knobs on the camera. Looked over at Corso.

"Did he just . . . ?"

"I believe so . . . yes," Corso said.

"About my . . . ?"

"Yes."

"Get her out of here," Himes insisted.

Dougherty shot a nervous glance at Corso, who still hadn't taken his eyes off Walter. "No," Corso said. "She stays. You want to get up and walk out, go ahead. But before you go, Walter Lee, you better think about how you've only got three days left and just about the only people in the world who think it's even remotely possible that you might be innocent are sitting here in this room."

Himes pointed over Corso's right shoulder. "Turn out the light," he said.

Corso looked to Dougherty. "Can you work with the light out?"

"Way better than with it on," she said.

Corso took two steps and flicked the switch down. The overhead bulb in the next room cast a dim yellow glow over the counter area, leaving the rest of the room in virtual darkness. "That better?" Corso asked.

"I guess," said Himes.

Corso took a seat. Pulled out his notepad. Himes beat him to the punch.

"So what you give a shit writin' about me and all?"

"It's news," Corso answered.

"Writin' 'bout how I ain't killed them bitches."

"I don't think you got a fair shake."

"And now the retard says I ain't done what she said I done."

Corso could feel movement in the air behind him and hear the clicking of the camera. "Yeah," Corso said. "She's told the police that she lied at your trial." Himes's shiny dome wrinkled as he thought it over. His eyes rolled in his head for a moment. Then rolled back down and stopped with a bounce like slot-machine windows.

"Then they gotta lemme go," he said.

"They may stop the execution or they may not. Lotta people don't like you, Himes. As for you walking out of here, the only way that's ever going to happen is if they've got the real killer."

"Ain't fair," he grumbled.

"There's still the cop who says you confessed to him."

"Lyin' dog. Never said no word to him. Not one. Never said a word."

"You be willing to take a lie-detector test on that subject?"

"Yep," he said without hesitation.

"What about on whether or not you killed those girls?"

"Offered to do that the first time."

"And they turned you down?"

"Nope. I took the test 'fore I ever went to trial. Let 'em hook all them tiny wires all over me." Himes shuddered at the memory.

"So where were the results? I don't recall any mention of a lie-detector test in your trial."

"Weren't none," Himes said. "Never come out."

"You know why?"

Himes spread his huge hands as far as the chains would permit. "Damned if I know." Corso scribbled furiously. "Warn't allowed to talk in court."

"That might have had something to do with the fact that you kept calling the jury cocksuckers."

"What's they were," Himes said stubbornly.

Corso looked back over his shoulder at Dougherty. "You know where I can find his first attorney?" She dropped the camera from her eye.

"I only got through the judge."

"Tomorrow, first thing," Corso said.

Himes's chair squeaked on the floor as he recoiled. "Doan wanna hear her voice."

"What's with you, Himes?" Corso asked. "Why are you always crapping in your own front yard?"

"Huh?"

"Why are you always trying so hard to make people hate you?"

Himes pursed his big rubbery lips. "I had me a bird once," he said after a minute. "An oriole. Found him all tore up by a barbed-wire fence. Took him home and nursed him back to health." Himes's eyes had a distant look. "But you know what?"

"What?"

"Soon as he was getting well . . . soon as he could fly again—just about when I was gonna let him go—he seen himself in a mirror. You know what he done?"

"What?"

"He started flyin' at his own reflection. Just throwin'

himself at that other bird in the mirror, like whatever
he saw there was surely his own worst enemy. Didn't
stop until he'd busted him a crack in the mirror. Little
guy kept peckin' until he covered the whole damn mirror with his blood and then fell over, stone dead. Just
like that." Himes's eyes locked on to Corso's. "I buried
him in the garden. In a matchbox. Later on, I asked my
uncle Emmett how come a animal do somethin' like
that. What he seen in that mirror that was worth dyin'
for. Uncle Emmett, he said he reckoned it was just the
critter's nature."

"So . . . you figure this is your destiny. Is that it?"

Himes wrinkled his nose and sneered at Corso.
"Doan matter what I figure. People doan care who you
are. Doan see nothin' but what they wanna see anyway.
Just somethin' bad about you so's they can feel better
about themselves. Doan gotta be true, neither. Just
gotta let 'em feel superior to somebody else."

"Am I supposed to feel sorry for you?"

Himes smirked. "If you askin' my advice, Mr.
Corso, I wouldn't feel nothin' at all. Me . . . I give it up
a long while back."

"I want to go back over your trial with you," Corso
said. "Starting from the moment you were arrested, until your conviction. Okay?"

Himes said it was. It took forty minutes and nearly
filled Corso's notebook. By the time Corso had finished, Meg had her gear packed and was leaning
against the wall, in the deep shadows. Corso pocketed
his notebook.

Himes got to his feet. Stretched. "They know damn
well I neva done them things they said I done. They
gonna kill me anyway, huh? Just outta spite."

The room felt thick and damp, as if it had suddenly filled with seawater.

"Could be, Walter. Could be," Corso said without looking up. He slowly got to his feet. "Anything you need?" he asked Walter Himes. "Can I put some money in your account . . . for cigarettes or something?"

Himes showed his ravaged teeth.

"Ain't no smokin' on the row. Wouldn't want us to get sick or nothin'."

Chapter 12

The eastern slope of the Cascades loomed like purple pickets. Mara Liasson's voice on "All Things Considered" sounded like somebody was blending margaritas in the backseat. Corso switched the radio off, leaving only the dull hiss of rain and the heartbeat slap of the windshield wipers.

"Thanks," Dougherty said. "The static was driving me crazy." She was huddled against the passenger door, using her jacket as a blanket. The digital dashboard clock read 5:41. Another hour to Seattle. They'd spent the past three hours mostly lost in their own thoughts and listening to National Public Radio. The Kosovo crisis. A guy flogging a book about the creation of *The Oxford English Dictionary*. Advances in fetal surgery. A recipe for peach cobbler.

Corso yawned. "Long day," he said.

She nodded. "Makes you wonder."

"What?"

"Why are we bothering about somebody like Himes?"

"The rationale, as I understand it, is that if we make sure to protect the rights of somebody like Walter Leroy Himes, citizens like us can be pretty damn sure our own rights are going to be secure."

She settled farther down into the seat, pulling the jacket closer around her neck.

"Mind if I ask you a personal question?"

"Yes," Corso said. "Actually, I do."

She laughed again. "So anyway . . . what I want to know is, how can this guy who lives inside this enormous personal bubble, who wouldn't piss on you if you were on fire, how can a guy like that get himself so in tune with other people's tragedies that he can write the kind of pieces you write?"

Her hands moved beneath the coat. Corso checked the rearview mirror and then slid the car over into the left lane, gave it more gas. Passed a tandem Allied Van Lines truck. Ahead, the right lane was clogged with trucks laboring up the slope. He stayed to the left, put his foot in it.

"Are you just going to ignore me?" she asked.

"Yeah," Corso said.

"How fast are we going?" she asked.

"You want to drive?"

"No. Don't change the subject."

"It's like they say . . . if you walk a mile in another man's shoes . . ."

"Yeah?" she prompted.

"You're a mile away, and you've got his shoes."

"Come on."

"What did you think of Walter Lee?" Corso asked.

"You're not going to answer me, are you?"

"No," he said. "Tell me what you thought of him."

As they crested the summit, the rain turned to slush, splatting on the glass, filling the night sky as if they were inside a paperweight. Corso turned the wipers up to high, tried the high beams, but that just made visibility worse. Clicked back to low.

"I'd say Walter's got some issues involving women," she said.

"Don't we all."

"Walter's issues may be a bit out of the mainstream."

"You noticed that, did you? What else?"

She thought it over. "When he was talking about that bird," she began, "suddenly he was like—"

"He was almost human, wasn't he? Like you could see the little kid in him. Carrying that matchbox out to the garden."

"Yeah."

She sighed and turned toward the side window. A reflection of the green dash lights was superimposed over the windswept trees of the summit. Short, thick firs. Nearly all the limbs on the east side of the trees, standing like tattered flags, retaining only those gnarly branches protected by the stout trunks from the howling Pacific winds.

On the left, the bright lights of the Snoqualmie Ski Area flashed by.

"How fast are we going?"

"You sure you don't want to drive?"

Corso couldn't be certain, but he thought maybe she growled at him.

"No wonder you're single," she said.

"Who says I'm single?"

She snorted. "You're not married."

"What—have I got some sort of mark on me?"

She laughed that deep laugh. "I've got the marks. With you, it's the marks you don't have."

"I'm in remission from women."

"Oh . . . nice word choice there. Makes women sound like a deadly disease."

"And your point is?"

She laughed again. "So what passes for your social life these days, Corso?"

"Fishing. And you?"

She made a rude noise with her lips. "Get a clue, Corso. I'm a freak."

"Lots of tattooed people around Seattle."

"Not the kind of stuff that's on me."

They rode in silence for a moment.

"Guy your age, never even got close to being married. Weird, Corso. Statistically aberrant, at best."

"You're not going to quit, are you?"

"Nope," she said. "I'm in therapy. I'm supposed to share."

"Therapy for what?"

"Recovering my lost self-esteem."

"If you ask me, your self-esteem is just peachy. It's your 'other esteem' I've got some questions about."

She snorted and said, "Don't change the subject."

Corso sighed. "Almost . . . once. A few years back." He waved a hand. "Tell you the truth, thought . . . it . . . wasn't so much that I wanted to get married as it was just what seemed to come next in life. Like I'd met her parents and all . . . and, you know, it seemed obvious to everybody but me that the next logical move was to get married . . . so I just sort of went along with the program."

"What happened?"

"My life took a left turn," Corso said.

"New York?"

He looked over at her. She had the coat pulled up over her nose. Her eyes looked like something out of *The Arabian Nights*. "Have you always been this pushy?" he asked.

"Since birth."

"And persistent?"

She dropped the coat below her chin. "I told you; I'm rebuilding my self-esteem. So what happened with the fiancée?"

Corso sighed. "About five minutes after I got fired, she was gone."

The oncoming headlights etched deep shadows in his face.

"Just like that?"

He ran a hand through his hair. "I was working a story in Miami. My editor, Ben Gardner, called me. Said, on account of me, the *Times* was being sued for ten million bucks. Said I was on unpaid leave until things got sorted out. By the time I got back to New York, she was gone. Took her stuff, half of my stuff, and hit the bricks." His mouth formed a bitter smile. "Not even a note," he said.

"What's she doing now?"

"She's a reporter for CNN."

"Really?"

"Cynthia Stone."

"The blonde with the big hair?"

"That's her."

She reached over and clapped him on the shoulder. "See now, you told me something about yourself. That wasn't so bad, was it?"

"Yes," he said.

Sometime earlier in the day, the road had been sanded. The rhythmic ticking of the sand on the undercarriage sounded like a jazz drummer using brushes on the high hat. He steered the Chevy back into the right lane.

"Corso," she said. "Let me help you out here. Now that you've disgorged a tidbit about yourself, this is the point in the conversation where you ask more about me and my story." She settled back in the seat. "Fire away," she said.

Corso sighed. "This morning you said your parents had other plans for you. What did that look like?"

"I was supposed to marry Dickie Wirtz."

"Dickie Wirtz?" Corso mocked. "What's a Dickie Wirtz?"

"His father owned the Drug Store. Four or five of them. All over the state. I was supposed to settle down and mow grass. Raise up a pack of little rat-faced Wirtzes. What about you?"

"What about me?"

"What were you supposed to turn out to be?"

Corso laughed. "My family . . . ," he started, "my family specializes in day-to-day survival. Where I come from, people don't spend any time wondering what you're going to be when you grow up. They just hope you last that long." He looked over at her, hoping for a laugh. Got only silence.

"Another half hour, and we're home," he said finally. He turned the flailing wipers back to regular speed. Then flicked the radio on. Del Shannon singing "Runaway." He turned it up. She pulled the jacket tighter around her shoulders. He could feel her eyes on him as he drove toward the bright lights ahead.

Chapter 13

He sat on the blacktop with one knee pulled tight to his chest. Rocking back and forth, Moaning. "Busted my goddamn knee," he whined. His ass was soaking wet, but he didn't care.

"You got over the damn wall wid it. Cain't be busted," Jared said. Actually he said "bufted" instead of "busted." Ever since he got that dumbass stud through his tongue, Jared couldn't talk worth shit.

"Shut the hell up. Ain't your goddamn knee. The hell you know about it anyway?" He hugged the knee tighter, glanced over at Tommy, who was standing on a barrel looking over the concrete wall.

"What the hell's he doing over there?"

"Fuckin', I think," Tommy said. "Every once in a while the whole van gets to rocking. Sounds like some bitch is moanin' and groanin' in there and then it stop for a while." Jared rolled a second barrel over next to the fence and climbed up.

"Noffin goin' on," Jared said.

"Wait a minute. It'll start again," Tommy assured him.

He rubbed his knee again and struggled to his feet. Limped over next to Tommy. "Gimme a hand," he said. Tommy reached down, grabbed his wrist, and helped him crawl up onto the teetering barrel. He put his arms over the wall to steady himself. Be lookin' at a little enclosed yard. Businesses on three sides. Shithole hotel on the other. The van come through the alley. Scare the shit outta everybody. Dropped two cans of spray paint on top of the Dumpster he'd been standing on. On the wall above the Dumpster, the flowery *F* of Fury . . . *UR* . . . no goddamn *Y* completing the circle. Damn van showed up. *FUR*—what kind of shit is that?

The van starts to move on its springs. Bouncing like a motherfucker. "Oooooooooooooooo," from inside the van. Worst damn sound he ever heard, and then bingo . . . it stops and then the van really starts to rock. A sound like somebody puking. And suddenly nothin'.

"Doan sound like no fuckin' I ever heard," Tommy said.

"Wid your mama, you done heard a lot of it too," he said.

"Maybe cops do it different," Jared suggested.

"I tol' you, dipshit—ain't no cop. Ain't no cop drivin' no piece of shit like that motherfucker."

"I seen the hat," Tommy insisted. "Mother either a cop or he in the army. Ain't nobody else be wearin' that kinda hat, man."

"Ain't no damn cop," he said again.

"How he get in frew the gate, if he ain't no cop? You fink of that?"

And then the noise started again. First like somebody humming really loud, then gettin' higher. Then more of the rockin'. And the sound get worse, like somebody dyin' in there. Then it stop again.

Tommy hopped to the ground. "I'm outta here," he say.

He had to brace himself on the top of the wall and scoot over to the center.

"I ain't leavin' without my paint," he said sullenly.

Jared jumped to the ground. "Let's go over Graffiti City and see what's happening. Gotta be better than this shit."

"What you be wantin' to go over there for?" he spat out. "Who the hell wanna be taggin' shit the city say you allowed to tag? What kinda bullshit is that? Take the heart right out of taggin', man. Ain't got no ghetto in it at all."

"You comin'?" Tommy asked.

"Not without my paint," he said again.

"Catch you later then," Tommy said.

He slid to a sitting position. Pulled his damaged knee to his chest. "No good worthless motherfuckers. No wonder they never gonna amount to shit." When he began to massage his knee, he noticed, for the first time, that his pants were ripped.

Shit! he thought. Gonna have to listen to her shit about the pants. Gonna put on that pissy face and run her lip on me forsure. *"Shit!"*

His knit hat was soaked through and sliding down toward his eyes. He pushed the cap back on his head and then rubbed his nose with his sleeve.

"FUR—what kind of shit is that?"

Chapter 14

Dorothy Sheridan massaged her temples with her fingertips. She felt as if her skull were being flattened by a steamroller. Her field of vision had narrowed, and objects were becoming blurry around the edges. Her tongue felt furry and too big for her mouth. On nearly any other day of her life she would have gone home, lounged in a hot bath, and then medicated herself into a stupor. Not today.

No. Today was the day when she got up in front of God and everybody and told them that the press conference that they'd been promised for this morning wasn't going to happen after all. And the whole damn alphabet soup was out there. Fox, CBS, NBC, ABC, CNN, CNBC—all of them. Hell, she'd refused an interview request from Geraldo Rivera's staff.

And that wasn't the worst of it. The survivors were the worst of it. Nearly a dozen of the murdered girls' friends and relatives had already been ensconced in the front row of the media room's spectator seats when Dorothy had peeked into the room at eight-fifteen this morning. Nearly two hours before the scheduled ten o'clock press conference. Sitting there in their Sunday suits, whispering among themselves and wringing their hands.

And she was stuck with it. Originally it was supposed to be a joint conference with the chief, the mayor, and the district attorney. No such luck. One by one they'd had their press people call to say they'd changed their minds. Finally Kesey called and told her to handle it alone. They'd have an announcement ready tomorrow. Handle it.

"You should have taken that job interview with Taylor and Abrams that Monica Stairs offered you," she whispered to herself. "Monica was right. Private-sector public relations has so much more to offer than this. I could have . . ." And then the familiar voices began to drone. The cowardly talk of security and old age and of making sure Brandy had the type of stable environment that she herself had never known.

She was fodder. Thirty-six hours until Himes's scheduled execution and Kesey was sending her out in front of the national media with a "no comment." Dorothy groaned. Something was wrong. Something they weren't telling her. She could feel it in her bones. She massaged her head and wondered whether or not Brandy's braces could be repossessed. They send who? A couple of unemployed Italian orthodontists named Carmine and Guido? Oh, God.

Half a dozen orange police barriers cordoned the front doors of the *Seattle Sun*. A pair of off-duty King County mounties patrolled the perimeter. Corso shouldered his way past a cameraman, ducked under the barrier. He held his press pass out to the nearest cop. "That's him," a voice said. "Mr. Corso," someone shouted. Suddenly the air was filled with his name. He walked faster. Cameras clicked and whirled. Above the din he heard a vaguely familiar voice call, "Frank." He had the urge to pull his coat up over his head like a Mafia don but resisted. Corso pulled open the glass door and stepped into the quiet of the lobby.

At the sight of Corso, Bill Post absentmindedly began to massage his right hand with his left. Catching himself, he busied his hands with a travel brochure full of palm trees. Corso watched as the brochure stubbornly refused to be refolded, forcing Post to use the heel of his hand to iron a new set of creases.

"Taking a trip?" Corso asked.

The guard gave a tentative grin. "Gonna take Nancy—that's my daughter—Nancy and my granddaughter, Rachael, gonna take 'em both to Hawaii for a little vacation. I been moonlighting down at the hotels in the evenings. Security. You know, banquets, things like that." He gave Corso a wink. "Food's darn good too."

"Been to the islands before?"

"Nope, never. Always wanted to but something always came up. The car always needed work or the house needed a new roof. Always something."

"Isn't that always the way?"

The old guy's eyes narrowed. "They was gonna go once a coupla years ago, when she was still married to that bum DeWayne. He promised he was gonna take 'em but that went by the board, like the rest of his promises."

"How long has the herd been camped outside?"

"I came on at seven and they were already here. So were the rent-a-cops."

Corso turned and headed for the elevator. Waited for the car. Then turned back toward Post. "Sorry about the hand the other day," he said.

Post waved a big paw. "No problem," he said. "Good as new."

The elevator arrived. Corso stepped in and pushed six.

The newsroom was empty. Corso crossed the room to the windows. Only Claire Harris, the arts and entertainment editor, was at her desk. She was about sixty-five. Face like a satchel. Prematurely purple hair and a big toothy grin that reminded Corso of a '57 Chevy. Always hitting on Corso. Always wearing tall boots of some sort: Corso figured she was probably a dominatrix in her spare time. As Corso walked down the aisle, she looked him over like a lunch menu.

"The prodigal returns," she said in a rough, scratchy voice that sounded as if her throat were lined with sandpaper. "I hope you've reconsidered the possibilities of older women." She gave him a lewd wink. Corso couldn't help himself. He laughed.

"I told you before, Claire, I think you overestimate both of us."

Before she could respond, he asked, "Where is everybody?"

"In the lunchroom. Waiting for the news conference."

Corso moved his eyes to the end of the aisle, to Hawes's glassed-in office. Hawes used one hand to press the phone to his ear and the other to frantically wave Corso forward. Hurry up. Hurry up, he gestured. Corso smiled and stood still.

Claire Harris checked over her shoulder to see what

was so funny. She narrowed her eyes and waved a bony finger at Corso. "You really shouldn't torture him, you know. He's very high-strung," she rasped.

"We deserve each other," Corso assured her, and started up the aisle.

Corso nodded at Mary Kenny and stepped into the managing editor's office. Closed the door. This morning's paper lay flat on the desk. "Lie-Detector Test?" Meg's photograph of Walter Leroy was unlike any other picture Corso had ever seen of Himes, whose feral visage was generally photographed while snarling or spewing invective. Instead, she'd caught him at a moment of uncertainty, as he was considering one of Corso's questions, and captured a wistful, almost childlike quality in his expression.

"What can I do for you?" Corso asked.

"Another two weeks of stories like today's lead."

Corso figured that was as close to a compliment as Hawes was going to get.

"I got lucky," Corso said. "I was just warming up. Himes coughed up the lie-detector test crap by accident."

"Yeah . . . well . . . get lucky some more. Have more accidents. Circulation's up a hundred forty percent over last week," Hawes growled.

"I'm going to need Dougherty for as long as the story floats," Corso said.

Hawes's eyes narrowed. He seemed surprised. "Okay . . . and?"

"And we ought to pay her at least whatever Newton's getting. No minimum-wage shit."

Hawes sneered at him. "You know what Mark Twain said about using the word 'we,' don't you, Corso?" Without waiting for an answer, Hawes said, "He said the only people who should use that word are the editors of newspapers and folks with tapeworms. I was you, I'd check my stool for a while."

"She's good," Corso insisted. "That's a hell of a picture this morning."

Hawes admitted how it was indeed one hell of a photo. Corso was ready for a fight, but Hawes said, "I'll take it up with Mrs. V."

Hawes tugged the bottom of his vest back into place and adjusted his tie. "Leanne's upstairs with Mrs. V. The cops are coming for her at ten-thirty. Gonna take her downtown for a deposition."

Corso had an image of Leanne Samples sitting in a straight-backed chair under a harsh white light. Two cigar-smoking homicide dicks, sleeves rolled up, leaning in close, breathing smoke and fear into her frightened face. She lasts what? Three minutes. Hell, substitute Richard Simmons for the homicide dicks and she only holds out for five.

"She's going by herself?"

"We got her a lawyer."

Corso breathed a sigh of relief.

"What have you got for tomorrow?" Hawes asked.

"Depends on what they say at the press conference."

Hawes rubbed the corners of his mouth with his thumb and forefinger. Put on a bland expression. "You seen the *PI* or the *Times* today?"

Corso said he hadn't.

"Both features are on you," Hawes said.

"I'll make it a point not to read them," Corso promised.

"Good idea. One of the papers went so far as to refer to you as a 'defrocked journalist.'"

"I've never been defrocked in my life."

Hawes cleared his throat. "So . . . I guess . . . since you're so worried about how she gets paid, then . . . Dougherty is working out okay for you?" Something in his tone put Corso on alert.

"Why wouldn't she?"

Hawes massaged the back of his neck. "Before I'd ever seen her—in the flesh, so to speak—you know, I'd seen some of her work, but I never put the name together with the tattoo story or anything."

"So?"

"So, I sent her out to a society shoot at the yacht club."

"The commodore find her a bit exotic for the yachting set, did he?"

Hawes whistled softly. "Not only that, but she ended up telling the commodore to go fuck himself." Behind his pale eyes Hawes relived the experience. "I mean . . . how the hell was I supposed to know?"

"She's doing fine," Corso assured him.

"What have you got her doing?"

"Finishing up some work at the courthouse."

"Looking for what?"

Corso told him. "I'm guessing we're going to find out Walter Leroy Himes never had a chance. That'll give us an instant backup lead anytime we need it."

Hawes gave him a smile thin enough to pass for a scar. "Nothing like proving yourself right, is there, Corso?"

Corso pretended to think about it. "There's simultaneous orgasms and a good piss when you really gotta go."

Hawes made a "maybe" face and said, "Yeah, but the glow doesn't last as long."

Corso allowed how Hawes had a point and said, "This afternoon I'm going to work on the lie-detector test results," he said. "I made some calls this morning. Tests are ordered by the SPD, but the results are held by the medical examiner's office. They keep it with the rest of the forensic material. I'm going down to ask for a copy."

Hawes emitted a short laugh. "I'll be holding my breath," he said.

"The sooner we start, the sooner they'll tell us it's lost or destroyed and we'll have a story from that end."

The Freedom of Information Act was a joke. Whether it was midtown Manhattan, or Husk, North Carolina, if what you wanted was something the folks in the courthouse didn't particularly want you to have, gird your loins, Bevis, because, like it or not, you were about to dance the bureaucratic boogie. Eventually, after enough attorneys fattened their retirement kitties, you'd get some part of what you'd originally asked for. The rest? Lost. Funny how they never lost parking tickets.

Hawes nodded his approval. "You know about the media circus downtown?"

"I'm guessing they're all over the place."

"Like ugly on an ape. Government Park is bumper-to-bumper remote feeds, do-gooders, and death fiends. You're getting a lot of negative national airtime from that quarter too." He cut the air with his hand. "Dredging up the whole New York thing and all."

Corso shrugged. "It was to be expected," he said.

"You've been getting a ton of calls from the networks," Hawes said. "I had Violet screen your calls and save the media requests separately."

"Thanks," Corso said.

Bennett Hawes waved him off. Walked around to the back of his desk and sat down in the oversize desk chair that he imagined made him look bigger, but which, in reality, had precisely the opposite effect.

"Mrs. V. would like a word with you," he said. As Corso started for the door he said, "Ask her about her chat with the mayor."

Corso took the elevator to the top floor. As he stepped out of the elevator car, Violet looked up from her keyboard. Smiled.

"So how was the room service?" Corso asked.

She frowned and shook her head. "Going to have to get myself right to the gym in the morning," she said. "And every morning for the foreseeable future," she added.

"It go okay with Leanne?" he asked.

"Oh sure," she said. "She's a very sweet girl . . . but . . . you know . . . for a girl her age, that poor thing has been nowhere and done nothing. Never stayed in a hotel room. Never ordered room service. Never been shopping without her mother. Never watched regular television. I mean . . . I'm all for keeping them on a short leash, but . . . really . . . I don't know."

"That's how those damn fundamentalist sects operate," Corso said. "The less stuff the kids are exposed to, the fewer things contradict the crap you're feeding them. You control the input, you control the kid. Self-induced ignorance in the name of religion."

Violet sat back in her chair and took Corso in. "You don't mind me saying, Mr. Corso, but sometimes you sound like you're mad at the Lord," she said.

Corso opened his mouth to protest but, instead,

stood staring at the woman, speechless. She bailed
them both out.

"I've got a ton of messages for you."

"Maybe later," Corso said.

She arched a thick eyebrow. "Several from a woman
at CNN name of Stone, who claims she was formerly
your fiancée."

Cynthia. Yeah. It figured. He almost laughed out loud.

"You can go in. Mrs. Van Der Hoven has been expecting you."

The red leather chair Corso had occupied on Monday was now full of lawyer. He was about fifty, with a
pair of upturned nostrils the size of dimes. Bald as an
egg, tiny ears lying flat against his head, and a set of
pinched features gathered in the center of his face like
they were having a meeting. The overall effect was an
expression of mild revulsion, as if someone had run
something rank right beneath his nose.

Mrs. V., from behind her desk, said, "Ah . . . Mr.
Corso. Come in."

Leanne was kneeling on a brocade settee, her back
to the door, looking out the window at the whitecapped
furrows of Puget Sound when Mrs. V.'s voice snapped
her head around. She dropped her feet to the floor and
hurried to Corso's side. "So there you are," she said.
She had a trendy new hairdo and a new set of duds that
looked as if they came from The Gap. She also had
dark pouches beneath her eyes and scaly patches
where she'd been picking at her lower lip.

"Returned from the land of the dead," Corso said.

Mrs. V. waved a hand. "Frank Corso . . . Dan
Beardsley."

The men exchanged disinterested nods.

"You've seen Bennett?" she asked.

"What's this about the mayor?" Corso asked.

"I received a rather contentious call from the mayor yesterday. Regarding both the conduct of the paper in general and your conduct in particular. Stanley seemed to feel that we have seriously outstripped the bounds of civilized journalism. He went so far as to remind me that newspapers were, in a sense, public trusts. Can you imagine? That little boot-licking toady preaching ethics to me! He actually suggested that it was my civic duty to clear stories with his office before going to print. He didn't quite say if I knew what was good for me, but it was most certainly floating somewhere nearby."

"Have they issued any public denials to anything we've printed?"

"Not a peep," Mrs. V. said. She made a rueful face. "They have, however, put their machine into motion."

"Yeah, Hawes told me. I'm a celebrity again."

"I've had to hire temps to answer the phones. We've been besieged."

"You wanted them talking about us," Corso reminded her.

"You've received nearly a hundred interview requests."

"Mr. Corso deeply regrets et cetera, et cetera," Corso said.

Leanne took hold of Corso's arm. She smelled like peppermint.

"What have you got for tomorrow?" Mrs. V. asked.

He told her the same thing he'd told Hawes. She looked up at the clock on the far wall. "Three minutes," she said.

"Is there a TV in here?" Corso asked.

"The lunchroom," she said. "Mr. Hawes sent Mr. Newton downtown."

"That's about what he's good for," Corso said. "I'm going downstairs to catch the news conference. Why don't I take Leanne with me? The cops get here, you can send them down." Leanne squeezed his arm tighter. Mrs. V. looked over at Beardsley.

"No problem," he said.

Corso waited until the elevator door slid shut. "How you hangin' in there?" he asked Leanne. She nodded a couple of times but didn't say anything. "Just tell them the truth, Leanne. That's all you've got to do. Your lawyer there will take care of the rest."

The elevator stopped at the second floor. "I'm scared, Mr. Corso," she said.

Corso pushed the Door Close button. He looked her in the eye. "That's because what you're going through is scary, Leanne You're not making it up. You're not having some sort of paranoid delusion. This would be a stressful situation for anybody. Not just you. Okay?"

She favored Corso with a wan smile, then said, "Okay." He released the button.

A head poked in the door. "One minute, Ms. Sheridan," she cooed. Dorothy answered with a wave of the hand. Went back to studying her notes. One stinking paragraph. When she looked up, her assistant still stood in the doorway. Leering . . . the way motorists rubberneck at particularly gruesome car wrecks. Sure. Why not? She was next in line, wasn't she? When Dorothy was long gone, forced to sell her ass down by the airport to keep out of the rain, her assistant would have her office. Sure. She'd fill the shelves with those goddamn Beanie Babies she collected. She'd picked up the vibe. The door closed. Dorothy sighed.

Dorothy crossed the room, grabbed the handle, and peeked out through the crack. Standing room only. Her eye fell on the front row, where Malcolm and Paula Tate sat holding hands. They were quiet people. Dairy farmers from Kelso. Their daughter Jennine had been a second-year nursing student when she became the Trashman's third victim. Every week for the past three years, they'd phoned the Seattle Police Department for an update on when they might expect Walter Leroy Himes to get what was coming to him. Just their little low-key way of saying it wasn't over for them until it was over for Himes, and that, for whatever it was worth, they were watching. Dorothy knew because she'd handled the calls. Always polite, always grateful for whatever information or solace she might be able to provide. They looked ten years older than when Dorothy had last seen them.

At the far end of the front row were the Butlers. Neil and Madeleine. Their daughter Sara had been number five. Found by the gulls amid compacted garbage at a city transfer station in south Seattle. Traced back to a Dumpster on lower Queen Anne Hill. Two blocks from the coffee shop where she worked part-time. Neil Butler owned some kind of electronics company, but that wasn't how he spent his time anymore. He'd become a highly visible supporter of appeal limits in death-penalty cases. Made the talk-show circuit. Testified before Congress. Started a foundation in his daughter's name to support candidates who favored an expeditious eye-for-an-eye approach.

In between the Tates and the Butlers sat Alice Doyle, who always wore the same print dress and always carried a picture of her murdered daughter Kelly. Her husband, Rodney, had been a King County police officer. One of those unfortunate souls for whom the rigors of policework had simply been too much. Fifteen years before his daughter's death, Rodney Doyle had put his service revolver to his temple and pulled the trigger.

Then the Nisovic family. All of them. Mother, father, two grandparents, four brothers, and a sister. Albanian refugees whose eldest daughter, Analia, had been the next-to-last girl killed. The father, Slobodan, despite his halting English, always spoke for the family. Always said that his family had seen enough killing for a lifetime. And that, despite having seen the very heart torn from his family, he had no wish to see Walter Leroy Himes put to death. He always asked, in his daughter's name, that the killing stop.

Dorothy squared her shoulders, patted herself down, put her index finger in her mouth, and then used it to smooth her eyebrows. The moment she pulled open the door and started for the forest of microphones, it was as if someone flicked a switch, as the low drone that filled the room quickly faded to breathless silence.

Cynthia Stone. Leaning against the wall with a CNN microphone in her hand. She never seemed to change. Corso remembered seeing her high school graduation picture and commenting that she even had the same hairdo. "If it works, I don't mess with it," she'd said. "If it doesn't work, it's history." If Corso had only known. Movement behind the bank of microphones pulled his eyes from Cynthia. The Sheridan woman. Looking ill.

"Ladies and gentlemen. I'm going to read a brief prepared statement, after which I will not be taking questions." She began to read. "Unanticipated developments in the case of Walter Leroy Himes have come to the attention of the Seattle Police Department. As we speak, SPD officers are in the process of investigating those developments. For that reason, the press conference that was originally scheduled for this time frame—" The buzz in the room began to rise like an airplane taxiing for takeoff. Sheridan looked around nervously. Corso knew the look well. His college roommate used to feed his pet python white rats. When you first dropped them in the cage they had that same "let-me-the-hell-out-of-here" expression. Sheridan collected her wits. "—which was originally scheduled for this time has been rescheduled for 1:00 P.M. tomorrow. The Seattle Police Department regrets any inconvenience this may cause, but feels it is in the best interest of the community that, in a capital matter such as this, all information be thoroughly investigated before further public statements are issued. Better to err on the side of caution—"

The room went postal. A well-groomed guy in the front row began shouting and waving a fist in Sheridan's face; his wife looked sadly about the room. Tried to pull him back into his seat. A dozen reporters shouted questions at Sheridan, who kept shaking her head and saying there would be no further comment until tomorrow at 1:00 P.M.

"What the hell is the matter with these people?" Bennett Hawes's voice came from behind Corso.

"What's the big deal? Am I missing something here? These guys are acting like they got evidence Chief Kesey is the Trashman."

On the screen, the room had erupted into chaos. Sheridan was shaking her head, sidling toward the door. On Corso's left, Leanne Samples looked to Corso for an explanation. "They're not going to let Mr. Himes go?"

"They're not going to do anything . . . until they talk to you."

She pouted. "I already talked to them."

"Officially," Corso said. "They want to take a statement and all." What they wanted was to see if they could bully her into sticking with her original testimony, but Corso wasn't about to tell Leanne anything of the sort. As if on cue, Corso caught sight of Beardsley, Leanne's attorney, and a couple of cops he hadn't seen before standing in the doorway of the lunchroom. He leaned over and put his face close to Leanne's.

"Just tell the truth, Leanne, and everything will be okay. Do you understand me?" She didn't answer. "I'll bet your mama told you that the truth will set you free, didn't she?" She gave him a tentative nod and then picked up the vibe from the doorway, turned toward the cops, went pure white, and then looked back up at Corso.

"Will you come with me?" she asked. "Please."

"I can't," Corso said. "This is for you and your attorney, Mr. Beardsley. I'd just be in the way." Their arms were locked together, but now it was Corso hanging on. "Come on," he said.

She locked her knees and slid the first four feet, then loosened up and walked on her own. "Please," she said

to Corso again. Corso shook his head and kept her
moving out through the door.

Beardsley put an arm around her shoulder. "It will
be fine," he assured her.

The cops stepped forward. "Miss Samples will
travel with me," the lawyer informed them. Corso
turned and walked back into the lunchroom.

On the screen, local anchor Laurie Dane had inter-
cepted Sheridan before she made good her escape.
"According to a story in the *Seattle Sun*, Leanne Samples has told the SPD that she lied during the trial of
Walter Leroy Himes?" Sheridan waved her off.

"Other than my earlier statement, I am not able, at
this time, to elaborate further."

Her eyes were nearly shut, as if a great weight were
pressing down on her head. Behind her, reporters jock-
eyed for interviews. "Try CNN," Corso shouted over
the din. At the front of the room, a woman's hand
reached up and changed the channel. A sea of eyes
turned to see who had spoken. Corso kept his eyes on
the screen.

Cynthia and the well-groomed fist-shaker. "Remind
me. Who's that?"

"Neil Butler. One of the parents," Hawes said.

". . . just a further example of the degree of ineptitude of the Seattle Police Department and of the decay
of the judicial system," Butler pontificated. He was
shaking a finger in Cynthia's face. "In no other civilized country could an animal like Walter Himes . . ."

"Try channel five," Hawes shouted to the front.
Same hand.

Another local commentator, Grant Hutchens, was
interviewing a couple. They wore matching red-and-

black wool coats. Both were fair. Redheads going
gray. Almost-white eyelashes. The wife was speaking.
"It's hard enough for us to take a day off from the
farm. Farms don't take holidays. Animals need feeding and milking whether or not you've got something
else planned. We had to hire people to work the place
today."

Her husband stepped forward. "But we'll be here tomorrow," he assured the camera. Whatever sense of
amiability his otherwise bland face might have suggested was belied by the flat look in his pale blue eyes.
"We'll be here for as long as it takes," he said.

"The Tates," Hawes said.

The hand at the front of the room switched the channel. Another local. Interviewing the dark-haired people
who'd been sitting front and center. "More parents,"
Hawes sighed.

"When in doubt, see if you can't get somebody to
cry," Corso groused.

"Great sound bites," Hawes offered.

"My fam-i-lee haf faidt een de Amerika systen," the
father was saying. Corso's eye was drawn to the grand-
mother. Beneath the paisley babushka, her weathered
face looked like ancient leather. Life-lined and eroded
into a serpentine, almost geometrical design of amazing natural complexity. "If dey need us to com bek tomor, ve com bek tomor." As he spoke, his wife, whose
dark eyes were filled with tears, whispered a transla-
tion to the grandparents, whose faces never so much as
twitched. "Ve haf seen nuf keeling." He swallowed.
"Nuf keeling," he said again. "De Amerika systen . . .
ov justees . . ."

Hawes cupped a hand around his mouth and

shouted, "All right, people. The head is officially dead. We've still got a paper to get out here." The hand snapped the TV off. Corso stepped back into the corner and fiddled with the Coke machine as the crowd hustled back to their desks. Their eyes felt like hail on his back. When they'd gone, Corso headed for the door.

"Where you going?" Hawes inquired.

"Gonna get Dougherty and then head up to the morgue."

Chapter 15

Thursday, September 20
11:40 A.M.   Day 4 of 6

Corso listened as the wolf-pack sirens moved closer.
Traffic was at a complete stop. Both directions. Despite a thick drizzle, people stood outside their cars,
one foot on the doorjambs, scowling up Third Avenue
as if to say, For this kind of gridlock, somebody damn
well better be dead. Not out loud, though. Much like
the weather, nobody talked about the traffic anymore.
Sitting for hours breathing catalytic converter fumes
had become such a fact of life that taking notice was
now considered positively rural.

Meg Dougherty struggled out of her yellow raincoat, threw it over into the backseat, and now sat with a
legal pad in her lap. She wore a black long-sleeved
blouse. Silk, it looked like. Through the cuff slits,
Corso could see more tattoos; thick, green tendrils and
leaves entwined both her forearms. From Corso's van-
tage it was hard to tell, but he thought text of some sort
was spaced along the tattooed designs.

"As long as we're not going anywhere . . . ," she
began.

"Good idea," Corso said. He told her about the press conference. "If we're gonna do a Himes-got-jobbed story, this is where it fits."

"Then you'll be pleased to know that Himes got jobbed."

The red Honda Accord in front of them had a bumper sticker that read: "I want to die peacefully in my sleep like my grandfather, not screaming like the passengers in his car."

Dougherty thumbed through her notes. "The judge . . . ," she began. "Spearbeck."

Corso turned off the radio. "A slug," she said. "His hours of operation are pretty much standard. It's just that nobody can figure out what he does with his time. Back in ninety-eight, he had the highest backlog of any King County Superior Court judge, an honor he still qualifies for. His backlog is about twice that of his closest competitor, a Judge David Heilman. Soooo," she said flipping the page.

"So," Corso said. "His caseload, then and now, was about twice what everybody else's was."

"Right . . . and that's not the good part."

"Oh?"

"The good part is his rate of overturn." She licked her thumb with a long pink tongue. "The state average is about seven percent overturn. Guess Spearbeck's."

"Fifteen," Corso guessed.

"Eighteen," she corrected. "Almost three times the average."

"So . . . he's not only slow, but sloppy."

She looked up from her notes, waited for the inter-mittent wiper to clear the window, and took in the grid-lock. "Where are we going, anyway?" she asked.

"To the medical examiner's office."

"What for?"

"I want to put in a request for the results of the lie-detector test."

Corso turned up the wipers. People were getting back into their cars. Three blocks up, brake lights were going out and cars were inching forward. Corso put the car in drive and crawled down the street behind the Honda.

"He actually issues fewer contempt citations than most of his colleagues."

Corso could tell she had a punch line, so he kept quiet.

"But I spoke to the proverbial attorney-who-wishes-to-remain-nameless, who says that's because nobody bothers arguing with Spearbeck anymore, because they know they can nearly always get a reversal in appellate court."

"Makes sense," Corso said. "Why mess with contempt citations or judicial complaints if you don't have to? Not to mention, of course, that the client now has to pay you all over again for the appeal."

She looked over at him. "And they say *I'm* cynical."

"What I am is paying attention," Corso corrected quickly.

"You know——" she began.

"Hey," Corso snapped. "What say today we skip the amateur psychoanalysis and stick to the job at hand?" He heard her catch her breath.

"No need to get nasty," she said.

Corso flicked a glance at her from the corner of his eye. "Sorry," he said. "Sometimes I can be a little too . . . I . . ." She'd turned away and was looking out the side window. Part of Corso screamed at him to let it go. He clamped his jaw shut so hard his teeth threatened to crumble, but it didn't help. Next thing he knew, he was talking again. "I'm just not warm and fuzzy. What can I tell you?" The silent treatment. Shit. "I don't make mewing noises whenever I see a baby-something. I think newborn infants look like boiled owls." He threw up his hands. "What can I say? I'm a terrible person. If I could find my inner child, I'd kick his little ass." He'd hoped for a laugh. But no.

When the northbound half of Fourth Avenue broke for a moment, Corso turned the wheel hard to the left, gunned it, and shot through the gap, roaring sharply uphill on James Street. Making all the lights. Under the freeway. All the way to the top of Pill Hill, until he had no choice but to turn left and cut over to Madison.

"You want to hear the rest of it?" she asked in a bored voice.

Corso said he did. He turned left on Madison. Coasted down the hill.

"The prosecutor, Alfred Palin. He's still with the district attorney's office. He's a full-fledged deputy prosecutor these days. The rumor mill says he's thinking about running for judge but is having trouble raising enough money." She wet her thumb again and turned the page. "His office cleared his calendar for him back at the time of the Himes trial. So, for the duration anyway, Himes was his only case. I talked to three lawyers who've recently gone against him. They say he's competent, but nothing special. A law-and-order man. The general consensus was that he was a better politician than lawyer. All three seemed to think his greatest talent was for getting himself assigned to the slam-dunk cases."

"And the defense attorney?"

"Richard Rivers. Mr. Rivers presently lives in Renton and sells adhesives for the 3M Company. Himes was his third and last assignment for the public defenders office. And the only capital case. He was zero for three as a defense attorney. Never stepped into a courtroom again after the Himes trial. I called him this morning and asked for a comment. He hung up on me."

"What about Donald?"

She checked her notes again. "Donald's the courthouse heartthrob. You mention his name to the secretarial staff and they get all dewy-eyed. He's got a filthy-rich wife who he married a mere three weeks after Himes was arrested. She's the former Allison Graves, whose parents have been rich for so long nobody I talked to could remember where the money originally came from. And who, in an amazing stroke of synchronicity, also happens to be Chief Kesey's goddaughter. I'll tell you, Corso, I'm gonna have to check this guy out for myself."

"He's a smooth package," Corso said.

She kept flipping pages backward until she got to the front.

"Donald's partner was a guy named Nance. He retired a couple of months after the Himes trial and lives somewhere down by Scottsdale, Arizona."

Corso took a deep breath. Then ran everything she'd told him around in his head. Decided he liked it.

"Good stuff," he said. "Gives us a lead nobody else has got. Nice work."

He waited for the left-turn arrow, turned the corner

onto Ninth Avenue, drove three blocks, and then rolled along the front of Harborview Medical Center to the far end of the building. He parked the car on the corner of Ninth and Alder. About ten feet too close to a fire hydrant and diagonally across Ninth Avenue from the medical examiner's office, which occupied the south end of the hospital's basement. He shut off the car. A silent mist made the windshield instantly opaque. The air inside the car was thick and humid.

"You can stay here or you can come inside with me." He would have bet the ranch that, annoyed as she was, she'd opt to wait in the car, but she surprised him by retrieving her raincoat from the backseat, grabbing the door handle, and getting out, camera bag and all. Slammed the door. No eye contact whatsoever with Corso.

She followed him across the street and down the five steps into the medical examiner's underground offices. The reception area was a long narrow room running the length of the building. A collection of institutional furniture and tattered magazines was grouped beneath the windows. Four sets of double swinging doors spaced along the far wall. A good-looking young woman with brown, turned-under hair sat at the desk, apparently doing homework of some sort. A sign said her name was Thane Cummings. She looked up and smiled. Closed the book on her mechanical pencil.

"Can I help you?"

"I hope so," Corso said. She was doing some kind of math assignment.

"I want to file a request for information."

"What kind of information?" she asked.

Corso told her.

"Autopsy information requires a court order, and an official request. The lie-detector test . . . I don't know," she said. "I've never been asked for lie-detector test results before." She shrugged and pulled open the bottom drawer of her desk. "There's only one request form, though, so I guess you put your copy requests here and then just check 'Other' "—she pointed to the list of frequently requested materials—"and then put the lie-detector requests here." She ran a bitten thumbnail over an empty patch of the form marked "Other (Explain)."

Corso took his time with the form. No sense giving them an excuse. He continually checked his notes as he worked. He had the eight autopsy dates down pat. It was the lie-detector date that had some play in it. The test was administered somewhere between Himes's arrest and his trial. The spread between February 17 and May 3, 1998, was as close as he could come to pinning it down.

Meg had wandered to the far end of the room. Had a black Nikon out, pointing back in Corso's direction. Decided she didn't like whatever she saw through the viewfinder and began moving closer. Checked the view again. Didn't like that either.

On Corso's left, one of the tall silver doors swung open. A woman, maybe fifty, wearing a long white lab coat, backed out through the swinging door. She was rubbing her hands together as if she was putting on lotion. She had short, curly, salt-and-pepper hair and wore a pair of black-rimmed glasses with thick lenses that made her dark eyes look tiny. A red-and-white name tag on her chest read "Dr. Fran Abbott."

"Oh, Dr. Abbott," the receptionist called.

The woman turned and raised her eyebrows. Rubbing at the backs of her hands now, she took a step in Corso's direction.

"This gentleman was asking about lie-detector test results," the girl said.

"What about them?"

"Do we keep those here?"

"Absolutely," she said. She wiped a palm on her lab coat and offered a hand to Corso. Her grip was moisturized but firm. She peered myopically from Dougherty to Corso and then back to Meg for another go-round. "And you would be?" she inquired.

Corso introduced Meg and himself. Showed the woman his press card. Behind the thick lenses, her eyes got even smaller. "What test would that be?" she asked.

"Walter Leroy Himes," Corso said.

Corso watched as the name went pinballing through her brain. The muscles along the sides of her jaw tightened. She jammed her hands into her coat pockets.

Behind Corso the phone buzzed.

"I'm not sure—" Dr. Abbott began.

"Dr. Abbott," the girl called.

The receptionist held the receiver against her chest. "There's a Sergeant Densmore on the line for you," she said.

Corso watched the color drain from Fran Abbott's face. Watched as she nervously licked her lips and then checked back over her shoulder. "I have to take that," she said. "Please excuse me."

As she turned and headed across the room, Corso strode quickly over to Meg. He pulled the car keys from his pants pocket, grabbed her by the left wrist, and slapped the keys into her palm. She jerked her arm from his grasp.

He leaned in close and spoke in a low voice. "Go get the car. Meet me outside. Turn it around. Make sure we're ready to roll."

Her first inclination was to tell him to keep his damn hands to himself and, while he was at it, to get the damn car for himself too. Something in his eyes, however, caught her attention. The usual vaguely annoyed sneer was missing, replaced by a steely-eyed seriousness she hadn't seen before. She dropped the keys into the pocket of her skirt, switched her camera bag over to her right shoulder, and started for the door.

When Corso turned back, Dr. Abbott was taking notes. "Airport Way," she muttered. Getting directions, Corso figured. Dr. Abbott held the receiver tight to her ear. "Yes," she said. "I understand." She breathed an enormous sigh. Caught herself and turned her back on Corso. "Yes. Twenty minutes. Yes. I'll hurry."

She handed the phone back to the receptionist and spoke to Corso. "I'm afraid I have to go," she said. "An emergency."

Corso watched as the woman bustled through the swinging door and disappeared, leaving only the smell of hand lotion in her wake. Corso stepped back over to the reception desk, signed and dated his request, and gave it to the young woman.

"Thanks for the help," he said.

She smiled. "It's nice to have something to do," she said. "Mostly I just sit around and do homework. Things can be pretty dead around here."

Corso chuckled and said, "I'll bet."

The rain had eased to something more akin to wet

fog. Not exactly falling, just sort of hitching a ride on the thick air. Corso felt the unseen moisture gathering on his cheeks as he walked across Ninth Avenue to the Chevy. He raised his collar against the dampness and slid into the passenger seat. "In a couple of minutes, a white van with a yellow light on top is going to come out from that garage door down at the end of the street." Corso pointed down Alder to the ramp and the white garage door at the end of the basement. "Probably going to turn that way," he said, pointing south on Ninth Avenue. "When the van shows, follow it."

"Why?"

"The cop who just called—Densmore—he's the one who wanted to punch my lights out at that meeting I interrupted. He's got something to do with the Trashman case."

"How do you know?"

He told her of asking the desk cops who had been in charge of the Trashman case. "So the young cop says this guy Densmore is the three."

"What's a three?"

"Homicide investigation teams are made up of three detectives. The detective in charge of the team is called the three."

"So?"

"So . . . that's all the guy said to me. That Densmore was the three. I did all my other talking to a Sergeant McCarty."

"So?"

"So . . . ten minutes later, as Donald is giving me the bum's rush out the door, McCarty is reading the younger guy the riot act and pointing at me. Like the younger guy really screwed up or something."

She looked over at Corso. "Weird," she said.

"And then there's the chief talking about how he doesn't want the Himes thing to compromise the ongoing investigation."

"What ongoing investigation?"

"That's a damn good question."

"Weird," she said again.

"What's really weird is how everybody is so uptight. Dr. Abbott in there damn near gets the vapors at the mention of Densmore's name. We've got the mayor making threatening phone calls to Mrs. V. An SPD sergeant seriously thinking about punching my lights out. Canceled news conferences. I mean, what's the big deal? Witness recants. Stop the execution. Get the lawyers together. Figure it out. Everybody comes out looking fair, and humane, and worth whatever ridiculous dole the county is paying them. Seems like a great big 'duuuh' to me."

Half a block away, the white garage door began to roll upward.

"Here we go," Corso said.

The van bounced up the ramp and out onto Alder. Rolled up to the stop sign. Turned right. Dougherty dropped the Chevy into gear. "How far back should I—"

"Just don't run into the back of them and we'll be all right. Stay close. They'll be focused on what they're about to find, not on the rearview mirror."

Corso saw the lightbulb come on behind her eyes.

"This is going to be a body, isn't it?" she said.

"And they said you were just another pretty face."

Chapter 16

South Doris Street. A little in-grown toenail of a lane, buried deep within the ten square miles of industrial squalor running south from the Kingdome. Beside the banks of the septic sump that was once the Duwamish River. The entrance to South Doris was blocked by orange police barriers. A baby-faced SPD officer pulled them aside for the medical examiner's van and now stood miserably in the rain, walking in small circles, stamping his feet, wishing he'd gotten his teaching certificate.

"Let's drive by nice and slow," Corso said.

Dougherty moved the car forward over the railroad tracks. As they came abreast of the cop, Corso rolled down his window. The young cop scowled and swung his arm in the international "move along" movement. Half a block down South Doris a King County officer got into his cruiser and backed it out of the mouth of an alley. The medical examiner's van eased into the space and disappeared from view. The cop slid the patrol car back across the alley opening and got out.

"Go straight," Corso said. "Let's go around the block."

They drove to the end of the block and turned right. Auto parts, forklift repairs. A scrap-metal yard along the whole left-hand side of the street. Down to the next block. The Aviator Hotel on the corner. Three stories of crumbling brick. Red neon sign, blinking. Rooms. A filthy South American blanket tacked over a cracked upstairs window. Long-forgotten flower boxes on a rusting fire escape. Rooms.

Another collection of cops was homesteading the north end of South Doris Street. Must have been the artsy-fartsy cop set. They'd added some bright yellow cop tape to their drab orange barricades. "What now?" Dougherty asked.

Corso pointed to the muddy shoulder of the road. A hundred feet in front of the car. "Park," he said. "Bring a camera you can climb with."

She pulled in behind a blue Ford pickup truck with the tailgate missing. Several greasy tires and rims were strewn about the bed. She pulled the Nikon from the camera bag. They got out. She locked the car and threw the keys over the roof at Corso, who snagged them one-handed and put them in his jacket. "Come on," he said. "Hold my hand, we'll look like a couple out for a walk."

Beneath a row of stunted, moss-encrusted oak trees, they strolled back to the corner, crossed South Homer Street in full view of a dozen recumbent cops, and then disappeared into the deep shade enveloping the east side of the Aviator Hotel. Rooms. Corso pointed to the bottom rung of the fire-escape ladder, about ten feet in the air. He laced his fingers together at knee level. "I'll boost you up."

Dougherty looked dubious. "You sure? You ask me, these cops really don't seem like they want any company."

Corso smiled like a wolf. "What about the public's right to know and all of that?"

She stepped into his hand and reached upward until she had both hands on the bottom rung of the ladder, her boots four feet above the ground.

"Hang on now," he said and let her go. For a moment, she hung, suspended by her arms. Then, with a high-pitched squeal and a hail of dislodged rust, the ladder began to inch toward the ground. When it got low enough, Corso grabbed hold and put his weight onto it, until the metal ladder clicked into the down position and Dougherty stepped to the ground. She brushed herself off and ran her hands through her hair several times. "Yuk," she said as flakes of rust fell to the ground.

She looked up at the rusted metal skeleton, switchbacking its way up the side of the building. "You think this thing is safe?"

"Hell no," Corso said. "Probably hasn't been inspected since the Eisenhower administration. You can stay down here if you want."

"Like hell," she said. *"Après vous."*

Corso stepped onto the ladder and started up. His weight made the fire escape quiver. On the first-floor landing, he stepped across an overturned flower box, whose spewed soil still supported a vagrant red geranium.

He moved up to the second floor and the blanket over the window, where he noticed that the entire contraption had come loose from the wall, that the bolts which supposedly tied the fire escape to the bricks had pulled loose, leaving the whole thing more or less leaning against the building. He looked down. Dougherty was on her way up. The air smelled of decay. Corso took a deep breath and continued climbing. Moving slowly now, as if he were walking on broken glass.

A pair of putrid cat boxes covered nearly the entire third-floor landing. The rain had filled them to the brim. Clumps of coated cat shit floated in thick, gray water. The sodden air was ripe and rank. Corso used the back of his hand to gingerly push them aside. Shuddered. He climbed the final three rungs holding his breath, stepped over the cornice and onto the roof. Dougherty's head was at cat-box level.

"Careful," he whispered.

"Ohhh," she groaned.

Corso hissed at her and held a finger to his lips. She skirted the cat boxes like they were a land mine. Corso offered his hand. She shook him off and stepped up onto the roof. "That's disgusting," she whispered.

The roof was L-shaped, the two segments separated by a three-foot wall. Mopped-on tar, cracked and grainy. A couple of dozen vents, some just pipes, some with little peaked metal roofs. The tops of the walls were covered by sheet metal, designed to keep the rain from eating away at the bricks. Corso pointed to the far side of the building. "We're going to have to go on hands and knees," he said. She nodded. Pulled the camera from around her neck and shortened the strap. "Ready," she said.

By the time he reached the far side of the building, Corso felt as if somebody were pounding nails into his kneecaps. He sat with his back against the bricks, rubbing his knees with both hands. Dougherty crawled to his side. They took a minute to regroup. She picked gravel from her palms. Let the camera strap out again. Corso kept massaging his knees.

Corso poked his head up slowly, as if expecting sniper fire. Found himself looking into an enclosed courtyard. Ran half the length of the block, in between South Doris and Homer, accessible only by the alley on South Doris. Nobody in sight. Corso grimaced as he rose to his knees. He quickly ducked his head. Caught Dougherty's eye. Pointed straight down. Mouthed the words, "Right under us." Dougherty nodded. She pulled the camera from around her neck and laid it on the roof. Together they leaned over and peered straight down three stories.

A woman. Dead. Naked. Blood all over her face. Spread-eagled on her back in a Dumpster. Her lifeless breasts flattened and falling toward her sides. Her black pubic patch thick with mist. Her left leg seemed to rest at an impossible angle. Dr. Abbott and a little Japanese guy in a red windbreaker poking around her. Densmore and another cop had their notebooks out. Talking to an elderly African-American guy wearing work gloves and short rubber boots. Probably the guy who found the body.

Dougherty pulled the lens cap from the camera and set it on the metal roof flashing. She leaned over the top, twisted the lens. Corso watched as she ran the telephoto slowly over the corpse, clicking off pictures as she moved, until she sat back down with her back to the wall. She used her sleeve to wipe moisture from the lens. "She's got purple marks around her wrists, ankles, and throat," she whispered. "And something really weird stuck to her ear."

"What color?"

"White . . . plastic, I think."

Corso felt a shiver run down his spine. "May I?" he asked.

She pulled the strap from her neck, looped it over Corso's head, and then handed the camera to him. He aimed the camera at the far side of the roof and fiddled with the focus, then got to his knees, leaned over the side of the building, and trained the lens on the Dumpster below. Focused again. Corso gulped air and returned to a sitting position. "Did you see it?" she asked.

He nodded. "Oh yeah," he whispered. "I saw it all right."

"What is it?"

"An ear tag," he said. "Ovine. Sheep."

"What's that mean?"

He told her about the holdback of the ear-tag evidence.

"It means they've got more Trashman murders," Corso said. "That's why everybody's panties are in such a wad. They've got a guy on death row, about to meet his maker, and all of a sudden, they've got new murders with the same MO."

"So . . . then . . . this can't be the first new one."

"Exactly," Corso said. "They've been keeping the new killings from the public. And then Leanne Samples shows up with a new story, which, as if it's not bad enough news in its own right, also threatens the official cover-up of the new murders."

Corso rubbed his hands together. "Take pictures," he

whispered. "Everything." She rose to her knees and began snapping pictures. Corso pulled out his notebook and began to scribble. 11:20, Densmore calls Abbott. He checked his watch and made more notes. Dougherty plopped back down onto the roof.

"Let's get the hell out of here," Corso said.

She reached for the lens cap on the roof edge but missed, sending the black plastic disk spinning out into space. Corso got to his knees. Watched as the disk floated on the breeze and finally landed on the stiff, directly in front of Dr. Fran Abbott. She looked straight up and made eye contact with Corso. In slow motion, her mouth formed a circle.

She pointed upward with a gloved hand. "Ooooooo," she wailed.

Corso sat back down on the roof. Looked over at Dougherty. A series of shouts and the slapping sound of running feet split the air.

"Oops," she whispered.

Corso gave it a minute, then got to his feet and ambled over to the fire escape. Half a dozen uniformed cops were clustered at the bottom.

"You get your ass down here, right now," one of them hollered. A chorus of threats and remonstrations followed.

Corso stepped back from the edge. "We might as well make it easy on them," he said to Dougherty. She shook her head. "I need two minutes," she said. "You don't look back this way, and you don't let them up here for at least two minutes."

Corso opened his mouth, but she shouted him down. "Just do it," she yelled.

The fire escape began to vibrate. Corso walked over

and looked down. Two-tone brown uniform. A King County mountie with a red face had dragged his beer gut as far as the first landing. He shook his fist at Corso.

"Don't make me come up there," he shouted.

Corso took hold of the uppermost section of fire escape and pushed. The whole thing moved three feet from the supporting wall and waved unsteadily in the breeze before banging back into the bricks. The cop's face went from beet red to stark white. He began to crawl down backward, showing Corso his palms whenever possible.

"This is awful dangerous, fellas," Corso shouted. "You need to be real careful here. Somebody could get seriously hurt."

He started to turn back toward Dougherty. "Not yet!" she whispered.

Densmore wore the same blue suit he'd worn the other day. He had his gun in one hand and the lens cap in the other.

His eyes dilated at the sight of Corso. "You!" he said.

Corso waved toodles with his fingers. "Hi, Andy," he said.

"You son of a bitch. Your ass is mine," he snarled. "I want that camera, and I want you down here right now," he yelled. "Let's go, asshole."

Corso smiled. "That the only suit you own?" he asked.

Behind him, he could hear the clicking of the camera and the sounds of Dougherty moving across the roof. Below, Densmore stuck the automatic back in his belt holster, grabbed the lowest rung of the ladder, and started up.

"Watch out for the flower," Corso shouted when Densmore reached the first landing. In a show of disdain, Densmore used his foot to sweep the geranium over the edge, scattering the uniforms below. Dougherty appeared at Corso's side.

Densmore had a rhythm going. He jogged up the ladder, crossed the second landing, and started up the final pitch. It was when he reached for the third landing with his left hand that things went terribly awry.

Instead of the metal support, his grasping fingers caught the edge of the nearest cat box, catapulting it completely up and over, sending the collected waste directly down into his upturned face. Instantly, the air was alive with the smell. Dougherty covered her nose and mouth with her hands. Corso winced and stepped back a pace.

Blind now, soaked and choking, Densmore groped upward for purchase, only to have his clawing hands dislodge the remaining cat box, pulling it over the edge, again raining tea and cat crumpets down upon his head. The smell was, by now, nearly unbearable. Densmore began to gag. He slid down the ladder to the second landing. Fell to his knees and dry-heaved a half dozen times before retreating downward. Looking for help that wasn't on the way. Down below, the posse had fanned out. Apparently, as far as local law enforcement was concerned, while bullets were to be considered an everyday occupational hazard, cat shit was way beyond the call of duty.

Corso pulled his cell phone from an inside jacket pocket. Pushed buttons until he found her private number. Auto-dialed. She answered on the third ring. "Yes?"

"It's Corso," he said. "Miss Dougherty and I are about to be arrested."

"Pray tell, what for?"

He gave her the *Reader's Digest* version. A hundred words or less. Heard Mrs. V.'s breathing stop when he told her about the new killing.

"We'll be waiting for you," she said and hung up.

Corso pocketed the phone and turned to Dougherty. "You ever been to jail?"

"No," she said.

Corso had a sudden image of Leanne Samples.

"Mama says there's a first time for everything," he said.

Chapter 17

Thursday, September 20
2:35 P.M. Day 4 of 6

"You stink," she said sullenly.

"You're not exactly springtime fresh yourself," Corso countered.

Densmore's drenching had left the fire escape slick and slimy. Despite their daintiest efforts, Corso and Dougherty had picked up a hint of eau de Garfield as they'd climbed down into the waiting arms of the law.

"Why haven't they put us in the regular jail yet?"

Good question. They'd been locked in a windowless underground office in the King County jail for what Corso figured was the better part of two hours. No prints taken. No mugs shot. Just a wooden bench to share and a pair of his and hers jailers stationed outside the door in case either of them needed to take a leak.

"I don't think they want us in with the regular jail population," Corso said. "They're probably worried we'll start running our mouths about what we saw today."

Corso checked his watch, and, for the umpteenth time, found it gone. Along with his wallet, his cell phone, the camera, the film, and everything else that

was loose on either of them. Strip-searched. Just short
of the rubber-glove routine. Corso hadn't asked. He assumed Dougherty'd gotten the same treatment. Probably why she'd been so quiet. He looked at his wrist
again. Still gone. Hadda be about two in the afternoon,
he figured.

He heard voices in the hall. The door opened. Lieutenant Donald and another cop entered the room. The
second man's gold shield hung from his suit-jacket
pocket. He had pale blue eyes, wiry red hair, and a humongous cold sore decorating his lower lip. Donald
started to close the door behind them, until his nose
twitched a couple of times, like a bunny, and he decided to leave it open. He looked at Corso.

"You got some knack for making enemies, man,"
Donald said.

"It's a calling," Corso said.

"You two better stay the hell away from Densmore,"
the other guy said, shaking his head. "On good days,
he's a pain in the ass. After this . . ." He let it hang.

"This is Sergeant Wald." Nods were exchanged all
around.

Donald leaned against the doorjamb. "They took
Densmore up to Harborview."

"They're afraid he might have swallowed some of
it," Wald said.

Corso held up both hands. "We had nothing to do with
it. He's the one brought the shit down upon himself."

"To coin a phrase," Wald said with a wink.

Donald shook his head sadly. "It's all over the
precincts. They're calling him Felix. You know, like
the cartoon cat."

"Never gonna live it down," Wald said.

"How many new killings have you got?" Corso asked.

The cops lobbed a look back and forth. Corso pushed.

"If you'll forgive me the phrase, fellas, the cat's already out of the bag."

Donald cocked his head, as if to say, What the hell. "This was the second."

"Started about two weeks ago," Wald added.

"Both of them ear-tagged?"

Another look passed between the cops. "Come on," Donald said, gesturing toward the open door. "You're wanted upstairs."

"The gods have assembled," Wald added.

Dougherty got to her feet and followed Donald out the door. Wald stopped, blocking the doorway, and turned back toward Corso. The cold sore glistened with some sort of yellow salve.

"How come on a homicide team with two sergeants and a lieutenant, the lieutenant's not the three?" Corso asked.

"Densmore's a desk jockey from Central. He's our political correctness officer. He's here to make sure SPD gets the glory when we catch the guy. And Chucky . . ." Wald snorted. "Chucky's got no major-crimes experience at all. You don't count the Samples girl throwing herself on the hood of his patrol car, I'm not even sure he owns a felony collar."

"Then why have him on the team?"

"Chief says it's as a liaison. Between the old murders and the new cases."

"What's everybody else say?"

Wald checked the hall. "Everybody else says

Chucky is the chief's boy. Say Kesey can't make him
captain without he has some high-profile major-crimes
time. So, we get him on the team."

"What's that leave you to do?"

"Catch the perp," Wald said with a grimace.

Before Corso could reply, Wald asked, "It true what
the matrons say?"

"What's that?"

"That Big Mamma there is tattooed all over?"

Corso felt blood moving to his cheeks. He kept his
voice level.

"Why don't you ask her for a little peek?"

He nodded at Dougherty and Donald disappearing
down the hallway. "Can't nobody compete with
Chucky for the ladies," he said with a smirk. "Say she's
got some pretty weird stuff all over her."

"I wouldn't know," Corso said.

"Stuff most people wouldn't want on them."

"Sounds to me like one of your bull dykes is
dreaming."

"Hmmm," was his only reply.

Corso stepped past him in the doorway and headed
down the hall. Donald was showing Dougherty his
teeth and holding the elevator door open. Going up.
Third floor. Office of the chief of police. At the far end
of the hall, Chief Kesey, the mayor, Marvin Hale the
district attorney, and Dorothy Sheridan were huddled
together like refugees.

Through the wavy glass, Corso could make out Mrs.
V.'s profile. Donald opened the door without knocking,
stepped aside, and ushered them in. Mrs. V. sat at the
far end with Dan Beardsley close at her right hand.
Bennett Hawes paced the narrow space behind them.

Corso and Dougherty headed for the friendly end of the table as Wald closed the door. "Are we under arrest?" Corso demanded.

"No," Beardsley said.

"Then let's get the hell out of here."

"There have been developments," Mrs V. said. She looked to the attorney.

"Miss Samples faltered rather badly, I'm afraid," he said.

Corso marinated the idea. "You mean she changed her story again?"

"And again and again and again," Beardsley recited. "Miss Samples's story depended entirely on who was asking the questions and in what tone of voice."

"What am I missing here? Isn't that what you were onboard for—to keep the cops from badgering her?"

Beardsley raised his porcine snout, as if sniffing the air. "I assure you, Mr. Corso," he said with great deliberation, "the young lady did not require coercion. She has, how shall I say . . . a terrific urge to please, which, when combined with difficulty recalling what she said last, makes for quite an interesting witness. Short of invoking her Fifth Amendment rights, I was completely helpless."

The door swung open and Hizhonor marched in. Followed by the chief, the DA, and the Sheridan woman. Beardsley waited for the scuffing of chairs to subside and said, "Mr. Corso has inquired as to whether or not he and Miss Dougherty are under arrest."

"No," said the DA.

"That could damn well change," Chief Kesey said quickly.

"Now, Ben," the mayor chided.

Beardsley made a disgusted face. "Don't be ridiculous. You have neither a complainant for trespassing nor a weapon for assault." The lawyer made a dismissive gesture with his hand. "Unless, of course, it is your intention to issue an assault indictment listing 'feline bowel effluent' as the weapon." Mrs. V. winced at the words.

"Neither of them is under arrest," the district attorney said emphatically. Marvin Hale was an athletic forty-five. Billiard-ball bald. Prone to pipes and sport jackets with elbow patches. "We're here in the spirit of cooperation," he said soothingly.

The chief looked like he was going to puke.

"Well, then . . . in the spirit of cooperation," Corso said, "Miss Dougherty and I want to leave. We've got a story to put together."

A ripple moved through the crowd, like "the wave" at the Kingdome.

Natalie Van Der Hoven sat forward in her chair. "These gentlemen feel strongly that it is our civic duty not to go to print with the story at this time."

"Time?" Corso sneered. "Time is exactly what Walter Leroy doesn't have." He checked his watch. "According to my watch, he's two days from the great beyond."

"You let us worry about Himes," Kesey snapped.

Corso laughed. "Oh yeah, if I were old Walter, you'd be just the bunch I'd want looking out for my well-being."

"After her performance today, the Samples woman can hardly be considered a credible witness," Kesey said.

"As I recall, she was considered credible enough when she was *your* witness," Corso said.

Suddenly the air was filled with threats and denials.

Hawes was yelling at the chief, who'd come up out of his chair and was stabbing the air with a finger. Dan Beardsley and Marvin Hale were trading snappy repartee in angry voices. Hizhonor was playing the peacemaker. The Sheridan woman rubbed her temples and stared disconsolately off into space. Meg Dougherty stood in the corner, her hands under her arms, her head swiveling back and forth as if she were watching a tennis match.

"Why in hell didn't you release Himes two weeks ago when the first new body turned up?"

"Because, Mr. Corso, we don't, for a second, believe the killings are related," Kesey said.

Corso was incredulous. "The body I just saw had a tag on her ear."

A knowing look passed among the powers-that-be.

"Different tags," the DA said. "Not from the same batch. The tags found in the latest victims are twenty years newer than those used in ninety-eight."

"MO's not the same either," the chief added. "The new murders have a significantly higher level of violence than the old."

Corso was taken aback. "So you guys are assuming what?"

The chief took over. "We're investigating three angles. I personally think we've got a copycat killer. Somebody who got all excited by the sensational crap he's read in the papers over the past couple of weeks and has decided he wants a little attention too."

"What else?" Corso prodded.

"The possibility that Himes has an accomplice. Somebody who's trying to muddy the waters. Trying to force at least a stay of execution."

"And?"

"We're also looking into some of the more radical members of the anti–capital punishment movement."

"Anti–capital punishment types are killing people?" Mrs. V. scoffed. "Sounds all rather self-defeating to me."

"Unlike newspapers," the chief said, "we have to do our homework before opening our mouths."

The DA leaned across the table. "Now, now. Let's see if we can't fix the problem rather than the blame." His green eyes took in the crowd at the other end of the table. He stopped and let it sink in. "Other than that unfortunate young woman who can't make up her mind whether or not she was raped or by whom . . . do you have anything?"

The room went silent. "Because"—the DA continued—"until and unless somebody shows us one scrap of hard evidence that the original eight murders were not the work of Walter Leroy Himes, we are going to continue to assume his guilt."

"Himes was convicted by a jury of his peers," the mayor added. "He's had three and a half years and several million dollars' worth of appeals."

"You don't think any of this constitutes reasonable doubt?" Corso asked. He could feel himself grasping for straws. "How would an activist or a copycat know about the ear tags?"

"*You* knew," Kesey said in a tone that suggested that if Corso could find out, anybody could find out. "In any organization the size of the SPD, leaks are to be expected. Considering how many people from the original task force knew about the tags . . . I'm amazed it hasn't hit the papers before."

"We'll be the first to admit that these new developments certainly cast something of a shadow," the DA said. "We are in constant communication with the governor, but as of this moment"—he spread his hands—"we have absolutely nothing that would warrant a request for a stay of execution."

"Not to mention that it's an election year," Hawes growled. "Governor Locke would rather be set on fire than have to stop the execution. He'll take less heat for juicing Himes by mistake than he would for letting him go, even if Himes really *was* innocent."

"And you want us to hold the story of the new murders?" Corso asked.

The chief was suddenly red in the face. "You have to. We'll be inundated. A hundred nuts will confess. We'll get thousands of phoned-in leads. The story will bring our current investigation to a standstill."

"What's in it for us?" Hawes asked.

"What do you want?" Kesey asked.

"We want access to information on all ten murders," Corso said. "We want copies of the field notes from the original detectives. We want copies of the autopsy results and the accompanying photographs, and we want a look at all forensic evidence."

Again the room erupted. Corso shouted them down. "And we want all of it between now and four o'clock this afternoon. If we don't have everything we've asked for by then, we go public."

The district attorney got to his feet and walked over two places. Put his arms around the chief and the mayor and pulled the three of them into a tight, muttering knot.

Dorothy Sheridan sat openmouthed. Hale straightened up. The chief was the color of an eggplant. The mayor's pallor was more like old custard. They exchanged disgusted looks.

"We keep the holdbacks," the chief said. "We have an ongoing investigation to consider here."

Corso agreed. Kesey worked his lips in and out a couple of times and then looked over at Donald and Wald.

"Donald . . . you and Wald see to it these people get what they need," he said.

Both cops opened their mouths to protest. "We can't let civilians—" Donald began. Kesey raised his voice. "Did you hear what I said, Lieutenant Donald?"

"But—" the cop started.

"Did you?" Louder this time.

"Yessir," Donald snapped.

"What about you, Sergeant Wald?" the chief asked. "Any questions?"

"No, sir," Wald said.

Without another word, the chief and the mayor joined Hale in the full upright position and marched out like Huey, Dewey, and Louie.

"You do have a way about you, Mr. Corso," Mrs. V. said the moment the door closed behind Dorothy Sheridan.

Corso turned to the cops. "How do you want to do this?" he asked.

Donald ran a hand through his hair, which, of course, fell perfectly back into place. He scratched the side of his neck. "Somebody is going to have to go to the medical examiner's office with one of us," he said, "and somebody is going to have to go across the street with the other, I guess."

Wald shook his head. "Densmore's gonna go ratsh . . ." He stopped. Flicked a gaze at Mrs. V. "He's gonna lose his mind," he finished.

Natalie Van Der Hoven got to her feet, scowling imperiously down at the detectives. "I'll leave it to you gentlemen to work out the details," she announced. Wald pulled the door open and stood behind it as the *Seattle Sun* contingent filed out. For a second there, just as Mrs. V. swooshed past him, it looked like Donald was going to curtsy.

Like the lady said, the details got worked out. After getting back their belongings, Corso and Dougherty would meet the cops across the street in Tully's coffee shop. Meg was going with Donald. Up to the medical examiner's office. Lie-detector results, autopsy reports, and photos. Corso was going with Wald, across the street to the Public Safety Building for detectives' notes and a look at the hard evidence. Wald stepped out from behind the door.

"Come on," he said.

Donald and Wald got off at ground level. Corso and Dougherty took the elevator all the way to the bottom. Walked down the long basement hall toward booking.

"I'd kill for a shower," Dougherty offered.

"You and me both," Corso said.

Corso bumped her with his elbow. "What'd you think of Donald?"

"Ooooh," she enthused. "That is one fine boy toy," she said.

"You really think so?"

She laughed at him. Women to the left, men to the right. The turnkey dumped the envelope out onto the battered counter. "Check your belongings carefully," he intoned. He pushed a clipboard at Corso. "Sign on line fifty-one."

Corso refilled his pockets and then scribbled his name on the dotted line.

"Sergeant Wald called down," the turnkey said. "Says you guys better go out the garage entrance down here, 'cause there's a herd of media types out front."

Corso thanked him for the tip and then followed his directions to the garage. Dougherty was already there. She had the back of the Nikon open.

"They get the film?" Corso asked.

"No film," she said with a smirk. "It's digital."

"They get the disk?"

"They got *a* disk."

"What's that mean?"

"They didn't get *the* disk," she said.

"What?"

"You heard me. I've still got the shots I took of the body."

"Where—" he began.

She shook her head. "Don't ask, don't tell," she said.

"I hope it was user-friendly?"

"Wouldn't you like to know."

Together, they followed the green exit signs through the bowels of the building, snaking back and forth among the patrol cars and the concrete pillars until they came to a gray steel door labeled "James Street." Dougherty grabbed the knob and stepped out, stopped in her tracks, and then suddenly turned and gave Corso a toothy grin he'd never seen from her before.

"Don't look now, Ken, but I think Malibu Barbie's here," she said.

Corso stepped out into a light drizzle. Overhead, dirty clouds had swallowed the tops of the buildings. Cars had their lights on. He looked uphill. Nothing. Then downhill. Cynthia Stone in a red plastic raincoat, little matching boots and umbrella.

"You still have my number?" Corso asked.

"Yeah."

"Call me when you finish at the medical examiner's office."

Dougherty said she would and then turned downhill, strode past Cynthia without making eye contact, and disappeared around the corner onto Fourth Avenue.

Corso had forgotten how Cynthia walked. That one-foot-in-front-of-the-other thing she did. The delicious way each step rustled with the silken sound of flesh passing flesh, until a guy was overcome and just had to see for himself what was rubbing together.

She held the umbrella tight against her shoulder with her right hand. The left she kept in the pocket of her raincoat. The heels of her red plastic boots clicked as she walked a circle around Corso. "You look good, Frank," she said. "The long hair becomes you."

Corso kept his mouth shut. On the one hand, she looked the same. Same surgically assisted profile and baby-blue eyes. On the other, she looked older than he remembered and more like her mother than he'd ever noticed before. Gonna end up with the same wrinkled, drawstring mouth that she'd be able to cinch up like a sack over everything she found in some way distasteful or disappointing.

"Aren't you going to tell me I look good too?"

"You know how you look, Cynthia. It's what you do."

She looked downhill toward the corner of Fourth Avenue. "Developing a fetish for big girls, are you, Frank?"

"They're easier to hold on to," Corso said.

She made a disbelieving face. "You didn't really think I was going to cling to the hull of a sinking ship, did you, Frank?" When he didn't answer, she said, "What can I say, Frank? When it was good, it was good." She shrugged with one shoulder. "Life goes on."

"You always were a sentimental fool, Cynth."

"I hear she's colorfully decorated."

Behind her, the sounds of car horns bounced off the damp air. The overhanging clouds gave the feeling of being in a low-ceilinged room.

"How'd you know to look for me here?" Corso asked.

She smirked. "I have my sources."

"No, Cynth, you have a *staff* that has sources. You, personally, couldn't find your own ass in the dark."

She twirled the umbrella and stepped in close to Corso. Same perfume as always. "As I recall, you never had much trouble finding my ass in the dark."

"Must have been the zeal of the organs for each other," Corso said.

She raised a sculptured eyebrow. "So you say now," she quipped.

"I've gotta go," Corso said.

She raised the umbrella and leaned her breast against Corso's arm. The insistent mist hissed against the plastic. "You've made quite a comeback, Frank."

He looked into her eyes and remembered what Bo Holland had once said about Cynthia, a couple of years before she and Corso became an item. Back when

Corso and Bo shared desk space at the *Times,* and she'd come waltzing through the newsroom, dragging every eye in her wake. Bo'd worked with her before. Someplace in Florida. St. Pete maybe. Said that she was like a beautifully appointed room, its walls lined with a series of doors, which presumably led to other wings of what must surely be a mansion. Surprise was, though, that it didn't matter which door you chose to open, because all doors led to the backyard. What you see is all there is. At the time, Corso had attributed the bitterness of Bo's tone to the pain of a spurned lover. You live and learn.

Corso stepped out from beneath the umbrella. "You come here to help me plot my progress through life or did you want something in particular?"

"I want in on the story, Frank. Because of you, that fish-wrap tabloid you work for has had the story all to itself for the better part of a week. You're all the buzz on every network, but you know it can't last."

"Why's that?"

"Because it's unnatural, Frank. Big dogs eat; little dogs go home hungry. That's just the way it is. You know it, and I know it." She took another step his way, covering his head again with the umbrella, leaning her hip against his. "Come on . . . ," she intoned in her silkiest talking-head tone. "We can still share, can't we? What have you got for tomorrow? I'll give you an attribution." The wind carried her scent to him again. He remembered the smell of her hair and how she liked to sing show tunes in the shower but could never quite remember the words.

Corso couldn't resist. "What I've got for tomorrow, Cynth, will blow those little red boots right off your feet." The raincoat crinkled as she leaned in it against Corso.

"Sometimes you used to prefer I leave the boots on," she said.

Corso opened his mouth to speak, felt a sudden dryness in his throat, and instead turned and allowed gravity to pull him down the hill toward Fourth Avenue.

Chapter 18

Never heard her comin'. Not till the crash of the door. Scared the shit out of him so bad he come off the bed like a rocket, seein' nothin' but this shape and the new hole in the Tony Hawk poster. Same goddamn place he'd spent a half hour taping up.

"You ain't neva moved," she said. "Your lazy ass is esactly where I left you this morning. Din I tell you to . . ."

Doan know what happened. It's like a dream or something, like suddenly I'm up off the bed standin' in front of her. With my right fist up, all shakin' and shit.

She stepped in closer. Talkin' right up in his face now. Her eyes bulged in her head. "You raise your hand to me? You?" She put hers on her hips. "What all the hell I done for you . . . and you raise your hand to me."

It's like my throat is closed and won't nothin' come out.

"The beatins I took so's he'd leave you be, an you raise your hand to me?" Got spit in the corner of her mouth. "They usta know my name down at Community

Health from all the beatins I took on your account."

"I din mean no—" he started.

"Where you learn that shit from, Robert? You learn that from him? Things doan go right, you just slap the bitch around some. You bust her lip, she shut the fuck up. That what 'Big Bobby Boyd' teach you? He teach you like that?"

"I din mean—"

"You neva mean, Robert. Neva. Shit just seem to happen while you mindin' your own buiness, doan it? Big Bobby Boyd neva meant it neither. You axed him, it was like it just slipped out and ended on my face. Come back all sweet and all. 'Sorry, baby, sorry. Neva gonna happen again.'"

He sat down on the bed and rubbed his face with both hands.

"I'll tell you, boy . . . may be time for me to revaluate my priorities. Yes, sir." She wandered across the middle of the room. "Doan need no two jobs to take care of myself. No, sir. I get by just fine on my market money."

No way he can tell her what he seen. The eyes on that motherfucker. Neva seen nothin' like that since Randy's big brother took all that fuckin PCP an run facefirst through the shoe-store window. Had his paint cans in his pocket and one leg over the wall when the back doors of the van popped open. Fucker come out, wearin' rubber gloves, went over and opened the top of the Dumpster. Both lids. That's why he didn't split. Wasn't the gloves. He stayed 'cause he couldn't figure why the guy'd need to open both of them. Damn near fell off the wall when that dude come out from the van carryin' somethin' in his arms. Real careful puttin' it in, leanin' in, like arrangin' shit. No way he can tell her about those fuckin' eyes and the feelin' he's had ever since.

He peeked between his fingers to see her looking at him like he'd never seen before, flopped onto his back on the bed, pulled the covers around his shoulders, and rolled over to face the wall. He listened to her labored breathing. Wanted to say something but couldn't force anything through his lips. In a minute, he heard the sound of her shoes on the stairs.

Chapter 19

Thursday, September 20
5:40 P.M. Day 4 of 6

The cab's headlights punched narrow channels into the dense fog. Dougherty must have had the window open. Corso could hear her voice as she told the cabbie to drive all the way down to the end. Heard the cabbie whine about how he was gonna have to back out blind, and then a minute later he heard the driver's voice again as he told her the fare was $9.75. The interior light flickered for a moment, and she stepped out with a pile of paperwork held beneath her left arm.

"Hey," he called as the cab began to back out of the lot.

The sound of his voice nearly lifted her from the ground. "Jesus—you scared me," she said. With her right hand, she swiped at the fog, as if she could brush it aside.

Corso started across the pavement toward her. "Sorry," he said.

She took several deep breaths. "I guess I'm a little spooked. Must be what happens when you spend an afternoon with the dead."

She'd changed clothes since he'd seen her last. Motorcycle jacket. Black tights, lycra top. Shorter skirt. Different pair of Doc Martens with thinner soles and shiny silver eyelets. A sorta Janet Jackson meets Morticia Addams look.

"You smell better," he said.

"I'll bet you say that to all the girls."

He laughed. "Yeah, just ask anybody. They'll tell you."

"I stopped at home after the morgue. About the time medical examiners start making it a point to stand upwind of you, ya gotta figure it's time for a shower."

Forty yards north, the fog had enveloped Kamon, the trendy Japanese restaurant at the north end of the lot. Out on Fairview Avenue, yellow cones of light poured down from the street lamps, only to be swallowed whole by the fog before ever reaching the ground. Rush-hour traffic was moving at ten miles an hour. Cold dinners tonight.

Dougherty shivered in the dampness. Used her free hand to pull the jacket tight around her. "I hate this damn fog," she said. "It goes right through you."

Corso nodded his agreement. "Come on," he said. "Let's get out of it."

He took her elbow and led her across the lot and down the ramp to C dock. As he used his key on the gate, she said, "A boat, huh? That's very you, Corso. Very you."

"You think so?"

"Sure," she said. "Like it's all disconnected from everything else. Just sorta like floating on the surface of things."

Corso grimaced as he pulled open the gate. "You really ought to consider a career in radio, you know that, Dougherty? You could do one of those advice shows . . . you know, like Dr. What'shername there."

"That Nazi bitch? As if."

They walked carefully down the dock. Ten feet ahead, the concrete disappeared into the fog. The air was heavy and still. On both sides, masts and rigging appeared ghostly in the filtered light, as if they were strolling among the skeletal remains of a drowned forest. In the empty slips, the water lay still and black, like obsidian. Another thirty feet and Corso's salon lights became visible on the right. He pulled her over in front of him. "Watch your head," he said, pointing at a dark shape ahead in the fog.

"What's that?"

"An anchor," he said. Over the weekend, some drunk had docked a forty-foot Carver way too far into the slip, leaving a sixty-pound Danforth anchor suspended, head high out over the dock. "Nice," she said.

"Home, sweet home," Corso said as he turned into his own slip.

She stopped at the stern. Hugging herself. Hopping from foot to foot. She read the name out loud. *"Saltheart,"* and beneath that, *"Foamfollower."* She furrowed her brow. "Where do I know that name from?"

"It's a name out of a fantasy book I read years ago," Corso said.

She snapped her fingers. "Yeah, those Donaldson books. There's three of them. What's it called . . . ?" she asked herself.

"The Chronicles of Thomas Covenant the Unbeliever."

"Yeah. And the Saltheart character . . . he was like the last of a race of seagoing giants or something."

"That's the one," Corso said.

"Cool name for a boat."

Corso shivered inside his coat. "Come on," he said. "I'm freezing."

He climbed onboard, turned, and offered Dougherty his hand. She plopped the pile of papers into his palm and then hoisted herself over the rail in a single motion.

Corso slid the door aside and then followed her in. "Oh," she said. "It's warm. Feels so good." She rubbed her hands together. Looked around. "Hell . . . it's bigger than my apartment," she said.

He took her coat and laid it on the chart table. Dumped his on top. Corso put together a pot of coffee while she gave herself the grand tour.

"It's definitely you, Corso. All tidy and self-contained," she announced.

"I'm thrilled you think so," he said, handing her a cup. "How'd it go at the medical examiner's?"

"I got everything except the lie-detector test results. They claim they were destroyed or maybe lost. They couldn't seem to make up their minds."

"That figures," Corso said. "Let's see what you've got."

It took a little over two hours and another pot of coffee to sort it all out. To get the paperwork and the photographs into eleven separate piles. When they'd finished, Corso took the primary crime-scene photos and stood them up along the pin rail behind the settee. Piled the paperwork pertaining to each case on the cushion directly below the picture. He left a space between the first eight victims and the more recent casualties.

Dougherty held her cup against her ample chest. She moved her eyes slowly along the row of standing photographs. "God, this is eerie," she said. "Seeing them all lined up like that. Makes me feel like I ought to cover them up so's nobody can see them all dirty and naked like that."

Corso walked over to the first photo. Picked up the crime-scene report. Susanne Tovar. Twenty. Last seen at about ten in the morning on January 7, 1998. Doing her laundry at the Sit and Spin Laundromat on Fourth Avenue. Found by a janitor twelve hours later in a Dumpster behind a bakery in the 2300 block of Eastlake Avenue. Raped, sodomized, and strangled. No fluid residue of any kind. Perp presumed to have worn a condom. Green polyester carpet fibers found beneath her fingernails.

The cops had worked their way back through Susanne Tovar's social life. Found an angry ex-boyfriend named Peter Nilson who looked good for a while. Then Kate Mitchell was found thirteen days later, this time in a Dumpster in Fremont. Same MO. Same fibers beneath the nails. So much for the boyfriend.

The words "serial killer" do not appear in the detective's field notes until the last day of January 1998. When Jennine Tate is found dead in the alley behind the Broadway market. Detective Sergeant Feeney notes that the crimes appear to be both random and stranger-related. Next to the notation he wrote "serial killer?" and drew a circle around the words, as if he was afraid they'd escape.

If Sergeant Feeney still harbored any doubts, they

were dispelled when Jennifer Robison disappeared from the Northgate Mall, in broad daylight. Wearing a pair of leopard-skin stretch pants, no less. Told her shopping companion Francine Limuti that she was going to run out to the car for a blouse she wanted to return to Nordstrom. Never seen alive again. Turned up the next morning, three blocks away, behind a Red Robin burger joint, sans the stretch pants.

Sara Butler's picture was the saddest of the lot. Only eighteen years old. The youngest of the victims. Not discovered until she'd made it all the way to the dump. Found by the gulls. Traced back to the Dumpster behind the coffee shop on lower Queen Anne, where she'd worked. Manager said she'd stepped out back for a smoke and never returned. He figured she'd quit— you know how these kids are—and didn't bother to report her missing.

Nine days later, it was Melody Williams. A tourist from Redfield, South Dakota. On her honeymoon. Strolling the Pike Street Market with her new husband, John, who ducked into the men's room, came out two minutes later to find his wife missing. Cops interviewed nearly a hundred people. Nobody saw a thing. She was found a day and a half later, in a First Avenue construction site less than a mile from where she'd disappeared.

To judge from the stubble, Analia Nisovic had shaved her pubic hair into a heart shape about three days before she disappeared from Westlake Center. The See's Chocolate Shop, where she had recently been promoted to assistant manager, was found unlocked, with the receipts still in the till. Of the eight women, she'd put up the most fight. Her nose and four of her fingers were broken in the struggle.

Then, on the night of April 2, while the city was suffering through the coldest spring in its history, Leanne Samples came staggering down that snow-covered service road and the city heaved a collective sigh of relief. The giddiness lasted for all of three days, until somebody drops a dime and says the body of Kelly Doyle can be found in a trash bin on Sixth Avenue South. Unlike the others, however, the tipster doesn't wait around for the cops to arrive. Dead body number eight was just different enough from the others to cause concern. Could it be they had the wrong guy in jail? Medical examiner said the cold weather made it impossible to pinpoint the time of death. The body was frozen solid. Same MO. Matching ear tag cinches it. Gotta be Himes. Another giant sigh whooshes through town.

Now, damn near three years later, they've got two more. Alice Crane-Carter and the girl they'd seen earlier today. Yet to be identified. Same fibers, different tags. Only difference between the old and new victims was that the level of violence had increased. The new victims had facial contusions. Number nine, Alice Crane-Carter, had suffered a fractured cheekbone and a broken eye socket. No report yet on the unnamed girl.

Corso walked into the galley and put his cup in the sink. Dougherty stood in the salon staring at the photos. "You okay?" he asked.

She shook her head. "I'll tell you what, Corso," she said. "If this is the kind of thing you do for a living, it's no damn wonder you're one weird dude."

"I used to think I'd get used to it," he said. "You know . . . like something inside me would scab over and I wouldn't feel it anymore."

"Did it?"

"No. All I got was the urge to be alone."

He lifted the coffeepot. She shook her head no. "What now?" she asked.

Corso thought it over. "They're running the new murders story tomorrow. Gives me a full day to pull something out of this stuff. So I guess we call it a day and go to bed."

He put his coat on and then held her motorcycle jacket out for her. She thought about snatching the coat from his hands, but instead turned her back and shrugged herself into the jacket. Zipped it all the way up. Corso pulled a set of keys from his jacket pocket. He swung the keys between his thumb and forefinger.

"Sometime tomorrow we're going to have to retrieve the paper's car."

She yawned. "I forgot about the damn car."

"Let's start early," he said. "Himes is getting short on time."

Corso again dreamed of the cobbled street. He stood on the uneven stones and watched, fascinated, as the three soldiers rudely turned one man after another away from the door. Sometimes providing a rough kick in the pants to speed the victim on his way. Laughing heartily among themselves at the joy of it all. Then—suddenly—the street is empty and the soldiers turn their leaden eyes his way. When he comes forward, the sound of boots and rifles snap around the stone walls. Without a word, they form a line to the right of the door and come to attention. They salute.

As Corso closes the door behind him and begins to

climb the narrow stairs, the walls on all sides seem to float away . . . leaving the building sheathed in rags. He steps up. His hands clutching the rails as he moves toward the light at the top of the stairs.

Chapter 20

"Stop," Corso said.

Apparently this command carried a far greater sense of urgency in North Africa than was customary in south Seattle. The Somali cabdriver locked up the brakes, rocketing Corso and Dougherty forward into the plastic shield separating the front seat from the back. Corso glowered at the driver, who was all shrugs and wide-eyed innocence.

Dougherty looked over. "You said stop," she said.

"I meant soon," Corso groused.

"You're never satisfied, you know that?"

The meter read fifteen and a quarter. Corso gave the guy a twenty and told him to keep the change. Corso and Dougherty stepped out onto South Doris Street. With a chirp of the tires, the cab continued west, turned left at the Aviator Hotel, and disappeared.

Dougherty looked around. "And why in hell are we stopping here anyway? The damn car's up around the corner."

Corso jerked his thumb back over his shoulder. The

alley gate to the murder scene was open. "Let's have a look."

"No way."

"Come on."

"The last time I listened to you I ended up in jail."

Corso swung a hand around. "All the cop stuff is gone."

"Smelling like cat shit."

"Come on."

The alley ran between a Peterbilt truck-parts distributor and a boarded-up auto-body shop. Ahead in the courtyard, somebody was whistling in between grunts, making it impossible to catch the tune. Dougherty tugged at the back of Corso's coat. Corso kept moving forward until he cleared the buildings.

A turquoise pickup truck from the late fifties was backed up to the rear wall of the Aviator Hotel. Next to the truck, a man knelt on the ground, pouring something from one red plastic bucket into another and then back. Grunting each time he hefted a full bucket. Whistling between grunts.

"Excuse me," Corso said, moving forward.

The man looked up. He was about seventy, a bit bent but still powerful-looking. He wore the same clothes as the day before when Corso had seen him talking with Densmore and Wald, red plaid shirt, jeans, worn through at the seat, short rubber boots, and long rubber gloves. He grunted as he levered himself to his feet.

"I hep you?" he asked.

Corso strode quickly forward with his hand extended. "I wanted to apologize."

"You best not be sellin' somethin'," the man said.

"No, sir. I just wanted to apologize for any trouble or

inconvenience we might have caused you yesterday when we . . ." He pointed upward. "The roof."

"That was you they busted up there?"

"Miss Dougherty and I."

The old man gave a hearty laugh. "Wasn't that just sumphin'," he chuckled. "That fella thinkin' I was gonna let him come in the hotel after. Cop or no cop, you ain't comin' in nothin' of mine smellin' like that." Just as suddenly as he'd laughed, his face fell into a frown. "Almost enough to make a body forget about that poor girl . . . layin' there like that. All by herself and such." He pulled the glove from his right hand and shook with Corso.

"Buster Davis," the old man said. "Given name's Clyde, but my mamma took to callin' me Buster, on account of how I always wanted a pair of them Buster Brown shoes I seen on the TV. Wid the kid and the dog inside the shoe. Name just sorta stuck."

Corso introduced Dougherty, then asked, "You the one found the body?"

"Sure did," he said sadly. "Damnedest thing to be findin' that early in the mornin' too. Doin' what I do every mornin', just comin' out see what kinda stuff I gotta paint over and I notice the Dumpster lid's open. I keep 'em shut on accounta the raccoons." He stroked his chin as he recalled the moment. "And there the poor thing was, laying there in her altogether and all. Damnedest thing."

Corso pointed at the gate. Eight feet of chain link with four rows of barbed wire decorating the top. "That gate lock?"

The old man eyed him narrowly. "Wouldn't be much point to it bein' there if it didn't lock, now would it?"

"Whoever left her there must have come through the gate."

"Same thing the cops said and I tell you the same thing I tol' them. Whoever it was musta climbed over and opened it from the inside. Ain't but two keys to that gate. I got one and the security company got the other." He waved a gnarled hand. "For all the damn good they doin' me for the money I'm paying 'em. Can't even keep the kids from paintin' on the damn wall. I got to come out here every damn day and waste my time painting over crap like that." He pointed up at the windowless back wall of the hotel, where someone had taken spray paint and written "FUR" in ornate, sweeping letters.

Dougherty stepped around the men and walked over to the wall.

"Just painted the damn wall, last thing Wednesday night, 'fore I went down to the Eagles for the evening. Get up in the damn mornin', find that poor little thing in there wid the rubbish."

"It's not finished," Dougherty said. Both men turned her way.

"What's not finished?" Corso asked.

"The tag." She pointed up at the letters on the wall. FUR in gold. "It's supposed to say 'fury,' with the tail of the Y making a circle around the whole thing. I've seen this one before. It's all over the place."

"Best not be all over the place for very damn long," the old man said. "City fine you a hunnered-ninety dollars you leave that stuff up on the wall."

"Really?" Corso said. "Even if it's your wall?"

"Specially if it's your wall. Were up to me, I'd just leave it up there. Looks better than them old bricks anyway. Not like anybody gonna see it back here. But the city says no. Got them an ordinance, you know." He threw up his hands. "Which reminds me, I better get myself to work here, 'less it starts rainin' again and I never get the damn thing done." He offered his hand again to Corso, who took it.

"Nice meetin' you folks," he said, nodding at Dougherty. "You-all try to stay out of trouble now," he said with a grin before turning back toward his work.

Dougherty took Corso by the elbow and steered him back through the gate. They turned left on South Doris and began walking west, toward the hotel.

"Did you hear what he said?" she asked.

"About painting over the graffiti on Wednesday night?"

"Which means the place was tagged sometime before Thursday morning, when he found the girl's body."

"And you're thinking the vandal might have been at work when the murder came down. Maybe saw something."

"No self-respecting tagger would leave his tag unfinished. The tag is their whole trip. It's their artistic identity."

"How is it you know so much about it?"

"I did a photo journal on taggers for *The Stranger*," she said, naming Seattle's most visible alternative paper. "Got to know quite a few of the artists."

"Artists, my ass," Corso scoffed as they reached the corner of South Doris and Homer and turned right under the bare trees.

"Lighten up, Corso. Expression comes in a lot of different flavors."

"Graffiti is hardly art."

"A hundred years ago they said the same thing about photographs."

The Chevy was right where they'd left it the day before. While Corso warmed the engine, Dougherty unlocked the back door, leaned in, and checked her camera case. Satisfied that everything was intact, she slid into the passenger seat.

"What now?" she asked.

"You think you could find the kid?"

"Probably," she said. "I know some people."

Corso wheeled the car around the block, turned left on Airport Way, and headed back downtown. "Where to?" Corso asked.

"It will have to be after dark," Dougherty said. "Taggers aren't morning people. The whole scene is kinda nocturnal."

"You want to come with me? I've got to work my way through that stuff we got from the cops."

Her eyes turned inward. She shook her head. "If I never see those pictures again, it will be too soon. Besides, I've got a treatment on my face this afternoon. Why don't you take me home? Pick me up again at . . . say . . . six or so."

She flipped on the radio. Rob Thomas singing "Smooth" in front of the Carlos Santana band. She began to move in the seat. Corso reached over and turned it up.

Chapter 21

Like Mad Fred said: The only thing the dead knew for sure was that being alive was better. Corso sat backward in the teak chair, resting his forearms across the top rail. He moved his head slowly, taking in the dead women one last time, as if, in their final eight-by-ten ignominy, they might yet have a tale to tell.

Outside, the wind had died. The slap of waves against the hull had stopped just after noon. By three, the fog had come rolling in from the Sound, advancing over Queen Anne Hill like a gray-clad army, reducing C dock visibility to twenty feet.

He'd been through it all. Just over two hundred pages. Ten women. All brunettes. The youngest, Sara Butler, had turned eighteen only a month before her disappearance. The oldest, Kelly Doyle, had been twenty-seven at the time of her death. Nine locals, one tourist. Williams, Mitchell, Crane, and Tovar had been married. The rest single. Each of the women still wore her jewelry, but no trace of the clothes or shoes had ever been found. No connection, be it personal or professional, had ever been found among the victims. Husbands, boyfriends, and bosses had been systematically eliminated as suspects. Every known sex offender within five hundred miles had been hauled in and questioned. The first eight ovine ear tags had been of a type not used since the late sixties, a fact that made the tags not only impossible to trace, but which, at the same time, squelched any possibility of a copycat killer. The new tags were sold in forty-four locations in King County alone. The cops were working that angle.

All total, nearly five months of investigation by the SPD, the Washington State Patrol, and the FBI had turned up nothing but some green polyester fibers and half a dozen stray pubic hairs, which any competent defense attorney would argue came from the Dumpsters.

Corso got to his feet. Stretched. Massaged the back of his neck for a moment and then ambled into the galley, where he dropped to one knee and rummaged around under the sink. He came out with a small cardboard box and carried it back to the salon, where, one at a time, almost reverentially, he put the photos and the files facedown in the box and then slid the box back under the sink. He checked his watch: 4:25.

"The stuff we got from the cops is a hundred-percent useless," Corso said. "I spent the day going over everything." He shook his head. "They've done what they could, but they've got bupkis. This guy's going to have to make a mistake before they get a line on him."

Mrs. V.'s face was grim. "How many more lives is that going to cost?"

Corso shrugged. "The good news is, his level of violence is going up. He's working himself up to a frenzy.

It's what these guys do. With each new killing, it takes more and more to get them off. They start to feel invincible. Next thing you know, even the organized ones start to get a little sloppy. Hopefully somebody in charge will be paying attention when it happens."

"Meanwhile . . . Mr. Himes," she began.

"Yeah," Corso said. "Meanwhile, Mr. Himes. We don't come up with a smoking gun, old Walter Lee's gonna buy the farm."

"And you're still convinced of his innocence?"

"Innocent"—he waggled a hand—"I don't know. I go back and forth about that. What I *am* sure of is that he got a bad deal in court. If nothing else, he ought to get a new trial."

A silence settled over the room.

With a sigh, she put her palms on the desk. Got to her feet.

"Guess who's on the payroll?"

"I'll bite, who?"

"Miss Samples."

"Doing what?"

"Subscription complaints. We needed some new help in a hurry. She said she'd like to try. Mr. Harris says she's absolutely marvelous. Totally unflappable. Seems she has a homily for every occasion."

Corso smiled at the thought of Leanne telling some irate subscriber who didn't get his paper how "Mama said . . . all things come to those who wait."

The grin faded when Mrs. V. said, "You wouldn't believe the volume of hate mail we've received in the past eight hours."

"Over what?"

"Over our suggestion that Mr. Himes may not be

guilty. It seems that a great many of our fellow citizens are in favor of executing Mr. Himes whether he's guilty or not."

"That's what idiots do, isn't it? Whenever reality fails to match their little preconceptions, they demand that reality forthwith be changed."

"You'd think they'd have *some* interest in justice."

"They can't," Corso said. "They'd have to admit that every day of their lives they're probably rubbing shoulders with the likes of Walter Leroy Himes. They like their villains remarkable. Evil geniuses who want to conquer the world or eat your liver with beans . . . something like that."

"I'm sure you have an opinion on why that is?"

" 'Cause the more remarkable the villain, the farther removed it is from them. They don't actually know anybody like Hannibal Lecter." He waved a hand. "Child-molesting rednecks. Hell, they've got relatives like that. That's what really scares the hell out of them."

She nodded. "What did somebody once say about how the law is practiced in courts, but justice is dispensed in alleys?"

"That's it, exactly," Corso said. "We ought to reinstate public executions." He met her amused gaze. "I mean it. Right out in the town square. Westlake Center. High noon. After church on Sunday. Everybody gets to see the system in action. Gets to let off a little steam. You know . . . bring a lunch. Bring the family. Make a day of it."

"You're terrible," she said with a chuckle.

"No . . . I mean it. It'd be like a weekly cautionary

tale. They could wire 'em up for special effects like that Porter guy over in Montana."

She winced at the memory. A couple of years back, triple murderer Stanley Porter had been electrocuted at the Montana State Penitentiary. As horrified witnesses watched, eight-inch flames had burst from Porter's ears. Several sensitive souls had fainted dead away. Turned out they'd had a dead short in the system. Not that it had mattered much to Stanley Porter. He'd had his fifteen minutes. For a while there, seemed like half the cars in Montana had one of those "Stanley Porter is alive and medium-well" bumper stickers.

"Way I figure it," Corso said, "you let a kid see a couple of dozen felons doing their impression of Bunsen burners, and we'll have a lot fewer of the little turds showing up at school with guns."

"I'd like to think we're too civilized for such spectacles."

"That's the problem. We're too damn civilized. We raise these kids out in little isolated patches of suburbia. Buy them any damn thing their diseased little minds can imagine, protect them from all harm, and what do we get? We get these lonely little nerd boys who blow our brains out over breakfast one morning and then go down to the high school and kill everybody who's feeling better than they are."

"You're feeling very passionate about things this afternoon," Mrs. V. noted. Corso rubbed the side of his face. "It's that—what did you call it the other day? That quixotic spark of mine."

"We're imperfect; ergo our systems are imperfect," she said.

Corso ran his hands through his hair. "I had a professor once who said the greatest trait a reporter could possess was a tolerance for ambiguity."

"You think he was correct?"

"Only up to a point. Too much tolerance and you become amorphous. You wake up one morning, everything's so friggin' hunky-dory that you're nobody in particular."

"How so?"

"Because things like intellectual certainty and moral outrage and righteous indignation are the engines of society. Self-satisfied tolerance never accomplished a damn thing except to muddy up the waters of what's right and what's wrong."

He opened his mouth to say something else, but instead merely laughed at himself. "Listen to me. Jesus. I must be tired." Corso turned and crossed to the door. "I've got to pick up Dougherty. We're following an artistic lead."

He tried to muster a final smile, but couldn't get his face to go along with the program. Opened the door and stepped out without a backward glance. Violet Rogers was tapping away at her keyboard. He walked past her desk and pushed the elevator button. Violet looked up. Gave him a wink.

"You know, Violet . . . I've been thinking about what you said the other day. About how maybe I was mad at God and all."

"And?"

"And I think maybe you're right. I think maybe I am."

A muted tinkle announced the elevator's arrival. The door slid open and Corso backed in. Violet shook her head sadly. "You better hope she don't get mad at you back."

Corso pushed the button. Rode to street level, where the little Hispanic guy was behind the security desk. They exchanged silent nods before Corso jerked open the door and stepped outside.

The night air clung to the skin like wet linen. He hunched his shoulders, crossed the sidewalk to where the Datsun was parked in a tow-away zone. Looked up toward First Avenue, where the fog had swallowed even the darkness, leaving the city puffy and whiter than white. He started the engine. Clicked on the head-lights. Watched the beams disappear down a black hole about twenty feet out.

She pulled the leather jacket tighter around herself as she stepped onto the concrete. Corso killed the engine and got out of the car.

"This will probably go better if I go in alone," she said.

He gave her a two-fingered salute. "I'll be right here. You have a problem, you just call my name."

In three steps, she was enveloped by the fog. Corso listened to the fading sound of her boots on the con-crete. Overhead, half a dozen orange lights cast a vel-vet glow. The school was gone, but the playground remained. What used to be the Martha Shelby Middle School was now nothing more than three concrete walls with a basketball hoop bolted to each wall. The city had dedicated the space for graffiti artists and skaters. "Graffiti City" the taggers called it. The de facto agreement was that the cops would leave Graffiti

City alone. Smoke your underage cigarettes. Toke on those pipes. Stay out late. Spite your parents. But . . . keep it off the streets and don't wake the neighbors. It starts leaking out into the streets or we get any complaints and the party's over.

As much as Dougherty hated the fog, the cool mist soothed her cheeks and forehead. Her face felt like it was sunburned and about to crack to pieces. The sound of a basketball slapping against the concrete echoed around the walls. To the left, a trio of preteens sat on the ground smoking contraband cigarettes. She heard voices ahead in the gloom. Three more steps and the outlines of two guys emerged. Shrill laughter erupted from somewhere deep in the enclosure.

They were maybe sixteen. One white. One Hispanic. Uniform baggy pants and oversize stocking caps. Plaid jackets buttoned all the way up. Passing a pipe.

"Hey, Cholo . . . look what we got here," the white kid said.

Her mouth suddenly felt as cracked and dry as her face. She knew better than to let them get started on their routine. Let 'em get worked up and they could be dangerous.

"I'm looking for Torpedo," she said.

Torpedo was the street name for one of the kids Dougherty had photographed for a piece about graffiti artists. They'd gotten along well. He'd been her guide through the underground world of taggers and skaters. His tag was the word "Boom" in the center of the rainbow-hued explosion. Made his taggin' rep puttin' his mark on cop cars, then made himself a legend tagging the space needle Christmas Eve, '98.

"I got a torpedo for you, baby," the other kid said.

The first kid stepped in close. He smelled of weed and stale sweat. He put a hand on her ass and gave it a little tweak. She slapped his arm away.

"Keep your fucking hands to yourself," she said.

"You hear that?" the Hispanic kid asked. "She gonna kick yo ass for you, boy." White boy laughed and grabbed his crotch. Moved his package up and down.

"Come on, baby. Got just what you need right here."

Dougherty felt her throat constrict as she checked out the area he was fondling and then stared him down.

"At best you got about half what I need right there."

The Hispanic kid bent at the waist and pointed at his friend. "Hoo hoo hoo."

White boy lost his sense of humor. Started bopping around like a spastic rapper.

"You got some mouth on you, bitch . . . you know that?"

She felt a finger of fear on the back of her neck. Much as it pained her, she was about to scream Corso's name when a figure stepped out of the fog.

"I hear somebody usin' my name in vain?"

Torpedo. Finely wrought features and some of the longest eyelashes she'd ever seen. Multiracial. A little of everything. Claimed to have been in seventeen separate foster homes. He'd grown since she'd seen him last. Tall as she was now. Still wore the biggest pants she'd ever seen. Obligatory plaid jacket buttoned to the throat and one of those knitted Scandinavian wool hats with the earflaps. Reindeer cavorting across the front. Festive like.

He stopped. Pointed at her. "The pitcher lady," he said. He walked over and slapped her five. "You gonna makes us famous again?"

"Maybe, if we can get rid of the stoner boys here."

He turned toward the pair. "You heard the lady," he said. "Take your weed-smellin' asses up the road." White boy opened his mouth to speak. Torpedo reached languidly into his pants pocket. Left his hand in there. Everybody got stiff all of a sudden. Had a little E. F. Hutton moment, until Whitey's friend reached over and put a hand on his pal's arm. They passed a look. "No problem," the Hispanic kid said, showing Torpedo his palms. Together, they backed silently off into the gloom.

Torpedo inclined his head to the left and then started walking that way. Dougherty followed. She heard shouts and the clank of the ball on the rim. More dribbling.

Torpedo walked all the way to the east wall. Leaned his back against it. He straddled a puddle. Dozens of bloated cigarette butts bobbed like an armada.

"I been thinkin' 'bout you lately," he said.

"About what?"

"'Bout how we need some more help to get our story out. To tell people what's really happenin' out here. Not that crap they put in the paper."

"Like what?"

"Like how they givin' kids a year inside for taggin'."

"A year?"

"No shit. I know three kids serving serious jail time for nothin' but taggin'. No dope. No resisting. No nothing but tagging."

Dougherty wasn't surprised. Seattle was as fat and full of itself as it'd been for a hundred years. Anything shabby had to go. You could walk around downtown and point at buildings and say, "That won't be there in a year." From Dougherty's Capital Hill apartment, the skyline bristled with construction cranes, almost as if the city were under siege. Turned out, affluence was the fifth column.

"What can I do?"

"Get us some space. So we can tell 'em."

"Tell them what?"

"That . . . that no matter how much they tear down, nothin' gonna change. People still gonna be shootin' dope and beatin' their old ladies. Guys gonna lose it behind whiskey and shoot some motherfucker for somethin' that don't make no sense to nobody but him. Ain't gonna be perfect . . . no matter how hard they try, how many poor people they lock up. City just ain't gonna be perfect."

"I can ask around the alternatives and see if anybody's interested."

"Somebody got to tell the story," he said. He pulled out a pack of Merit cigarettes, offered her one, took it himself when she refused. Fired it up.

"What you needin' from me?" he asked.

"The kid who tags 'fury.' "

"What about him?"

"What's his real name?"

"Bobby Boyd."

"I need to find him."

Torpedo bumped himself off the wall. "He doan come down here much. Doan like painting where it's allowed. Kid's a taggin' animal," he said with obvious admiration.

"You know anybody who'd know where I could find him?"

"Sure," he said. "His two main homeboys are Tommy and Jared." He pointed in the direction of the invisible basketball game. "Them two little shits shootin' hoops right over there."

Chapter 22

Hear the car door. Figure it be that fat Korean she work for. King, Kin, Kim, whatever the hell it is. Stop by sometime to bring her little presents and shit. But there's three voices. Hope like hell it ain't the cops. Can't hear shit through the door. A woman's deep voice say "fury." His mama sayin' how he ain't been out the house at all. They go back and forth, real quick like, but he can't make out the words.

"Robert." The voice. Maybe if he don't say nothin' . . .

"Robert, you come down here, right now."

Shit. Shit. Shit. Must be the damn cops. His stomach contracts and the tears start from his eyes. That bitch judge told him. Gonna get a year inside like Manny, if they catch him at it again. Gonna admit nothin'. Not one goddamn thing. That's where everybody blow it. Listen to that cop crap about how they'll feel better if they tell the truth. End up down in county lockup givin' it up to stay alive. Don't tell 'em nothin'.

He checks himself in the mirror on back the door.

Lookin' nappy as hell. He pats at his hair. Just look worse. Shit.

"Robert." Real loud this time.

"Comin'," he calls.

He steps over the hole in the stairs. Take his time. Gettin' his shit together on the way down. No way they gonna see him sweat. All you got to do is just be cool, fool. Just be cool.

Two of 'em. Standin' there in the front room. Ain't no cops neither. Big mean-lookin dude with a ponytail and one of them Capital Hill sun-hater chicks with the black all-over shit. Maybe seen her before somewhere. Hard to tell. All them Addams family hos look the same. "Yeah?"

She's standin' there with her arms folded across her chest, big-time pissy look on her face. "These people here from the newspaper. Want to talk to you."

"You remember me?" the chick ask.

He don't say nothin'.

"I took pictures of your artwork, last year sometime. Remember?"

"Oh yeah," he say. "You come wid Torpedo."

Before she can say somethin', Pissy Face start flappin' her lip. Right up in Goth Girl's face too. "Don't be talking about no 'art' here, lady." She turn her head and lay the brow on him. Almost as bad as the voice. "What we talkin' about here is vandalism. 'Bout defacin' people's property. 'Bout the kind of choices this young man is making wid his life. Choices if he ain't careful gonna follow him around for the rest of his days. So doan be talking bout no spray can 'art.' Not here in my house, you ain't."

"We're not here to make any trouble," the big guy say.

"Good, 'cause Robert doan need no help wid trouble."

"Why don't you tell us about the yard behind the Aviator Hotel, Robert?" Ponytail say. Felt like all the blood drained down to his feet. Musta looked that way too. Next thing he knows everybody lookin' at him like he hurled or somethin'. She unfold her arms and put a hand on his shoulder. "You all right, Robert? What's this man here talking about? Aviator yard or something."

He's feeling shaky but sacs up. "What about it?"

"About the guy in the black van," Goth Girl say. And now he feels cold all over. Got goose bumps up and down his arms. He don't say nothin'.

She's sweepin' her head around like a searchlight. "What's this van?" she want to know. "This guy?" The big guy ask her if she been watchin' the thing wid that Himes guy on the tube all week. She say "yeah" 'bout what a shame they got to let him go and all. How the likes of that Himes fella ought to be either dead or in the jailhouse.

Big guy say, "We think maybe Robert got a look at the real killer," and all of a sudden, it sound like somebody pulled the plug. Real quiet like. Then she say, "You know what this man's talkin' about, Robert? You see somethin' like that?" He don't say nothin'. Just tryin' not to piss his pants. She gives him the brow.

"You know what he's talkin' about, doan you?"

"This had nothing to do with tagging," Ponytail say.

Goth Girl tell him, "The tag's already painted over."

"Wasn't no tag. Just some damn letters."

"'Cause you got interrupted," the guy say.

"You know all this shit, why you down here talkin' to me?"

She reach over, slap him in the ear. "You watch your mouth," she say. When he don't say nothin', she get all up in his face. Grab him by the chin, make him look in her eyes. "You know somethin' about this, doan you?"

Ain't no point in tryin' to lie. He nods. She puts the voice on him. "You better tell these people what you seen." She lets go of his face. "Maybe all you stayin' out all night finally do some good for a change. Go on . . . tell them."

"I seen him," he say, "after he put somethin' in wid the trash, he come around the front and I seen what he looked like."

All of a sudden, they the ones not sayin' shit.

Chapter 23

Friday, September 21
8:23 P.M.   Day 5 of 6

"Skinny little white guy. Weird eyes. Somewhere around thirty-five or forty. Wearing some kind of blue or black uniform. Driving a primer-gray van with quarter-moon bubble windows in back."

"Maybe a cop. Maybe not. Depending on which kids you believe."

Corso nodded as he forked the last piece of hot turkey sandwich into his mouth. They were ensconced in a booth in Andy's Diner, a landmark greasy spoon consisting of an interconnected maze of converted railway cars. Dougherty had long since inhaled an order of meat loaf and mashed potatoes, followed by a humongous piece of cherry pie à la mode. She sat leaning against the wall, squeaking her thumb along the rim of her water glass.

Corso washed the turkey down with a healthy swig of milk, then gestured toward Dougherty with his fork. "You remember what Buster Davis told us about the gate?"

"He said somebody must have climbed over."

"But all three kids say no."

"So?"

"So . . . he also said that there were only two keys. Said he had one and his security company had the other."

"So you're thinking what?"

"Security guard," Corso said. "It fits with the guy wearing a uniform, and it's consistent with the FBI profile. Not only is it a perfect job for a loner, but it explains how somebody could be familiar with all the different locales where the bodies have been found."

"What do we do?" she asked.

Corso thought it over. "We call the cops. Like the god-fearing citizens we are."

Behind the counter, a short-order cook in a stained white T-shirt was flipping eggs and hash browns. The place was deserted.

"I hate giving that Densmore asshole anything," Dougherty groused.

"No argument there," Corso said. "If Himes wasn't sitting on death row and I wasn't sure this guy was going to kill again real soon, I'd be inclined to let them figure it out for themselves."

"You're right," she sighed. "We can't take the chance. I couldn't live with myself if it turned out to be this guy and he killed again."

Corso dabbed at his lips with a white paper napkin. Pulled his phone from his pocket and pushed a few buttons. Asked for the general number of the Seattle Police Department. Said thanks and dialed again. Asked for Lieutenant Andrew Densmore. Said it was an urgent matter of police business. Waited with the phone held an inch from his ear. Dougherty heard

Densmore come on the line. "Densmore," he barked.

"It's Frank Corso."

Silence for a moment, then a bitter laugh. "What is it, asshole?" the cop asked. "After tonight's fiasco you still don't think you've fucked things up enough yet?"

Corso wasn't sure exactly what Densmore meant but said, "I think I've got something for you."

"You haven't been listening to me, have you, Corso?"

"I may have a line on the real killer."

"I'm gonna tell you one more time, Corso. If you and circus girl so much as sniff at my investigation, I'm gonna ream the both of you."

"Listen to me—" Corso began.

"No," Densmore said quickly. "You got something to say, why don't you say it to Tiffany Eyre or maybe to her parents."

Corso felt a steel ball bearing roll down his spine. "Who's—" he began.

"We found Tiffany this morning in a Dumpster on Union Street." Corso had to force the phone against his ear.

"Why don't you talk to her parents?" Densmore sneered. "If you think you've got something to say, say it to them. Tell 'em how you and that rag you work for muddied up an ongoing investigation. Tell 'em how we might have had the guy by now if you'd kept your goddamn nose out of it." The line went dead.

Corso sat for a moment, staring at the phone.

"They've got another dead girl."

Dougherty brought both hands to her mouth. "Oh . . . God . . . so soon."

"Motherfucker," Corso said.

The word had barely escaped his lips when he no-

ticed the waitress scowling by the side of the table. Big
red hands on half-acre hips. "Earlene," the badge said.

"You kiss your mother with that mouth?" she
wanted to know.

"Sorry," Corso said. Across the table, Dougherty
grimaced.

The waitress pulled the check from her pocket. "Anything else?" she asked. When they said no, she dropped
the check onto the table and squeaked out of view.

"Well?" Dougherty said.

"He's winding up. The killings are going to get
closer together. He's working his way into a murder
frenzy."

Suddenly Dougherty's expression froze and she was
pointing one of her black-tipped fingers out over
Corso's head. He looked back over his shoulder. The
cook had come out from behind the counter. He was
sitting on a stool, shoveling eggs and hash browns into
his mouth, gazing up at the silent TV mounted against
the ceiling in the corner of the room.

Split screen. Photo of Walter Leroy Himes. Another
of the death chamber. Cut to CNN logo. Washington
State Penitentiary, Cynthia Stone reporting . . . gold
graphic "LIVE." Cynthia behind her serious face. "We
are now less than thirty hours from the event . . ." The
screen went black. The cook dropped the remote,
wiped his mouth. Spoke to Earlene.

"World'd be a better place without that Himes fella,"
he said.

"Amen," she said.

"We've got a problem," Corso said.

"What did I tell you about using 'we'?"

"A serious problem."

Hawes scoffed. "Let me tell you about problems." He waved his arm toward the newsroom. "I've got to be ready. I've got to pretend that Himes might get a stay. Which means I've got thirteen people I can't send home on a Friday night. All of whom had plans and who now hate me, and all of whom I've gotta pay time and a half while they're out there, cursing me under their collective breaths and wishing I was dead."

"I think I've got a serious lead on the murderer."

"So . . . call the cops."

"I did. They don't want to hear about it. Guess what?"

"I'll bite."

"They've got another dead woman. Number eleven."

Hawes sat forward in a hurry. "Says who?"

His face darkened as Corso filled him in. "But the kid didn't actually see a body," he said when Corso had finished.

"No."

"What was your impression of the kid?"

"If I had to guess, I'd say he was being straight with us."

Hawes blew the air from his lungs. "Then we've definitely got to notify SPD."

"I did," Corso said again.

Hawes reached for the phone, stopped his hand in midair. "Maybe Mrs. Van Der Hoven ought to . . . ," he said after a moment.

"You ask me, our mutual popularity is at an all-time low."

"Funny, but subscriptions are at an all-time high," Hawes mused.

"You suppose there's a connection there?"

"I prefer not to think about it."

"We could go public. Save our asses by writing the story."

Hawes rolled his eyes. "And if we're wrong?"

"Then it's like the Atlanta bombing all over again. The poor bastard in the van becomes the new Richard Jewell."

"And if we're right?"

"Then we just gave away one hell of a story."

"At least our asses would be covered."

"That's the Pulitzer spirit," Corso said.

"You got a better idea?"

"We've still got a full day. Maybe Dougherty and I can turn this guy."

"And where is the indispensable Miss Dougherty?"

"I took her home. We've been at it since the news conference yesterday morning."

"The news business is tough that way."

"We've gotta do something."

Hawes rocked in his chair as he thought it over. "You got a plan?" he asked finally. Corso told him what he had in mind.

Hawes winced and nodded simultaneously. He folded his stubby arms across his chest and leaned so far back in his chair his feet came off the ground. Corso watched his lips move in and out as he tried to square the idea with himself. "You know what it's like to go to the American Society of Newspaper Editors conference every year as the managing editor of the *Seattle Sun*, Corso?" Corso said he didn't. "I'm like"—he searched for a word—"plankton. The absolute bottom of the food chain. The bar conversation stops every time I slide onto a stool. The big-timers look at me with a combination of pity and something more like terror. As if my presence reminds them of how bad things could actually get." He sat forward. "I stopped going a few years back. Got to the point where if one more of those guys gave me that patronizing little smile, I was going to pop him one." He looked up at Corso. "This year's event is in Denver, right after the Pulitzers in April. I was thinking this morning that I might just go. Maybe do a little smiling of my own."

"Then we better hope like hell I'm not right and that he doesn't kill again between now and tomorrow night."

Hawes folded his arms even tighter. Full straight-jacket hug.

"Bite your tongue," he said.

Chapter 24

Yuppies love brunch. Especially on weekends, when, having survived yet another week in their cubicles, they come lurching out of their high-priced hovels to migrate purblind toward the bistro du jour, where, after an hour or so of waiting in the rain, they're awarded a table at which they languish well into the shank of the afternoon, sipping oceans of latte and picking at divine goat cheese omelets.

Julia's Bakery was packed to the rafters. Headline on the *Seattle Times* read "Judgment Day." The *Post Intelligencer* blared: "And One to Go!" The clock on the wall read 9:21 before Corso and Dougherty squeezed inside, shuffled their way through the service line, and then, for want of a table, back out the side door into the parking lot.

Corso set his coffee atop a blue mailbox and zipped his coat. The fog had disappeared. Leaving acrylic-blue skies, marred only by occasional patches of fast-moving clouds. "You look remarkably status quo today," he offered. Beneath her full-length black

leather coat Dougherty wore a white blouse and a pair
of blue jeans tucked into black cowboy boots. She'd
changed her lip and nail colors from the usual black to
fire-engine red. She looked like a bigger version of
fifties pinup girl Betty Paige.

She glared at him and grunted.

He retrieved his coffee. Blew away the steam. She
rolled her cup between her hands. "Where do we
start?"

"Four crime scenes each." He recited the list from
memory.

"What about the other locations?"

"We'll do this one together. Just to make sure we're
on the same page."

"This one?"

"Yeah, remember? Susanne Tovar, the first victim,
was found out back of here in the bakery's Dumpster."

"What about the hotel?"

"Buster Davis is our control group. Since he's the
one got us started on this thing, I want to call him last.
That way, whatever we find out today won't be tainted
by what we already know."

She stopped a strip of cinnamon roll just short of her
mouth. "I don't understand."

"If we call Buster first and ask him what security
company he uses, then we'll have that company im-
planted in our heads while we're out there knocking on
doors. It's better to do it blind. It's just human nature to
try to prove what you already know. When we're all
done, we'll see how many duplicates we get, and then
we'll call Buster."

He gestured with his cup. "Come on."

They crossed Eastlake Avenue and stood on the

sidewalk looking back at the bakery. Corso pointed north. "We're going to have to do everything commercial within a square block of each dump site."

Dougherty stuffed the last of the roll in her mouth. Held up a finger as she chewed and swallowed. She spread her arms. "Across the street like this too?"

"Yeah. If it's a neighborhood like this, you know, mostly residential with its own little business district, try to do every storefront. We've got one woman found three blocks from the Northgate Mall. If it's like that, wall-to-wall businesses for ten blocks all around, then we're going to have to do the best we can."

Together they walked to the far end of the block. Holiday Travel on one corner, Rory's pub across the street. Corso opened the door to Holiday Travel and stepped aside, allowing Dougherty to enter first. A young woman. Thick, wheat-colored hair, held back from her face by a tortoiseshell clip. Tapping away at the computer. She swiveled a one-eighty in her chair. Found a big smile.

"I'll bet you two want to get out of the rain," she said hopefully.

"Sounds great to me," Corso said. "But unfortunately, right at this moment, I don't think time is going to allow."

"I've got seven days, eight nights in Mazatlán . . . airfare, hotel, continental breakfast . . . four forty-nine ninety-five, double occupancy . . . plus tax, of course."

He gestured toward Dougherty. "My friend and I were thinking about renting that vacant storefront up at the end of the block."

"Oh," the woman said. "I hadn't noticed anything was empty."

"Up past the Italian restaurant," Dougherty said.

"We were wondering whether or not the building owners provide security or whether it was something we'd have to pay for out of our own pockets."

"Oh no," she said. "We can barely get the real estate corporation to fix the plumbing. Security comes out of the individual merchants' pockets."

"Who do you use?" Corso asked.

She pulled out a sliding shelf in her desk. A business card was taped to the wood.

"Reliable Security. In Shoreline. Same as everybody in the building. They supposedly give us a group discount." She waved an unbelieving hand. "Supposedly gets us a discount from our insurance companies too. So, I guess it probably evens out in the end."

Corso thanked her. She pulled a business card from a silver holder on her desk.

"Holiday for all your travel needs," she said.

Corso thanked her again, stuffed the card in his jacket pocket, and followed Dougherty out onto the sidewalk. "At this point," he said, "a week on a beach sounds pretty good."

Dougherty's laugh was anything but amused. "Yeah. I'll break out my thong."

"Don't be so hard on yourself, Dougherty. As far as I'm concerned, you're the very flower of American womanhood."

"I'm the whole goddamn garden."

"I'm serious," he said.

"So am I," she said. She bopped him on the arm. "But thanks for the thought, big fella. What now?"

Corso pointed across the street. "Let's start over there."

They split up. Corso did the florist, Dougherty the tavern. Corso the pizza joint, Dougherty the café. It took an hour and fifty-five minutes to work the neighborhood. Corso pulled the car keys from his pocket and held them out. "You take the car. I'll cab it." He checked his watch. "Where do you want to meet?"

"This is going to take forever," she said.

Corso pointed north along Eastlake Avenue. "Half a mile up the road there's a place on the left called Bridges."

"I know it."

"How late are the stores open?"

"On a Saturday night? Till nine probably."

"Let's meet at Bridges at nine-thirty."

5:56 P.M. Day 6 of 6

"Move to the front of the cell." The voice clattered through the concrete and steel, like a dry stick drawn along a fence. Walter Leroy Himes rose from his bunk and shuffled toward the light. He remained expressionless as he leaned his back against the cell door and stuck his arms out through the bars. Practiced hands snapped a cuff around each wrist. "Clear," a metallic voice called.

The door at the opposite end of the cell slid open on greased wheels. A guard came in carrying a tray, which he set down on the bunk. "Here's what you wanted, Walter Lee. Two bacon cheeseburgers, fries, and a couple of Cokes." He gave Himes a grin.

"Enjoy," he said.

The cell door closed behind him with a click. "Clear."

Himes stood still for a moment after the cuffs had been removed. Waiting for the sound of the footsteps to fade before ambling over and sitting next to the tray.

Forty yards away, in the red-zone security area, a pair of corrections officers stared at a grainy black-and-white picture. "Watch him," one said. "He'll touch everything on the plate, then check the room before he eats."

As if on cue, Himes used his right forefinger to probe the items on the tray. Seemingly satisfied, he got to his feet again and took a leisurely lap of the cell, moving from corner to corner, peering here and poking there, finally checking inside the toilet before returning to the bunk.

"Like there's somebody hiding in there with him," the other said.

"Old Walter always acts like somebody's gonna run up and take his grub from him. Just hates anybody watching him eat."

"Ain't gonna have that problem much longer, is he?"

Himes reached over and delicately slid a single french fry from its white paper wrapping. He put the end in between his lips and sucked it in like spaghetti, then grabbed the nearest burger and bit it in half. His jaw muscles worked like pile drivers as his mangled mouth mashed the burger. As he was about to swallow, Himes cast his eyes upward at the camera, and, mouth still full, opened his mouth. Wide.

"Jesus," said one of the guards. "That's disgusting."

"I count myself as a decent Christian, but I can't say I'm gonna be too sorry to see him go," said the other.

9:40 P.M. Day 6 of 6

On the opposite shore of Lake Union, the defunct ferry
Kalakala lay beached in the gloom, like some festering
carcass run aground by the tide. Once the pride of the
Puget Sound ferry fleet, the old Art Deco vessel now
lay derelict, listing hard to starboard, her hundred-car
deck yawning out at the lake like an invalid bird waiting to be fed.

Corso got the waiter's attention. Pointed at his cup.
The front door burst open and Dougherty came strid-
ing in. She swiveled her head, caught sight of Corso
sitting in a booth overlooking the lake. She slid in opposite Corso. He showed the waiter two fingers.
"How'd it go?" he asked.

"I had no idea there were so many security companies in one city," Dougherty said. "I stopped counting
at forty."

"The paranoia business is booming," Corso said.

"Or how many people just flat wouldn't discuss it
with me."

"Let me guess . . . for security reasons."

"Amazing, huh?"

"Or how many businesses don't have any type of security at all."

She nodded. "I must have had a dozen people tell
me that since the rest of the strip mall was paying for
security, they figured they'd just ride along on the other
tenants' coattails." She threw a dozen or so pages of
notes onto the table.

Corso read from his notes. "Lockworks, First Response, ADT, Homeguard, Proline, Washington Emergency Services, Entrance Controls, Security Link."

Dougherty retrieved a page of her notes and took over. "Intelligent Controls, Silver Shield, Protection Technology, Allied, Northwest, Lock Ranger. It goes on and on. How in hell are we going to sort all this out?"

"What we need to know is whether any of the companies appear on all ten lists." He tore the first page of notes from his notebook and slid them over the table toward Dougherty. "Here's the one we did together this morning. Now we've each got five."

The waiter set a mug of coffee in front of Dougherty and refilled Corso's. "Get you anything else?" he asked. Dougherty shook her head. Corso told him no, then took another sip from the cup and started working on his notes. Alphabetizing each site. Making it easier to compare notes. Then going back looking for matches.

Corso finished first. Ten minutes later, Dougherty made a couple of final scribbles and looked up.

"So? How many did you get?" he asked.

"Three."

"Me too."

She covered her paper with her hand. "You go first."

"No. You go."

"You first," she insisted.

"Indian poker," he said. "Together."

Dougherty laughed out loud. "You're getting silly on me, Corso."

"Ready?"

"Okay . . . on three."

"One . . . two . . . three . . ."

They each held their lists up over their heads. Dougherty's read: Reliable, Metro, Silver Shield. Same as Corso's. "Bingo," she said.

" 'Let's see what our studio audience has to say,' "
Corso intoned.

He crossed the room to the pay phone and jimmied
the directory from its metal moorings. Rasta Boy behind the counter opened his mouth to protest, but
Corso waved him off. "I'll put it back in a minute,"
Corso said.

Corso slapped the book onto the tabletop. Turned to
the beginning of the yellow pages. Worked his way
back to H. Hotels. The Ambassador. The Atrium. The
Aviator. Six-eight-two, four-five, eight-five. He pulled
his phone from his pocket and dialed.

"Mr. Davis," he said. "This is Frank Corso. I spoke to
you yesterday." Corso listened. "Yeah, the guy from the
roof. Yes, sir. Yes, sir." Again he listened intently. "Just
wanted to run a quick question by you, sir. Yes . . . thank
you. The other day you said that the only other key to
that gate was in the hands of your security company.
Yes, sir. Yes. What company is that?" Corso winked at
Dougherty. "Yes, sir. I sure will. Thanks again."

"Well?"

"Survey says . . . Silver Shield," Corso said.

"I'll be damned."

Corso fingered his way deeper into the yellow
pages. Security. Flipped two pages. Moved his finger
down the page: "Silver Shield Security, See our add on
page 1,438." Corso thumbed back one page. Half-page
ad. Red border. "Nationwide—America's first choice
for security. Over three hundred offices across America. For instant response, call . . ."

Corso dialed.

"Silver Shield. This is Kramer. Your address,
please."

"This isn't a security matter," Corso said quickly.

Kramer sounded disappointed. "How can I help you?"

"I'm looking for some information on a Silver Shield employee."

"You'd hafta call the people in personnel. On Monday. The number is—"

"I can't wait that long," Corso said.

"Then you're out of luck with me, buddy. Nobody but personnel—or maybe Mr. Gabriel himself—could tell you anything personal like that."

Corso mustered a hearty laugh. "Gabriel," he intoned enthusiastically. "Why, I had no idea Sam Gabriel owned Silver Shield. Thanks a lot, Mr. Kramer. I'll give Sam a call at home."

"Whoa, whoa," Kramer said. "I don't know who this Sam guy you know is, but before you get going off half-cocked, it's Vincent Gabriel who's the owner here."

"Jeez. Thanks for stopping me. I could have made a real fool of myself there." He hung up.

Dougherty raised an immaculate eyebrow. "It's scary how well you lie."

"Owner's a guy named Vincent Gabriel."

"What good does that do us?"

Corso pulled up the phone book and worked his way back to the *G*'s. Two Vincent Gabriels. One down by Southcenter with a Military Road address. A strip mall wonderland. Strictly red necks, white socks, and blue-ribbon beer. The other was hard by the lake in Madison Park. Big-time, old-time, high-rent district. He remembered the yellow page ad, "Nationwide—America's first choice for security."

Chapter 25

Saturday, September 22
9:40 P.M. Day 6 of 6

Dorothy Sheridan was keeping her mouth shut. She
had no doubt about it. She was there to take the fall.
She wasn't sure exactly when or how they were going
to shift the blame her way, or, for that matter, what
blame there was to shift. She was, however, certain it
was going to happen.

Kesey tugged at his collar. "The governor is
adamant. No smoking gun . . . no stay."

"He's right," the mayor said. "Even if, god forbid,
Himes turned out to be innocent, the backlash would
be less than if he stopped the execution without
cause."

"I've gotta go," the DA said. "I've got a flight at
ten-fifteen."

"You better take Sheridan here with you," the chief
said. "She's been the survivor liaison the whole time.
You handle the press, and she'll handle the survivors
for you."

It took everything Dorothy had not to groan out
loud. Prison. An execution. Where in her job descrip-

tion, she wondered, did it say anything about maximum-security prisons and lethal injections?

Hizhonor scowled. "What survivors?"

"The victims' families," the chief said. "We've got . . ." As usual, he looked to Dorothy for a number.

"Eight," she said.

"We've got eight family members scheduled to witness the execution," he finished.

"Shit," said the mayor. "I suppose that Butler asshole is one of them."

"You can count on it," said Kesey.

"Himes's mother is there too," Dorothy said. The mayor looked horrified. "To watch?"

"No, sir," she said. "To say good-bye . . . you know, last respects and all."

10:00 P.M.   Day 6 of 6

"Ain't neva give none of you-all a hard time. Not all the years I been here."

"We got procedures, Walter."

"Ain't neva asked none of you-all for nothin'."

"No . . . you haven't," said the new one they called Smitty.

"Wanna see my mama like a man. Not chained up like some cur dog."

Smitty looked up at the sergeant, who pursed his thin lips and shook his bullet head. "Gotta chain you up, Walter. It's the rules," Smitty said.

"Ain't right," Himes said. "You gonna let them freak people come in here and watch me die, but you won't let me see my mama like a man."

Smitty reached to slide the waist chain around Himes's middle.

"Wait," the sergeant said.

Smitty stopped, genuflected, with the chain dangling from his hand.

"Clear," the sergeant said suddenly.

The cell door rolled open. "Come on, Walter," he said, stepping aside. "Let's go down the hall and see your mama." Himes looked down at his ankles as he shuffled out of the cell, at first short-stepping out of habit, then lengthening his stride as he left his cell without ankle chains for the first time in about three years.

Himes had nearly mastered his unencumbered gait when he stopped outside the second door on the right. Smitty pulled a key from his pocket and unlocked the door. Pulled it open. Himes stepped inside. Smitty shut the door behind him. Snapped the lock. The sergeant gave Smitty a bored look that said, What the hell?

Loretta Himes had her face buried in a wad of tissues as Walter slipped into the worn wooden seat. He leaned close to the screen. "Mama," he said gently.

She looked up. Her eye makeup lay in pools on her cheeks.

"Doan neva let 'em see you cry," he said.

10:10 P.M.   Day 6 of 6

Scared, Dorothy knew. For fourteen years, she'd watched denying defendants as their facades had finally flickered. Seen them in that moment right after sentencing when the bailiff takes them by the arm.

When they peer at their lawyers like furtive children begging to be held tightly and assured it was all a bad dream.

Yeah. She knew the look all right, and the pilot had it.

"A little foggier than we usually fly in. But . . . I understand it's an emergency, so we'll just take our time getting out of here. Weather's supposed to be clear on the other side of the mountains." He'd said it hopefully, but without conviction, before he'd disappeared inside the cockpit.

Across the aisle, she saw Marvin Hale peer out the tiny window into the gloaming. These days it didn't actually get dark; it merely segued to deeper shades of gray. She'd called home. Left a message for Brandy. She'd stopped just short of telling her how much she loved her. Afraid something in her voice would give away her terror.

Classic no-win situation. Either she was going to be forced to watch an execution or . . . What should she call it? What was the proper euphemism for something like this? Should she call it . . . a change in plans? Technical difficulties? A glitch? What?

The pilot revved the port engine, spun the plane on its axis, and started toward the invisible runways. For the first time in a week, her head was comfortably numb.

10:21 P.M. Day 6 of 6

The circular driveway ran slightly uphill, curving steadily left beneath arches of ancient oaks as it wound its way toward the shimmering lights a hundred yards ahead. Corso brought the Chevy to a halt in front of a three-story French Colonial mansion, whose elegant stone facade and slate-roofed turrets spoke eloquently of another age.

Dougherty whistled softly. "Aren't we just swell," she said.

A tall blond kid wearing a green Silver Cloud Valet Service jacket skipped down the front stairs and pulled open the driver's door before Corso got his seat belt unfastened.

"Evening, sir," he said.

Corso left the car running as he eased himself from behind the wheel and stepped out onto the driveway. Somewhere in the castle, a door opened and closed, allowing a slice of music and laughter to escape momentarily into the night. Along the front, the light from a dozen tall, transomed windows cast a golden glow down upon the entryway.

The sight of Dougherty stepping out onto the bricks seemed to startle the kid. His head swiveled from Corso, to Dougherty, to the house, and then back to Corso.

"Excuse me, sir. Don't mind me asking, but are you guys sure you've got the right place?"

"This the Gabriel residence?" Corso asked.

"Yes, sir . . . it is." His voice was tentative.

"You happen to know what Mr. Gabriel does for a living?" Corso asked.

"Some kind of security thing."

"Then we're in the right place."

The kid looked embarrassed. "You-all came for the reception, then?"

"What reception?"

"The wedding. Mr. Gabriel's daughter."

Corso handed the kid a ten-dollar bill. "Keep it handy," he said. "We're not going to be long." He turned to Dougherty. "You bring your gown?"

"As if . . . ," she huffed and headed for the door, where she grabbed the brass knocker and gave it three sharp raps. Inside the house, what sounded like a four-piece combo was playing Horace Silver's "Song for My Father."

Out in the driveway, the kid had made no move to park the car. He stood, slack-jawed, resting his fore-arms on the Chevy's roof. The front door opened.

Blond Margaret Thatcher hair. Her taut face suggested thirty-five, but the guile in her green eyes said fifty. She wore an ankle-length silver sheath. Silk. Understated and elegant. Highlighted by a double string of perfectly matched pearls. The minute she blinked them into focus, she swallowed the toothy welcome smile. Took her time looking them over, as if she couldn't decide whether she should call the cops or an exterminator.

"Yes?" she said icily.

"Very sorry to intrude," Corso said.

"How can I help you?" Her tone suggested she would have liked to add the words "off my front steps" but was far too well-bred.

"I need to speak to Vincent Gabriel."

She folded her arms against the chill. "I'm Mrs. Gabriel."

Corso handed her his press credential. She scanned it and handed it back.

"Whatever it is will have to wait until Monday." She stepped back and began to close the door.

"It could be a matter of life and death," Corso said quickly.

She searched his eyes for irony. Took in Dougherty again. Frowned.

"You're serious, aren't you?"

"Yes," he said. "I'm afraid I am."

"If this is about one of his security clients, you should—"

"It's not," Corso interrupted.

"My daughter . . . ," she began. Then stopped and heaved a sigh. "Life and death," she said again. Corso confirmed this.

She rubbed her upper arms as she stepped out onto the top step. "Go around that way . . . that side of the house," she said, pointing. "The solarium door is open. Wait in there. I'll get my husband."

Corso and Dougherty followed a flagstone path around the north end of the house. As they reached the corner and turned right again, Lake Washington came into view. Across the lake, the high-rises of Bellevue flickered like candles in the night, their fractured reflections dancing piecemeal across the rough surface.

The solarium ran perpendicular to the house. All glass. Round on top like a Quonset hut. Corso pulled open the door, stepped aside, and allowed Dougherty to enter first. In the center of the space, a palm tree nearly brushed the twenty-foot ceiling. A forest of exotic potted plants were scattered around, giving the impression that someone had strewn lawn furniture about the jungle. Overhead, a pair of brass ceiling fans twirled languorously.

Dougherty turned in a circle, taking it all in. "Great room," she said.

Before Corso could agree, Vincent Gabriel stepped into the room. A powerful-looking man in a tux he sure as hell hadn't rented. What used to be called swarthy. Six-two, maybe two-ten or so, with a thick mustache and a head of wavy salt-and-pepper hair he was never going to lose. His bearing and stride gave off an air of tightly controlled aggression. He crossed the room to Corso and Dougherty with a champagne glass in his hand and a scowl on his face.

"What's this?" he demanded.

"We're very sorry for the intrusion," Corso said.

Vincent Gabriel's expression suggested they were about to get sorrier.

"And who might you be?"

Again, Corso handed over his press credential. Unlike his wife, Vincent Gabriel read every word. Front and back. "Corso, huh?" he said. "You're the one who's been writing the Himes story for the *Sun*."

"Yes. I am."

"The one used to be with the *New York Times*."

"That's me," Corso said.

Gabriel waited, as if affording Corso an opportunity to defend himself.

Instead, Corso inclined his head and said, "This is my associate, Meg Dougherty."

Vincent gave her a curt nod. "I've got ninety-five guests inside, Mr. Corso. So, real quick here, you better tell me what is it you find so damned important that it requires interrupting my daughter's wedding reception."

"The Himes story," Corso said.

Gabriel stiffened, then reached over and set his champagne on a glass-topped table.

"And what might that awful mess have to do with me?"

"We've come across a piece of information that"—
Corso chose his words carefully—"that suggests it
might be possible the real killer is a security guard."

"What piece of information might that be?"

Without naming the Aviator Hotel, Corso told him
the kids' story. The locked gate, the taggers. The van.
The supposed guy in uniform.

"You're here on the word of vandals?" His tone carried an understood "you idiot."

"No, sir," Dougherty piped up. "We're here because
we took what the kids told us and ran with it."

"Ran with it how?"

"We divided up the murders and canvassed the
neighborhoods where the bodies were found." She
gave him the blow-by-blow. Halfway through, he
checked his watch and interrupted. "I still don't see
what this has to do with me."

"Only three security companies had clients in the
immediate neighborhoods of where all eleven bodies
were found," she said.

"Reliable, Metro Link, and you—Silver Shield,"
Corso added.

Vincent Gabriel made a disbelieving face. "I'll bet
you could canvass any three square commercial blocks
in the Pacific Northwest and get much the same result.
Reliable, Metro, and Silver Shield are the three biggest
players in this part of the country."

"Then Corso called down to where this whole thing
with the kids started," Dougherty said.

"The guy who says the only key other than his belongs to his security company," Corso prompted.

"And where the kids swear the guy had a key to the
gate."

"And he's a Silver Shield customer?"

"Yessir," Corso and Dougherty said in unison. For the first time, Vincent Gabriel's tanned face showed concern.

"Interesting," he said, picking up his champagne glass. "Tell you what. You two come down to the office on Monday morning and we'll see if—"

Corso interrupted him. "That could be too late, Mr. Gabriel. Have you read the paper today?"

"What? No . . . with all the—"

"He killed another young woman yesterday afternoon," Dougherty said.

"The killings are getting closer together," Corso added. "It's only three days since the last one."

Gabriel's complexion lost some of its glow. "You can't expect me to—"

Before he could finish, the door connecting the solarium to the house swung open. The bride, looking internally radiant in that way in which only brides are capable.

She looked like her mother. Same height. Same hair. Same frank green eyes. Her gown trailed across the terra-cotta tile floor to Vincent's side.

"Is everything all right?" she asked her father.

He patted her arm and assured her that everything was just peachy.

"Well, then, come on," she pleaded. "The Lunquists want a picture with us." She tried to tug him along by the forearm, but he stood his ground.

"Tell them I'll be in in a minute."

When she started to protest, he put a finger delicately on her lips. "Just a minute, Princess," he said softly. "Tell them I'll be right there."

She kissed him on the cheek, leaving a silver-pink signature on his face, shot Corso and Dougherty a quizzical look, and flounced out the way she'd come. Her father watched her cross the room and close the door behind herself. He stood for a moment staring at the air in her wake, as if she'd left a vapor trail.

"I can't imagine losing her," he said.

"Most people can't imagine it even after it happens," Corso said. "Something in them refuses to believe it's possible to outlive a child."

"I don't know what I'd do," he said. "What I'd get out of bed for in the morning." He waved his arm around the room. "You get to a point in life where you've got everything you thought you wanted and when you think about losing a child or a wife . . . it's like all of a sudden you realize none of it really means a damn thing to you. That only the people in your life are worth a goddamn thing. All the rest of this . . ." His voice got husky as it trailed off. "I have to go," he said almost apologetically, as if suddenly embarrassed and overwhelmed by the magnitude of his blessings. "I can't—"

"One minute," Corso said. "Give me one minute."

As Vincent started for the door, Corso kept on talking to his back. "The FBI profile of this guy says he's a white male, somewhere between twenty-five and thirty-five. A loner. The kind of guy who eats lunch by himself and has a hard time getting along with his fellow workers. Bad interpersonal skills. Single, but probably lives in a dependent relationship with a woman—maybe a sister or a cousin, something like that. Maybe has a history of petty crimes. Fires, assaults, things like that. He may have some sort of strict religious background. The Bureau thought there was a ceremonial element to the way the bodies were left. And, if the kids are to be believed, he drives a primer-gray Dodge van, with quarter-moon bubble windows in the back."

Vincent Gabriel had stopped with his hand on the door handle. When he turned back toward Corso, his face was like concrete. "That's it?" he asked tentatively.

"He's probably had some stressor in his life lately. Something that's set him off on another murder spree," Corso added.

Gabriel blew air through his pursed lips and then ran a hand through his hair.

"Sound like anybody who might work for you?" Dougherty asked.

Vincent Gabriel shrugged. "Could be," he said in a low voice. "Not what he drives or anything . . . but I might—" He stopped himself. "I'm not usually involved in the day-to-day operations." He shrugged. "Tell you the truth, most of the time, I couldn't tell you who works for me and who doesn't, let alone what they drive."

"But . . . ," Corso pressed.

"But lately . . . the local office . . . had . . ." He searched for the right phrase. "They had a really weird scene."

"Weird how?"

Gabriel stared at his patent-leather shoes and nodded almost imperceptibly.

"Guy that's worked for us for years. I get a call from his supervisor. Says the guy's been getting increasingly weird lately. Says he's concerned . . ." He looked up at Corso. "You know—the guy's a gun nut. What with all the workplace violence . . . the supervisor thinks this guy might be dangerous or something. So he calls me."

"This guy have any unusual stressors in his life lately?" Corso asked. "Something that could push him over the edge?"

"Yeah, the guy I'm thinking of . . . he has," Gabriel said. "Two, in fact."

He absentmindedly touched the lipstick on his cheek and then looked from Dougherty to Corso, as if pleading for absolution. "His mother died a month or so back and then . . . two weeks ago"—he looked up at the twirling fans—"I fired him."

"What for?" Dougherty asked.

Vincent Gabriel took a deep breath. He looked tubercular. "Threatening to kill another employee." He spread his big hands. "He was completely out of it," he said. "He kept claiming the guy was stealing from his locker."

"Any chance he was right?"

"We don't have lockers."

Chapter 26

"Got no damn use for no preacher," Himes said to the sergeant. "Don't be bringin' his sorry ass in here."

"You sure, Walter? I seen him bring comfort to a lotta men."

Himes laughed. "He doan come in here to comfort the likes of me. He comes in so's he can comfort the likes of you-all. So's you can go home tonight, have dinner wid the Mrs. tellin' yourself there's some kinda difference between the killin' you-all do and the kind they say I done."

The sergeant folded his arms and looked over at Smitty. "Walter's got a point there," he said to the other man. "Not a whole lotta difference . . . not from Walter's end anyway, is there?"

"No, sir," said the younger man. "I guess there isn't."

11:04 P.M.   Day 6 of 6

The windows stood as dark and gray as tombstones. 1279 Arlen Avenue South sat a hundred yards back

from the road. Junkyard to the north. Five acres of
halogen-lit mini-storage to the south. At the back
oozed the Duwamish River. Could have been a small
farm at one time. Might have owned one whole side of
the block, way back when. Probably sold off the street
front to make ends meet. Nothing left now but a driveway easement and a narrow strip of ground along an
acrid river.

From the end of the muddy drive, a single yellow
porch light revealed a peeling two-story facade cow-
ering beneath a stand of mossy oaks. The clapboard
siding now forming a shallow V as the structure
sagged inexorably downward. In the distance a siren
wailed its plaintive song. Closer, a junkyard dog
picked up the note and rolled it into a long miserable
howl.

"That's gotta be it," Corso said.

"What are we doing here, anyway?" Dougherty
asked.

"I've got to be sure."

"What? You think he's going to have a sign or
something?"

"I'd settle for a van with bubble windows."

"You're nuts."

Corso shrugged. "All we've got so far is a big
maybe. I want to be sure."

He gave the Chevy some gas. Rolled past the driveway and parked in front of the junkyard, between a
battered flatbed truck and an orange VW beetle. He
killed the engine and the lights. Grabbed the door handle. "Come on," he said.

"What if he shows up while we're walking down his
driveway?"

"Then we claim to be broken down and stupid. We saw a light and were looking for help."

"You're out of your goddamn mind," Dougherty whispered.

"Come on. The driveway's empty. Let's just poke around a little."

"What if he's parked behind the house?"

"If it's a van, we hot-foot it out of there and call the cops."

"No way."

"Okay," he said. "Wait in the car . . . I'll be right back."

She grabbed him by the elbow. "You're not leaving me out here alone," she said.

"Come on, then."

"I hate you."

"Take a number."

She punched him in the arm. Hard. "You go first," she hissed through her teeth.

Corso pointed to the grass-covered berm running between the worn tire ruts. "Up here."

The ditches on either side of the drive were a forest of dead dandelions, the unmowed summer stalks standing stiff and still in the unnatural light as Corso and Dougherty edged their way up the driveway toward the house.

As they came abreast of the house, it became obvious that no vehicle was present. Corso felt his breathing become deeper and more regular. Despite feeling like his throat was full of dirt, he managed to swallow a couple of times.

The end of the drive was worn in a circle. A well-trodden path led from the circle to the back door. To

the right, what had once been a long outbuilding running across the back of the property now lay collapsed
upon itself. Fallen to the left, with its walls and roofs
fanned out along the ground like playing cards. At the
far end, the tines of a rusted hay rake lay like the rib
cage of some ancient metal beast.

The weed-covered backyard sported a pile of partially burned furniture. Corso walked over to the pile.
Probed it with his toe. In the dim light, he could make
out the soot-covered remains of a brass bed. A partially
burned mattress and box spring, their floral prints
scorched in some places, melted in others. Blankets
and bedclothes. A couple of lamps and shades.
Smashed picture frames. An end table, maybe two. A
charred collection of old women's clothes and underthings. All piled together in a smelly heap. Corso
reached gingerly into the pile, pulled aside the pieces
of a broken picture frame, and extracted the picture between his fingers. Turned it over. A color rendition of
Christ expelling the moneylenders from the temple.
Carefully, he put the picture back on the pile.

He dusted his palms together as he crossed the lawn
to the back door. Grabbed the handle on the screen
door. The rusted spring shrieked as Corso pulled open
the door. In the junkyard, a trio of dogs began to bark.
Corso rapped on the door with his knuckles.

"Hello," he called tentatively.

The door swung inward.

"Did you . . . ," Dougherty sputtered.

He raised a hand. Scout's honor. "I just knocked. It
opened on its own."

"Hello," he sang again.

She read the gleam in his eyes. "Don't even think about it."

He elbowed the door open. Poked his head in. "Anybody home?" he called.

Silence. Corso turned a dull red as he stepped across the threshold. Dougherty poked her head in the door. She could see past the room they were in, up the hall and into what must be the living room. Everything was a familiar red. "Darkroom bulbs," she whispered.

They were in the kitchen. The room smelled of rancid milk and decay. The old-fashioned sink was piled high with dirty dishes. The counters awash in paper plates, takeout containers and empty beer cans. Rainier Lite mostly.

Corso started forward. She grabbed him by the belt, but he kept moving, towing her over the threshold and through the kitchen into what probably had been the dining room. A window on the left had been covered from the inside. Rough-sawn plywood had been nailed over the opening, the edges dented and split from the force of the hammer blows. To the right of the window, a gun case sat catty-corner. Full. Maybe a dozen weapons. All chained together through the trigger guards. From among the shotguns and deer rifles poked the priapic banana clip of an AK-47.

Corso moved forward. Peeked into the living room. Thrift-shop furniture along the perimeter. Knicknacks on the shelves. A rag rug on the floor. Big color portrait of Jesus—blond-haired and blue-eyed—over the mantel. Everything shipshape. Same red bulb burning overhead. Same window treatment. Half-inch plywood and ten-penny nails.

"Let's get out of here," Dougherty whispered.

Corso headed toward the stairs. "Let's have a look upstairs." Before she could protest, he said, "A quick cruise upstairs and then we'll be gone." He held out his hand. Dougherty released her grip on his belt and laced her fingers through his.

The stairs popped and groaned as they climbed, moving quickly now, like children running home after dark. No plywood over the windows up here. Tattered curtains over old-fashioned shades.

One bedroom on either side of the second-floor landing. Two rooms of some kind down the hall. Corso opened the door on the right. Hit the lights. Regular bulb. The room was bare. Completely empty, right down to the pine boards covering the floor. He pulled Dougherty across the planks, pulled open the interior door. Found the light switch to the right of the door. A bathroom. Similarly empty. Spotless and smelling of chlorine bleach.

Still pulling Dougherty along by the hand, he retraced his steps across the room, crossed the landing, and pulled open the opposite door. About half the size of the master bedroom across the hall, the room was military spare. A single bed along one wall was made to a precision seldom seen in civilian circles. Shoes stood in a perfect line in the mouth of the closet, where each hanger was precisely equidistant from its mates. The walls were bare except for a single marine corps poster: "The Free, the Proud, the Brave."

Dougherty balked in the doorway, so Corso let go of her hand and crossed to the bookcase. What must have been every issue of *Soldier of Fortune* ever printed. Gun manuals. *Police Digest. Guns and Ammo.* Police manuals. The NRA newsletter. "A regular Charlton Heston," Corso said under his breath.

"What?" Dougherty said from the doorway. Corso didn't answer. Just moved from the bookcase to the dresser.

The top of the dresser was arranged with the same precision. A silver comb and brush set perfectly aligned. A candy dish full of change. Pennies, nickels, dimes, and quarters, each in its own little space. Exactly in the center of the coins sat a brass skeleton key. Six huge bullets, fifty-caliber at least, stood like teeth along the back edge. At the right, half a dozen condoms, stretched out straight and neat in red foil packs.

"Corso," Dougherty hissed from the doorway. "Come on."

He nodded and returned to her side. She followed him down the hall. Another bathroom. Same precise arrangement. Bright, gleaming fixtures. Towels so neat the bathroom looked like one in a motel. Corso pulled open the medicine cabinet. Lined up like little soldiers stood a dozen or so pill bottles. Corso scanned the labels: Risperdal, Zyprexa, Haloperidol, Clozapine, Olanzapine, Sertindol. "What's all that?" Dougherty whispered.

"Antipsychotic medication," Corso said.

Back on the landing, they skirted the stairwell to the door of the remaining room. Locked. Corso shook the knob. Then stepped back and lowered his shoulder.

"Don't you dare," she said, wagging a fist in his face.

Instead of arguing, Corso turned and jogged back to the furnished bedroom. Dougherty stood transfixed. He reappeared a few seconds later with an old fashioned brass key in his hand. He put the key in the lock, turned it one way—nothing—then the other, and the lock snapped. He pushed the door open. The room was dark. Over Corso's shoulder, Dougherty could see a plywood-covered window.

He reached inside, groping for the light switch. Found it. The room lit up like a ballpark. A dozen track lights hung from the ceiling along three sides of the room, spilling fans of white light down along the bare walls and boarded-over windows. Corso walked out into the middle of the room and looked around. On his left, a floor-to-ceiling curtain hung bunched in the far corner. His eyes followed the aluminum track around the room. Back to where Dougherty stood in the doorway. To her left sat a brand-new leather lounger and an oak end table. On the table, a crystal ashtray glinted in the harsh overhead lights. Beneath the odors of stale smoke and nicotine, something sickly sweet hung in the air.

Corso gestured toward the chair. "So, what? Somebody comes in here, pulls back the curtain, sits in their favorite chair, puts their feet up, lights up a smoke, and then what, stares at the walls?"

Dougherty took three steps into the room. "Weird," she said. "It's like a home theater or something, except there's nothing behind the curtain."

Corso walked to the far wall. Running his hands over the rotting plaster and splintered plywood, feeling for something not available to the eye. Nothing. He turned to Dougherty and shrugged. "Beats me," he said.

"Let's go," she begged.

Corso started for the door. Then suddenly stopped. Tilted his head. "Or maybe," he said tentatively, "maybe you come into the room and close the curtain."

He walked to the corner, grabbed the edge of the curtain, and began to pull the heavy material along its overhead track. As he walked along the wall, he heard Dougherty catch her breath. And then again, as he moved along the far wall, rounded the corner, and turned back her way, something stuck in her throat.

She began moving toward the center of the room as if she were remote-controlled. Corso let go of the curtain and looked around.

Clothes. Women's clothes. Complete ensembles. Pinned neatly to the inside of the curtain. Outerwear on the left. Underwear on the right. Nine complete sets, with room for at least one more.

Corso pointed to the set directly in front of him. "Victim number four. Jennifer Robison," he said. Matching black bra and panties. A black, sleeveless blouse, silk maybe, and a pair of leopard-skin stretch pants. "That's what she was reported to be wearing when she disappeared from the Northgate Mall."

"You catch this?" Dougherty asked, pointing upward.

Written along the top of the curtain in bold black letters: "Behold the ten brides of Christ . . . who having strayed from his ways are now returned to the fold of our master, like lost sheep." Then it started over. "Behold the ten . . ."

"Jesus," he said as he moved around the room. The garments were attached to the curtain with little color-coordinated safety pins.

"Can you smell it?" Dougherty asked. She rubbed a white sports bra between her fingers and then held the fingers to her nose. "Smells like my grandfather."

Corso leaned in close to the closet set of clothes. Recoiled. Then leaned in again. "Old Spice," he said.

Dougherty looked ill. "You don't suppose he—"

"Let's get the hell out of here," Corso said.

They moved quickly now. Doused the light and re-locked the room. Hurried down the hall. Turned left into the occupied bedroom, crossed the room, and set the key carefully in the bowl of change.

Abandoning any pretense of stealth, they thumped down the stairs. They went the way they had come, to the back door. Corso peeked out. The yard was empty. He grabbed Dougherty by the hand. As they double-timed it around the house and back down the driveway, Corso pulled the phone from his pocket and dialed.

He kept it short and sweet. Didn't give Densmore the chance to say anything other than his name. "Densmore . . . this is Corso. You listen to me, goddamnit. We got him. Dead to rights. He killed all of them. Past and present. His name is Patrick Defeo." Corso spelled it. "He lives at twelve seventy-nine Arlen Avenue South. The driveway between Arlen Auto Parts and the Cascade Self-Storage yard. Call the chief and get the execution stopped and then get down here. Hurry. And bring the goddamn marines. He's armed to the teeth. Lotsa backup. You hear me?"

He pocketed the phone.

Dougherty was dragging him now. Pulling him headlong over the rutted tracks. Ten yards from the end of the drive, Corso heard the squeal of tires, tried to stop and listen, but Dougherty wasn't buying. She dropped his hand and began to run, her long strides eating up the ground. Good thing she was wearing boots. If she'd been going any faster, she'd have plowed facefirst into the gray van that slid to a stop in the mouth of the driveway.

Chapter 27

Saturday, September 22
11:16 P.M. Day 6 of 6

The van's engine shuddered slightly at each revolution. The rhythmic tick of a bad valve seemed to be the only sound moving in the air. Behind the nearly black windows, the figure leaned to his right, as if fetching something from the glove compartment. From where he stood in the driveway, Corso could see the rear bubble window puffing out like a blister from the van's flat profile.

Dougherty was backing toward Corso, who began moving quickly toward the van. He swallowed and put on his best Jim Rockford smile.

"Look, honey, we got lucky."

Dougherty's expression suggested she was not familiar with English. Corso hooked her around the waist and forced her forward. Skidding her over the grass.

"What . . . you can't read the sign?" Defeo said in a nasal tenor. He couldn't have weighed more than a hundred fifty pounds. A pipsqueak. "Somethin' about the sign you two didn't understand?"

Corso kept smiling. Mr. Jovial. "What sign is that?"

Corso had no intention of squinting into the head-lights. He kept moving, forcing Defeo to step aside as they made their way past the van, out into the street. The guy smelled of Old Spice. Corso nearly gagged. Defeo's hand trembled as he pointed to a tattered sign hanging askew! "No Trespassing."

"Sorry," Corso said. "It was dark as hell when we walked down. I never even saw the sign." He turned to Dougherty. "Did you see it, honey?"

She managed to stammer out, "No."

"Well, what the hell are you doing here anyway?" Defeo asked. He walked around Corso, taking him in from all angles. "Nobody comes down here at night no more. No reason to." He made eye contact for the first time.

You had to pull your eyes from the twitching mus-cles around his mouth before you could process the face. Patrick Defeo appeared to have been made of spare parts. His right eye was fully an inch higher than its counterpart. Same thing with his cab-door ears. Off-set. Angular, the effect was of a head that had been welded together. The expression lost and desperate, like one of those long-ago *Life* black-and-whites of gaunt Dust Bowl refugees.

He wore a blue baseball cap. "FBI" in big gold let-ters. The hat was sized down as far as it would go, leaving a four-inch piece of strap sticking out the back. Otherwise it was all camouflage. Fatigues with a pack of Marlboros rolled into the left sleeve. Tiny spit-shined boots. Pants tucked into the boots. Marine in-signia on his chest. Special Forces patches sewn on his narrow shoulders.

"We broke down," Corso said. "Up the street." He pointed toward the Chevy. "We were going along just fine and then just like that"—he snapped his fingers—"it quit."

Dougherty regained her wits and said, "We saw the house light and thought maybe you'd call a tow truck for us."

It wasn't just his mouth. Defeo was twitchy all over, as if his limbs had a life of their own. He seemed to be incapable of standing still. Constantly moving from one foot to another, shifting his weight, as if he was about to walk off and then suddenly changed his mind. He folded his arms across his chest to keep them still. Beneath his arms, his fingers fluttered like wings.

"Can't imagine what might have happened. Always been a real reliable car. Nothing like this ever happened before."

Defeo rolled his neck, like he was working out a kink. "Just quit, you said."

"Just like that," Corso said. "I'm terrible with cars. Don't know a thing about 'em. Never have."

Defeo looked Corso over like he was measuring him for a suit. "What was you doing down here anyway?" he demanded. "The old woman sent you two down here to spy on me? Still can't keep her damn nose outta my business."

Dougherty began to stammer, "Oh . . . no . . . we . . . not to spy . . . we—"

"We just took a wrong turn somewhere," Corso said quickly.

Defeo cocked his head, as if listening to distant voices. Rolled his neck again.

"Lemme have a look at this broke-down car of

yours," Defeo said, gesturing up the road with his chin. "Lemme see it."

"We were desperate," Dougherty said as they moved toward the Chevy. "Yours was the only light on the whole street."

Defeo's eyes rolled in his head like a horse's. "Nobody out here no more," he said. He swung his arms in an arc. "Used to be nothin' but farms." He pointed at the mini-storage yard. "That was Jorgenson's dairy." He looked up at Corso. "Will be again too. Someday. When the final turnaround comes. Everything's gonna be like it was before."

He looked from Corso to Dougherty and back, as if daring them to disagree.

Suddenly, Defeo stopped walking. Reached over and grabbed Dougherty by the arm. Squinted at the gold bracelet tattooed around her wrist and the red letters in the palm of her hand. "What the hell you go and defile yourself like that for?" he asked. "That's a hell of a thing. Let a woman defile herself that way." He dropped her arm and looked to Corso for an explanation, as if to say, "You let her do that to herself?"

Corso kept grinning and walking.

Dougherty hung back now. Rubbing her arm where he'd touched it. Corso pointed to the Chevy. "Here it is," he said. Defeo looked the car over as if he were going to salvage it for parts. "All parked nice and neat," he commented. "You push it in here?"

"Just rolled it right in," Corso said.

"Get in. Pop the hood," Defeo said.

Corso slid into the driver's seat. Found the hood release. Pulled it. Dougherty slipped into the passenger seat and locked the door. Still massaging her arm.

Defeo fiddled around for a moment and then opened the hood.

Dougherty shot Corso a panicked look. He made a "stay calm" gesture.

"Try it," Defeo said.

Instead of turning the key to the right, Corso turned it to the left. Got a series of electrical clicks. "Nothing," he said out the window.

"Try it again," Defeo called back. Corso did it again.

"You sure you turning it the right way?" Defeo asked.

"Positive," Corso assured him.

They kept repeating the process for what seemed to Dougherty an hour, until finally Defeo dropped the hood. He walked around to the driver's side and leaned down. Peered into the car. Gave Corso his version of a smile. "I'm gonna run up the house, get my toolbox," Defeo said. A muscle in his cheek fluttered like a butterfly.

He looked back over his shoulder twice as he hustled back to the van. Smiling all the way, like he'd just heard a good joke and couldn't wait to tell it to somebody else. The van began to roll. Corso checked his watch. Thirteen minutes since he'd called Densmore.

"Did you smell him?" Dougherty asked.

Corso nodded. "Let's get the hell out of here. From now on he's Densmore's problem." He turned the key in the ignition. Nothing. Tried it again. Still nothing. His stomach was suddenly ice cold.

"He . . . ," was all Dougherty could get out.

He grabbed the door handle. "Come on."

In the junkyard, the dogs were growling along the fence. He grabbed Dougherty by the hand and sprinted diagonally across the street, running along the fronts of the buildings, trying doors, looking for a place to duck in and hide, finding nothing until, fifty yards up the street, they came to a narrow alley separating a welding shop from something called Fircrest Fabrication. A pair of fifty-five-gallon drums were chained together in the mouth of a grimy alcove. One barrel was marked "Oil." The other, "Solvents." He peered over the top into a narrow space between the recycling drums and the metal wall behind. Maybe three feet wide. Big enough.

He grabbed Dougherty by the elbows and lifted her completely over the drums. Set her gently on the littered ground.

"Get down," he said. "Stay down."

Chapter 28

Saturday, September 22
11:38 P.M. Day 6 of 6

His knuckles glowed white around the phone. Again, he paced over and peered down the driveway. Nothing had changed. The van still sat facing the street. Lights on. Engine running. The tired yellow bulb over the front door carved the same deep shadows into the yard.

"Come on," he muttered to himself.

Corso jogged back to the alley. Dougherty sat huddled against the north wall, her usually ruddy face now the color of cement.

"What if they don't come?" she wheezed.

"They'll come," he said, with a good deal more conviction than he felt. He checked his watch. Sixteen minutes since he'd hung up on Densmore. Four since Defeo went for his tools. This time of night, if they were coming, it shouldn't be long.

He ran to the edge of the driveway and looked down. Status quo. On his way back to Dougherty, he heard the sound of studded tires snapping on the pavement. He turned. No lights. The snapping drew closer, until out of the darkness a dark blue Ford Crown Victoria rolled around the corner and pulled to a stop, with the front half of the car blocking the driveway. Wald was driving. Densmore shotgun. Donald in back, behind Wald. Densmore was out of the passenger door the second the car came to a stop. Circled the hood of the car. Got right up in Corso's face.

"Where's the backup?" Corso asked.

"You just don't know when to quit, do you?" he said.

"The guy's got automatic weapons, fellas. You guys are gonna need some serious help here. Lots of it."

Behind Densmore's back, the two cops exchanged worried looks. Densmore held up a moderating hand. He turned to his fellow cops. "We don't even know if this is the guy. All we've got is the say-so of the world's most notorious liar here."

"Still, Andy . . . we better—" Wald began.

Densmore was having none of it. "Last I looked, Wald, I was still the three. You got any complaints, you better take it up with somebody downtown."

Corso stared disbelievingly at Densmore. "Did you call the chief? You didn't, did you?" He turned to the other cops. "Did he call about Himes?"

"What makes you think this is the guy?" Donald asked Corso.

Dougherty was out of the alley now, walking across the pavement toward the men, her eyes the size of hubcaps. "He's got the victims' clothes on display. He's got, like, this really sick little shrine set up in there," she said.

The cops exchanged another long look. "And you know this how?" Wald asked.

Dougherty covered her mouth with her hand, looked to Corso.

"We were inside the house," he said.

Densmore bared his teeth. "You broke into . . . ?" he barked.

"It wasn't locked."

"You realize . . . you asshole"—he stomped in a tight circle—"you realize you've tainted every piece of evidence inside that house, don't you? We're not going to be able to use anything in there."

Densmore jabbed a finger, first at Corso, then at Dougherty. He had a smile on his face. "You two are under arrest. As soon as we get this sorted out, I'm having you transported downtown on charges of—"

Whatever charges Densmore had in mind were lost when Donald suddenly said, "We've got movement up at the house."

He was right. The light over the front door had been turned off, leaving only the headlights and the ghostly purple reflections of the mini-storage yard to illuminate the scene. As Corso squinted into the gloom, Defeo clicked on the high beams. No doubt about it. He could see the cop car across the front of the driveway. After a moment, he threw open the door of the van, jumped out, and ran back into the house.

"He made us," said Donald.

Wald popped the trunk on the cop car and began shouldering himself into a Kevlar vest. Donald stood dumbfounded for a moment and then hustled over and followed suit; his long delicate fingers shook as he pulled the Velcro fasteners tight across his chest. By the time Wald had the vest settled over his suit, he was alternately thumbing shells into a shotgun and peering nervously down the muddy track toward the van.

Densmore fixed Corso with a final feral stare,

stepped around Donald, and leaned into the trunk. Instead of a vest, he came out with a bullhorn.

"Call for backup, Chucky," Wald said.

Donald had gotten one step toward the front of the car when Densmore snapped, "No, we'll handle this."

Wald started for the radio. "Fuck you, Densmore," he said. "You want to risk your own ass, that's okay by me. But—"

He didn't get to finish. Up at the house, Defeo was back in the van. Wald squatted in front of the driver's door, holding the shotgun in his left hand. Thumbed off the safety.

"The van's moving," Donald chanted.

He was right. The van was rolling forward down the drive. The bright lights and dark-tinted windows made Defeo completely invisible.

The van stopped. Seventy yards from the cop car. Densmore arranged his gold shield over his heart like it would make him bulletproof. He got to his feet and faced the van over the hood of the car. He held his service revolver in his left hand and the bullhorn in his right. He straightened his spine and brought the bullhorn up to his lips like a carnival barker.

"Jesus, Densmore, get down," Wald said, tugging at his partner's pant leg. "Are you fucking crazy?"

Densmore's electronic voice crackled through the darkness.

"This is the Seattle Police Department. You are surrounded. Turn off the car and put both hands out the window."

Defeo raced the engine. Corso thought he might have heard high-pitched laughter. Wald got to his knees, in firing position. Donald rested his forearms on the roof as he aimed at the windshield. His face was taut. His mouth hung open.

"This is Detective Sergeant Andrew Densmore of the Seattle Police Department. Turn off the car and—"

Defeo came up through the sunroof. Fired half a dozen rounds before anyone could move. The force of the slugs moved Densmore backward, like he was on tracks. Moon-walking in reverse. The bullhorn arced back into the darkness. Corso threw himself into the ditch beside the driveway. The assault weapon began to spit bullets in sixes and eights. Tearing the windows from the car, sending the glass showering down onto the pavement. The force of the multiple impacts rocked the car on its springs. Gaping holes appeared on the far side as flattened slugs began to punch their way through the sheet metal. And then it stopped.

Donald crouched behind the rear tire, his arms thrown over his head.

Wald kept the engine block between himself and the van. Densmore lay in the road, one foot twitching, his arms outstretched above his head, as if he were basking on the beach. His service revolver lay in the middle of the street. Corso thought of trying to drag him from the line of fire, but, before he could force himself into action, the assault began anew. Again the flat sound of the muzzle filled the night air. The cop car began to disintegrate as the bullets tore the metal to pieces. Pieces of metal began to fall noisily to the street. The car squatted on its rims. Then silence again.

"He's coming," Donald shouted. The roar of the van's engine filled the air. Corso jumped to his feet, took one step to the right, and retrieved Densmore's revolver from the pavement. When he turned, the van was no more than fifty feet away, its worn fan belt screaming as it rocketed down the rutted track.

Wald was on his feet, pumping the shotgun. The windshield of the van was a shattered mess. Corso raised the revolver and began pulling the trigger. Over and over as the van lurched onward. He was still pulling the useless trigger when Wald dove out from behind the car and tackled him back into the ditch.

The van hit the police car doing about forty miles an hour, nearly lifting the Crown Victoria up onto its side. Six tons of scrap metal hovered in the air for a moment and then slammed back to earth. An eerie silence settled over the scene. Only the soft ticking of cooling metal was audible above the buzzing of the streetlights.

Wald scrambled up from the ground, keeping the shotgun trained on the van as he worked his way between the two cars, inching toward the driver's door. The van's windshield had torn loose from the frame and was about to collapse inward. Except right above the steering wheel, where a red dimple of impacted glass bulged outward like a boil.

"Put both hands out the window," Wald screamed.

Corso gulped air, snapped his head around looking for Dougherty. She lay fifteen yards to his left. Facedown in the ditch. Unmoving. His legs were loose-jointed and seemed to have a will of their own as he covered the distance and knelt by her side.

"Hands out the window," Wald screamed again.

Corso took her by the shoulders and carefully turned her over. Her eyes popped open in terror. She raised a hand to strike out, recognized Corso and instead threw her arms around his neck and pulled him down upon her.

"Is it over?" she breathed into his neck.

Corso said it was. "You okay?" he asked. She said she was. Corso disentangled himself and got to his feet. He took her hands and pulled her from the ground.

"We're going to jail, huh?" she said. Corso looked back over his shoulder.

Wald had the driver's door open. He rested the shotgun on his hip while he felt for life on the driver's throat.

"Maybe not," Corso said.

"Is he?" she asked.

"I think so, yeah," Corso said, taking her by the elbow and turning her away. She wobbled, like the heels weren't connected to her boots.

"Perp's dead," Wald announced. The sound of his own voice seemed to bring him around. He swiveled his head. "Chucky," he hollered. "Andy."

The force of the collision had driven Donald all the way across the street. He rose from the grass wiping at a nosebleed, his trousers blown out to reveal a pair of peeled, bloody knees. His unfired gun was still in his hand. "Over here," he yelled.

Wald was breathing heavily through his mouth. His lip was bleeding; his bright yellow tie had escaped the vest and now lay flopped up over his shoulder. The shotgun hung from his limp right arm. He found himself looking at the soles of Densmore's shoes and stopped in his tracks. He gulped air and shouted to Donald on the far side of the street.

"Chucky! Call for an aide car. Officer-down call."

Donald holstered his gun. "For Christ's sake, Wald . . . come over here and look at the poor bastard.

He doesn't need an aide car. Half his head's gone." As if sickened by his own words, he suddenly began to retch, sending the contents of his stomach spewing out onto the pavement in a dozen raspy spasms.

Donald was right. Densmore's head was gone from the eyebrows up. Nothing but a couple of shiny gray dreadlocks hanging down over the ears. What was left of his skull looked like a broken lava lamp.

"Listen," Corso said.

Wald looked confused. "What?"

Corso gestured with his hand. "Listen, no sirens. No nothing."

"So?"

"So Dougherty and I are getting out of here."

"No," Wald said. "You can't . . . we—"

"This scene doesn't play with us in it."

"He's right," Donald croaked. "We keep this simple. An anonymous tip. We follow up on a phone tip and walk into a hornet's nest. We've got a hero. We've got a villain. All nice and simple like."

Corso jumped in. "Otherwise, somebody's gonna want to know why an experienced cop like yourself found himself facing a mass murderer without backup. Especially after you'd been told what to expect."

"Jesus," Donald muttered. "We're fucked here, Wald. This is a career killer."

"Same people are gonna want an explanation of why Lieutenant Donald here never managed to get off a shot."

Wald shot a disgusted glance at Donald and then returned his gaze to Corso.

"You think I'm betting my ass—my career—on you two keeping your mouths shut?" Wald sneered.

"There's nothing in this for either Dougherty or me, except some time behind bars. We broke and entered. We interfered with an ongoing investigation. Tainted evidence. Maybe even recklessly endangered. It's as much in our own best interests to keep our mouths shut as it is for you two.

"We beat it, and you guys tell the story any way you want." He hesitated. "If not for your own asses, then maybe do it for Densmore."

Wald looked down at Densmore. Winced. "God knows he paid for his lunch."

"Paid in full," Donald said.

Wald swiveled his head. Donald nodded.

"Somebody gonna call about Himes or what?" Corso demanded.

Wald pulled a phone from his inside jacket pocket. Checked his wrist.

"What you say is in that house is in there?"

"I swear."

Wald opened the phone and dialed. "This is Detective Sergeant Steven Wald. I need to be patched through to Chief Kesey, immediately." He began to shake his head. "Don't start that not available crap with me. This is an emergency." He looked up at Corso. "Wald," he shouted into the phone, exasperated now. "Detective Sergeant Steven Wald. Don't tell me you can't—" He listened for a moment. "Get me a supervisor," he snapped. He covered the mouthpiece with his hand. "She says all the circuits are busy."

"Oh, Jesus," Donald moaned.

Wald looked at Corso again. "Get outta here," he said, then turned back to Donald.

"Make that radio call, Chucky."

Corso moved quickly, grabbing Dougherty by the hand. "Let's get the hell out of here."

He didn't have to ask twice.

Chapter 29

It was like a small-town carnival. Bright ballpark
banks of mercury vapor lights threw an unholy purple
glare on the overhead coils of razor wire. The blaring
music made the ominous front gate of the Washington
State Penitentiary look like the clown's-mouth entrance to the fun house. Closest to the wall, an irregular
midway sported food stands, T-shirts, souvenirs, and
sno-cones. The remaining commercial sprawl was
spread haphazardly about the parking lot, as if the ven-
dors had been unable to agree on any pattern of
arrangement whatsoever. Farther back in the shadows,
a herd of motor homes grazed placidly among the
bands of vans and packs of pickups. Maybe a dozen remote TV feeds, parked hip to hip inside the first chain-
link fence, pointing their blank white eyes at the sky.
The seething crowd was nervous and constantly on the
move. Hard to count. Two, three thousand anyway,
Dorothy figured. The air was electric.

Warden Danson was a short, contentious-looking
man with eyes like rivets. He'd met them just inside the

west gate, his breath rising toward the orchard of stars in the night sky, his small hands massaging each other for warmth.

Without bothering to introduce Dorothy, Marvin Hale had pulled Danson aside. They'd spent the past five minutes forty feet away, gesturing like spastic mimes and hissing at each other in stage whispers.

What, from the outside, had appeared to be a single stone wall was actually two parallel walls, with the guard towers spanning the gap at intervals. A prisoner scaling the inside wall, instead of facing a mere half dozen steel fences, two of which were lethally electrified, found himself trapped between the proverbial rock and the hard place of song and story. Almost wasn't fair.

Hale used one hand on Dorothy's elbow and the other to point to the right. Dorothy looked down his arm. At that moment, a red light came on over the door at the far end. "Go down to that door," Hale said. "They're expecting you. Whoever's there will take you to witness orientation."

Dorothy pushed the little button on the side of her watch and the dial lit up: 11:40. Twenty minutes to go. Without a word she turned and began marching toward the light, stepping along, her arms swinging smoothly at her sides, her chin held high. Inexplicably, "Onward, Christian Soldiers" began to play in her head.

11:40 P.M. Day 6 of 6

"I seen seventeen of 'em go now," said the sergeant. "You see enough of them, you learn to tell the difference." Smitty looked reverentially at the sergeant. This was Smitty's first execution. He'd requested the death-watch assignment because they said it was quiet in the death house. None of that screaming-in-their-sleep babble of the cell blocks. Everybody said, Hell, the state of Washington never offs anybody anyway. Easy duty, they'd said. Now Smitty wasn't so sure. During the past week his dreams had turned increasingly grue-some. Turned to nightmares of such severity that, on three occasions, some primal instinct had been forced to intervene, shouting at him from the darkness of sleep, "Wake up; you don't have to die; it's just a dream," catapulting him upright in bed, his lungs empty from gasping, his cheeks washed with tears.

"Seen the big mouths who talk a good game. They're always the ones we got to stop halfway down the mile and hose out their pants for 'em. Seen the mealymouth little bastards you gotta carry the whole damn way. Little fuckers get so strong at the sight of the table, takes eight of us to strap 'em in."

"How do you figure old Walter's gonna go?" Smitty asked.

The sergeant chuckled. "Walter's gonna walk down that hall like he's goin' out for an ice cream cone."

"You really think so?"

"Count on it, kid," the sergeant said. "That guy's known nothin' but hate his whole life. No way he'd give anybody the satisfaction of seeing him crawl. He'll jump up on that damn table like Cindy Craw-ford's waiting up there for him."

For reasons he couldn't explain, the image made Smitty feel better.

11:52 P.M.   Day 6 of 6

"Please remember that Mr. Himes has a right to make a
final statement," the woman was saying. "We have no
control over the content." She looked up from the page
in her hand and noticed Dorothy for the first time. "Are
you . . . ," she began. Eight heads turned Dorothy's way.
Two Butlers, two Nisovics, two Tates, Alice Doyle,
clutching a picture of her daughter Kelly in her lap,
and on the far left, John Williams, come all the way
from South Dakota in search of something without a
name. Dorothy waved a hand at the woman, as if to tell
her to carry on, which she did. "Sometimes inmates
express contrition, sometimes not." She checked the
crowd. "You'll need to be prepared for whatever he
might say."

She looked from person to person again. "We in-
sist that you refrain from saying anything to the inmate. Although I am given to understand that Mr.
Himes will not have family members in attendance,
I believe his ACLU attorney, Mr. Adams, will be
there. So for the sake of Mr. Adams, at least . . ."
She let it go.

She turned the paper over in her hand. "On the
back," she said and waited for her stunned audience to
follow suit, "on the back is a description of the inmate's final hours. "At ten-thirty this morning, Mr.
Himes was transferred to a segregation cell adjacent to
the death chamber. At six o'clock this evening, Mr.
Himes had a final meal of cheeseburgers and French
fries. Between ten o'clock and eleven, he spent an hour
with his mother. Subsequently, Mr. Himes was af-
forded the opportunity to consult with clergy . . . an

opportunity which Mr. Himes rejected." She checked her watch. Dorothy did too. Ten minutes.

"So that you'll know what to expect, let me tell you what's going to happen." Again she paused to let the audience catch up. She began to read from the sheet. "In the state of Washington, lethal injection comes in three phases. The inmate is first injected with thiopental sodium which many of you know as sodium pentothol, or truth serum. The first injection immobilizes the inmate."

The first injection would immobilize a rhinoceros, Dorothy thought.

"One minute later the inmate is injected with Pavulon. Pavulon is a curare derivative that immediately halts the diaphragm."

Mrs. Butler's shoulders began to shake. Her husband rubbed the back of her neck. Whispered in her ear.

"One minute later the inmate is injected with potassium chloride, at which point the heart can no longer beat. Inmates generally emit an audible gasp at this point." She checked the crowd again. "A minute later the inmate is pronounced dead."

Sounded almost serene. Except that Dorothy had once heard a couple of medical examiners discussing the process.

"They make it look like the guy's just gone to sleep," one of them said.

The other had laughed out loud. "Are you shittin' me? All three of those drugs have a pH higher than six. Must feel like the fires of hell are being injected into your veins. If they could, they'd sit straight up and make noises like nobody's heard on earth since the Spanish Inquisition."

The other guy had nodded grimly. "Except, strapped down, with the lungs immobile, the closest you can get to a scream is that one little gasp they all let out."

"Yeah," said the first guy. "In the end, all they leave you with is the whimper instead of the bang."

And then, on the other side of the glass, Himes stepped into the death chamber. Standing there. Bald. No eyebrows. He cast a contemptuous glance at the white-covered gurney and then stood glaring at the viewing window.

"You all got your popcorn ready?" he asked.

Warden Danson now entered. "Mr. Himes would like to exercise his constitutional right to make a final statement," he said.

Himes stepped closer. "I ain't neva killed nobody," Himes said. "So I know where I'm goin' from here." He took them in again, moving only his eyes. "Probably the same place you-all think you goin'. So if we both right, old Walter Lee'll see you when you get there." He showed the stubs of his teeth. "And if we ain't . . . I'll see you-all in hell."

Alice Doyle got to her feet and pressed the picture of her daughter Kelly tightly against the glass. She turned back toward Dorothy, her pouchy eyes streaming.

"I want this to be the last thing he sees. The very last thing," she cried.

Somewhere in the room somebody was making noises like a gored animal.

Dorothy turned and ground her face into the wall.

Chapter 30

Sunday, September 23
10:15 A.M. Day 6 + 1

Corso dreamed of that cobbled street again. Of the soldiers and the door intended solely for him. Only this time, in the moment when he closed the door behind himself, before putting that first foot on the tread and watching the walls fall away . . . this time someone began knocking on the door. The knocking got louder. He hesitated, foot in the air, torn between the insistent sound at his back and the bright promise waiting above.

Corso sat up in bed. More knocking as he struggled into a Mariners T-shirt and a pair of black sweatpants. Slipped on boat shoes. Up three steps, into the galley.

Corso checked the clock over the nav station: 10:15 A.M.

With a yawn, he pulled open the door and stepped out on deck, rubbing his eyes. The wind was up. Overhead, the sky was electric blue. No clouds at all. He checked the tops of the masts. Six, eight knots from the south. All over the marina, loose halyards banged against masts like drunken tinkers.

Wald and Donald. Cleaned and pressed. Showered, shaved, and swapped suits.

Hadn't helped Donald as much as it helped Wald, though. On Wald, the extra lines seemed to disappear into his already pouchy face. Donald, on the other hand, looked like he'd been snorting speedballs for a week. For some reason, Corso was cheered by the sight.

"A little early for protecting and serving, don't you think?" Corso said.

"We never rest," Wald assured him.

"You seen the papers?" Donald asked.

"Not yet."

"I'll bet you missed our press conference too."

"Next time I'll set the alarm."

Both cops checked the area. "We kept it simple," Wald said. "Phone tip. We go out for a look-see and, out of the blue, the guy attacks us. Densmore and Defeo get offed in the struggle."

"Works for me," Corso said, rubbing his face with his hands.

Donald stepped in closer to Corso. His blue eyes were filigreed with red. "You sure?" he asked. "Last night isn't going to show up in a book or something, is it?"

Corso looked him over. "I don't know what you're talking about. I spent last night right here." Corso yawned. "Read till about midnight."

"Nothing like a good book," Donald said.

Corso agreed and then yawned again. Covering his mouth this time.

"You ready for a little mirth?" Wald asked.

"I love the smell of irony in the morning," Corso said.

"The lab says Defeo had a bullet in his head."

"Couldn't happen to a nicer guy."

"They say the bullet's the cause of death."

"So?"

"They also say the slug came from Densmore's piece."

"No shit," Corso said.

"Who taught you to shoot? I may want to take lessons," Donald joked.

"I learned from the KGB," Corso said with a straight face.

"We told 'em Andy must have gotten a salvo off on the way down," Wald said with a grimace.

"Was that before or after the top half of his head got vaporized?"

"We opted for before," Donald said.

Corso shrugged. "It'll look better on his record than on mine."

Wald shook his head. "Amazing, ain't it? Densmore makes every mistake a cop can make, damn near gets us all killed, and he comes out of this thing looking like Rambo."

"Radio said Himes had already said his final words when the call came from the governor," Corso said.

Wald whistled silently. "Six more minutes and your boy Himes was history," Wald said.

"He's fired his ACLU attorney and hired Myron Mendenhal," Donald said, naming Seattle's most successful personal-injury specialist.

"He's gonna get millions," Wald offered.

"Got a press conference called for this afternoon."

"What about you guys?" Corso asked.

Wald looked as if he was going to puke. "I'm getting

promoted to lieutenant. Chucky here's getting a commendation for valor."

"The public does *so* like a happy ending," Corso sneered. He got to his feet. Stretched. And then sidestepped up the slip, past the cops.

The good weather had the weekend warriors out. Four boats up, a red-haired woman he'd never seen before was scrubbing the deck of a Morgan Out-Island. Farther along on the far side, a couple of boatyard types were replacing the roller furling on a Catalina thirty-six. The new cable and fittings ran nearly the length of the dock. Half a dozen other boats had people crawling over them. Sunday on the dock.

"What about this Defeo guy?" Corso asked.

Wald shrugged. "The usual. School record full of shrinks and counselors. Been through the mental-health system and back. Diagnosed as schizophrenic when he was sixteen. Applied to the Seattle and King County police departments, about three times each. Took the tests for all four branches of the armed services. Nobody wanted any part of him."

"A regular super criminal," Corso said.

"His current doctor and his therapist are both playing hardball. Claiming doctor/patient privilege. Holding out for court orders. It'll be a week or so before we can be certain, but we're pretty damn sure Defeo must have told his mama what he was doing back in ninety-eight."

"Either that or she figured it out on her own," Donald added.

"You guys see that pile of burnt stuff in the backyard?" Corso asked.

"His mama's stuff," Wald said.

"Interesting relationship there."

"Freud'd have a field day," Donald agreed.

Wald rolled his eyes. "Anyway . . . instead of dropping a quarter on her own flesh and blood, Mama took away his genuine lambs of God ear tags, got him on medication and into therapy. Which, if you don't count eight murders, worked just peachy until she died a couple of months back."

"At which time, he, of course, stopped taking the meds," Wald added.

"And the killing started again," Donald finished.

"You find the rest of the clothes?"

"One set was still at the dry cleaners. He had 'em all cleaned before he mounted them. Thoughtful of him, don't you think?"

"We've identified six sets for sure," Wald said. He ran down the list from memory. Kate Mitchell, Analia Nisovic, and Jennifer Robison from ninety-eight. And all three recent victims, Alice Crane-Carter, Denise Gould, and Tiffany Eyre. "The other four we're working on," Wald concluded.

"Five," Corso said.

"Five what?" Donald demanded.

"The other five sets of clothes. You said you'd identified six. That leaves five." He looked from cop to cop. "There's eleven victims, right?"

"We've got ten sets of clothes," Wald said. "Nine from the house and one from the dry cleaner."

"Where's the other set?" Corso asked.

"You read the shit in that room, didn't you?" Donald said. "That crap about the ten brides of Christ. He only needed ten sets."

"Which," noted Wald, "our Bible-toting brethren in the station house assure us is a notion not to be found in the Bible."

"So there's a missing set of clothes, then?"

"Who the hell knows?" Donald said. "Maybe they got torn up during the attack. With that crazy bastard anything could have happened."

"The dry cleaners only cleaned ten," Wald said.

On the Catalina, one guy was winching the other guy up the mast in a yellow canvas boson's chair. "Pretty weird," Corso noted. "You'd think with Defeo so fixated on his ten brides of Christ thing . . . you'd think he could keep track of the damn number."

Donald moved toward Corso with a stiff-legged gait. His face suddenly red. His voice suddenly loud. Along the dock, all work stopped.

"What the fuck is the matter with you, Corso? What is it? The only way you can get up in the morning is if you feel superior to everybody else? You can't feel good about yourself unless you see something that nobody else sees? Is that what floats your boat, Corso?" Donald was close now, crowding Corso.

"Just wondering," Corso said affably.

"You know what I think? I think you're a big-time loser. I think you're such a loser, you don't even have sense enough to know when you've won, and that's the biggest kind of loser there is."

"Hey, hey," Wald was saying. "We're all on the same side here."

He stepped between the two men, stood facing his partner.

Corso kept his eyes locked on Donald. "Wald," he said, "you better take the lieutenant here home for his nap. He seems to be a bit out of sorts this morning."

Donald made a show of trying to swim his way past Wald to get at Corso.

"You're a loser," he was yelling. "A loser."

Corso stood his ground, smiling as Wald began shoving Donald down the dock. Halfway down, right after Donald took to walking on his own, Wald stopped for a moment and threw a long quizzical look back Corso's way, then turned and followed his partner toward the gate and the ramp beyond.

"Two Killed in Trashman Battle." Big as headlines get. Picture of Wald and Donald standing beside the bullet-riddled car in their spiffy Kevlar vests. A sidebar on Densmore and his career. Corso folded the paper beneath his arm, pulled open the front door of the *Seattle Sun*, and stepped into the lobby.

Behind the security desk, Bill Post looked up and smiled. "Hey, Mr. Corso," he said. "You seen they got him, huh?"

Corso crossed the room. Leaned on the desk.

"I saw," he said. "I hear Himes is already out."

Post nodded. "I'm workin' security at the Hilton this afternoon. Himes and his new mouthpiece are havin' them a press conference."

"A guy can always use a little extra Hawaii money," Corso said.

"Yeah," he beamed. "Leavin' next Wednesday. Ten glorious days and nights on Maui."

Corso said, "Congratulations," and started for the elevator. Post waddled out from behind the desk, following Corso down the hall. "You shoulda seen my granddaughter's face when I told her. Never seen the kid so happy before. Nancy says she's already packed and ready to go."

Corso stopped his finger just short of the Up button. Turned to Post. "Where do the people who answer the phones work? What floor is that?" he asked.

"Down two," Post said. "That's basement, B."

Corso thumbed the Down button. "If I don't see you again," he said to the guard, "have a mai tai for me."

"Thanks," Post said. "I'll make it a couple." They shook hands.

The door slid open silently. Corso stepped into the car. Pushed B. Post waved.

Basement B was just that. A windowless room filled with cubicles. The dull roar of a hundred conversations rolled like waves just below the ceiling. Corso had to ask three times before he found the right row. Three desks up. Leanne Samples wore a white plastic band in her hair. She was making conversation with the stout African-American woman at the next desk when Corso turned the corner.

"Mr. Corso," she squealed when she saw him.

She tried to jump to her feet but the cord on her headset wasn't nearly long enough and jerked her right back into her chair.

"Oops," she said, dropping the headset to the desk- top and throwing her arms around Corso's waist. "It's all done, huh? They got the guy."

"They got the guy," Corso repeated. Changed the subject. "You're looking great. I hear you're a regular whiz at your job."

She took him by the hand and led him to the next cu- bicle. "Georgeanne, this is my friend Mr. Corso." Georgeanne, whose last name turned out to be Taylor, allowed how it was a great pleasure to meet the famous Mr. Frank Corso and how she faithfully read his column. Leanne dragged him on. They zigzagged the length of the room in a frenzy of rushed introductions and hurried handshakes. Fifteen minutes later, they stumbled out of the maze, directly in front of the elevators.

She pulled at his elbow. "And you must meet my friend Ellie over here . . ."

Corso resisted. "I've gotta go," he said. "I need to have a few words with Mr. Hawes."

Her eyes widened. "Oh . . . ," she said. "We mustn't keep Mr. Hawes waiting." She was suddenly flustered. Looked around the room as if she'd never seen it before. "I probably ought to get back to work myself." She managed a wan smile. "After all, they're not paying me to stand around and talk to famous writers, are they?" Corso managed a smile of his own. They shook hands. Changed their minds and hugged. Said goodbye and then hugged again.

Corso turned and rang for the elevator. "Mr. Corso," Leanne said, "thank you for everything." He nodded. "Everything is different in my life now. Better. It's like, for the first time, I actually have a life of my own."

Corso held up a hand. "That's your doing, not mine," he said.

She started to argue, but he cut her off.

"You know what *my* mama used to say, Leanne?"

"What?"

"She used to say, 'If a miracle takes place within five miles of you, take credit for it.' That's what she used to say." Corso stepped into the elevator, pushed six.

The car slid upward. Corso watched the numbers turn red until the car bounced to a halt on six. Corso

held the door open with his arm. The newsroom. Nor-
mally, on a Sunday, they'd be down to a skeleton crew
and the building would be silent. Last night's developments cost people another day off. He stepped out of
the car and started up the aisle toward Bennett Hawes's
glassed-in office, leaving silence in his wake as phone
conversations suddenly ended and coffee cups stopped
short of lips. Claire Harris waved. Corso gave her a
salacious wink.

"Hey, Claire," he said, stopping by her desk.

"I'll tell ya, kiddo . . . whatever your other failings
may be, you sure know how to set the woods on fire."

"Thanks, Claire."

"You're not going to upset poor Bennett, are you?"

"I'm too tired."

Hawes gestured him in with a nod of his head.
Corso continued up the aisle toward Hawes. Pulled
open the door and stepped in. He dangled a set of
keys from his thumb and forefinger for a moment before tossing them across the desk. Hawes snatched
them out of midair and put them in his top drawer.
"Once and for all," Corso said. "Here's your car
back."

Hawes rocked back in his oversize chair and took
Corso in. "Seems your security-guard angle was right
on the money."

"A lucky guess," Corso said with a smirk.

Hawes searched his eyes for a story. "Am I missing
something here?" he asked.

"Yeah," Corso said. "And it's gonna have to stay
that way."

Hawes furrowed his brow. "Were you—"

Corso held up a hand. "I can't," he said.

"Dougherty's okay?"

"She's fine," Corso assured him.

A silence settled over the room. "You make your reservations for the American Society of Newspaper Editors conference?" Corso asked.

"Sent the registration form in yesterday."

"If it wasn't for me, you'd sure as hell get a Pulitzer nomination."

Both men knew it was true. Small papers that break major stories are usually rewarded with Pulitzer nominations. Corso's presence on the story, however, made that impossible. As far as the committee was concerned, nominating Frank Corso for a journalism award would be like nominating Jeffrey Dahmer for a culinary medal.

Hawes shrugged. "I've got no complaints."

"Everybody's got the story they want. Big shootout at the O.K. Corral. At great personal cost, brave cops kill despoiler of virgins. What else could anybody ask for? It's positively mythic."

Corso walked over to the desk and stuck out his hand. Hawes got to his feet. Made eye contact and took Corso's hand in his. "I stand corrected," Hawes said.

Corso raised an eyebrow.

"About you," Hawes said. "You ever get tired of writing books and want to get back into the newspaper business full-time, you be sure to give me a call."

"Tell Mrs. V. I'll give her a jingle one of these nights," Corso said.

Hawes said he would. "What's for you now?"

Corso thought it over. "Finally got some decent

weather; I think I'll wash my boat. Maybe putt over
and pump the heads and top it off with diesel."

"Sailing off into the sunset?"

"Something like that."

A dock is a special type of community. Diverse beyond
reason. Filled with everything from millionaires who
barely remember they own a vessel to lifetime live-
aboards who have every dime they own tied up in the
rig. Moguls, morons, and misfits, all of whom find
common ground in the mystique of the water. All of
whom, it seemed, wanted to drop by and chat of a
sunny Sunday afternoon as Corso washed *Saltheart*.
Everyone mentioned the weather, of course, and then
immediately segued into how they'd heard there'd
been some excitement down here this morning. Corso
handed out quite a few Heinekens but precious little
information.

Others bitched about the Carver's anchor hanging
out over the dock. Wanted to call management. The
guy in the green Cruisahome wanted to push the
Carver back in the slip and retie it with a springline,
but nobody would lend a hand. You just don't touch another man's lines.

Corso had worked up a full sweat. He'd started in
the dinghy with the sun hot on his shoulders. Paddling
himself around, scrubbing the hull. Worked his way
back onboard, where, as the last rays of the day had begun to slide behind Queen Anne Hill, the wind quickly
died and the fog appeared from nowhere to take its
place. As the mist settled on his bare shoulders, Corso
moved the broom in a single-minded frenzy. He'd been
at it so long the soft blue bristles had begun to hum in

his head, like a mantra. A low Gregorian chant. "Behold the ten brides of Christ . . ." it intoned, ". . . who having strayed from his ways are now returned to the fold of our master, like lost sheep. Behold the . . ."

Chapter 31

Sunday, September 23
1:57 P.M. Day 6 + 1

Why, she used to wonder, would survivors subject themselves to this? She knew why *she* was here. That was easy. She was covering her ass. Making sure when Chief Kesey called she'd be able to say, "Yes, Chief, as a matter of fact, I did hear what Himes and his attorney had to say. Actually, I was there in the hotel for the press conference, Chief. And you?" On a Sunday too.

But them. The Tates and the Butlers, Mrs. Doyle and the Nisovics. Right there in the front row again. After the week they'd had. Dorothy Sheridan shivered, because, after fourteen years and a daughter of her own, she finally understood. Same as her, they were covering their asses. They were doing everything they could. Making certain that no stone was unturned, no step untaken, no opportunity to remember lost. Fruitful . . . futile . . . it didn't matter. Because somewhere down the road, when the headlines and memories had faded, nothing was going to be more vital to their long-term survival than being able to tell themselves they'd done everything humanly possible.

She'd made up her mind. First thing Monday morning she was calling Monica and setting up an interview. Anything had to be better than this. What good was security if it killed you? First thing Monday.

She was still lost in thought when the buzz in the room suddenly subsided, pulling her attention to the dais. She'd never seen Myron Mendenhal in person before. Only on TV. Not that he looked particularly good either way. The man was a gnome. A bandy-legged troll with a head about four sizes too big for his body. Bald on top, grown out long on the sides. Big Moscow snow-cutter eyebrows.

Mendenhal tapped at the bank of microphones. Flashbulbs twinkled all over the ballroom. TV cameras began to hum. "Ladies and gentlemen," he began. "It seems my client has been unavoidably delayed, so why don't we begin." He had a wet mouth. Everything he said sounded a little juicy. "As most of you well know, my client Walter Leroy Himes was unjustly convicted and sentenced to death for the series of murders commonly known as the Trashman killings. Whether this gross miscarriage of justice was a matter of official ineptitude or indifference will be decided in a court of law. What cannot be denied, however, is that even at this late date, it is not too late for some measure of justice to be done."

Dorothy allowed his voice to settle into a drone. Her head no longer throbbed. Instead, the pain had become a cold river of pressure flowing directly behind her eyes, making her feel as if her eyeballs might unexpectedly pop from their sockets like champagne corks. She massaged the bridge of her nose with her thumb and forefinger.

Mendenhal stopped talking as the buzz in the room began to rise. Himes, in maybe the worst suit in the world. An orange-plaid pattern that could have been used as the international symbol for bad taste. Way too small. Oh, god, look at his ankles.

Himes pulled out the other chair on the dais and sat down hard enough to make the bank of microphones belch. Weaving back and forth. Obviously shitfaced drunk. Sitting there surveying the crowd with this big loopy grin on his face.

"As I was saying," Myron Mendenhal continued, "on behalf of my client Mr. Himes"—whom he acknowledged with the smallest of nods—"I have today, in state superior court, filed a lawsuit alleging willful and malicious prosecution in the amounts of . . ."

Thirteen million. If they got even half of that there'd be big-time layoffs. Might get all the way down to her. She pressed at her eyes, as if to keep them in place. She heard the scrape of a chair and then another belch from the mikes.

Himes leaning over the microphones. "Now that them no-good bitches got what they deserved . . . now old Walter Lee gonna get somma what he deserves for a change."

Mendenhal whispered furiously in his client's ear. Himes sneered and kept on talking. "Gonna buy me evathin' I want. Might even git me a little"—he winked—"you know . . . a little . . . poontang."

Malcolm Tate rose from his front-row seat. He pointed at Himes.

"Don't," he warned. "Don't you dare."

Himes pointed back at him. "I seen you there. Eva

time, in the front row, with your clean clothes and your old woman and all . . . up there in the good seats."

"You shut your mouth," Tate warned at the top of his voice.

All around the room, security guards hustled toward Malcolm Tate. His wife pulled at his pant leg, then rose to put herself between her husband and the dais.

"I'll bet one of them bitches was yourn, wasn't she?" Himes taunted.

Paula Tate put both palms on her husband's chest and gently tried to force him back into his chair. Malcolm Tate, however, was having none of it. Instead, he stepped around his wife and wagged a blunt finger in Himes's face. "You shut your filthy mouth," he said.

Himes leaned forward over the table, grinned at the audience, and then spit on Tate's blue denim shirt. A collective intake of breath was followed by dead silence. Malcolm Tate's mouth fell open as he stared down at the yellow glob of phlegm now welded to his shirtfront.

"Ladies and gentlemen, please, ah. . . ." Myron Mendenhal sputtered. "Could we perhaps . . . at this time—"

Tate went berserk. With a bellow, he lurched forward, toward Himes. His fingers extended like talons, as if he intended to go for the eyes. Tate took a single stride and then attempted to hurl himself upward onto the dais. He'd have made it too, except that his trailing foot became entangled in the maze of cables running along the front of the platform, stopping his ascent in mid-flight, jerking him down onto the cluster of microphones. Myron Mendenhal fell backward from his chair. An electronic shriek tore the air.

A female security guard arrived first, grabbing Tate by the belt and jerking him to the floor. Malcolm Tate got as far up as his knees before he was buried beneath an onrushing pile of uniforms. The amplifiers screamed like a jet on takeoff. The audience was on its feet, hands cupped over ears as if playing some deranged version of Simon Says. Without willing it so, Dorothy Sheridan found herself hurrying toward the front of the room. "Malcolm," Paula Tate cried. "Oh . . . please, Malcolm."

By the time Dorothy arrived, Tate had been pulled to his feet and was being led stiff-legged down the central aisle by four rent-a-cops. Somewhere in the scuffle, he'd suffered a cut on the bridge of his nose, sending a single crimson rivulet rolling down over his upper lip and into his mouth. "Mr. Tate," Dorothy said. "Please, Mr. Tate."

He bellowed at the ceiling, launching a spray of blood and spittle as he was muscled past her down the aisle. She turned and trotted along behind Paula Tate, who repeatedly called her husband's name as he was dragged from the room. Dorothy patted at the pockets of her dress until she found her SPD ID badge.

Out in the hallway, Malcolm Tate had been forced to his knees. The female guard had disengaged and was whispering into a handheld radio. Holding her SPD ID badge before her, Dorothy Sheridan ran to Malcolm Tate's side. "Don't hurt him," she said.

The nearest guard turned his sweaty, pockmarked face her way. "Listen, lady, why don't you—"

She waved the ID in his face. "Don't hurt him . . . you hear me? Don't."

Malcolm Tate hiccuped once and then vomited onto

the carpet. The security guards released their grip and scrambled to their feet as his body convulsed, over and over again, until he was empty, left with nothing but a single silver strand connecting his lower lip to the carpet below. His wife knelt at his side. Put her hand on his back.

"Malcolm," she said again.

Dorothy pointed to a bench against the wall. "Put him there," she said. The pockmarked guard started to protest. "Do it," she screamed.

Carefully avoiding the puddle, two of the guards helped Malcolm Tate to the bench, where he sat heavily, holding his head in his hands.

Someone brought a glass of water and some paper towels.

Ten minutes later, Paula Tate was till dabbing at her husband's face and whispering in his ear when a pair of uniformed SPD officers came jogging around the corner and down the hall.

Dorothy held up her ID and met them halfway. As she explained the situation, they began to relax. "Poor guy," the younger one said.

"Would you please help them to their car?" Dorothy asked.

"Sure," they said in unison.

Paula Tate looked Sheridan's way with red-rimmed eyes. "Come on," Sheridan said. The Tates rose from the bench together and shuffled over. "Are we . . . is Malcolm being arrested?" Mrs. Tate wanted to know. Dorothy shook her head. "These officers are going to see you to your car," she said. Paula Tate's eyes filled with tears. "Did you hear what that man said?"

Dorothy said she had.

"How could this happen?" Paula Tate asked, as much to herself as to Sheridan. "I don't understand."

"I'm so sorry," was all Dorothy could come up with. "If there's anything I can—"

Paula Tate turned away. Her words echoed in Dorothy's head as she watched the officers lead the couple up the stairs and around the corner.

Dorothy walked over, eased the ballroom door open, and stepped back inside. A trio of techies were putting the microphones back in order. Myron Mendenhal was still straightening his suit. Himes sat there, looking pleased with himself, rocking his chair up onto its back legs and then letting it slam back down.

A voice on her right asked, "Everybody all right?" Another guard. Fat and fifty. About to burst the buttons on a Hilton security uniform that obviously didn't belong to him. Handwritten name tag read "Bill Post."

"Fine," she said.

He made a gesture as if he were mopping his brow. "Gotta leave that kinda rough stuff for the young guys," he said. "Me, I'm just moonlighting for a little vacation money. Didn't expect anything like that. No, sir, I didn't."

Mendenhal was talking again. Same thing he'd said before the excitement. Thirteen million. Civil suits to follow. "How do you compensate a man for three years of his life?" he asked. "Is there some dollar figure that can repair the heart of a man who has lived for years under the specter of his own imminent death? Who has lain upon the table of death? I think not. Can we—"

Dorothy held her breath as Himes leaned toward the mikes.

"If it ain't me or him, just gonna be somebody else, you know."

"Excuse me?" a big-haired blonde along the wall said.

"Said there's always gonna be somebody out there killin' bitches. Bitches and mo' bitches is gonna be dyin' all over the damn place, till you-all up to your damn ass in dead bitches."

Up front, Slobodan Nisovic slowly got to his feet. Brushed at his face, then turned his back on Mendenhal and Himes. The little man leaned over and appeared to whisper in his mother's ear. She nodded and handed him something.

On Dorothy's right, Bill Post muttered, "Holy shit," under his breath and started hustling toward the front of the room with an awkward, rolling gait.

When Slobodan Nisovic straightened up, he was holding an automatic in both hands. He had tears in his eyes as he looked out over the crowded ballroom.

"No" was all he said before turning toward the front of the room and pulling the trigger. The roar of the gun ripped the air. Dorothy stood transfixed as, all around her, people threw themselves to the floor. Screams and more shots. Himes was down on his side on the dais, his chest a mass of red. Nisovic turned to face the crowd. He stuck the gun in his mouth and pulled the trigger. Dorothy watched the side of his face explode and waited for him to crumple to the floor.

To Dorothy's amazement, however, Slobodan Nisovic flinched but didn't fall. He just stood there jerking the trigger, over and over. Nothing happened. Not even a click. Just the silent finger flexing and unflexing inside the trigger guard, until old Bill Post hit him with a flying tackle and drove him to the floor. First thing Monday. Call Monica.

Chapter 32

Monday, September 24
1:35 A.M. Day 6 + 2

"Guess what's missing?"

He pointed to the series of photos pinned to the drapes. Victim number two. Kate Mitchell. Dougherty checked her watch and scowled. She wanted to punch him in the mouth. He looked so goddamn pleased with himself. Standing there in the salon, moving from one foot to the other, like some smart-ass schoolboy who'd stolen the answers to the algebra final. She stepped in close, poked him in the chest with a long red fingernail.

"What gives with you? I finally get last night's disaster out of my mind and sleep for the first time in forty-eight hours and what happens? You call me at one in the morning. Then, without being consulted, next thing I know, there's a cab calling me from downstairs. What kind of shit is that? You think I'm your dog or something?"

Corso tried to look as if his feelings were hurt, but she ignored him. "In return for being dragged out of bed, I get fifteen minutes in the back of a drafty taxi, driving at two miles an hour through the worst fog I've ever seen and you think I'm going to play goddamn guessing games with you. Get a grip, Corso. If you've got a point, you better get to it."

"How about a glass of wine?" For the first time since she'd known him, he looked vaguely embarrassed. She wanted to take advantage of the situation, to stay in his face, to puncture that veneer of his but couldn't muster the energy. Instead, she sighed and said, "White. Dry." He hesitated, waiting for her to step aside. She held her ground.

Corso squeezed by her, slowly, belly to belly, slipped into the galley, and opened the refrigerator. Dougherty slid the coat from her shoulders and threw it over the back of the teak desk chair. Aware of her un-encumbered body moving beneath the dress, she folded her arms across her chest and leaned back against the built-in bookcase. She tried to focus on Corso pulling the cork, but couldn't keep her eyes from drifting to the glossy black-and-whites of Kate Mitchell. From the way her arranged body seemed to fall away from its center. From the knot of angry bruises encircling her narrow throat. From the rubbery film covering her eyeballs like milky sandwich wrap. She pulled away. Hugging herself harder now. Her mouth felt as dry as wood.

"I can't believe you dragged me down here in the middle of the night to look at photographs," she groused. "This thing is over. The good guys finally won."

"Nobody won," Corso countered. "Himes is up in Harborview sitting in bed, stuffing his face and telling anybody who'll listen what he's going to do with the money he gets from the state. Old man Nisovic's the closest thing we've got to a hero and that poor bastard couldn't even blow his own brains out. Sticks a gun in his mouth and only manages to shoot off half his jawbone. Not only that, but whenever he gets out of the hospital, he's going to have to stand trial for trying to off Himes. Excuse me if I'm not feeling all warm and fuzzy over this one."

"What's your problem, Corso?"

"Ten brides. Eleven bodies," he said while pouring wine. "Do the math."

"You saw that place. Defeo was a hundred-percent stone nuts. What makes you think anything he did has to make literal sense?"

"He seemed pretty firm on the number ten to me."

She thought about it and, although unwilling to admit it to Corso, couldn't help but agree. The amount of trouble Defeo had gone through to play out his deranged "lambs of God" and "brides of Christ" scenario, no matter how loony it might seem to the rest of the world, suggested that he probably wasn't going to be confused about the size of his flock.

"So how come you're the only one bothered by the disparity?"

"The cops have already got what they want. They've got themselves a serial murderer, a martyr, and a couple of heroes. Cue the memorial service and the awards ceremony. End of story."

Corso came back into the salon offering a glass of wine. She took it. Stuck her nose into the glass. Okay, not fruity. She took a sip. Then another, sipping halfway down the glass. Just the way she liked it, but she wasn't telling him that either.

"Okay?" he inquired.

"Um," was all she said. She waved at the photos. "So what is it I'm supposed to notice is missing?"

The glint in his eye said he was going to try to make her guess.

"Don't," she warned. "I'm not in the mood."

He took her seriously, tucked his lower lip in, and said, "The ear tag." He reached down onto the settee cushion, picked up the list of the items in Kate Mitchell's evidence bag. He read the list: " 'One watch, Timex. One gold bracelet. One gold cross and chain. Two toe rings. One plastic ear tag, ovine,' " he intoned finally. Corso let the list float back to the cushion, then pointed to Dougherty's photos of the evidence. Pointed.

"No tag," he said. "Not in any of them."

Dougherty drained her glass and handed it to Corso. She put one knee on the cushion and stuck her nose close to the pictures. Picked up the list and mouthed the words as she slowly scanned the pictures. He was right. No ear tag in any of the prints.

When she looked back over her shoulder, Corso had refilled both glasses. She stood upright, plucked the glass from his fingers. "So . . . what? You think I made a mistake? You think I missed something, don't you? That's why you dragged me down here at one o'clock in the morning, to tell me I missed something."

"Matter-of-fact, I don't think any such thing," he said. "I think you got everything that was there."

"Which means what?"

"Which means somebody removed it from the evidence room."

"Stole it?"

"Yep."

"Why in God's name would anybody want to steal an ear tag?"

"Good question."

"For a souvenir, maybe?" she offered.

"Hell of a risk for a trinket."

Grudgingly, she agreed. "What then?"

"Damned if I know."

"You're paranoid. You know that? You could find a conspiracy at a yard sale, Corso."

He didn't say anything. Just stood there rolling his wineglass between his palms, staring back at the photographs.

"How could someone get into the police evidence room and . . ." She stopped herself. "Unless the person was—"

"Somehow associated with the Himes case," he finished for her.

"You mean in some kind of official capacity?"

"Absolutely. The SPD evidence room isn't part of the building tour."

"Maybe they used it for testing purposes or something."

"If they did, it'd be noted in the file. Besides which, they'd never use up one whole tag. They take little pieces from all of them."

"And all the rest of the victims still have their tags?"

"Yep."

"You still have the rest of the files?"

"Yep."

"Lemme see."

She watched from the far side of the salon as Corso retrieved the cardboard box from beneath the sink and

then, once again, covered the pin rail with glossy visions of murder most foul. She handed him her glass
and knelt on the cushions, studying the prints. Moving
a fingertip from list to photo and back. Halfway
through the gallery, she heard the muted pop of a cork.
He was right. Except for Kate Mitchell's missing ear
tag, the evidence lists matched the photos she'd taken
on Thursday. Kate Mitchell's crime-scene photographs, however, clearly showed the tag in her left ear
at the time when the body was found. Now, her tag was
gone. Ergo what?

Corso slipped her glass between her fingers. "So?"
he said.

She took a swallow. "So . . . then . . . what you're
saying is that maybe one of the women wasn't killed by
Defeo after all. She was killed by somebody connected
to the original investigation, who then arranged it to
look like she was just another victim of the Trashman."

"You're a quick one, you are," Corso said.

"And you think the odd victim was Kate Mitchell."

He shook his head. "It can't be her."

"Why not?"

"Because Defeo had her clothes."

"They know that for sure?"

"It's the outfit she was reported missing in. The dry
cleaners by Defeo's house has records for cleaning all
ten sets of women's clothes found by the cops. They've
identified five sets of the clothes. Mitchell's was one of
them."

"Can't be one of the new victims," she said out loud
to herself. "That wouldn't make any sense at all."

"If there's something haywire with any of the original victims, it's gotta be the Doyle girl," Corso said quickly.

"The one they found after Himes was already in jail?"

"Gotta be."

"Mother carries the picture with her all the time."

"Yep."

"Why her?"

"She's the only fly in the ointment. Found two full days after Himes was arrested. Frozen solid, so time of death couldn't be pinned down. The only victim where whoever called the cops about the body didn't stick around until they got there."

"If you ask me, that's pretty damn weak."

His expression said he wasn't prepared to argue the point.

"I suppose you think you know who did it."

"Not a clue," he said with a flicker in his eye that said maybe he did.

Dougherty made a rude noise with her lips. "You're a regular engine of conflict, you know that, Corso? Where others find answers, you find only questions."

"It's possible that—" he began.

She waved him off. "I'm not onboard here, Corso. I've gone along with the program. Haven't I gone along with the program?" He nodded but didn't speak. "I've been shot at, shit on, thrown into jail." She looked at the floor. "I saw a man get killed last night," she said in a low voice. "All in the name of getting to the bottom of this thing. But"—she hesitated—"this is way too out there." She waved a hand. "Let well enough alone, for criminey sakes. Win some friends. Influence some people."

Her hand dropped to her side with a slap. "It's like you're always striving . . . looking for some sort of moral high ground or something. Like you don't think anybody but you can possibly get things right."

He stood silently, his eyes turned inward, looking tired and lonely.

She turned her back on Corso, ran her eyes over the pictures again, shivered, and looked away. She felt Corso's eyes moving over her back like long fingers. Without turning, she said, "Get rid of those pictures, will you, Frank? They're giving me the damn willies."

He said, "Sure." As Corso busied himself with the photos, she pulled the right half of the aft door aside and stepped out onto the stern. Unbelievable that a glorious day like today could end like this. Like being closed in a box of cotton. The air was stark white, floating seamlessly around the boat like chowder. She looked up. Not even the tops of the masts were visible. Then down. The water beneath the swim step was flat and still, like black ice.

From somewhere within the fog . . . the sharp sound of shoes and then the voice. A woman's voice. "Frank?" And the hesitant clicking of high heels.

She watched as Corso reached above the navigation station with his left hand. With a single twiddle of his fingers, he simultaneously activated the boat's exterior spotlights and doused the cabin lights. "Frank." The voice again.

Corso turned Dougherty's way. Put a finger to his lips. She nodded in the darkness. And then peeked around the corner, toward the bow. The spotlights made it possible to make out the iceberg outline of the cruiser in the next slip. Nothing else. Corso's head poked out into the fog just as a figure appeared at the end of the slip. Cynthia Stone. Same red plastic raincoat she'd been wearing the other day.

"How'd you find your way down here?" he asked.

"I told you, Frank. I have my sources."

She had this way of squirming around while standing still. Like she had ants in her dress or something. "Aren't you going to invite me onboard?" she asked. She didn't wait for an answer. Stepped up onto the dock box, threw a leg over the rail, then the other, until she had Corso pinned against the doorway with her crotch.

Corso took his time escaping. The raincoat cracked and crinkled as he backed slowly out of the doorway. "What do you want, Cynth?"

She slid the door closed behind her. "Do I have to want something to see my ex-fiancé?"

"Pretty much. That's the way it works. Yeah," Corso said.

"You're getting to be such a cynic, Frank," she teased.

Corso shook his head. "Nah," he said. "Cynics think they know all the answers. I'm not even clear on the questions."

"That's remarkably humble," she cooed. "Especially for you, Frank."

"I was just buttoning things up for the night, Cynth."

She stepped up close to him again. "I'm leaving in the morning."

"Where to?"

"D.C.," she said. "The Hartman hearings."

"Lot of good dirt there."

She leaned against him now. "Speaking of which, Frank."

"Yeah."

"You know what my downtown source told me tonight?"

"It's late, Cynth."

"The story is that you and Officers Donald and Wald had quite the spat earlier today. Right here on this very dock. In front of God and everybody. The way I hear it, if Detective Wald hadn't intervened, you and Donald might have actually come to blows."

"And your point is?"

"My point is that you've been one step ahead of the rest of us for the past week and a half and, when I heard that story . . . I don't know . . . suddenly I had this niggling feeling that you *still* know something the rest of us don't." She put her arms around his waist and searched his eyes. "Come on, Frank. Talk to Mama."

"I don't know what you're talking about, Cynth. You know me. I've never been good with authority figures. Especially cops."

She smiled and began to pick at the belt of the raincoat. "A trade," she wheedled.

"One good turn deserves another." She gave him a piranha-like smile and pulled the coat back to reveal scanty red silk underthings. "You used to like it when I surprised you like this." She swayed from side to side, as if dancing to silent music. "Remember?"

From the darkness of the stern, Dougherty's hands clenched as she watched Corso's Adam's apple bob a couple of times before he spoke. "I remember," he said.

Her dancing had turned her back to Dougherty. Corso looked out over Cynthia Stone's head. Found Dougherty's eyes. Covered his mouth with his hand.

"You haven't been sleeping with that cow, have

you? She's had her shots, I hope. You haven't caught anything dreadful?"

"Maybe you should ask her."

Corso pointed toward Dougherty in the stern. Stone turned her head. ˙

"Mooooo," Dougherty said from the darkness.

Cynthia Stone's mouth dropped so far open her fillings gleamed in the dull light. She spun back toward Corso. Pulled back her right fist and let it fly. Corso caught it in midair. She brought up a left, but Corso caught that one too. When she tried to knee him in the balls, he deflected the blow with his thigh and pinned her against the sink.

"Don't," he said evenly. "Way I see it, Cynth, you don't have a free one coming from me. You hit me and I'm going to knock you on your ass." He let go of her hands and stepped back.

"You son of a bitch," she spat out. "You're a loser . . . you know that, Frank? A small-time loser. You and your freak there . . . you two . . . you deserve each other."

Cynthia Stone crossed the galley, jerked open the door, and stepped out on deck.

Dougherty walked back into the salon, closing the door behind her.

"That we deserve each other is the best she can do?" she asked.

"She works best from a script," Corso said.

Cynthia Stone's high heels pounded a frantic staccato beat on the slip. Then came a sound, like the dull ring of a cracked bell . . . followed by the rustling of plastic and a sudden sob. Dougherty raised her eyebrows, looked to Corso. His thin lips curled into a smile.

"The anchor," he said.

Dougherty loped across the boat, pulled open the door on the opposite side of the galley just in time to see Cynthia Stone's murky silhouette struggle back to its feet. The apparition swayed for a moment and then began crabbing down the dock. Slowly, placing one foot at a time on the concrete, holding her forehead with one hand while using the other to probe the fog for other unseen impediments. A moment before disappearing into the fog, she stopped and wobbled, as if she might lose it and fall in the lake. Dougherty felt Corso tighten against her back. "Shouldn't we . . . ," she began.

Then Stone was moving again, moaning slightly with each measured step.

Mewing under her breath as she disappeared from view.

"Nah," they said in unison and laughed out loud.

They stood close in the doorway, listening to the scrape of her shoes.

"If she'd hit you, you were going to pop her one, weren't you?"

"Absolutely," he said without a hint of reservation.

"Some folks wouldn't think much of that."

"Some folks don't know Cynthia Stone."

"She was really something in those red undies."

"If you don't think so, just ask her."

"You think you'd have been so holy if I wasn't here?" she asked.

He chuckled. "I'm a slow learner," he said. "But not that slow."

"Hmmm."

They stood in the narrow doorway until they heard

the metallic clank of the gate. Dougherty slid the door closed. Corso's breath tickled the back of her ear. She turned and put her palm on his chest. She watched his eyes fall down the slope of her neck and stop at the top of her breasts. He brought his eyes up. Put his hand on top of hers. She took a breath. Sharp, quick. Tried to pull her hand away, but he held on. She felt the movement of her flesh beneath the dress. How long had it been?

"Don't screw with me, Corso."

A slow smile inched its way across his face, sad and lonely. He reached up and touched her hair. "I don't screw with anybody," he said.

She searched her mind for a sentence. Something with thorns. About how just because Stone had gotten his dander up didn't mean she was going to step into the breach. She opened her mouth to speak but couldn't get past Corso's eyes or the way his hand felt against her hair. She wanted to move away but instead moved closer. Wanted to hide, without relinquishing his gaze.

"Corso . . . it's been . . ." She felt her lips moving closer to his. His hands moved around the back of her neck and pulled. "Corso . . ." Her voice was lost in his mouth. In the crush of lips and teeth, she nearly forgot herself. Pulled away. "If you want me to stop the ama- teur psychoanalysis, all you have to do is ask," she said. Then his mouth was on hers again. She felt his hands run down the curve of her breasts, felt his fingers at her waist. She tried to call out. To tell him to wait. But her voice faded to a whisper. He looked into her eyes and wrapped his fingers around the top button of her dress. One button. Two buttons.

She gulped a bucket of air. "The lights," she said. Corso released her. Reached up. Snapped them into total darkness. In the black, she searched for his lips and pressed herself against him. Their hips met, folded into one another. She felt her body move in the slow give and take of passion. Corso grabbed her hips and backed her against the wall.

Without warning, her knees buckled and she began to slide down the wall. He seemed to have too many hands. He moved with her, rolling the dress from her shoulders as they slid to the floor. She felt her arms pulling free of the fabric, felt his hands reading the tattoos like Braille. Felt the pads of his fingers pause over the occasional welts, trying to follow the design. She groaned.

She raised her hips; the dress disappeared and suddenly they were on the floor, with his lips tracing the etchings on her flesh, moving across the arch of her right breast. Somewhere in the gloom a car alarm began to bray. She felt his breath on her belly and his hand along the inside of her thigh. Her pelvis reached up to meet his touch, pressing her warmth against the soft pad of his hand.

She pushed her hand into Corso's crotch, worked her fingers through the button fly of his jeans. His breath came faster. Louder. He moved against her hand.

She thought she might have called his name. She couldn't be sure. Next thing she knew she was unbuckling his belt, raising her mouth again to his, aware of nothing but the tangy burn between her legs and the continuous shiver shooting past her navel.

Stronger, faster, louder than the shock of memory. She squeezed her eyes shut, almost pushed him off.

And then, he slipped between her thoughts. Inside her, and suddenly she thought of nothing but the slow swing of his rhythm. Felt nothing but the moment's pulse and the skin of a man dancing close to hers.

Chapter 33

She put on the big-time pissy face when he say he doan wanna go to no damn whistle-blower ceremony. "What you mean, you doan wanna go?" Like she got a earwax problem or something. Start puttin' the voice and the brow on him at the same time. "You goin', Robert. You just get that in your mind right now. You goin'. And you getting up there and acceptin' that award all nice and polite like. You hear me, boy?"

He doan say nothin'. Doan help. She keeps on wid the voice.

"For once in your life you do the right thing. Do somethin' make somebody proud of you and you think you ain't going." She wave a finger all up in his face. He feel like breaking the goddamn thing off, chewing it up, and swallowing it.

"You goin'," she say. Like he didn't hear it the first fifteen times she say it.

She told every damn neighbor on the block. "My Bobby getting an award from the mayor himself. Gonna be on TV and all. Two thousand dollars. In the papers. Hepped 'em catch that Trashman guy. Gonna get him a whistle-blower award. Right down at the courthouse. Wednesday morning at ten. Havin' them a big ceremony just for him."

Called Grandma down in Riverside too. Told her the same damn shit. Tell her how that fat Korean, King, Kin, Kim, whatever the hell it is, gonna give her the morning off so's she can go. Said he gonna pay her for the time too, 'cause of having a hero in the family. She promised she'd take pictures and send them on down south to Grandma soon as she got 'em developed.

Shoulda never told Goth Girl and the tall dude nothin'. Assholes sent all them damn cops over here wantin' to know every motherfuckin' thing he saw that night. Askin' the same shit over and over like a bunch of fuckin' retards can't remember what he told 'em five minutes ago. Makin' him sign a paper full of his own words. Shit.

And now she out shoppin' for clothes. So's he'll look like a gentleman, she say. He say he ain't going. She say, "Fine, I'll buy 'em widout your ass." Shit. Shoulda gone with her. Might maybe could have talked her into some of that Tommy Hilfiger stuff like the downtown brothers always sporting. Shit may be lame, but it at least got some ghetto to it.

Screw that whistle-blowing, stoolie-of-the-year, rat-out-your-damn-friends award. Who needs that goddamn thing anyway. Whistle-blower my ass.

Chapter 34

Tuesday, September 25
11:11 A.M.   Day 6 + 3

A husband and a daughter . . . both dead and gone. Alice Doyle wasn't planning on losing anything else. Herds of furniture crammed the rooms. Leaving only narrow, plastic-covered trails to navigate as one moved from place to place. In the living room, the furniture and lampshades had likewise been sealed in plastic like leftover stew.

While she'd busied herself in the kitchen, Corso had toured the room. A million knickknacks and trinkets. Half a dozen photos of Kelly. None of which Corso had seen before. Several of which showed her in a different light than the "Little Miss Vivacious" shot the papers had all been using . . . unsure of herself. Maybe even a bit melancholy.

Two pictures of her late husband, Rodney. One as a young police officer in his dress blues. Another as a middle-aged man in a cardigan, holding a pitchfork, scowling into the lens. The man had changed but the chin remained the same. "Disappointed" was the word that came to mind, as if here was a person who felt slighted because time and circumstance had, for reasons unknown, conspired to grant him less than his allotted share.

His badge lay on the shelf next to the pictures on the wall. Corso had reached to pick it up, but it was stuck to the surface. He'd reached for the glass cat on the shelf above. Same deal. He'd crossed the room and tried elsewhere. Everything was glued to the shelves. Yeah. Alice Doyle was keeping what she had left.

Corso sat back on the couch. He brought the cup to his lips and sipped. Tea. Didn't taste like much of anything. Like the pipes were rusty, maybe.

"Roddy wasn't happy," she was saying. "Not for a long, long time."

They were on their second pot of tea. He hadn't had to ask a question in half an hour. Apparently, Alice Doyle didn't get many visitors.

Corso inhaled just enough tea to wet his teeth. "Not since the war," she went on. "Never had a happy day in his life since he came back from that godforsaken place."

He'd heard it all before. More times than he could count. Something about Vietnam had poisoned half a generation. Taken their visions of heroic charges across open ground and mutated them into long-drawn-out, duck-and-cover jungle skirmishes, around bends in the road and across the rivers, up the sides of slippery hills, which they were ordered to "take" in the face of snipers and mines and machine guns. As if the ground really mattered and they weren't just going to walk back down later, fewer than before.

"You could see . . . as soon as he got back. He was different. Angry. Like somebody I'd never seen be-

fore." She set the cup in the saucer in her lap and stared
off into space. "I remember once . . . right after he got
back. We went to a dance in Volunteer Park and this
man said something—maybe to me, maybe to Roddy, I
don't remember—and Roddy just went off on him. I
can still see the man covering his head and trying to
crawl under a car while Roddy kicked him and spit on
him and called him a son of a bitch. I can still see the
blood on the man's yellow shirt and his pocket change
spilled out on the pavement where he lay." She sighed.
"Just like it was yesterday."

"How old was he when he . . ." Corso let it hang.

"He was thirty-nine. Kelly was fourteen." Her eyes
clouded over. "He took his revolver, went out by the
compost heap, and shot himself in the head. No note.
No good-bye of any kind. No anything. We got half his
pension. The station house took up a collection. Paid
off the house for us."

"How did Kelly take it?"

She set her cup and saucer on the table. Sighed.
"Like girls that age take things like that, Mr. Corso.
They blame themselves. She grew up too fast. Got a lot
wilder. For about five years there, I hardly knew my
own daughter. It was the only time in our lives we
weren't close."

"So . . . at the end . . . you and Kelly were close
again?"

"Like sisters," she said.

"She'd never been married?"

She shook her head and smiled. Started reciting the
lines she'd said so many times before. "She was so demanding. She knew just what she wanted and wasn't

going to settle for anything less. My Kelly was a girl
who knew where she was going."

Corso took another sip. "At the time of her death,
was Kelly involved with anyone?"

She shook her head. "She'd been between
boyfriends for months. She said she was fed up with
relationships that weren't going anywhere."

"You sure?" he asked gently. "You know, sometimes . . ." He waggled a hand. "Sometimes people
don't always share everything with their parents."

She cast Corso a pitying glance and began to clean
up. "There was no reason for Kelly to keep anything
from me. I didn't try to run her life for her. She was a
grown woman." She put Corso's cup and saucer on the
tray and got to her feet. "I didn't care who she dated, as
long as she was happy." She headed for the kitchen.
"She always knew she could have brought home a doctor, a lawyer, or an Indian chief and I'd be happy as
long as she was." She turned around to back through
the swinging door. She cocked an amused eyebrow at
Corso. "As long as it wasn't a cop. There's nothing but
sorrow being married to a cop. Ask me. I know."

She came back through the door wiping her hands
on a black-and-white dish towel.

"You've let me prattle on for over an hour. You're
quite a listener."

Corso smiled.

"In your business, that must be quite an asset. So tell
me, Mr. Corso, do you mind if I ask a question?" He
said he didn't. "So why . . . at this late date . . . what
interest is any of this to you now? The story's over,
isn't it?"

"I thought I might write a book about it," Corso lied.

She brought a hand to her throat. "Lord knows it had enough twists and turns."

"It sure did," he agreed. "A few more than anybody needed," he added.

She had a faraway look in her eyes. "A book would be good," she said. "When it's written down, people don't forget so easily."

"Did she have a best girlfriend? Somebody her own age she was close to?"

Alice Doyle took a deep breath. "Paula Ziller . . . I suppose. They'd known each other since middle school."

"You know where I might be able to find her?"

"She's moved away," she answered absently. "Down to Portland somewhere."

"That's Ziller." He spelled it. She nodded.

"Ah," she said softly and left the room.

When she returned, she carried a Ziplock freezer bag full of greeting cards. Lots of snowflakes and mangers. Alice Doyle sat in the chair opposite Corso, the bag in her lap. "She sent me a card last year," she said, pawing through the bag. "Paula's a nice girl. The kind who remembers to send cards," she mused.

She pulled an oversize red card from the bag and handed it to Corso. The return address sticker had been snipped from the envelope and scotch-taped to the front of the card. Paula Ziller—1840 Harrison Street, Portland, Oregon. Noel.

"You used to be a journalist," Alice Doyle said suddenly.

"At one time, yes."

"Did you ever cover a war?"

"Yes, ma'am. The Gulf War."

She paused to collect herself. "What was it about that Vietnam War that sent them all home so damaged?" she asked finally. "So damaged."

"I think all wars are like that," Corso said. He looked up into the woman's liquid brown eyes. "My family talks about how whatever was kind or decent about my father must have gotten lost in some Korean foxhole. About how the only thing the army shipped home was his whiskey thirst and his mean streak."

"I'm sorry," Alice Doyle said.

"Don't be," Corso said. "He wasn't worth it."

Chapter 35

Tuesday, September 25
6:36 P.M. Day 6 + 3

Maybe losing a friend to a monster permanently heightens the senses. Or maybe she was merely prudent by nature. Either way, Paula Ziller was an exceptionally careful young woman. She stopped the red Ford Taurus well back in the driveway, pushed the garage-door opener, and waited, allowing first the low and then the high beams to play over the empty interior of the garage before easing slowly forward.

Once parked inside, she took her time. Corso watched her eyes play over the rearview mirror as the garage door slid down behind her. A full minute passed before the side yard lit up like a ballpark. Only then did she scurry from the side door of the garage to the back steps, her purse clutched in one hand and her keys at the ready in the other. Little white Mace canister dangling from the key chain. In door. Out lights.

The radio in the rented Ford Explorer had already been tuned to the Portland NPR jazz station when Corso got it from the airport. He'd left it that way.

Tuesday-night blues program. Hank Crawford and
Jimmy McGriff jamming on "The Glory of Love."

Corso groaned as he stretched. His back was tight.
He thought of Dougherty. Remembered the taste of her
mouth. And again felt the imaginary draft he'd felt all
day on the back of his neck, as if he'd left a door ajar
somewhere and the wind had suddenly found access.

Corso checked his watch: 7:40. Two hours since
he'd knocked on the front door and then peeked in the
side window of the garage and found it empty. He
counted to a hundred. And then again. Enough time for
a careful girl to get settled and maybe take a leak. Not
enough to climb into bed.

1840 Harrison Street was a small, postwar starter
home. One story, probably two bedrooms, with a detached garage. The kind of no-frills home once intended to shelter returning GIs and their expectant
families.

Corso stepped up onto the front porch and knocked
twice on the screen door. He heard the padding of feet
and then suddenly the front porch lit up like a runway.
He remembered the Mace and moved as far back from
the door as possible without stepping off the porch.
Held his press credential out in front of him. Winced.

He hadn't noticed the intercom speaker mounted
over the front door. The electronic "What do you
want?" startled him.

"I'm Frank Corso, from the *Seattle Sun*. I got your
name and address from Alice Doyle." He waited, holding the card in front of him like a supplicant and
squinting into the spotlights.

A series of snaps and pops and then the inside door

opened on a security chain. She was short and had at least one brown eye. Maybe five foot three in her stocking feet. Red hair the color of an orangutan. "What do you want?" she said again.

"I'd like to talk to you about Kelly Doyle."

"Put your ID up against the door so I can see it," she said.

Corso stepped forward and pressed the card against the glass of the screen door.

"I'm going to call Mrs. Doyle," she said and closed the door.

Corso could sense that she hadn't walked away. A minute passed; the interior door opened. She reached out and flipped the lock on the screen door.

"If that didn't send you scurrying off, you must be who you say you are. Come in," she said. Corso stepped into the vestibule.

She was built like a gymnast. Not quite stocky, but hard all over. Big close-set ears, big brown eyes, little tiny nose. Maybe a little surgery, Corso figured.

She picked apologetically at her battered flannel nightgown. "Sorry about the frumpy," she said. "I had a bad day at work. I was going to nuke something to eat and then get in bed and read."

"It's stunning," he assured her.

She looked down at the orange sweat socks on her feet. "Especially the socks," she said. "Very haute."

"My thoughts precisely," he said.

She looked him over. "Are you always this easy to please?" she asked with a teasing twinkle in her eyes.

"I'm a prince," Corso said. "Ask anybody."

"Yeah." She laughed. "I'll just bet you are. Come on." She led him down a central hall to the brightly lit kitchen at the back of the house. Yellow fifties dinette set. Bright blue dishes and glasses inside four-pane kitchen cabinets. New appliances and sink, old linoleum and light fixtures. Ethan Allen meets Ikea.

She gestured toward one of the chairs. Corso said he'd rather stand.

She leaned back against the counter. "You said you wanted to talk about Kelly."

"If you don't mind."

"But . . . I saw on the news that . . . the police killed the guy."

"They did."

"Then what's to talk about?"

"It's pretty complicated . . . but to make a long story short, I'm not altogether sure I think Kelly was killed by the same person who killed the rest of the girls."

Her dark eyes flashed. "They said there was no doubt about it."

"Who said?"

"The Seattle police."

"You spoke with them?"

"I sure did."

"When was this?"

"Over three years ago. As soon as I heard Kelly was dead. I called to tell them what I knew, but they said they had evidence that made it certain Kelly was killed by the same person who'd killed all those other poor girls."

Corso spread his hands. "I'm not sure," he said.

"Neither was I," she said. "That's why I called and sent the letter."

"What letter?"

"About Kelly's mystery man."

"Maybe you better start at the beginning."

"Coffee?" she asked.

He said no.

She poured herself a cup, and again leaned back against the counter. "You have to understand Kelly, Mr. Corso." Paula Ziller sighed. "Kelly had a knack for losers. I never understood why. She was beautiful and smart and vivacious and everything most girls wish they were and yet . . . if you put her in a room with a dozen men, she'd always pick the loser. The guy who hadn't had a job in five years . . . the guy with five kids who claimed he wasn't married. Every time." She waved her coffee cup. "Like on some level or other she was looking for something she just couldn't find."

"Like a father, maybe," Corso suggested.

She nodded. "I never thought of it that way. But . . . yeah . . . maybe," she said.

"So anyway."

"So . . . it was right at the time I was in the process of moving from Seattle down here to Portland. Kelly had this hot and heavy romance going on with some guy." She made a wry face. "Very hush-hush. Her mother couldn't know about it or anything. I figured the guy must be married. One of those 'My wife doesn't understand me, we'll be divorcing soon' types."

"Mrs. Doyle says her daughter shared everything with her."

"That was one of the weird things about the whole deal. Usually she did. Kelly dated African Americans. She was engaged to a Chinese guy for a while." She made a face. "All of which was okay with her mom.

But not this one. For some reason, this one was strictly off-limits to everybody . . . even me."

"Then how come you know?"

"Because it started to get ugly."

"Ugly how?"

"Ugly like all of a sudden, out of the blue, he says he's going to marry somebody else. He says it was some sort of family obligation or something. Like he had no choice. Like he had to do it or else."

"And?"

"Kelly was crazy about him. Desperate."

"So?"

She raised her eyebrows. "She told him she was pregnant."

"She wasn't."

"How do you know?"

"I've read the autopsy report."

She looked away for a moment and then took a long sip from her cup.

"Then she told him she was going to his girlfriend. When she told him that, I guess he came unglued and threatened her. Said he wasn't going to let her ruin his life. Said he'd put a stop to her if she tried."

"How?"

"I don't know. That's all she said."

"And you have no idea who this guy was?"

She shook her head. "A name . . . no . . . but I think I may have seen him once," she said. "Right before I moved. I stopped in some little hole-in-the-wall deli in Wallingford. Inside that old school they renovated into a shopping center."

Corso said he knew the place.

"She was sitting at a table with this guy I'd never seen before. A fox. They were arguing. You could feel it in the air. The other people in the place were embarrassed for them." She let a hand drop noisily to her side. "I backed right out the door. I felt like I was intruding on something."

"And you never mentioned it to her?"

Her eyes clouded over. "That was the last time I ever saw her alive." She turned and emptied the dregs of her cup down the drain. "I'll tell you though, Mr. . . ."

"Corso," he filled in.

"I've carried Kelly and what happened to her with me every day of my life since then." She searched him with her eyes. "I've never quite felt safe since."

Corso knew the feeling. The moment when the last remnants of childhood optimism finally disappear down the drain like tepid coffee.

"So when she turned up dead, you notified the police."

"I called and sent a letter."

"You have a copy of the letter?"

"Somewhere."

Corso reached into the inside pocket of his jacket, pulled out a handful of newspaper. Folded both the headlines and the captions over, so only the photographs remained visible.

"The guy in the deli. Was it any of these guys?" he asked, turning the first picture her way. She shook her head. He showed her another picture. Same result. Then the third. She nearly put her nose on the paper. Pointed.

"Second guy from the left," she said.

Chapter 36

Wald slipped onto the stool next to Corso. Ordered a cup of coffee and an English muffin from the gold-toothed counterman.

"What? There weren't enough shit-hole eateries downtown? You had to drag me all the way out to hell and gone?"

"I figured you might not want to be seen with me."

"At last," Wald said, "an area of agreement." He took in the place. Sighed. "Nice ambience. Kind of retro–industrial waste."

Hector's Lunch was nestled in the shadow of the West Seattle Highway. Catering to the longshoremen of pier eighteen, it opened at five and closed at two. At 11 A.M. on a Wednesday, they were too late for breakfast and too early for lunch. Except for a bearded senior citizen snoring in a booth over by the men's room, they had the place to themselves.

The counterman set Wald's order on the counter and disappeared through the door to the kitchen. "So . . .

you and your girlfriend decide you don't want to go
along with the program anymore?"

"Nope," said Corso. "A deal's a deal."

Wald took a bite out of his English muffin. Washed
it down with coffee.

Corso slid the picture across the counter at Wald.
Crime-scene photo. Head shot.

"Kate Mitchell. Victim number two."

Wald gave it a cursory glance. Bit off another piece
of muffin. "So?"

"Notice the lovely ear tag."

"The accessory no girl should be without."

"Here's the SPD list of what's supposed to be in the
bag: 'one watch, Timex; one gold bracelet; one gold
cross and chain; two toe rings; one plastic ear tag,
ovine.' Here's Dougherty's picture of what's *actually*
still in Kate Mitchell's evidence file. Day before yesterday. Two toe rings. A gold cross and chain, and a gold
bracelet, and a wristwatch." He waited. "No ear tag."

More muffin, more coffee. "She musta missed it,"
the cop insisted.

Corso plopped two more pictures on top of the first.
"Here's two other angles. No ear tag. She didn't miss it."

This time Wald studied all three photos, then turned
them upside down on the counter. "Anything could
have happened. Maybe it got sent for testing and never
got returned. Maybe it's in somebody else's file. Who
the fuck knows?"

"Whoever took it out of the file knows."

Wald's posture stiffened. The implication was clear.
The SPD property room wasn't exactly the public library. "Now why would anybody want to do a thing
like that?"

"So they could accessorize Kelly Doyle with it."

Wald stopped mid-munch. "To what purpose?" he asked tentatively.

"To make damn sure she was listed as a Trashman victim."

"Who says she wasn't?"

"I do."

He finished chewing. Finished the coffee. Looked Corso in the eye.

"You got somebody specific in mind? Or you just talking out your ass?"

"I'll tell you a little story, and then you tell me."

"Have at it."

"I talked to a woman named Paula Ziller last night. She's a securities analyst, lives down in Portland. Used to be Kelly Doyle's best friend." Wald stopped swirling the dregs of his coffee and locked his eyes on Corso, as if daring him to continue. Instead, Corso pulled two pieces of folded paper from his coat pocket. Held them between his middle and index fingers and offered them to the cop. Wald pulled his head back, as if Corso was trying to hand him a weasel. Then finally reached out and plucked the pages from Corso's fingers. Flattened them on the counter and began to read. He read both pages once and then started at the beginning and went through them again.

"Sound like anybody we know?" Corso asked.

"Sounds like a whole lotta people."

"That letter isn't in Kelly Doyle's file."

"How—" he began.

"I've got a copy of the file, remember? You and I xe-roxed it with our own little hands."

Wald went silent.

"You know her father?" Corso asked.

"The Doyle girl?"

"Yeah."

"He was just before my time. I hear he went sideways with his piece."

"The Ziller woman says Kelly Doyle dated most of the known world and none of it was a problem for her mother. Both she and the mother claim they were real close. Shared everything."

"I'm touched. I really am, but you got a point here, Corso?"

"Mama Doyle told me there was only one kind of man her daughter best never bring home."

"What kind was that?"

"A cop."

Wald shrugged and turned away. "Who can blame her? I'm bettin' my wife feels the same way about our daughters."

Wald winced when Corso pulled a newspaper photo from the same pocket.

"I showed the Ziller woman this."

Wald looked like he wanted to close his eyes and put his fingers in his ears.

"She says the second guy on the left is the guy she saw Kelly Doyle arguing with, a week before she died."

Wald shot the photo a quick glance and then pulled a napkin from the dispenser and dabbed at his lips.

"What did I ever do to deserve you?" he muttered.

"I want to see the property room log books for the two days between when Himes was arrested and Kelly Doyle was found."

Wald blew a long whistle. Scratched the back of his neck.

"You realize what you're asking me to do?"

"I'm asking you to put a murderer where he belongs."

"Says you."

"We can sure as hell find out, now can't we?"

"There's gotta be some other explanation."

"I'm all ears, Wald. What you got in mind?"

He used his forefinger to pick at the sore on his lip. "Lotta people have access to the property room."

"Do they all sign in?"

"As far as I know."

"And they have to sign out for specific items. Just like you and I had to do the other day."

"Far as I know."

"Then why not have a look?" Before he could object, Corso went on. "If you're right and you have a look and his name's not there, then we can let this whole thing settle. If you find what I'm saying you're going to find, then it's a grounder, right? I mean . . . what are the chances? We've got a two-day time window from the day Himes was arrested till the day Kelly Doyle was found. How many people can have signed out for that particular piece of property, within that period of time?"

"And if it's there?"

"Then have a look at the sign-outs for Kelly Doyle's file. If we get a doubleheader, then it's a slam dunk. We explain all the ten brides stuff. We explain the missing set of clothes. We explain the missing tag and the letter. Neat as can be. End of story. Our boy inherits Himes's seat on the gurney."

Wald wiped the corners of his mouth with his thumb and forefinger.

"This is bad juju, Corso," he said. "In case you forgot, we got a funeral for a dead cop this afternoon." He wagged a finger Corso's way. "A cop who, at the time of his death, was my partner." He paused to let it sink in. "We got a general public still wants to fry Walter Himes. A million people who don't give a rat's ass we took the real perp down. They still want Himes dead. Period." He waved a thick hand. "Instead, they turn on the tube and there's Himes sitting up in Harborview on their dime. Stuffin' his face and talking to the press about what he's gonna do with all the money he gets from the city." He waved again. "Downtown is like a fucking circus. Kesey tried to fire a secretary for dripping coffee on his desk. Everybody is out of their minds. Scared shitless." Wald looked away. "I've got eighteen years of my life into this. I'm thirty-six hours from being promoted to lieutenant when I really ought to get fired or sent back to foot patrol and, all of a sudden, the whole department looks like a joke. A sideshow. Like we're the fucking Keystone Kops or something."

"You know I'm right," Corso said.

"Oh . . . you're a mind reader now too. You know what I'm thinking."

Wald's face was blank, but the tips of his ears were bright red.

"Holy Mary mother of God," he said. Checked his watch.

He threw a five-dollar bill on the counter. Pinned Corso with his glare.

"Shift changes at twelve-thirty. I'll have a look then,

but I'm telling you, man, I hope to God you're wrong," he said.

"Tell you the truth, Wald, I kinda hope so too. This story doesn't need any more twists and turns."

Wald jammed his hands in his overcoat pockets. "Gimme a number. I'll call you after the funeral."

Corso watched him leave. Pulled the phone from his pocket and dialed Dougherty's number again. Same deal. Just rings forever. Unplugged.

The counterman reappeared; he pulled a gray plastic tub from beneath the counter and set Wald's dishes inside. "How's the chili?" Corso asked the kid.

"Canned," the kid said with a glint.

"Gimme a bowl and a large glass of milk."

Chapter 37

Butler Parking Garage. All the way down to the bottom, he'd said. Five floors. As close to three o'clock as he could make it.

The oily grit on the floor caused Corso's shoes to slip with nearly every step. The place smelled like they'd used urine instead of water to mix the concrete. The only parked car was a '69 Pontiac convertible. Red. Ghetto sled extraordinaire. All fins and flourishes. The four flat tires and the inch and a half of dust suggested it had been a while since this baby had cruised the Malt Shoppe.

Two thirds of the way down his esophagus, the glass of milk was losing a titanic battle with the chili. Felt like he had a candle in his chest. Shoulda held the onions.

It was seven after three when a dim green bulb came on over the elevator. The door slid back with a bump, but nobody stepped out. From where he was, Corso could just make out the tip of a toe holding the door open.

The sound of his slipping shoes ricocheted around the walls as he made his way over. Wald. Standing at the front of the elevator car. Fresh from the funeral in his dress blues. Sick expression on his face.

"I want two promises from you," he said.

"Like?"

"First I want to make damn sure I'm clean on these." He waved a large manila envelope. "They're clean from my end. You make sure they stay clean from yours. It gets out I had anything to do with this, I might as well just transfer to internal affairs with the rest of the rats."

"You have my word on it. What else?"

Wald stared at Corso long and hard. "I want to hear that I won't be seeing you again. Or hearing from you. Or anything. This needs to be the last time I ever lay eyes on you."

Corso grinned. "You could hurt a guy's feelings talking like that, Wald."

The cop stiffened. "I'm not in the mood, Corso. I buried a fellow officer this afternoon. The fact that I didn't much like him or that you didn't much like him or that he wasn't much of a cop . . . you know . . . somehow, when it came to putting him in the ground, none of that mattered. He still had parents and a sister and her kids sitting there. And his dying still"—he searched for a word—"diminishes . . . his death diminishes all of us. Individually and as a department." He held out the brown envelope. Grimaced. "And now I'm going to contribute to this debacle," he said disgustedly. "As if we don't look bad enough already."

Corso took hold of the envelope. Wald hung on. The envelope swung between them, like one of those old pictures of the Great White Father and the Indians signing a treaty and then holding it up for all to see.

"I thought about lying to you. Telling you it wasn't there. But you're so goddamn insistent, you'd just get somebody else to check it out for you. I thought about tearing out the pages. Burning them. Telling you to go fuck yourself."

"So . . . what stopped you?"

"I don't know," he said after a moment. "I really don't."

Wald released his grip on the envelope. Corso let it fall to his side. Wald opened his mouth to speak, thought better of it. Punched the button.

She picked it up on the tenth ring.

"Yeah."

"Hey," he said.

"Hey yourself."

"How you doin'?"

"Fine. You?"

"I'm a little sore," he said. "Musta used a few muscles I haven't used in quite a while."

She laughed. "One in particular."

"That one's fine. It's the rest of me that's broke down."

"Must be middle age," she teased.

A crackle of static ran through the line and then faded to silence.

"I've been calling—" he began.

"I had it unplugged."

They both spoke at once; he heard her laugh.

"About the other night . . ." she began.

"What night was that?"

"Don't start with me, Corso."

"You always say that."

"I don't generally drink that much."

"Do we have to talk about it?"

"Yes, Corso . . . I know it's your worst nightmare, but we do."

"Then let's do it in person," Corso said. "I'd feel better about it that way."

"I've got a lot to do today."

"Dinner?"

Pause. "Where?"

"Depends on what you're in the mood to eat."

"Red meat," she said. "And thick red wine."

"Metropolitan Grill. Eight o'clock."

"Corso . . . you know, just because we . . . we . . . you know . . . doesn't mean we have to make like we're going steady or anything."

Longer pause. "Look . . . if you don't want to . . ."

"I didn't say that."

"Eight o'clock."

"Hawes."

"Corso."

"What—you've had a change of heart and want to get back into the newspaper game?"

"Maybe we get you that Pulitzer nomination after all."

"How so?"

"Maybe help your boy Newton make his bones while we're at it."

"I'm all ears."

Except for a single "holy shit," muttered about halfway through, he stayed that way until Corso finished talking.

"Wait a second," he said. A series of clicks came over the line. Two minutes passed. Then Hawes's voice again. "Mrs. V.'s on with us," he said.

"And you've got all this documented?" she wanted to know.

"Big as life. I've got copies of the evidence room sign-out sheets for both files. He signed the Mitchell woman's file out the day after Himes was arrested. He's checked the Doyle file nearly twice a month for over three years."

"Will your source come forward, if necessary?" she asked.

"No. My source is untouchable. If we're not prepared to go to the wall to protect the source, then we should drop a quarter and give the story away."

They thought it over. "What did you have in mind for breaking the story?" she asked.

Corso told her. Hawes whistled. "You are a trouble-maker, aren't you?"

"It's more dramatic that way. They always field questions at the end. All the local affiliates will have a team there. That way, Newton's face ends up all over the evening news. Get his name in the lead paragraph in every paper, coast to coast."

"And what do you get out of this?" Hawes asked.

"I get to crawl back under my rock."

"I wish we had more," Mrs. V. said.

"Don't we always."

"You're doing that 'we' thing again," Hawes said.

"I've got an idea, though."

"Shoot."

"Let me ask you a question, Hawes. If you were stepping out on your wife, how would you handle it."

"I'd double my life insurance. Louise ever caught me—"

"Seriously. If you were conducting a little liaison on the side, where would you meet your sweetie? Would you find a little love nest, where nobody knows either of you and stick with it? Meet there all the time? Or would you move around from place to place, for a little variety?"

"I'd find a place and stick with it."

"Me too," said Corso.

"Wallingford."

"That's it. Send Newton and anybody else you can spare. Have them show pictures around. Especially the hotels and motels. She lived with her mother. He was creeping around on his girlfriend. They had to be doing the hokeypokey somewhere. Chances are that if the Ziller woman saw them together, so did somebody else."

"You know, Mr. Corso . . . whether Mr. Newton or anyone else breaks the news, the smart money is going to figure the story came through you."

"They'll have to find me."

Chapter 38

Thursday, September 27
9:23 A.M. Day 6 + 5

At the Fairway buoy, less than fifty feet of water slipped beneath the hull. He reached up and set the autopilot for 3:39. Magnetic. The twin Lehman diesels purred at two thousand RPMs. Turning into the wind at a stately twelve knots, the bow plowed contentedly into endless rows of rising green waves, which curled but did not break. Overhead, the sun looked like a tarnished nickel trying desperately to assert itself in a silver sky. The water ahead shimmered with silver light.

The depth sounder began to question itself as the bottom fell away. Sixty-five feet and then a hundred and five. One-fifty. And then suddenly the sounder lost touch. Its ultrasonic impulses no longer able to bounce off the rapidly retreating bottom.

To the east, the Magnolia Bluffs loomed white against the haze. He lifted the binoculars. Picture windows and planter boxes. Glass-topped tables and furled umbrellas. Hawaiian torches around the patio. An empty hammock hanging thick and wet between two trees.

The sounder chattered again at two hundred feet, began to spew random numbers and then slid into a sustained electronic beep. He reached up and switched it off.

"What's that thing's problem?" she asked.

"The bottom's too deep to read."

"So how do you keep track of how deep it is?"

"You read the chart."

She sat and peered at the chart for a moment, then pointed with a long fingernail. "Is this where we are?"

He bent and looked down at the chart table. "Yeah. The depth is the black numbers."

"Six hundred feet," she said tentatively.

"That's about right," he said. "It falls away in a big hurry."

She rolled open the starboard door and gazed out at the blots of half-million-dollar houses covering the side of the hill, half a mile away. "You think they know?" she asked. "You know, that they're like sitting there and right out here under the water it's like the end of the world. Like the abyss."

"Nah," he said. "They're just pleased to have front-row seats for the surface of things."

They were across the shipping channel now, pointed directly at Kingston and the Kitsap Peninsula, where a pair of ferries looped gracefully around each other. She got to her feet and put an arm around his waist, slid her hand down inside the right-hand pocket of his jeans. He moved his left hand up under her hair to the back of her neck. With his right hand, he disengaged the autopilot. Took the wheel, aiming at an imaginary point in the silver foam between the ferries.

Chapter 39

Dorothy Sheridan straightened the red-white-and-blue bunting, tapped the microphones one last time, and then stepped down from the stage. The interview with Taylor and Abrams had gone well. Monica had called Tuesday night to say T. and A., as she liked to call them, were going to make Dorothy an offer, but it was Thursday, and she hadn't heard anything. A timid voice in her head kept saying that maybe it was all for the best.

She checked her notes. First it was the kid. Robert Boyd. He was Seifort's baby. The mayor's Whistle-blower's Award. Stanley'd say a few words, hand the kid the plaque and the check, and then it was her turn with the Post guy. Good Citizen Award. That was easy. She'd seen it for herself. Been there when he'd tackled poor Mr. Nisovic. Give him the check and the medal and then hand off to Chief Kesey. Promotion for Sergeant Wald and a valor commendation for Chucky Donald. She shook her head in wonder. The only thing funnier than a *Seattle Sun* employee getting an award

from the mayor was Chucky Donald getting anointed
for valor.

"What if somebody see me," he demanded, "lookin'
like a goddamn FBI agent?" Put on the pissy face right
away. "Those down-at-the-heel little bums you hang
out wid." She bust up laughing. "Tommy Hutton's
mama din bring so many 'uncles' home, him and his
sisters woulda starved years ago. None of them you
hang out wid got any room to talk. Them people
oughta be happy jus havin' 'somethin' new for a
change." She laughed again.

Bitch really think she funny this morning. True
about Tommy's mama, though. Woman ought to have
her one of those little red dispenser things like in the
bakery. Numba nineteen. Nineteen. He put a hand over
his mouth so she couldn't see his lips. They hadn't
talked about the money yet, neither. Know she gonna
want him to put it in the bank . . . for college or some
such shit. He smiled behind his hand. Check gonna be
made out to him, though, so there's hope.

Her fingers worked at his throat.

"Daddy, we have *got* to fix that tie."

Bill Post squinted into the bathroom mirror. "What's
the matter with it?"

"It only comes halfway down your shirt, for Pete's
sake. It's supposed to reach the top of your belt buckle.
You look like Oliver Hardy."

"Is that the fat one or the skinny one?"

"The fat one."

Rachael ducked between his pants legs and came up
under the pedestal sink. With the three of them jammed

into the tiny bathroom, all Bill Post could do was turn
in a circle. Nancy slid the tie out from under his collar.
Tied it around her own neck and then slipped it over
his head. She turned up his stiff collar. "You look like a
conductor," she said.

"Railroad?"

"Orchestra."

She rearranged the collar. Slipped the knot into
place at Bill Post's throat. "There," she said, patting his
jacket into place. "Now you look like a hero."

It was going well. The police auditorium in the Alaska
Building was only about a quarter full, which was fine
with Dorothy. She figured the recent hurricane of excitement had kept the crowd down. No parents of survivors, either. Thank goodness.

She'd done the introductions without flubbing anything. Seifort was working his way up to handing the
Boyd kid the loot. Dorothy Sheridan pulled a single
blue notecard from her pocket. Bill Post. Post no Bills
came to mind, and she smiled.

"What we need, ladies and gentlemen," Hizhonor
was saying, "is more young men like Robert Boyd.
Young men with a sense of purpose and a sense of
community." The kid sat there scowling into his lap. "It
is with great pride that I introduce the recipient of this
year's Whistle-blower Award—Mr. Robert Boyd."

The mayor offered the plaque. The kid reached over
and grabbed the check instead. He carefully stashed
the check in the inside pocket of his sport coat and then
accepted the plaque from Stanley. Big photo-op hand-
shake. The kid exits stage left. His mother's been saving a seat for him at the end of the third row. She

throws an arm around his shoulder, drawing him close.
He looks embarrassed. Just like Brandy.

"And now, ladies and gentlemen, to present our next
award, Seattle Police Department spokesperson
Dorothy Sheridan."

Seems the big old doofus tackled some guy with a gun.
Same guy shot that liver-lips Himes asshole. She
sayin' he might have saved the lives of a whole room
fulla people, but he can't figure out why they make a
fuss about anybody for saving that piece-of-shit
Himes. Oughta give the fucker wid the gun the medal.
Oughta give me the money.

She ain't said nothin' about the money, but that sure
as hell ain't gonna last. She kept tryin' to talk in his ear
but he's making like he's digging every word they say
onstage and can't listen to her right now.

The red-headed lady was saying, "On behalf of the
Seattle Police Department and the people of King
County, I would like to present the Good Citizen
Award to Mr. Bill Post."

Doofus bust a move up to the front, grab his loot,
thank about three hundred fucking people and then, finally, they're applauding again.

We should go now, he's thinkin'. No reason to sit
through this cop shit. He looks up at her. She's reading
his mind. Pissy look. Shit.

Bill Post hung the silver medal around Rachael's neck.
She pulled it back off and dropped it on the floor with
a clang. He grunted as he bent to retrieve it. He
dropped it in the breast pocket of his sport coat. She'd
been sitting quietly for a long time now and was get-

ting itchy. He pulled her into his lap, where she squirmed like a fish. Just about done. Both cops had gotten their awards. Chief Kesey was going on. "Without the efforts of dedicated professional law-enforcement officers such as these, we would no longer have a society in which we could reasonably have any hope of realizing our dreams or the dreams of our children." Rachael slid onto the floor and began playing with her shoes. The applause rose and then faded as the police spokeslady, whose name Bill Post couldn't, for the life of him, recall at the moment, came forward and called for questions. What was the current status of Slobodan Nisovic? Mr. Nisovic was still in Harborview Medical Center. In serious but stable condition. Charges? Charges would be decided by the district attorney's office. What about Himes? Was either Donald or Wald being reassigned? Another half a dozen questions and then a lull. Post picked Rachael up and bounced her on his knee. Nancy grabbed her purse from the floor.

"If there are no further questions," the woman said, "I'd like to thank you all—"

A pink-cheeked guy rose from the audience. "Blaine Newton from the *Seattle Sun*," he said. "I have a question for Chief Kesey."

A Pound of Cure

God only knows what he was thinking. There must have been eighty people in the room. Forty of them cops. Maybe the collective pressure just got to be too much for him and he slipped a cog or something. Or maybe, as rumor around the department had it, he'd had a sudden vision of what his life in prison was going to look like. Either way, anything would have been better than what he did.

Chief Kesey stepped up to the microphone. Blaine Newton turned a page on his clipboard, cleared his throat, and said, "Chief Kesey, I was wondering if you were aware of the fact that at the time of her death, victim number eight, Kelly Doyle, was conducting an affair with Lieutenant Charles Donald?"

Kesey went white. "Excuse me, what did you—"

"I asked you if you were aware of the fact that Lieutenant Donald and Trashman victim number eight, Kelly Doyle, were conducting an affair at the time of her death, in nineteen ninety-eight."

The Sheridan woman stepped forward. "Surely, Mr. . . ."

"Newton."

"Surely, Mr. Newton, there must be some more ap-

propriate venue for these sorts of unfounded allega-
tions, than a moment such as—"

Newton had begun to sweat profusely. His voice
rose an octave. He was reading now. "You might be interested to know that the *Seattle Sun* has obtained depositions from nine past and present employees of the
Emerald Inn on Stone Way attesting to the fact that in
early nineteen ninety-eight Detective Donald and
Kelly Doyle met for afternoon liaisons on an average
of three to four times a week. Sometimes more."

"You're a damn liar," Kesey shouted.

Every camera in the room was grinding. Newton
wiped his brow with his forarm. Kesey turned away
from the audience. Said something. Neither the microphones nor the cameras picked up what he said. Those
on the stage at the time later agreed that he'd been
talking to Donald. "Tell him he's a goddamn liar,"
he'd said.

Newton was talking again. "Copies of the Seattle
Police Department's evidence room log books reveal
that—"

At that point, Donald lost his marbles. Grabbed the
Sheridan woman by the back of her hair, pulled her to
his chest, and put a gun in her ear. "Keep away from
me," he said as he backed down the stairs, dragging
Sheridan along with him. Her eyes were squeezed
shut. Her lips moved as if in prayer. "Keep away from
me," he said again, grinding the pistol into the
woman's head.

"Let her go," someone screamed.

"Now," another voice shouted.

Most of the civilians were either huddled on the
floor or sprinting for the doors at the back of the room.

The rest of the crowd had guns out. The screaming to let her go came now from a dozen throats as Donald began to back down the aisle.

That's when the Post guy got to his feet and started for Donald. Musta thought his shiny new silver medal made him bulletproof or something. "Now listen here . . . ," he said, reaching a big red hand out for Donald.

Donald shot him once in the heart. The old guy clutched his chest in disbelief, staggered backward into the row of folding chairs, and went down in a clatter. A woman dropped to her knees beside the old man. A little girl in a pink dress and white tights began to cry. A chorus of shouts. To put down the gun . . . to let her go now . . . roared, octaves below the girl's high-pitched wail.

From there on, it was like a collage. Each of the three television cameras in the room was focused on something different. The local ABC affiliate stayed with Donald as he continued to edge toward the side door of the auditorium, with the Sheridan woman locked behind his forearm. He reached back and grabbed the door handle.

Some instinct in the Sheridan woman told her she'd be better off in a room full of cops. For the first time since the ordeal began, she opened her eyes. What she saw was the black nostrils of a dozen gun barrels pointed her way. Her reaction to the sight saved her life. She fainted dead away. Dropped to the floor so quickly that Donald was left staring down in disbelief at her motionless body.

Except for Donald, everybody in the room who was holding a gun used it. Sounded like some sort of salute.

Donald was dead before he hit the floor. Calls for aide wagons and backup were being shouted in from all over the room. Cops were herding civilians and news crews out the back of the room. The woman and the girl pitched a fit, wouldn't leave the old man. The cops let 'em stay.

Outside in the hall, CBS filled its feel-good quota with pictures of Robert Boyd—recipient of the mayor's Whistle-blower's Award—with his arms around his sobbing mother, patting her back and reminding her that they were both all right.

NBC was still inside the auditorium when the first gurney arrived and was waved toward Bill Post. NBC swung its camera in time to see a pair of EMTs push their way through a circle of cops to reach Dorothy Sheridan's side. They quickly checked for wounds. Found none. Pulse. Strong. One lifted up Sheridan's head. The other ran something under her nose. She frowned and shook her head. Ran a hand over her face and then suddenly sat up. She looked over her shoulder. A circle of feet obscured Donald's mangled body. She hiccuped once and covered her mouth.

When she turned back, Chief Kesey had taken one of her hands. The camera mike wasn't close enough to pick up what she said, but even amateur lip readers could plainly make out the words. "I quit."

When he swung back to Bill Post, they were performing CPR. Fifteen and a breath. Fifteen and a breath. Serious head shaking. Fifteen and a breath. Fifteen and a breath. Suddenly the chest compression guy stopped. Put his hand flat on the chest. Then replaced his hand with his ear. "He's breathing again," he announced.

His partner clapped an oxygen mask on Bill Post's

face and then began carefully separating the folds of
the old man's clothes. Gently probing for the wound.
Sport coat unbuttoned and parted. Same for the shirt.
Undershirt ignominiously pulled up along his torso
and bunched beneath his southernmost chin. The EMT
frowned. He looked up at his buddy and said, "Nothing. Not a mark on him."

The other guy checked his pulse and then listened to
his heart. "He's doing fine."

Together they carefully rolled him over. Same deal.
They pulled his undershirt back down and rolled him
onto his back. Felt around in the shirt. Then in the sport
coat. The chest compresser's hand came out of the coat
with the silver Good Citizen Award in it. The once-
symmetrical silver disk had been warped into the
shape of a wavy potato chip.

"Bullet hit this," he announced. "Saved his life."

By the time they had Bill Post strapped to a gurney
and rolling toward the doors, his eyes were open and
the room was empty. Most of the throng had followed
Donald's body out the door. The stragglers left with
Post. An officer poked his head in.

"We need to seal the room," he said.

NBC nodded, gathered his stuff. As he stepped into
the hall, the Boyd kid came sauntering over. "Left my
jacket in there," he said.

"Sorry . . . you'll have to—" the cop began.

"Robert here won the mayor's Whistle-blower
Award today," NBC said.

"Did you, now?" the cop said.

"Sure did," the kid replied.

The cop smiled down at Robert. Pulled the door
open. "Hurry up, now. Go get it." The kid ducked inside.

"It true what they say? We had cops killing cops in there?"

NBC nodded. "You wanna see it?" he asked.

The cop looked around the chaotic hallway. "Sure," he said.

NBC turned the camera on. Rewound to when Kesey stepped up to answer the question, then turned the screen to face the cop. His face sagged as he watched the three minutes of tape.

"Jesus," he said.

The door opened and Robert Boyd appeared, wearing a brown-plaid wool jacket. As the door eased closed, NBC noticed a sudden flash of gold, like a fish rising in a stream. He watched Robert Boyd kindly take his distraught mother by the arm and help her down the hall to the corner, where he looked back with a barracuda smile before steering his mom toward the front doors.

NBC pulled open the auditorium door and peered inside. Right between the state seal and the city seal. Big, thick, gold letters. The tail of the *Y* looped around to make a circle.

In Frank Corso, G. M. Ford has created
the kind of character who allows you to get to know him
just enough to ensure that he's got your attention,
but not enough to guess what makes him tick.
If you're dying to know Corso better,
you won't want to miss

Black River

Available in hardcover
from William Morrow

What starts out as a botched "hit"
turns into the beginning of a complex and twisted trail,
as Corso pieces together some shady dealings
involving a local thug who's facing 63 counts of murder.
When Corso's friend Meg Dougherty ends up in the ICU,
Frank is determined to make sense out of the madness
and dish out his own brand of justice . . .

Wednesday, July 27, 2000
5:23 A.M.

Like nearly everyone born in the tin shacks that line the banks of the Rio Cauto, Gerardo Limon was short, dark, and bandy-legged. A textbook cholo, Limon was less than a generation removed from the jungle and thus denied even the pretense of having measurable quantities of European blood, a deprivation of the soul which, for all his adult life, had burned in his chest like a candle. That his partner, Ramon Javier, was tall, elegant, and obviously of Spanish descent, merely added fuel to the flame.

Gerardo shouldered his way into the orange coveralls and then buckled the leather toolbelt about his waist. A sticky valve in the truck's engine ticked in the near darkness. Twenty yards away, Ramon spaced the trio of orange traffic cones across the mouth of the driveway leading to the back of the Briarwood Garden Apartments.

The kill zone was perfect. The driveway had two nearly blind turns. This end of the building had no windows. To the North, a half a mile of marsh separated the apartments from the Speedy Auto Parts outlet up the road.

"You wanna pitch or catch?" Gerardo asked.

"Who was up last?" Ramon wanted to know.

"We turned two, remember."

Last time out, they'd encountered an unexpected visitor and had to play an impromptu doubleheader. Ramon's thin lips twisted into a smile as he recalled the last time they'd worn these uniforms. As he settled the toolbelt on his hips, he wondered how many times they'd run their "utility repairmen" number. Certainly dozens. He'd lost count years ago.

Ramon Javier liked to think he might have become a doctor. Or a jazz musician. Or maybe even a baseball player. If things had been different. If his family had made it to Miami the first time. If they hadn't been dragged back to that stinking island and treated like pig shit for five years.

Ramon settled the yellow hard hat onto his head and then checked the load in the twenty-two automatic, screwed the CAC22 suppressor carefully onto the barrel and then slipped the weapon through the loop in the tool belt generally reserved for the hammer.

He checked his watch. "Three minutes," he said. "What will it be?"

"Whatever you want," Gerardo said. "I don't care."

"Don't forget, we got orders to lose the truck," Ramon said.

Gerardo shrugged. "You pitch. I'll catch."

Wednesday, July 27, 2000
5:24 A.M.

The kitchen floor squeaked as he made his way over to the refrigerator. He removed a brown paper sack, set it on the counter and checked inside. Two sandwiches. Olive loaf and American cheese on white. A little salt, a little pepper and just a dab of Miracle Whip. Satisfied, he grabbed the plastic water bottle from the refrigerator, stuffed it into the pocket of his jacket and headed for the door.

Overhead, the Milky Way was little more than a smear across the sky. Too many lights, too many people, too much smog for the stars. He used his key to open the truck door. The seventy-nine Toyota pick-up, once bright yellow, had oxidized to a shade more reminiscent of uncleaned teeth.

The engine started at the first turn of the key. He smiled as he raced the motor and fiddled with the radio. The on-off knob was going. You had to catch it just right and even then, first time you hit a bump, it would switch itself off, and you had to start all over again.

He caught two bars of music. Chopin, he thought, when the light in the cab flickered. As he sat up, a movement caught his eye. He looked to his left, thinking it was that sorry ass troll who lived in the basement. Guy never slept. Never washed either.

Wasn't him, though. No, it was old hang-dog, himself. Standing there with his hands clasped behind his back, staring in the truck window like he's the messenger of doom or something.

He rolled down the window. "You want something?" he inquired.

"How do you live with yourself?" the guy asked. "Have you no shame?"

He raced the engine three times and then spoke. "Don't you ever give it up man? It's over. What can I say? Shit happens."

Given a second chance, he probably would have chosen his words more carefully. As last words go, "shit happens" left a great deal to be desired. Those three syllables were, however, the last mortal utterance to pass his lips, because, at that point, old hang-dog pulled a gun out from behind his back and shot the driver four times in the face.

As he stood next to the truck, trying to absorb the gravity of his act, the truck radio suddenly began to play classical music, scattering his thoughts like leaves. He looked uncomprehendingly at the weapon in his hand, then lobbed it through the window into the driver's lap and slowly walked away.

Wednesday, July 27, 2000
5:26 A.M.

"What was that?" Ramon asked.

"Shhh." Gerardo held a finger to his lips. The pulsing yellow light circled them in the darkness.

"Sound like shots to me," Ramon whispered.

Gerardo slipped the gun from his tool belt and held it close along his right leg as he worked his way along the side of the building. All the way to the back, where he could see out into the parking lot. He peered around the corner and then came running back.

"He's sitting there warming up the truck, just like always."

"Musta been backfires," said Ramon, without believing it.

They'd been following him for a week. Memorizing his schedule. Getting to know his habits. Gerardo checked his watch. "One minute," he whispered.

Whatever his other failings, and the quality of his life suggested they were many, their victim was always on time. Left his cruddy apartment just before five-thirty each morning. Warmed up his truck for three minutes and then left for work in time to arrive at five minutes to six. The only time he'd varied from his schedule was Friday night, when he'd stopped for gas and groceries on the way home.

Gerardo's thick lips began to tremble as he stared at his watch and counted time. "Thirty Seconds," he whispered. "Twenty-nine . . ."

Wednesday, July 27, 2000
5:31 A.M.

He signed his confession, checked his watch and then dialed
nine-one-one. "There has been a killing at the Briarwood
Garden Apartments. Nine fifty-nine Marginal Way South,"
he said. "In the back parking lot. I'll meet the officers there."

"Let me have your . . ."

He hung up on the dispatcher. Then smoothed his confession out on the counter and read it over. It began: "This night
of March 27, 2000, I killed a man who deserved to die. For
this act I am prepared to suffer whatever consequences society sees fit to impose upon me." It was followed by his signature. He'd thought of explaining his crime, but felt certain
they wouldn't understand. They knew so little of honor.

The more he looked at the word "consequences" the more
convinced he became it was spelled incorrectly. To be
thought a killer was one thing; to be thought ignorant was
another.

"He's late," Gerardo said.

This time it was Ramon who scurried up to the corner of the building and peeked around. In the ghostly overhead light, he could see the mark sitting behind the wheel, hear the sounds of music and the engine running. He wondered if perhaps the driver had fallen asleep at the wheel. Something about the situation didn't feel right.

When he looked back, Gerardo had doused the emergency light and was throwing the traffic cones into the back of the truck. He hurried along the side of the building.

"He's still sitting there," he whispered to Gerardo. "Maybe we should wait for a few more minutes."

Gerardo's face was grim. "Something's wrong," he said. "Get in."

Ramon hopped into the passenger side just as the truck sprung to life.

"You play center," Gerardo said. "I'll play third."

They'd done it so many times before, nothing more needed to be said. Gerardo gunned the truck up the narrow drive, swung left around the parking lot and slid to a stop with the bed of their pick-up blocking the mark's. Both men leaped from the truck and ran to their respective positions.

Ramon out onto the grass in front of the truck, where he assumed the combat position, holding his silenced automatic in two hands, pointing directly at the dark windshield. Gerardo a half pace to the rear of the driver's side window, where, by the mere extension of his arm, he could place the end of the suppressor behind the victim's ear. "What the fuck is this?" Gerardo said.

When Gerardo returned his weapon to his belt and leaned down to peer in the window, Ramon hustled across the grass to his side. The mark sat openmouthed. Four separate rivers of blood ran down over his face and disappeared into his collar. He'd been shot twice high on the forehead, once in the right eye and once again just to the left of the nose.

"Somebody shot him," Gerardo offered, in that literal manner of his that drove Ramon crazy.

"No shit," Ramon said. He pointed down at the twenty-two target pistol in the dead man's lap. "Shooter dropped the piece," he said.

"What the fuck are we gonna do? *We* was supposed to shoot the guy. What kinda fuck would do something like this?" Gerardo demanded.

"Lemme think, will ya?"

Ramon looked around the parking lot. Nothing. Apparently nobody had heard the noise. "We gotta finish this thing," he said after a minute. "Just like the plan."

"But we didn't pop him."

"Don't matter," Ramon said quickly. "We still gotta finish." He checked the area again. Still nothing. "We finish . . . just like it was us who offed him."

"It ain't right," Gerardo said. "We was supposed to do it."

Ramon knew the muley look. He pointed the silenced automatic through the window and shot the lifeless corpse twice in the side. The body toppled over in the seat.

"There . . . we shot him," he said. "You feel better now?"

Gerardo didn't answer. Just stared sullenly off into space.

"Go ahead," Ramon said. "Give him a couple."

Gerardo shook his head. "It's not right," he said again.

"Go on," Ramon coaxed.

Gerardo hesitated for a moment, gave a small shrug, and then leaned into the cab and shot the body three times in rapid succession.

Ramon began to move. "I'll drive his truck. You follow behind. We do it just like we planned."

"What if . . ."

Ramon cut him off. "You gonna go back and tell the man we struck out?" he asked. "You gonna tell him how we was sitting on our thumbs out front while somebody else was earning our money for us?" They both knew the answer was no. In their present positions, failure was not an option.

Ramon pulled open the driver's door and used his foot to push the body down onto the passenger side floorboards. "Let's go," he said. "Nice and easy like always."

Gerardo hustled over to their truck and moved it forward, allowing his partner to back out into the lot. He began to sweat, as he followed the flickering taillights out the drive, around the corner and into the street, where they drove north at forty miles an hour.

A mile down the road from the Briarwood Garden Apartments, flashing lights appeared in the distance. Blue and white. Both men tensed at the wheel, watching the lights grow closer, until a pair of white police cruisers came roaring by in the opposite direction. Both men smiled into their rearview mirrors and watched the lights disappear into the darkness.

Wednesday, July 27, 2000
5:41 A.M.

The swirling light was captured in the iris of a single orange
eye. Then, a moment later, the static crack of a radio
scratched the air, and the great bird began rushing forward
through the water, curling its long neck for flight, beating its
indignant wings against the cold night air. He watched as the
heron forced itself upward into the black sky and then pulled
his confession from his jacket pocket and read it once again.
He stayed in the shadows as he made his way toward the
pulsing blue and white lights ahead. At the final corner, he
stopped. Everything was as he had imagined it would be. A
pair of police cruisers sat in the middle of the lot, doors
open, light banks blazing. Four policemen stood in a knot in
front of the cars, the harsh glare of their headlights turning
their legs to gold. Everything but the truck and the body.

The yellow truck was gone. He leaned back against the
building to steady himself. Then looked again. Still gone.
He blinked his eyes in disbelief and then, afraid he might
have fallen asleep, checked his watch. Eleven forty-two.
Ten minutes since he'd called 911. No way the slime had
lived and driven off. No way the cops towed it away so
quickly. His pulse throbbed in his temples and his knees

were weak. He'd never been more confused in his life. Without willing it so, he began to move. As if in a trance, he pocketed his confession and hurried back the way he'd come.